KANGAROO HOLLOW

Thomas Hal Phillips

KANGAROO HOLLOW

University Press of Mississippi / Jackson

Books by Thomas Hal Phillips

The Bitterweed Path, Rinehart, New York and W. H. Allen & Co.,
    London, 1950
The Golden Lie, Rinehart, New York and W. H. Allen & Co., London,
    1951
Search for a Hero, Rinehart, New York and W. H. Allen & Co.,
    London, 1952
The Loved and the Unloved, Harper, New York and W. H. Allen & Co.,
    London, 1955 (reprinted by University Press of Mississippi, 1998)

First published in 1954 by W. H. Allen & Co., London
Copyright © 2000 by Thomas Hal Phillips
Manufactured in the United States of America

08   07   06   05   04   03   02   01   00   4   3   2   1

Library of Congress Cataloging-in-Publication Data

Phillips, Thomas Hal, 1922-
    Kangaroo Hollow / Thomas Hal Phillips.
        p. cm.
    ISBN 1-57806-260-8 (alk. paper)
    1. Fathers and sons--Fiction. I. Title.

PS3566.H524 K36 2000
813'.54--dc21   99-054642

British Library Cataloging-in-Publication Data available

CONTENTS

This book is for
Debbie

BOOK ONE

PART ONE: 1916. THE HOLLOW

I

THE Hollow had been a beautiful place before the sawmills came. In autumn, the rim of hills blazed with hickory and oak and deep red gum, so that children in the cold and gloomy days of February could look through the windows of the unpainted houses and remember the colour of October.

In his young days, Jesse Shannon had been a lover of trees; he would no more think of cutting a tree unnecessarily than he would think of burning a barn. But in the last year of his life, he brought a sawmill to the Hollow and left acres of his fine timberland as bare as a new-cut sorghum patch. There was no accounting for the sudden destructive urge that raged within the old man. Perhaps it was mere coincidence that it had started during the same fall his daughter, Anna, went off to Blue Mountain College. The next fall, when she returned to school, he ordered another mill, as if the one he had could not eat his trees fast enough. He died before the second mill arrived, and his son, young Jesse, inherited a good many affairs, about which he knew nothing.

When the funeral was over and old Jesse was buried beside his wife in the cemetery near the chapel he had built, Anna returned to school with the premonition that she would not be there long. Jesse might be five years older than she, and the accepted head of the household, but she was aware that he hardly knew the difference between a mare mule and a horse mule. She was also aware of the various feminine tongues who said it was high time that Anna Shannon, already twenty-two, caught herself a man. (If the truth was out, the tongues said, Old Jesse had sent her off not for an education, but for a husband; as if nothing in the Hollow was good enough for his Anna! Evil old man that he was: obviously share-cropper stock who had hit a lucky streak somewhere.)

Jesse did not like his new responsibility: a sawmill, a farm, and croppers who when winter set in converged on the huge old house in the centre of the Hollow. He needed Anna. It seemed to him that the croppers were always asking for another sack of flour or meal, another side of meat; and the mill hands were always asking for money. He marvelled that such things had never troubled his father.

The lean days grew leaner, and at last Anna was forced to come home. She was disgusted with Jesse's management, but she had learned early from her nagging mother never to nag about anything. She had been born with a certain amount of frankness.

"Jesse," she demanded, "am I extravagant?"

"No. Of course you're not."

"Blue Mountain College is not full of sharecroppers and orphans. It is expensive. But explain to me why there's not enough money for me to go to school."

"Because . . . the taxes are due."

It was January. That settled the matter; told her what she already knew; left her at her row's end. She did ask herself a few questions. Was Jesse lazy? No. Did he waste money? No. He simply had no love for the land, the stock, the crops. He would fare better on a ship at sea. But she had learned to keep a still tongue. No doubt she always came first in his heart, and one had to be considerate of such devotion.

With the sawmill had come a dozen itinerant families: sawyers, loggers, cutters, boilermen, and even off-bearers. Rough, two-room shacks had been quickly built, and the old gin-house had been converted into a boarding house called the Kangaroo. Even Burke's store, above the small grey railroad station, had put on an extra week-day clerk and two extra clerks on Saturday. The Hollow had buzzed like a hive. At Christmas-time there had been much celebrating and a proportionate number of casualties: most serious case being the Streeter boy, who, on a dare, had let a firecracker go off between his toes.

As winter broke and spring began to appear, the toll of the sawmill was more apparent. There were spots that lay like the disembowelled and scraped white bellies of hogs. Anna did not like the sight, but it was too late then. Already the new mill was being set up and the families who would feed its hungry teeth were moving in one by one.

When the second mill was installed, a slight problem arose as to where the crew would get its noon meal. The Kangaroo was already filled at noon, and though the hands could have carried sack lunches with them, there was complaining that ants always found the sacks, no matter where they were hung or hidden. The solution fell upon Anna. Each day at twelve o'clock she delivered lunch for fourteen men to mill No. 2.

What commenced as a chore quickly became a delight. From one of the itinerant families, Jesse hired a girl named Todda to help out at the house; and already there was Ursa, a huge Negro woman who had been in the house before Jesse was born. Preparing the meal was not nearly as much trouble for Anna as the men supposed; nor was the bringing of it. Though Todda could have done the errand, Anna never missed a day bringing the meal herself, stopping the buggy a few yards away, and watching the silent team-work of the men.

She knew the mills had come to stay. She also knew that for the first time in his life Jesse enjoyed something. He arose early and worked about the mills until late afternoon. He read less and less at night, and their conversations at the table were often of logs, conveyor belts and sawdust. A few times he suggested that they drive to a Saturday-night barn dance, and on occasions he had actually made a feeble attempt to dance. Even stranger, when he arrived from the mills every evening he frequently drove Todda home. So frequently, in fact, that the Hollow was quick to surmise a love affair. Anna looked on the matter with curiosity, but without judgment. Poor Jesse, she thought. He had been so quiet and unhappy all his life, never had a girl; and he was almost twenty-eight years old. Let him marry Todda: she was agreeable enough, and certainly pretty. (Here Anna could not help but compare herself to Todda, who was a year or two younger. They were strikingly alike, with yards of black hair, fiery black eyes, and fair complexion. Anna was easily an inch taller and an inch larger in the waist; their voices were quite different: Todda had a slightly wild lilt in her speech, except when she was angry.) Still, it never seriously crossed Anna's mind that Jesse was going to marry.

Spring had arrived. Jesse drove Todda home almost every night and Anna made her daily trip to the mill. The smell of resin, of new sawdust, the grind and choke of the saws fastened upon her like a drug. Often she prolonged, much more than necessary, the gathering up of empty plates, cups, and utensils. As she drove away in the buggy, she would look back for one last image. When she was out of sight she continued to hear the sound beating through the sweating men like one giant pulse. She understood why some of them had left their homes, their wives, for the sight and sound of a miraculous circle spewing its yellow dust.

One day Anna stopped the buggy at the usual place and with little attention toward the men set out the food on a rough table in the shade of an elm. As she walked from the buggy to the table with a huge pot of coffee, her glance happened to fall on the No. 1 off-bearer. She stopped still in her tracks. The new face startled her. She had the curious sensation of imagining exactly what the face had looked like as a child and what it would look like when it was old. She saw both images clearly, as if a strange power possessed her. At the same time, it seemed to her that he stood and stared though his arms were loaded with slabs and the carriage was bearing down upon him. Weather-hardened face, she thought, straight from the earth, immobile. The carriage bore down. He stepped aside, unhurried, threw his load of slabs down the chute, as if the weight had not taxed his huge body. The whistle sounded for noon. The coffee-pot dropped from Anna's hand. She made a lightning recovery, but not before half the coffee had splattered her foot and seeped into the sawdust-covered ground.

Then she got into the buggy and drove away. She stopped at Clear Creek and for a long time sat on the sand and let the water flow over her slightly burned foot. In the middle of the afternoon she returned to the mill for the empty dishes. The mill was in full swing, so that none of the men noticed her arrival or departure. When she reached home, her foot was burning more than ever and she was afraid it might blister. Todda was solicitous. She smeared the foot with a thin layer of salve and gave instructions to leave the foot uncovered. Ursa took one look at the foot, screwed up her large black face, and asked, "How come?"

"I spilled some coffee on it."

"You ain't no business eatin' with them mill hands." And Ursa turned away without sympathy, wanting no further explanation. She was a bit jealous of Todda.

It had never been Anna's custom to lie abed, even to take a nap, in the daytime. However, she went straight to her room, closed the door, and lay down across her bed. When her foot became easy she went to sleep. At dusk she awoke with the feeling that something tremendous had happened to her, something that needed a great deal of consideration. Yet she could not call to mind what it might be.

For some time she had been worrying about the way Jesse was neglecting the farm. April was already upon them and not a plough had been stuck into the ground. Naturally, Jesse had his hands full with the sawmills; but in turn, he must realize how little profit they had brought. It was true that many hands had work, especially the farmhands, who found little to do during the winter and early spring months—now that old Jesse was gone. It was hers and Jesse's duty to take care of them, and no doubt she worried more about the hands, the farm, and the mills than Jesse did. But at the moment she could not worry about anything. She felt a deep satisfaction. Bending slowly forward, she examined her foot. Much of the redness was gone; a faint soreness had appeared. That was all.

Ursa pecked on the door and called, "Supper."

Anna had taken her seat at the long table when Jesse appeared. With absolute grace, he withdrew his chair, seated himself like a prince, and stretched his long, thin hands beside his plate. For a greeting, he smiled. No one could possibly suspect that he was the owner—or half-owner with his sister—of two sawmills. He wore a white shirt, monogrammed in blue, and wide red suspenders, because his gangling pale body did not have flesh enough to properly support his trousers.

He looked exactly as he had looked on his first trip home from the University ten or eleven years before. Not a hair in his black bushy head had changed. On that occasion, old Jesse had said, "Son, you made up your mind what you wanta be?" "Yes," young Jesse had answered. "I'd like to be a dilettante." Whereupon the old man tightened his puzzled face and said, "I reckon that's all right if you can make a living at it." Two years later, however, Jesse was back on the farm, once again in his dull, secluded pattern, because he had refused to study law.

"How's your foot?" Jesse asked.

"Who mentioned my foot to you?" A glimmer of fire kindled in Anna's eyes, for she had the distinct impression that Jesse was amusing himself at her expense.

"Todda," he answered, surprised at her outburst. "I drove her home."

She felt ridiculous. She must make some move to hide her agitation. "Jesse, you're being unfair to Todda!"

"In what way, please, ma'am?"

"She's a nice, sweet girl. People talk. They're already talking. And I know you haven't the slightest urge to marry her." There. It was out, and she had meant precisely every word. She was a woman; she had to be on Todda's side.

Jesse got up. His pale, thin face quivered; feverish spots of red appeared on his cheeks. "Will you leave me alone?" he cried. "It was always Papa. Now it's you." The trembling grew to a shake. He pushed at his chair and left the room.

He threw himself across his bed and wished his consciousness could rock him into the world of ghosts. Only the ghosts left him in peace. The billion-eyed world cared nothing of what happened to him, except the few beaks that pecked at his secrets, scratched at the corner of his heart. No, that was not true. He must calm himself, regain the cool, impartial feelings of early morning. Sometimes he woke up in the cool of the morning and thought: "Love is waiting for me in the heart of some city." And he imagined the city, dead, empty, the way he had sometimes seen Memphis at dawn; he saw himself walk through daybreak along newly washed streets to find his love, by chance, at a fountain in the heart of the city.

A soft knock shook his door. Anna entered, sat on the bed, and threw her arm around him. The smallness of his body shocked her. "Please forgive me," she whispered. "Please listen to me." At once she knew she must pour out her heart to him, something she had never done before. She must make him understand what had happened to her to-day. No, that was impossible. "Jesse . . . are you mad at me? Look at me. I want to ask you something."

Slowly he turned his face toward her, like a child. He smiled weakly.

"Who was the new hand at the mill to-day?"

"I forget his name. Frost, I think."

"How could you forget a name like that?"

"How? What's the matter with you to-night? You've fussed about everything."

"I didn't mean to. I just wanted to ask if he knew anything about a farm."

"He was raised on one, he told me."

Anna's heart quickened. "Why . . . why don't we let him see after the crop? You've got your hands full, and if we're going to make one we've got to start it right now."

"I guess that would suit him."

"Will you arrange it to-morrow?" Her voice was urgent.

Jesse's face brightened. He had completely recovered. A suspicious smile crept into his face. "I knew you would like him."

"Is there any reason for me to dislike him? He doesn't look like a criminal."

"Do criminals look a certain way? But go ahead and like him. He followed Todda here. He's in love with her."

"Who told you that?"

"Todda. She told me two or three days ago." The smile on his face exploded into a curious, repulsive accusation. She felt a very unnatural need to strike him; not him, but the smile. At the same time, she was sorry she had sided with a woman against her brother.

2

RUFUS FROST sat on an oak stump and looked down at the lumberjack houses before him. House by house, soft coal-oil light appeared through the windows. In a little while he would whistle for Todda, but he was not certain she would meet him. How strange it was that this long-time magic between them should disappear like snow under sunlight.

An hour before, he had watched from the same spot as Todda rode gaily through the dusk beside another man. Not an ordinary man, but one who owned horses, buggies, land, and sawmills. Fighting a man like that meant trouble. You had not only to defeat him, but also everything he owned as well. And besides, it was all Todda's fault.

To his left, he could hear the noise at the Kangaroo. The men might be in a poker game. He had a great notion to return and join them; there would be less trouble in that direction. The darkness increased; the night grew still and briskly cool. Flocks of sparrows cut strange patterns, disappeared and returned. The noise and laughter from the Kangaroo increased; good-natured threats and accusations flew into the night. For half an hour, Rufus remained undecided in his movement. Then he made a simple decision. He would choose Todda first. If she did not respond, he would return to whatever had blossomed at the Kangaroo.

A hundred yards from Todda's house, he leaned against an elm and whistled like a quail. As he repeated the call he saw figures moving in the kitchen. One of them was Todda's twin brother, Howard, a sun-hardened, nervous little fellow who had engineered the family's move to the Hollow primarily to get Todda away from Rufus. Howard had never been friends with any of Todda's suitors. He met all of them with distrust in his steely grey eyes; he spoke hardly at all and continually lurked in the background, listening, waiting. Rufus was not afraid of Howard, and yet he avoided him, often reflecting that a little man with guts is the kind you have to kill. It was perhaps more because of Howard than anyone else that the whistle signal had been arranged between Rufus and Todda. After a while it became a part of the ritual and added to the mysterious strength of their love affair.

Rufus sat down at the roots of the elm. He had no doubt that Todda had heard. It was now a question of response. He picked up a small rock between the roots of the tree, fingered it like a baseball, remembering the two summers he had pitched in a semi-pro. league before hurting his arm. Arm was all right now; plenty of good strength. When he thought of growing old, he did not consider that his perfect set of teeth might decay, that his shaggy mane of blond hair might fall out, that his Viking face might sag into furrows and grow pale; he thought only of losing the power in his body, the explosive energy that flowed through him as steadily as an artesian stream. He whistled again.

A figure left the lamplight and came towards him, but it came slowly, not with the fervour of other days. They caught hands without a word, almost without a smile, and turned into the path that led to acres of pines. The old magic was not there, not in the seizure of their hands; and both understood it would not be in their kisses nor in their tenderest caress. On their faces was a splendid sadness, and they enjoyed it almost as much as they had once enjoyed a passionate embrace.

"You worked hard to-day?" she asked quietly.

" 'Bout like usual," he answered.

Not another syllable passed between them for some time. They entered the woods, selected a comfortable place, where she sat down and received his head into her lap. Patiently she stroked his face, his hair, pulled gently at his ears. After a quarter hour he raised up and kissed her throat, her lips. They believed the old magic had returned in all its force to tear away this new sadness and smash it to pieces.

Then a wave of doubt crept between them. They were afraid the old magic would not stay. They hurried their love. It was a mistake;

the sadness came back again. They had spoken briefly in whispers. Now they were quiet, hearing only the slight breeze in the branches above them. The day had ended. What happened next belonged to nothing or to another day.

Suddenly Rufus burst out in a mechanical and unnatural way for him. "Todda . . . I'm gonna take a two-by-four and beat his brains out if I ever see you in the buggy with him again."

"Will you?" she teased.

"Yes; if ever I see you put a foot in his buggy . . . just one foot."

"Darling," she mocked, "how am I gonna git home? You coming after me in *your* buggy?"

The moment had been fulfilled; now they could be brutally honest with each other. Their stares met. Neither would give way. "You women're just not like men," he said.

"That's the only power we got in this world. Not being like men."

"What're you gonna do, Todda? Run away some night with your little man in the buggy?"

"You couldn't stop me—if I took a notion."

"Pore little Todda. I thought I learned you a few things. Don't you know he's not going to marry you?"

"What you worrying about, then? If he don't, I might talk trade with you."

"Aye god, but ain't that a fine note! You better make up your mind purty quick, less you wanta call some day and me not answer."

"You the one's been calling. I know what I want."

"You don't act like it."

"Stop fussing at me!"

"I'm not fussing. I'm telling you straight a few things. Things you need to know. What you're going after you won't git, and anybody with half-sense knows. . . ."

She got up and ran away from him. For a while he lay in anger, refusing to think or move. Then he got up and went like a moth toward the noise and laughter of the Kangaroo. The men were not playing poker.

Miss Lillie, who operated the Kangaroo, was not against a bit of friendly gambling. Occasionally, she grabbed the spotted cubes herself and rolled them with a great deal of confidence. She was a large woman, past fifty, still an extremely hard worker, and honest. For twenty years—commencing the year her husband died—she had run a boarding-house for men. From place to place she followed the timber trade, moving every five or six years. Her one mission was to make every boarder happy. When she found one who was incapable of appreciating the hundreds of motherly tasks she performed for him, he was immediately dislodged. Ingratitude was not permitted in her house. Sin, however, often received her approbation or at least a kind turn of her back.

She was sitting on her front porch, apron across her lap, when Rufus Frost appeared out of the darkness. She took one look at his face and said, "They're on the wash-porch. Tell 'em they got one more hour."

With no break in his stride, he turned and walked to the south side of the house, where the men crouched about a smoky-globed lantern. There was a mad scramble as Rufus stepped on to the porch. One of the men looked up, squinted, and said, "Don't do us thataway, feller. We thought you was a Gover'mint man."

Rufus could smell the excited, nervous sweat from their bodies. He could feel the charged air, the thrill of winning, the throb of losing. Something about the crude, knee-wearing game was like an endless scene of love-making. He would roll for one point, no more.

"Git in here," Barney said. "We'll clean of plough."

Rufus threw down four one-dollar bills. If he won he could get a ticket home; if he lost, another matter. "That's it. All my eggs in one basket."

"Don't be scarit, men," Barney said. "We'll jist share-crop it." Four men put down a dollar each. "Now shine," he added to Rufus. Barney was the fun-maker, the fiddler, the live wire of the Kangaroo. Without question he occupied the warmest corner of Miss Lillie's heart, possibly because his small, malarial-looking body consumed more food than any two other men at the house. When it came to good whisky, he could find it with the ease and innocence that some children discover Easter eggs. At the dice, he was a splendid loser.

"Don't I git in?" Sterling Temple said. Sterling was dull and slow; he depended on Barney to think for him. He was always good-natured, laughed frequently, made silly jokes which drew fewer laughs than his uncommonly tall, freakish angles.

"Jist squat down over 'air in the corner," Barney said to Sterling. "You ain't in this."

Rufus fingered the dice, hesitated, as if realizing for the first time that his total fortune was at stake. Max Muller, a pleasant, sturdy German millwright, touched his arm. His blue eyes winked encouragement to Rufus. "You vill throw seven, first time." Max, nearing forty and growing bald, still loved baseball like a kid. As manager and catcher of the Hollow team, he had quickly found out that Rufus was a pitcher. He touched the arm again, hoping to give his hero luck.

Rufus knelt, threw quickly: a nine.

"Iss easy! Iss easy!" Max said.

Rufus threw four more times and grunted at the sight of a seven. Max breathed heavily. "Iss too bad."

"That's the crop," Rufus said. He brushed off his hands and went upstairs, forgetting to mention that Miss Lillie had set a time limit on their game.

He felt relieved that he had lost every dollar he had. Now there was no immediate question of going home, or going any place else: not before a pay-day. But he had to admit he probably wouldn't have gone home, anyway. Why should he? For a stingy old mountaineer father who worked the guts out of his children share-cropping a forty-acre cotton and tobacco farm; then hired them out to a neighbouring farm or a sawmill to buy their own clothes and shoes for winter? To two long-nosed, inquisitive sisters, already old maids though neither was more than a year away from thirty? Well, there was poor, little freckled-faced Bee, a year younger than he. But she was married to a good boy, and heavy with child. She was the first person he had ever cared deeply about. Sid was turned like her; but he and Sid had not had a chance to get into much together—Sid was so young, only eleven. No; Sid would be twelve in a few days. For a few minutes he suffered for Sid, so hemmed by those pious voices: "Allus remember your pore mother gave her own life to bring you into this world."

He got up, went downstairs and asked Barney for a dollar. Puzzled and curious, Barney lifted the bill to him without rising from his knees or saying anything. Then Rufus borrowed pencil and paper from Miss Lillie and went to the dining-room. He wrote:

"DEAR SID BOY,—I come on down here on the train and got here without no trouble. I been working at a sawmill some. Not too hard. Filed saws till today I off beared some. It is alright. How are papa and Gay and Vivian and Bee and yourself?

"Listen Sid, I'm going to tell you how it is but don't you tell the others. I'm not no closer to Todda than when I left. I mean there's somebody else about to beat me, but I ruther you wouldn't tell a soul. I would leave but looks like I can't walk off and leave a man I just hired to. You write me a letter and tell me how everybody is. I would like to see you.

"Your brother,
"RUFUS.

"PS.—Here is one $ for your birthday."

The letter took some time. When he returned to the sleeping hall upstairs, most of the men were already in bed. Sterling Temple was saying, "If the war gits me an' I have to go 'cross the waters, I'm shore gonna tie into me a Frenchwomen."

"She couldn't understand you," Barney said. "Less'n she's a mind-reader."

"Ain't most Frenchwomen mind-readers?" Sterling demanded.

"Why shore, man," Barney said. "Fact is, I can read a body's mind myself when they ain't but one thing on it."

A few men laughed. From the corner a man groaned, "I shore Lord hope it ain't no war. Don't you, Frost?"

Rufus looked toward the man; it was too dark to see. "It don't make me no difference," he answered.

3

AT first, Rufus did not quite understand. He was sitting on a pile of slabs, a few minutes before whistle time, when Jesse Shannon rode up. Half an hour later he was on his way to the old house which was the heart of the Hollow. Any day of the week he would take the farm instead of the logwoods or a sawmill. He preferred the smell of horses to pine resin; he preferred the steady creak of harness to the frantic grind of saws. Besides, farmhands made things grow; timbermen were like a drove of locusts, laying everything bare. The thought of working in the rich, black land of the Hollow made his hands sweat, eager for the feel of hickory plough handles. He had always wanted a chance to farm where he would not be forever stumbling over rocks; the idea of being an overseer was like inheriting a small fortune, except for one big consideration: the matter of taking orders from a woman. He understood from Jesse Shannon that the farm was more or less in the hands of his sister, Anna.

He was into it, good. But there was nothing to do but walk on, stick his foot into something that would more'n likely take his shoe off. His feelings were eased, however, as he pictured the envy and surprise that would show on Todda's face. He tried to recall what Anna Shannon looked like: he had got but a faint glimpse of her at the mill the day before.

A few minutes later he had his first clear look at Anna. She was standing beside the garden gate pointing out something to two Negro men. In her left hand was a wide-brimmed straw hat with which she occasionally fanned herself. As he approached, she had her back to him, so that his eyes dwelled unconsciously on her white neck and the huge bun of black hair at the back of her head. When she turned, he studied her face; it was pleasant enough, mostly because of her neatly curved nose. But the first thing he thought was, "Shorely to God she ain't left-handed."

As if to answer him, she casually slipped the straw hat into her right hand. "Mr. Frost?"

"Yes'm." He took off his hat.

Her quick, fiery eyes inspected him, apparently surprised that he had on khaki pants instead of overalls. He refused to return the inspection, deliberately averting his eyes.

"Jesse wanted the garden done this morning, before you started in the fields."

He believed that was a lie; a nice one, but still a lie. Jesse hadn't wanted anything done. She wanted it. He nodded.

"Jim and Peter Cat here will help you."

He inspected the two men: one a barrel-chested, squatty figure with huge hairy forearms; the other a tall, stooped figure with the thin face of a prophet. While he tried to decide who was Jim and who was Peter Cat, Anna went on, "Just the upper half this morning; the lower half, I think, is still too wet. You understand to break the ground first, Jim? . . ."

The squatty figure nodded. Rufus could not help smiling; for he had got their names right.

"Then fix me up several rows and put in lots of barnyard fertilizer. I expect it'll take two big wagon loads. Don't you think so, Mr. Frost?"

Rufus nodded, frowning slightly. He still had a suspicion of an urge to insult this woman who was so pleasantly giving him orders. If she had been ugly, it would be a totally different matter. In any case, he had not come all the way from Tennessee to haul manure into a garden—for a woman.

"On second thoughts," she said to Rufus, as if reading his mind for the second time, "while you're breaking the ground, Jim and Peter Cat can haul the barnyard fertilizer."

She might as well have said "manure." "No'm," he said, just to stop her. "I'll help haul the manure."

She left them and went back into the house.

But Rufus was not satisfied. Twice that morning Anna came to see how the garden was working. Each time, Rufus searched for something unpleasant to say, if not directly to her, then in her hearing. But she gave him no chance to part his lips: she asked nothing, advised nothing. A fog of anger burned in him, making his sweat clammy instead of bright, crystal drops; he suspected that Todda might be watching him from a window in the big house.

Near noon, he and Jim were loading the second wagon of manure. Spade by spade they broke off huge smoking slabs and pitched them into the wagon in the alley of the barn. As Rufus stopped to see what loading was left to be done, he caught a glimpse of Anna at the end of the alley. Thrusting his shovel downward again, he began to speak loudly to Jim of their cargo, giving it its most vulgar name.

Anna, on the supposition that horse manure is much finer for a garden than any other animal waste, was checking to see that the correct stall was being cleaned; she turned quietly toward the house. She was somewhat excited, having heard no language of that sort since her father died. Except—she remembered now—from that girl at Blue Mountain College: the girl's name was Sandra. How odd it was that such words from Sandra were so nauseating, and

yet from this man each syllable seemed to filter through muscles
and layers of strength until it came out at last purified. It was—she
hated to admit it—rather thrilling.

In the kitchen, Anna helped Ursa and Todda pack the lunch
for the mill hands. She was in a delightful humour, but as she was
usually pleasant neither of the other women noticed her mood. The
baskets were placed in the buggy, which Peter Cat had harnessed
and brought to the back door. Anna climbed into the seat and
drove away smiling. As she turned from the driveway into the main
road, it occurred to her that Rufus Frost would be eating at her
table, with Todda, while she fed a group of hungry mill hands.
She slapped at the mare, feeling that she had been completely
duped.

At exactly twelve o'clock, Todda stepped on to the back porch
and pulled a long clothes' line device that rang the huge dinner
bell beside the smokehouse. Within a few minutes, Rufus and half
a dozen Negro hands appeared at the house. Ursa provided wash-
pans, warm water, and towels. Todda waited like a prim hostess;
she motioned Rufus into the dining-room.

It was a beautiful room, ceiling and walls papered with a small
green-checked paper. Three huge windows opened from the south,
and against the north wall were three pieces of simple old furniture:
a buffet and two chests. The table was long, egg-shaped, surrounded
by hand-carved chairs attractively out of order. Two places were
set near the windows, near enough that a few rays of sunlight
glinted on the silver.

Todda's eyes danced; her face wore a curious smile. She could
not hide the peculiar pleasure the scene afforded. Rufus was at first
piqued, then touched with anger. He surveyed everything; he
rubbed his forefinger over a silver spoon; he mocked at the sharpness
of a knife; he demanded, "Miss Queen, where do I sit?"

Todda was suddenly afraid she had gone too far. "There," she
said plainly, pointing to the place at the head of the table.

They sat down. She began to pass the food. She waited for him
to say something, but he remained sullen. At last he pointed to the
huge linen napkin beside his plate. "How come all this?"

"We allus eat in here," she said. "These folks don't high-hat
people. They just like me and you, except they own stuff, a good
bit of stuff."

Ursa came in with hot cornbread. For a few minutes, Rufus ate
hungrily. A good deal of confidence returned to Todda. She leaned
forward and tapped the small service bell before her plate. Ursa
reappeared in the doorway.

"Yessum?"

"Butter, please, Ursa."

Ursa quietly brought the butter and returned to the kitchen, to the sound of the Negro hands scraping their plates. Todda smiled, a faint, haughty, teasing smile. She gazed at the napkin which remained untouched beside Rufus's plate.

"What you lookin' at?" he asked.

"Oh, nothing." Gingerly, she wiped at her mouth with her napkin, then unfolded his. "Go ahead. Use it."

Rufus got up. His thick neck and jaws turned red and swelled with pressure inside him. He slapped his napkin on to the floor. "Goddam all this finery! It ain't like us. All this ain't like us. Let's git out. We'll git us a place, all ours. I'll work. I can work hard. Can't nobody work harder'n me, Todda. You can git whatever you want. Know how we used to think about it? Everything and kids. A house and good mules; and some land we could find purty cheap some'eres. Don't you remember . . . ?"

She was moved. She had dropped her head on to the table. "I remember. . . . But you know and I know . . . we just know. . . ."

"Know what, Todda?"

"We can't never have it. Not us. . . ."

He put his arm around her; clumsily he kissed the hair that hung over her face. "If you don't love me . . . just say it."

"It ain't that. Please leave me alone. I'm tired."

"Tired?"

"Tired of gittin' up way 'fore daylight, tired of cooking and washing and ironing, tired of moving, tired of eatin' molasses and fat-back meat and sawmill gravy. . . ." She laid her face on her forearm and cried.

He started out. She dried her face and looked after him. "Come back and finish."

"I finished." He went out the front way and sat under an elm tree near the garden, and looked out toward the rim of hills. He didn't know exactly where to turn. If you had a field to plough, or a thousand feet of mixed-up lumber to stack in the sun, there was nothing to it. You got up, and you started, and after a while it was done. But which way did you go when things got mixed up inside you? Not only in you, in somebody else too? Which way did you walk and where did you put your hands? He gripped at his thighs. A hand touched his shoulder. He did not move.

"What you thinking?" Todda said.

He stretched out his arms, flexed them for her to see. "I was thinking 'bout how stout I am. I could take Jesse Shannon and bend him into a staple. Done more work with my left hand than he's done with both legs and both arms. But he owns ever'thing in sight and I ain't got a real decent pair of Sunday pants to hide my hind end. Couldn't buy you a dress to hide yours either. And it ain't bad luck caused it. I ain't never had no real bad luck 'cepting when I hurt my pitching arm. I'm just dumb. But I'm going to git smart. . . ."

"Now you understand me. You know how I feel, don't you, Rufus?"

"We may see the day when we wisht we hadn't got so smart."

"I'm not going to be sorry," she said. "I know what I want and I'm going to git it, and when I git it I'm not going to be sorry."

He would not look up at her. "I hope you git it, Todda."

It was a bitter, stubborn seal for both of them. The curtain was completely drawn. Yet their faces showed a calmness devoid of emotion, for each had drawn his own half; the ends had met, the curtain fused into one grey entity. They talked from either side of it, softly.

"You won't be leaving, will you?" she asked.

"Yes. I guess I'll go some'eres in a few days." He would have to wait until Saturday: pay-day.

"Where?"

"No telling yet."

"Back home?"

"No."

It seemed to him that their conversation continued, quietly, in short vapid words. But Todda had returned to the house and he was alone, his eyes closed, leaning against the elm. All about him was the full smell of spring, like the distant smell of rich food. At that moment he longed for autumn and dry leaves. Which way now?

He did not often see situations clearly because he did not often give his mind to them. He had worked hard all his life, from sun-up till sundown (except the two summers he had pitched in the Smoky Mountain Semi-pro. League), and the only thing he had ever thought very much about was a woman, with a home and kids somewhere in the background. He had earned some faint title to manhood at the age of fifteen with a wash-woman who was twice his age. He did not think she was pretty or ugly; he did not think of her at all, except to sense that she was a woman and he was a man and they were alone in a house together. Others followed, younger and prettier. At nineteen he fell in love with Todda. That was somewhere behind the grey curtain.

A man could not sit still and wait. He wanted to start walking and go over the rim of hills and beyond. If a man was to do that, surely some day he would come upon what he wanted: maybe a vast stretch of rich, black land, half in crop, half in pasture, filled with untamed horses; not far away a girl, a pretty farm girl with sun-browned skin and shining hair, who knew what it was to get up at four o'clock and help with the milking.

A breeze moved from the rim of hills down across the Hollow. He rose, as if to begin his journey at that very minute. Actually, the sound of a buggy had unconsciously brought him to his feet.

Anna stopped the buggy near the garden gate. "Would you help me with these boxes?" she asked. "I've got everything here: cabbage and onion sets and tomato plants. . . ."

He went toward her. Her hat was high on the back of her head, and her plain print dress made her look cool and comfortable. Closer, reaching up to take the boxes from her, he could smell her clean body, and odour not sweet nor strong, but faintly citric. The way she stood, it seemed that her body, particularly her throat and breasts, drank up all the day's sunlight. He had the feeling of being in the presence of someone who never slept.

"Now," she said, and with a brief dust of her hands she descended from the buggy. Her movements were neither delicate nor mannish; they were quick and positive. "I hope we can get everything set out this afternoon. It may rain to-morrow." She looked up at the sky. "Yes; I think it may be raining in the morning."

Well, Rufus thought, I'm leaving; I might as well shoot straight. He cleared his throat. "I don't never hep set out a garden."

"You mean . . . ?"

"I don't never hep set it out, and I don't never hep hoe it."

Anna began to laugh, her voice lilting, her eyes dancing. "Why, that's funny! That's so funny! I'll have to tell Jesse you don't like a garden. . . ."

He wanted to make it clear that he was drawing a line between the work of men and the work of womenfolk. "I don't mind ploughing it."

She had stopped laughing and was looking at him. The point was clear to her. "Why, my goodness. . . ." She hesitated over his name. "You'll find plenty to do in the field. You don't have to bother with the garden. I just never thought. A garden is about the only thing Jesse likes on a farm. But, of course . . . you're not like Jesse." She started toward the house, wading through the high spring grass which had not yet had its first cutting.

Rufus was furious: with himself, with her laugh, with Todda, and with the bright, busy world spinning madly past him, giving him no proper hand-hold to control his share. "One other thing," he called. "I don't never mow nobody's yard." Stupid, yes; but it was said now.

She was on the front step. As she looked back toward him, the wind blew at her hat. She removed it calmly. "That's perfectly all right, Mr. Frost. When people know where everybody stands, they get along better. You take the hands this afternoon and work on the early cornland, or wherever you choose to start. Peter Cat and I will take care of the garden . . . and the yard."

He looked at the barn; he made a few steps and thought of his hat. He hoped to God Todda had not heard them. Aye, god, which way was Saturday? He walked blindly.

4

WORD spread that Rufus would be leaving at the end of the week. Todda had unwittingly started it in the presence of Anna and Ursa. By nightfall, every farmhand on the Shannon place, every sawmill worker at the Kangaroo seemed to know. It became the topic of the hour, a grave issue; across the Hollow it hung like a heat wave. Even those who hardly knew his face (for he had been there less than a week) expressed concern and demanded regretfully: "You ain't leaving us?"

Miss Lillie went out of her way at supper to serve Rufus extra helpings.

Sterling Temple, in his dull, half-witted tone, declared, "You musta come atter a coal of fire."

Barney remembered his dollar and kept silent.

Max Muller, thinking of his baseball team, was deeply disappointed. He had counted on Rufus as the main pitcher for the Hollow. Even in the face of misfortune, he still insisted that after supper Rufus should come out with him and pitch a few warm-up balls. Rufus obliged, and all the men respectfully followed the two, hoping to see some miraculous feat. After a hundred slow, lobbed-over pitches, the men grew impatient. Sterling Temple yelled again and again for something faster, for a fireball, until Max rose from his catcher's stance to shout, "You vont the man to hurt hees arm? You peeg!" He raised his mitt and brought it down squarely upon Sterling's head. Then he walked calmly toward the house, leaving Sterling buckled to his knees, stunned, but unhurt. Why had they always to break into his dreams? A fine pitching arm brought fire into him quicker than the legs of a beautiful woman. Pigs. It was they who would cause this man to leave.

Voices called after Max, "Kaiser! Kaiser!"

He looked back from the wash porch. "Some day you vill fall into the saw. Zzzipp . . . half in two. Not like thees mitt, hnnnh?"

"I ain't gonna fall," Sterling said.

"I vill push you!"

After a minute the men broke into roaring laughter. Then they turned their attention to Rufus again and focused their concern on his leaving.

He did not understand their concern; neither did they.

He did not know that people gave way to him, without resentment. He did not know that his huge frame, his hard, pleasant face, his unkempt mane of blond hair, his grey, undoubting eyes, his peasant voice, his boyish grin worked on the hearts of people. He did not understand what it was to be different, because he earnestly wanted to be one of the great herd. He did not understand that within him was some of David and some of Goliath, and observing eyes saw what they wished to see.

The men broke into small groups. Most of them talked about the sawmills or the logwoods. A few spoke of the Kaiser and the coming war.

Rufus went to bed early, still counting the remaining days before his departure. The sleeping hall was quieter than usual, giving him a chance to review in peace his brief sojourn in the Hollow. Never had he been received with such warmth—even Todda had been warm about everything, hadn't she? And it was a man's duty to remain a respectable length of time after he was hired; though, of course, he had had his jobs switched. Yet, that very afternoon, he had been ploughing the kind of land he had always dreamed about owning. (Not to mention that a farm any day was better than a sawmill.) To-night his arm felt almost as good as the day he had pitched a two-hitter against Kerryville—and Kerryville was leading the League. His memory hopped from incident to incident. He remembered the white foam sweat on the mules he had ploughed; the mellow, jocular voices of the Negroes (he'd rather work with Negroes than white men, for they made things seem natural and easy and they never complained); the wet streak around his shoulders where the checklines had worn; the smell of the barn and old alfalfa; and the feel of clean corn-shucks. He guessed he'd rather shuck corn than do most anything under the sun; and aye god, the Shannons had a crib full! It seemed a pity he had committed himself to leave.

He went to sleep thinking about early morning and his hands ripping off shucks in the corn crib. He slept fitfully. He tossed and groaned, smacking his lips and swallowing at regular intervals. He dreamed of the war and the Huns coming down upon him with swords and daggers. Barney, a light sleeper, was awakened two or three times, and remembering his dollar again, said, "Aw, shet up, Rufe!"

Max heard it. "Iss too bad," he whispered to himself. He had not closed his eyes. He lay awake thinking of the strong right arm. He was still awake when Miss Lillie began to ring her bell for five o'clock breakfast.

Rufus avoided the Shannon house. His lunch was brought to the fields each day by Peter Cat, and as he already knew what must be done to the land, he had no need to appear for instructions. If Anna Shannon wished to instruct him, she would find him at the barn early in the mornings and at dusk in the afternoons. He saw no sign of her other than a distant glimpse as she drove at noon toward the sawmill. As for Todda, he saw her each evening riding home beside Jesse Shannon. He was glad he did not encounter them, for his heart was committed against women.

In order to forget the sight of Todda riding primly in the master's buggy, each day after supper he willingly tossed a few pitches with Max. It was a great help, until he went upstairs and got into bed. There, he lay awake considering all the aspects of his leaving. Who would take over the farm? He had not been fired. The old, inborn, share-cropper feeling of belonging to the man he worked for rose again and again in him. He had not a single proper and authoritative reason to consider himself free. For the first time in his life, his nerves were on edge. He began to worry.

On Friday morning, after a night of tumbling, Rufus got up an hour earlier than usual. He shook Max awake, and the two went down with ball and mitt. Miss Lillie was already up and at work in the kitchen; the smell of coffee and bacon was beginning to fill the air. She looked at them curiously, but twenty years of boarders had stifled her nature to inquire. Later, in the grey twilight, a leather-cracking sound exploded at ten-second intervals. The smell of the coffee and bacon grew richer and richer; the twilight explosions grew sharper and louder. A few sleep-choked faces appeared at windows upstairs and yelled down insulting and vulgar threats.

Rufus and Max walked off toward the creek a hundred yards away and sat down. "Iss too bad," Max said.

"What?"

"You got to leave."

"I don't have to leave!" Rufus said heatedly.

Max was not offended. "No. I know. She no good to you. She got the boss in her eye. You get no sleep. Vell, iss too bad. Hnnh?" He caught Rufus's right arm and shook it. "Very fine arm. To-morrow you vill pitch. You leave? Vhere do you go?"

Rufus shook his head, and handed the ball to Max. "Don't count on me." He went off to the barn without breakfast.

His hunger whetted his senses. Never had his hands ripped more eagerly into the shucks; never had the sharp, sweet smell of alfalfa penetrated so deeply; never had the section-harrowed land looked so vital. If he should lift a pinch of it to his tongue, he believed it would taste like rich tobacco.

The morning sun bore down upon him, June weather in April. His clothes were soaked with sweat. His stomach rolled and growled in hunger. There were four teams going, breaking from the edge of a six-acre rectangle. Every hour the other three teams lapped Rufus. Each time he threw his plough aside to let the other teams pass, he cursed his own mules bitterly, though all hands knew he had the fastest pair in the fields.

He drank water by the quarts. It poured through his body, alleviating none of his hunger pains. By mid-morning, he was forced to stop one of the ploughs and send for more water. That single interruption seemed to spoil the whole morning's work. Rufus drove his mules harder. He was in a panic. One minute the fresh earth crumbling from the wing of his plough excited him, brought forth the image of green crops soon to be; the next minute he would have welcomed a wind that would blow away every loose inch of the soil around him.

At last he drove his mules to a small willow shade at the creek bank. One glance at the sun assured him that the dinner bell would ring in a quarter of an hour. He signalled for the hands to take out. They unhitched, pretending the bell had rung, and led all the mules toward the barn. Rufus stretched out beneath the willow and waited for Peter Cat to bring his food. Finally, it occurred to him that he was not terribly hungry, that something else had hounded him all morning long. Aye god, he thought, I'll shore be glad when I git away from here so I won't have to keep on thinking 'bout leaving.

Peter Cat appeared with a water bucket full of food. "They done fixed extra," he explained. "Said you never had no breakfust."

"How'd they know that?" Rufus asked.

"Musta been a little burd told 'em."

"Don't mock at me," Rufus said, still partially hounded.

"Nossuh. You knows how women is. You ain't never been married, is you, Mister Rufe? Well, you ain't met no trouble face to face yet. But 'scusing the trouble 'er not 'scusing it, a woman is a mighty powerful joy. I figure the good Lawd sho' knowed what He was doing when He made this ole world and all's in it. No longer'n last Saturday the Lawd said to me, 'Peter Cat, heah is two roads: one lead home to yo' good wife, Ursa, and the other lead rat down to the Holyoke boys with all that sinful liquor and evil bones.' Seems like I got to find out iffen the Lawd really knows. I wakes up Sunday mawning and I says, 'Lawd, you was sho' right; hit was a mighty evil road.' And I puts my arm 'round Ursa, so iffen the Devil reach at me again he can't pull me away. Ain't nothing but a wife can keep a man outa trouble; and when he take his eye offen her, the devil got his eye on him. I brung you some fresh water too, Mister Rufe." He uncorked the jug and held it out. Then he sat down and waited while Rufus ate, disappointed that complete silence had settled between them.

The silence brought to Peter Cat's mind the picture of his son Mansell, who was now in Texas because he had been accused of stealing two hams. His intuition had, from the first meeting, sensed a struggle in this young white giant, who had perhaps been driven here by theft or rape or murder. Whatever the charge, just or unjust, Peter Cat wished to help. He grew bold. "Mister Rufe, is you in trouble?" Somewhere, somebody might be doing such a thing for his son.

"Trouble?"

"Yessuh. Trouble," Peter Cat whispered. His eyes were beginning to dilate, because he believed he had struck a telling chord.

Rufus, with his stomach quieted, was feeling better. He caught the vibrations from Peter Cat. "Plenty. I don't mind telling you, Pete, the law's on my heels. I'm gonna have to skin outa here soon. You could tell they was after me, couldn't you?"

"Yessuh."

"You felt it, didn't you? You could see it in my eyes. You could tell they was tracking me down; don't tell me you couldn't."

Peter Cat nodded.

Rufus's voice became lower, sensuous, depraved. "They gonna git me this time. I can feel them gittin' closer and closer. At night when I git into bed. . . ." He suddenly shivered, jerked his body around as if someone stalked behind them. Peter Cat leaped halfway to his feet, let out a stifled scream, settled to the ground again with a thud. His body trembled.

"Nerves," Rufus said. "Feels like they always creeping up to my back. They gonna git me soon."

"What . . . what was it you done?" His eyes were huge, unblinking; his body still trembled slightly.

"Stuck up a bank . . . Chattanooga. Ain't that a fine-sounding word? Chattanooga . . . Chattanooga . . . Chattanooga . . . like a train. I had to shoot a woman in the leg . . . and shoot a bank-teller right through the Adam's apple, right there. . . ." He reached over to show Peter Cat, who drew back from the pointing finger and got up.

"If you was to see any strange men hanging around here," Rufus went on, "aye god, you better git to me and hep me git outa here."

"I sho' do it." Peter Cat's hands worked quickly at putting the empty dishes into the water bucket. When he was gone, Rufus stretched out and slept for fifteen minutes, waiting for the hands to return with the teams. He smiled in his sleep.

The afternoon was sheer pleasure. He laughed over his story to Peter Cat; the hands, picking up his mood, hummed and sang and yelled crude jokes to each other. The land, which was becoming drier, pulverized better; sparrows and jays swooped down in search of worms; kildees squalled and feigned broken wings in a vain attempt to preserve their nests from the ploughs; the flicflac of harness was steady and soothing, reassuring as cow-bells at dusk.

In the late afternoon, a few rounds before quitting time, Peter Cat came running toward the fields. Under the spur of emergency, his gangling body whipped over obstacles like a young hurdler. From some distance away he yelled, "Don't go, boss! Hit's a trick! Hit's a trap to ketch you. . . ." Coming to a standstill, he calmed himself enough to explain, "Miss Anna sent fer you. Somebody at the house wants to see you."

Rufus was puzzled as well as curious to discover who could want him. He put the checklines around Peter Cat's waist and started off, undisturbed, toward the house.

Peter Cat shook with fear for his brave friend walking into a nest of danger. To the hands, he muttered foolish warnings about traps and tricks and officers in hiding.

After crossing the first fence, Rufus decided somebody had come for him to file a bunch of saws. The thought was irking. A man worth his salt didn't like being switched from job to job. The anger pushed him on rather than held him back; his long strides ate up the ground.

He entered the yard frowning. A second later, a small figure emerged from the front of the house and stopped at the end of the porch. The figure stood in faded and threadbare knickerbockers, innocent and frightened, leaning heavily on his twelve years for poise and the right thing to say. Rufus jolted to a standstill a few yards away. He was vaguely frightened too, because his mind did not quickly grasp this small miracle. He stared at Sidney.

Then his face seemed to splinter like tapped ice, and he began to laugh. His arms slipped forward in a gesture of welcome. Sidney made a few cautious steps toward Rufus, paused, as if he might run in any direction. Then with a burst of confidence, he leaped forward and locked his arms around the giant, sunburned neck.

"How'd you come?" Rufus whispered.

"On the train. Are you mad at me? . . ."

"No. You run off?" Rufus felt the face nod against his neck. "You'd better slip down. I'm wet."

Sidney slipped to the ground and looked up with wonder and awe at this great man who was his brother. "To-day's my birthday."

Rufus reached down and grabbed both ears; it was an oldtime gesture with Sidney. "I remembered it, didn't I?"

Sidney nodded. "That's how I had enough to buy my ticket." He looked down at his clothes, ashamed. "I didn't have much . . . that was fit to bring."

In his enthusiasm and tenderness, Rufus closed his hands too roughly on Sidney's ears. Sidney struggled to show no sign of pain. "Can I stay?"

Rufus's hands became more gentle. He was overcome by that small frame of pride and innocence and honesty. In a temper of generosity, he seized Sidney's arm and led the way across the fields, across the creek toward Burke's store.

For convenience, they entered through the back door of the store. Rufus pulled shirts, pants, overalls, socks, underwear, and shoes from the rear shelves and pushed them into Sidney's arms. Azel Burke stood with mute attention until the final selections were made. With some misgivings, he began to wrap the clothes.

When the wrapping was finished, Rufus said, "Charge all this to me—to Rufus Frost."

Azel rolled the pencil on his tongue, stalling; he had been fooled before by honest, clear grey eyes. "You work for Jesse Shannon, don't you?"

"That's right."

Azel was still wary; the years of general merchandising had taught him several lessons. Again he rolled the pencil, unaware of its flat, chalky taste. "You not fixing to quit him?"

"Nossir. I ain't fixin' to quit nobody."

"Well, lemme see. . . ." He made a quick calculation of the total. "That's all I wanta know. Hand it to me whenever you can." Sometimes a man had to gamble.

That night, just before Sidney climbed into bed beside Rufus (in a double bed which Max Muller had willingly given up with the repeated comment, "Iss fine boy, iss fine boy, Rufus") he picked up each new item and smelled deeply. His enormous blue eyes followed the men who welcomed him with awkward, friendly stares; his ears drank in their rough, uncensored banter; his heart was full of a memorable day. Never before had he owned more than two shirts or two pairs of socks. He would work hard, he would try his best to repay Rufus. He felt done with childhood.

The lamp was turned out; the men settled on their hard mattresses; all was quiet, but for deep, masculine breathing. Rufus placed his arm across the small body beside him. It was a gesture of gratitude more than affection: Sidney had settled a tremendous thing for him.

5

RUFUS FROST had none of the expressive faculties of the artist, yet he had an insatiable will to create. It was morally and spiritually necessary for him to build with his own hands and body. Building a fence or a chicken coop, growing a field of corn or cotton, raising a calf: these activities satisfied his nature to some degree, giving him an excitement similar to that received by Barney and Sterling while felling a tree.

But building alone did not begin to fulfil the enormous desires of Rufus Frost. After the creation, he needed to possess; not intimately, but in a vague, ruling manner. The new crops gave him endless pleasure. The cotton seemed to leap by inches overnight, and already the corn was tall enough to shadow-strip the ground from row to row. All was his: the barn, the stock, the fields. No one interfered. Except at the Saturday afternoon ball-games, or the Saturday-night barn dances, he rarely spoke to Anna and Jesse Shannon. His weekday discussions with either of them were of the briefest nature, usually ending with, "Back your own judgment." He had done so, to the last stalk, and the achievement was his own.

The heart of the Hollow stretched out in a miraculous pattern of growth. Nowhere within a day's walk could one find comparable fields. The lush growth, the certain promise of autumn plenty, the smell of the rain-ripe earth drove him on, like an athlete who draws the last cruel drop of energy so that thousands of raw-throated devotees can boast. The fire in him burned with the sun.

At night, however, instead of heavy fruited rows, he often saw wood-smoke and dying leaves, brittle skeletons probing the fog and mist of winter. To put his arm around the slim, exhausted body of Sidney gave him only a momentary sense of peace. Night by night and week by week, his masculine desires whetted intemperately. He cursed Todda; he tried to hate her; failing, he drove himself and Sidney harder and harder, as if they were both lost and the coming harvest was their only salvation.

Miss Lillie, sensing the desperate demands Rufus made of Sidney, brought her mother instinct into the battle. "You working that child too hard. He ought not to work but half-time since he don't get but half-pay. You make it lighter on him, else I'll hire him myself." She meant her threat. Though Rufus agreed with her—and slackened his demands immediately—he resented her intrusion and her struggle for Sidney's affection. Unconsciously, he knew that if she won Sidney now, he would have nothing left. He was not one to live with nothing.

The hot days wore on in high key, broken each evening by a few minutes of practice pitching with Sidney or Max. (Sidney had somewhere discovered an old catcher's mitt which he hid in the barn loft; occasionally he and Rufus had a pitching session while they waited for the hands to finish with the feeding.) The sultry June nights worked magic on the cotton; slow, soaking rains came at perfect intervals for the corn. An air of abundance flooded the Hollow. Though many hands had left to tend their crops, the saw-mills were still running full-scale. Yet, a sense of ponderous waiting hovered. Those who noticed—as Anna Shannon—and analysed, laid the cause at the feet of the Kaiser and the coming war.

Rufus had matters other than war to weigh and consider. With monotonous regularity he saw Todda as Jesse drove her home each evening. It seemed that Fate turned his head at the right moment and he beheld them: Jesse, a doting suitor, and Todda, a veritable queen. But he had made up his mind that none of it would give him pain, and he succeeded, with some irritation.

When it was clear to all that Rufus, for one reason or another, was no longer Todda's suitor, a strange affinity developed between her twin-brother, Howard, and Rufus. Howard sought out Rufus, followed his heels like a faithful dog, laughed at Rufus's infrequent jokes, and gave warm attention to Sidney. He suggested fishing trips with such pleading enthusiasm that Rufus could not handily refuse.

On those trips he occasionally mentioned his regrets that Rufus and Todda had "broken up." Then he proceeded to describe in detail Jesse Shannon's actions toward Todda, mocking his looks, his grin, his pale, awkward body (which was not really awkward at all), and sometimes his self-conscious courting words. If Rufus continued to listen, Howard would clinch his small, calloused fists, squint his steely grey eyes, and hurl feverish accusations at that rich, anæmic beanpole who had stolen his sister from her childhood sweetheart. Todda, Howard said, was blind, pore thing.

Rufus usually found the conversations amusing. Whether there was any truth in the details Howard recounted, he could not decide; for he recalled clearly the scalding anger those steely grey eyes had hurled at him only a few weeks before. He no longer tried to presage what would happen between Todda and Jesse Shannon; he merely wished that the event, if foreordained, would occur soon and settle something for him, as Sidney's arrival had settled his intended departure.

At last the days lost some of their fury; a layer of green faded from the fields. Work slackened; the crops would soon be finished. The Negroes began to talk of watermelons and the Fourth of July. Baseball raised its head in full force. To the Saturday afternoon affair was added a mid-week game. Rufus reigned on the mound for the Hollow, and the people turned out almost as faithfully as for a funeral.

The games were held in Holyoke pasture, with a small clump of trees serving as grandstand. The infield was kept in excellent condition, though in the outfield patches of bitterweeds had tripped many a fly-chaser trying for a hero's role. The ground rules were vague, causing many squabbles with the umpire, who stood six feet behind the pitcher's mound instead of behind home plate. But arguments were usually mild for fear the unsalaried umpire would resign in the midst of a game. No averages were kept, but the spectators—women and men alike—spoke of hits and errors and earned runs as if each player's record were kept to four decimal places.

The women spectators outnumbered the men, who came primarily to see the game. Some women came because it was a chance to flee from the kitchen for a few hours; some came to show off their babies; others came because it was simply somewhere to go. Todda came because she loved baseball; Anna came because Rufus was the pitcher.

By the second or third game, Anna began to comprehend. She always chose a position near Sidney and whispered questions to him. His lean, finely sculptured face lit at the chance of answering. Between Sidney and Anna, no eye could have judged accurately which body trembled more, which uncoiled more energy, which suffered more in the static, futile agony of helping Rufus each time his arm pumped and sent the ball blazing toward the enemy's bat. When he walked the enemy, when he failed to gather in their bunts, when he threw wild past the catcher, he still remained their hero. There he was on the mound, tireless, fed by the sunlight, a lean, victory-hungry giant. When someone sent his best curve into the bitterweeds, he paused, pushed back his cap, and wiped the sweat from his face; or he spat a golden stream of tobacco juice toward third base. He was never disconcerted, Anna thought; he was invincible, regardless of who won or lost. His incidental grin while on the mound, his few casual words to her and Sidney after winning a game (and if he had lost one, it was not his fault), his strolling off to join the team and rehash each play (taking even Sidney from her) was enough to undo her for days. Yet she was certain his eyes fell on her at times with far more than passing interest. She lived in a restless state; her most sacred energies fed a steady and consuming hope. Never was her agony greater, never was her hope stronger, than when she watched him, towering on the pitcher's mound like something on Olympus.

Rufus was not a good pitcher: it was simply that he never got too tired, he had control, and he used his head. But his big frame and steady nerve made him look quite professional. When a batter drove one of his pitches over the head of an outfielder, the comments fell one of two ways: if the hitter was a good one, they said, "Why, feller, that boy could hit anybody"; if the hitter was mediocre, they said, "Watch big Rufe. That boy ain't had a hit in so long, Rufe jist got sorry fer him."

Gradually word spread that Rufus Frost was a demon with a baseball. He had phenomenal success; because the batters, who had heard tall tales, kept looking for knucklers and sinkers and sliders, while Rufus threw the only things he could throw, a wide-breaking curve and a three-quarter fast ball. As July approached and his success continued, he was asked to pitch, for a 10-dollar fee, in Cross City's Independence Day game. All of the Hollow awaited the appointed day, sharing the anticipated glory.

Work in the fields was finished except for a few acres of late corn and the hay crop, which would not be ready for another two weeks. As nothing was pressing, Rufus and Sidney spent many off-hours with the baseball. Late in the afternoon before the big game, they stationed themselves behind the barn for a final practice session. Sidney crouched with the mitt swallowing his left hand, and imitated Max Muller: "Chunk it on in here, baby . . . you the von . . . you the von. . . ." He was thrilled to have even that much of a part in the coming show. For an hour Rufus threw, not much harder than Sidney himself could have thrown. Then gradually he increased his speed, asking from time to time, "Is that too hard?"

"Nope," Sidney said, and, still in imitation of Max Muller, he called for more and more.

Rufus was having almost as much fun as Sidney, but the sun was setting and it was time to quit. Before making his last pitch toward the mitt hanging bravely on that small left hand, he looked by chance past the corner of the garden toward the road. There against the dying rays of the sun rode Todda and Jesse. The sight was absurdly infuriating to him. Under the spell of fury he gripped the ball tighter and tighter, leaned back and fired a sharp-breaking curve ball. By the time his wrist snapped and the ball shot forward, he knew he had done a terrible thing. His tongue, half-paralyzed, yelled, "Let it go, Sid boy! Let it go!" But his words hung in his throat. The ball went straight for the mitt, broke sharply, and cracked, instead, against the naked right palm. For a few seconds, Sidney staggered blindly, the way a killdee will flounder to lead something away from its nest, and then he fell face forward across his shattered right hand.

Rufus was white with fear; he went into a cursing rage, staring in the direction of Todda. Then, breaking from his trance, he scooped Sidney into his arms, kissed the broken hand, which was already twice its normal size, and rushed toward the house: to Anna or Ursa or anyone who could offer motherly protection for Sidney.

Almost within a matter of seconds, Anna had her own buggy rigged and was driving madly for Cross City, while Rufus held Sidney in his arms and mopped streams of sweat from the small, feverish face. Sidney writhed fitfully, but he made no whimper, except the occasional complaint, "I'm sick at my stomach, Buddy."

When the town's water-tank came into sight, Anna said, "We'll go to Dr. Fitzwanger. He's a cross-grained old fool, but he knows more about bones than anybody this side of Memphis."

Rufus nodded, now in a temporary lull. He had quit blaming Todda, and was weighing the blessing of having Anna along, who knew exactly what to do.

They found the doctor in his many-gabled grey house (which served as office, home, and hospital) slowly chewing tobacco and waiting, it seemed, for a casualty. Without rising, he watched the three enter. He was a tall, angular man, well past sixty, who had seen so much sickness and death that nothing would startle or hurry him. His chief stock in trade was two short coughs, a long breath, and "Ah, you can't beat Nature."

"Well, now," he said with a cough. Then a second cough, "What you got here? A sick boy?"

"His hand," Rufus said gruffly, completely outdone with the doctor's poking, unconcerned manner.

A nurse wheeled Sidney into another room; the hand was inspected, while sharp cries split the room. It seemed to Rufus that hours went by and nothing had happened. Then followed a nightmare of screams, of turning white walls, of drifting ether (Anna had made the decision for an anæsthetic), and funereal whispers. Rufus crouched by a window, a hungry ghost of himself. He had never been in a hospital before. His eyes felt too large, his head weighed heavily, and his right arm seemed to be pitching the ball over and over again. At last he whispered, "I'm sick, Anna. Lord, I'm sick!"

She took him outside. "You get some fresh air. I'll stay with Sid."

He sat down under a huge oak and leaned against its trunk. The wind dried the sweat from his face, from the palms of his hands, but his mind was a tangled mass of ifs and whys, a curious arrangement of scenes showing that small hand warm and healthy, reaching for bread from Miss Lillie's table or grasping a hoe-handle in a field owned by a stranger. Suddenly he realized that darkness was all about him, and he could not remember when dark had come. The thought of returning into the house made him sick again. He made bitter accusations against himself, against Todda, and pressed his right palm against the bark of the tree to erase the feel of the ball. His head began to ache and it seemed that he was coming down with chills and fever. He wished mightily for a long stretch of black land and a pasture of untamed horses. If a horse had stepped on the hand, it would be different.

Someone called his name.

He staggered to his feet and recognized Anna. "Is it bad?"

"Not quite as bad as the doctor first thought. He got a good set. Sid woke up, but he's back asleep now. He can go home in the morning."

"In the morning?" It had not occurred to him that it might be necessary to spend the night. He had, in reality, seen the whole thing as a needless tragedy in which time was not involved.

Anna led the way to the north wing of the house, which served as a six-room hospital. They entered a room, bare except for the tall hospital bed, a table, and one chair. At the end of the table, a coal-oil lamp burned dimly. Rufus knelt beside the bed; the benumbing aroma of ether struck his face, but he knew it would not bother him now that everything was safely over. After a few minutes, Sidney opened his eyes. "Where's Buddy?" It was a quick, jerky question.

"Here he is," Anna said.

"Are you mad at me?" Rufus whispered.

Sidney shook his head weakly. "Is there an animal named ether?" He made the smile of those with nauseated stomachs. "When I was going to sleep, you-all laughed at me and said an animal named ether was going to tell me a secret. I saw him. He looked like a rabbit, but he didn't tell me anything. He ran away. . . ."

The nurse leaned over and put a drop of castor oil into each eye.

Rufus's big hands clutched the sheet; he pressed his lips against the helpless throat, a gesture to erase the thought of what he had done. Sidney closed his eyes and went back to sleep. Rufus remained kneeling, staring at the bundlesome, splinted hand, until the nurse suggested that they leave.

Together, in the heavy night, Rufus and Anna walked aimlessly. By accident, they crossed the railroad, approached the depot and the only all-night café in town. A small boy ran barefooted over the cinders toward them, held out a Memphis paper. Rufus bought one.

"Want one too, lady? Only got one left. See?"

Anna bought one. The boy rushed back toward the corner of the depot, where his sack lay still half full.

The café, a small dingy room smelling of strong coffee and bacon, was frequented by railroad men who ate breakfast there at all hours of the day and night. Anna and Rufus chose a corner booth; they pushed their papers aside without a glance even at the war headlines. Each remained on guard, withdrawn, afraid. Lurking in Rufus's mind was his own poverty-stricken background and crude manners. He remembered that first day at the barn when he had found pleasure in those vulgar expressions; he was ashamed. He remembered the times he had come face to face with her and would quickly pull his fingers across the corners of his mouth for fear she might see the ugly stains of Old Apple. Any man might chew—it was the custom—but only the crude and careless went about with stained mouths. (He had learned that from an old Negro man named Vivian, from whom he had learned to chew and with whom he had cut a thousand cords of wood. What were the other things he had learned from old Vivian? He needed them now. What was the thing the old man had said again and again? No man knows where he is going until he gets there. Yes, of course, but that was no help now.) The neat, unruffled appearance of Anna caused him to look down at his work-clothes. "I'm sorry about these clothes. . . ."

"Nothing wrong with them," she said. "You didn't have time to think about changing clothes."

"No; I didn't. It was awful quick. You know how much that ball curved? That much." He measured a wide space with his hands. He could feel the baseball tight within his fingers. He touched her hand and the feel of the ball slipped away.

A waitress came. They ordered only coffee. A group of railroad men entered, one carrying a lantern and singing good-naturedly:

> "It seem like to me
> She come from Tennessee;
> I wouldn't be for sure,
> 'Cause I don't know.

Some good day
I'm gonna check,
Gonna ask,
Or break my neck;
But I'll never ask
Without my forty-fo'."

The man looked at Rufus and Anna and smiled. The waitress brought coffee.

Rufus felt a sudden release of energy in his body. The penned emotions of a long, desperate summer began to stir in him. He was aware, now, of all the times he had looked at Anna as if she were forbidden to him. He saw, now, her strength, her plain attractiveness, her passionate smile; he saw the real truth imprisoned in her shining black eyes. The crisis was formed. Energies rose slowly in his body, as if he were a giant tree with a hollowed heart, through which bright-eyed animals climbed. In a violent motion he leaned forward, thrust the palms of his hands over her ears, and crushed her lips beneath his own. The act was both wild and tender.

Without a word they got up and left the café. Still silent, his arm around her, they turned along the railroad tracks. Behind them was the glare of the station lights; ahead were the grey, unlit houses and a blanket of clouds ripped by heat lightning. Even in the darkness, the rails glistened like two endless swords. The houses were so near the tracks, and the July night was so still, they could hear intimate whisperings as they went along. Their hearts beat fiercely; neither had any question of what would happen to them: it had been decided long ago, as naturally, inevitably, as two streams flowing together.

The enchantment was upon them, leading them beyond the grey houses and the voices into a darkness which, on most nights, belonged to other and darker lovers.

6

WHEN Anna spoke to Jesse of the bond between her and Rufus, his first reaction was one of envy—the natural envy that all people outside the magic circle have for those in love. Like a dart to the keenest point of his mind came the recollected expression of his favourite schoolmate, a wit who always pretended to be suffering at the hands of a young co-ed.: "My dear, I care not if you fling your caresses like the mad Ophelia scattering her flowers." Remembering, Jesse smiled.

The sight of his smile brought a storm of anger to Anna's face. "You think it's funny!"

Her anger shocked him back to seriousness. "Anna! I wasn't

laughing. . . . Please believe me, I'm glad for you." To prove his good faith, he repeated his words, asked questions about Sidney, and finally insisted that Sidney should be brought to their house, where there was ample help to care for him: Ursa, Todda, and Anna herself.

That day, Sidney was transferred to the Shannon house while Miss Lillie protested and was openly offended. She had looked forward to showering her affections upon him.

Sidney uttered no preferences. He was almost as enchanted by his second new world as by his first one. Ursa attended him with infinite care; she put a small service bell beside his bed, insisting that he ring for the slightest item. "And whut's more," she said, "iffen you gits jist plain lonesome, you pound on it, baby, and I be heah."

Ursa loved to wear dilapidated old shoes discarded by Jesse, and cover her head with stockings discarded by Anna. In contrast, her uniform was always meticulously clean and starched to the point of breaking. She worked diligently when she could find no one to talk to; alone, she often recounted the troubles she was suffering from Peter Cat, who was enough to make a woman "rat discouraged" with men. In general, she did not like people. But she loved the sick and helpless, and took to Sidney immediately and more completely than she had taken to anyone since Jesse was a child.

One afternoon she came into Sidney's room, dropped into a chair beside the bed, for the climb upstairs had winded her. "You rang fer me, honey?"

"No; I don't want anything."

"I thought you rung."

She continued to sit, and he knew she had come to talk.

"I guess they ain't tole you nuthing 'bout it, Mista Sid-baby, but ain't gonna work . . . shore Lawd ain't gonna work. Me? I ain't saying it ain't gonna work . . . ain't me. It sumthin' else come telling me, come saying to me, No! Mista Jesse ain't gonna kick up. He been good all his life . . . he a sweet man. But it ain't gonna work."

"What, Ursa?"

She could see the brightness in him and that was why she wished to tell; she wished to see what would happen to the brightness. "I guess they ain't tole you Miss Anna gonna marry Mista Rufe?"

Sidney laughed. The brightness did not flicker. He was not in a position to be surprised, not with a broken hand in a second new world. And besides, it seemed far-off, like a rain cloud that never brought rain.

"Well, they is. But it ain't gonna work. A thing comes telling me. An' I know why."

He waited for her to go on, but she withdrew, sullen, distant. She gazed out the window. If the big man had in his face the brightness before her, it would be different. With her, where there was no brightness, there was uneasiness.

"Why, Ursa?"

Still, she did not come back for a while, until suddenly she turned her eyes on him, leaned her shoulders forward. "You like . . . uh . . . strawberries?"

"Yeah."

"You like . . . uh . . . choc'late pie?"

"Yeah?"

"They both good, ain't they?"

"Yeah."

"But they ain't good mixed together. Lawd, how mercy, honey. . . ."

Sidney burst out laughing again. "Which one is the pie, Ursa? Which one is the pie?"

"Hush," she warned.

"Make me a chocolate pie," he cried. "Please make me one, Ursa!"

"Hush," she warned again.

They heard someone coming up the stairs. She got up, took his splintered hand, touched the tip of his fingers, inspected his fingernails.

Anna entered the room, smiling. Her face had a new energy, a radiant quality like that in the faces of people who are preparing for a pleasant journey. It made Ursa sad to see it, for she was certain about her premonition; it was plain as the wind though there were no trees or weathervanes to tell its direction.

"Now, what've you two been plotting about?"

"Nuthing," Ursa said, and slipped out of the room as quietly as a cat.

Anna sat down on the side of the bed, a gesture which she hoped would establish a certain intimacy between her and Sidney. "In a few days, I've got something to tell you."

Sidney did not want to help her by saying he already knew. She was, after all, taking his brother, leaving him in an uncertain status. How could he know now whether he liked such arrangements? "When can I go home?" he asked.

She was surprised. "Don't you like it here?"

"I like it. But I'm well enough to go home."

"The quieter you are the more rest you have, the quicker your hand'll be well."

"I think," he announced with finality, "I ought to go to Miss Lillie's to-morrow."

Later in the afternoon Rufus came by, grinning, his voice in a

ringing good humour. "They tell me you gitting homesick. How
come? Miss Lillie's awful busy. Would you stay if I was to ask
you to?"

"Yes."

"But I ain't going to ask you to less you don't mind."

"I'll stay if you'll get Ursa to make me a big chocolate pie."
Seeing that he had stopped his big brother, he burst out laughing
again. "When you gonna marry Miss Anna?"

A flaming grin chocked Rufus's face and his words too. "You
see. . . ." Failing for words, he shook Sidney's knee roughly. He saw
the brightness too.

A little while before supper-time, Jesse Shannon came into
Sidney's room for his usual daily visit. He sat in profile, his left side
to Sidney, for on the right side of his chin was a tiny mole, hardly
noticeable, except that during any moment of stress he always
drew attention to it by constant rubbing with his thumb. His brief
daily visits had acted on him; Sidney's innocent gaze had been like
warm sunlight after a long dark winter. A few minutes ago, when
Anna remarked that Sidney was getting homesick, he had been
completely unnerved. Until then it had not occurred to him that
Sidney would ever get well and leave their house. Quickly he had
gathered up every boy's book he could find and had rushed
upstairs as if he carried some vital medicine. In the presence of
Sidney, his unnecessary rush seemed foolish. He placed the books
on the bed table and sat down quietly, completely at a loss for
words. He remembered the books. "You like to read, don't you,
Sid?"

"I'd rather fish."

Jesse was hurt, but he did not blame Sidney; he blamed something
else, out of the house and far away.

Sidney leaned forward, with his dark eyes shining. "Could I fish
much with my left hand, reckon?"

"You want to go fishing? I'll take you fishing."

Sidney nodded. "You rig up for us to go. I want to go soon as I
can." He spoke exactly as he pleased, for Jesse Shannon was to
him like another little boy.

"I'll rig it up," Jesse said, smiling, and rubbing the mole on
his chin.

"Do you like secrets?" Sidney asked, and now he felt older than
the man beside him. "My brother is going to marry your sister. Did
you know that?" His eyes were huge and glowing, a world where
tiny creatures lived.

"Yes," Jesse whispered back, under a spell.

His secret was not a secret; the light faded in his eyes. "Would
we be kin, me and you?"

"Yes," Jesse whispered, and the brightness blinded him.

"I bet they go off and stay a long time. Will they, you reckon?"

Jesse could say nothing. He forgot the mills and the men. He forgot his secret city. He forgot that Todda was waiting for him.

Sidney glanced at the books. "I never read that many books in all my life put together. How many books you ever read?"

"I couldn't count them."

"That many!"

Ursa called that Todda was waiting. He went down the stairs slowly, and on the road he drove slowly and silently; but returning, watching the light in the room upstairs, he began to feel better. He was laughing as he sat down at the table. It was a bit unusual for him. He glanced at Anna, saw the new thing burning quietly in her eyes. It seemed that in the last few days he had been to the secret fountain in the heart of his secret city; he had drunk and its water had worked a miracle. For the first time in his life he understood Anna; he understood how the springs of her being flowed toward one person, alone; how perhaps she hungered for his words, sought the faintest glimpse of his face in sunlight or shadow. He knew, and he wished to shout his knowledge, let the world know that he understood.

"Anna, I've never tried to advise you, have I?"

"No." She grew tense; her eyes were apprehensive.

"I think you're doing right. Marry him. They're good people. I know . . . I feel it. Other things don't matter. Don't be afraid."

"I'm not afraid."

"No . . . you're not. I might be. But you're not. It'll all work out."

Ursa came out of nowhere, mumbling, "Shore Lawd ain't gonna work neither. Ain't me saying it. A thing comes telling me. . . ."

Jesse prepared himself to hush her, but she disappeared into the kitchen. To dispel any shadow Ursa had cast over the room, he said again to Anna, "I think you're doing right."

When the meal was finished, Jesse went to his room, which was directly below Sidney's, and reclined on his bed. Lately he had not used his imagination, except when he thought of his secret city. But it seemed to him now that the future was settled: it was bright and pleasant, and the earth was ruled by a queen like Anna and a king like Rufus, who smiled and bowed to each other. And there was a prince also, a clever, smiling, bright little prince.

From the very beginning he had liked the man's face, his hands, his voice, his way of standing, his way of going. Surely he would have known, without asking, that such a man came from a land where rocks lay buried, a land which might have given him those things too. Not that it mattered, not that he would ever again let those things matter. He smiled and felt a breeze which did not exist. He was utterly proud of himself, proud that he understood Anna in a matter concerning the heart. An easiness was upon him, a strange, comfortable feeling that all roads led toward him rather than away, as if he were some strange device or unfinished work of art, perhaps, which people came to gaze upon.

He got up, and standing before the mirror in semi-darkness, he undressed for bed. He inspected his smooth white body, unbroken by muscles, devoid of power and the strength to hurt. He neither liked nor disliked the looks of himself, but in the faint light he was superbly graceful. "Ah, well," he said, "I was never meant to be king."

He got into bed and turned his face toward the windows. A real breeze came out of the night and covered him. How long since he had felt such peace? His mind worked backward along a tenuous passage until light broke through, into his cave of golden dreams.

7

THEY were married in the Shannon house, without music and with little ceremony. The minister, a heavy-set young man with thick glasses, conducted the occasion with obvious dignity. He was a Presbyterian and well aware that his flock was an economic notch above the Baptists: in general in the Hollow, the small landowners were Presbyterians, while the share-croppers and mill workers were Baptists—and more numerous. There were only two witnesses, Sidney and Jesse. Todda had stayed at home that morning on the pretence that her mother was sick. Ursa was not really a witness, though she saw it all by standing in the corner of the dining-room and peeping through the double doors. During the brief ceremony she remained in the corner, shaking her head from side to side.

An hour after the ceremony, they were on the train for Memphis. "Poor Sid," Anna said, "I felt sorry for him. He worships you and we just walked off and left him."

"Sid's all right. He'll get along." Rufus spoke with assurance, but within him there was a touch of misgiving which had nothing to do with Sidney. He got up and went into the smoker so that he could look at himself in a full-length mirror. The image he saw pleased him: his new suit was well cut; his shoulders were straight; his face was angular and ruddy; his eyes were clear and firm. No man could tell by looking how far he had been in school, how far he had failed to go. He returned to his seat beside Anna.

"You're certainly dressed up," she whispered.

"No. It's just because I don't never wear suits. People who wear suits all the time don't look dressed up . . . or can't never really feel dressed up."

She smiled. The truth was, she too liked this man's face, his hands, his voice, his way of standing, his way of going; she liked as well as loved.

They made no plans, other than reservations at the Loyola House. The first evening they went to the Showboat on the river; the next afternoon they went to a baseball game, which Memphis lost. Anna had the wisdom to say, "Rufus, they need you to pitch for them." That single remark helped them over several difficult moments, as when Anna bought a dress and paid for it out of her own purse. Another thing helped too: Rufus knew that he outlooked any of the pudgy-faced planters who gathered in knots in the lobby of the Loyola House and smoked long cigars; he not only outlooked them; he was taller, stronger, and his wife was prettier than any of those old men's daughters. For all they knew, he owned every foot of the Hollow. They could go to hell. He regarded Delta people with the same measure of suspicion with which they regarded him, a hill-billy. If one of their julep-drinking pollywogs had a mind to test a corn-fed mountain fellow, let him come on, give him room. He would give them a lesson not available in books—grammar, high school, or college. Damn their blackland bones; they would not spoil his honeymoon.

And they did not. He laughed as well as the next man, or better, and laughter was a master key in their world of doors. Within two days he had become attached to three or four planters, and Anna had fallen in with their wives. He was delighted with them; he no longer saw pudgy faces, but instead wise, agreeable faces, grown a bit thick with age; he was surprised that their repertory of talk closely paralleled his own: the coming war, the weather, cotton, and pretty women. He smoked cigars with them; he said crops were good in the Hollow; a manly blush flowed in his cheeks when the dean of the planters, a widower of some years, spoke of Anna. "I'll be damned, Frost, but you've got a charming wife, and my God, she's a sensible woman! That's a splendid asset for anybody, particularly for a woman, suh. Don't ever forget it."

And, holding Rufus's sleeve, he added, "I can count on my fingers the number of sensible women between the lobby of this hotel and the National Cemetery of Vicksburg, which is one hundred and seventy-five miles as the crow flies, two hundred by rail, and I dare say two-fifty by water, and in that fertile stretch of land which will—as you may know—grow cotton to hide a mule, not twelve sensible women! Why? I'll tell you why, young fellow. We've spoiled them. Spoiled!" The word rolled in his throat and jumped out. He tightened his grip on Rufus's arm; he was transported in part by his own words, in part by the feeling that he had once been young and strong and grand in the eyes of women. "My God, how could men so misunderstand women? Well, suh, for one thing, a woman is inherently more sensible than a man. I cite you history. Women are not poets; they are not the dreamers of this world. The basic concern of woman is life and the act of making life; man is concerned with anything placed six inches before his nose or six light-years away. In order to free himself, to escape censure, he has encouraged her remotest and most unnecessary whims. He has dreamed and made of her an untouchable doll. Why, suh, a woman does not wish to be a doll; she wishes to be a woman! My God, it's refreshing to see a young man who understands that. . . ." He patted Rufus affectionately and dreamed once more of his own lost youth and the women he had spoiled. The conversation moved casually as smoke to a younger planter who was eager to make his impression on this uninitiated man from the hills.

Rufus liked being married; he liked the aura of the hotel, the bellboys in their blue uniforms, the gay ladies who came for lunch, the business transients, the leisurely planters; he liked the choices Anna made: her quick and decisive rejection of what displeased her as well as her spirited acceptance of what she liked. He was under a spell, conscious enough to reap all its benefits, but not quite aware enough to cast the spell away. The day of departure came like a shock, and in one final blow the spell was shattered completely; the bill he received at the cashier's window was three times every penny he had in his pocket. Anna quietly dissolved the emergency before anyone could realize there was one. Rufus had intended to tell all his planter friends goodbye, enjoy their good wishes, and insist that they would meet again. But he walked out of the lobby, directly past them, without a word.

The train gave him no comfort; the dry hills of July burned across his vision. The image of his sitting among the planters, laughing, smoking cigars, made him sick. He slouched down into his seat and closed his eyes.

Anna said nothing. She was tormented by his sealed lips and drooping shoulders. The thought of losing him was unbearable, and yet it seemed to her that he was gone, as if some omnipotent hand had arranged the cards against them, had dealt his strongest blow against the tender and fragile pride of a man from the hills. It was inconceivable that to-day's funereal silence should follow yesterday's laughter.

By the time they had reached home, matters were less painful, and at least the cloud of total silence had somewhat lifted. They remembered a funny man on the Showboat and laughed together over one of his silly jokes. Still, Anna was afraid—not that Rufus would walk off and leave her, but that she might lose him though he was there beside her.

For one wonderful moment, as they sat in the buggy which Peter Cat had brought to the station for them, he grasped her hand passionately; and the gesture was so spontaneous, so warm that their fingers seemed grafted together. At those times she had no misgivings.

It was late afternoon when they reached the house. Anna went immediately inside and, after a few words, upstairs to the room she and Rufus would occupy. Rufus had walked toward the barn and had stopped at the lot gate looking out over the crops. The sight of tall cotton and golden-topped corn made him feel better; it was really his. But he could not keep his mind on the crops, for there were certain other matters he had to face. Not Jesse. He and Jesse would get along well enough. As for Todda, he was blind as to where she stood—with Jesse, with himself, with anybody. He had never once talked to Anna about Todda. His mind drifted back to the crops again. The Negroes had said openly that no such crops had been seen on that place since old man Shannon died. He, Rufus, had directed every move, and had made a good many of them himself. Why shouldn't he feel the whole thing belonged to him, to the Negroes, and to Sidney. Not the money each bale and ear would bring, but the crops themselves: every blade and tassel of corn, every leaf, stalk, and lock of cotton. He wanted to go out and gather it all into his arms, fling it at the feet of the pudgy-faced planters in the lobby of the Loyola House, and cry madly, "I raised this on land not even mine! That's why I can't pay my hotel bill. Damn your bale to the acre! Damn you to hell and all your spoiled women! Don't you ever laugh at me." A sobering thought came into his head: he could not remember any of their laughter.

He saw Peter Cat coming from the barn, and called to him. "Where's Sid, Pete?"

"He not here, Mista Rufe."

"Where is he?"

"He at the Kangaroo. It seem like to ever'body he got mad and lef'."

"Got mad? What'd he git mad about?"

"I don't know, suh. Ain't nuthin' I done."

The day was still hot, though the sun was almost gone. Nothing moved, and the only sound was the endless peeping of late chickens. August was two days away. Already in the air was a touch of fall, a favourite time for Rufus, but also a sad time because it was so close to winter. He looked at the coat across his arm; he could not use it much longer: it was too thin even for late fall winds. He was thinking of Sidney and beyond him, remembering how at the end of fall during lean years he had often wondered how his father could feed all of them during the winter: Vivian, Gay, Bee, himself, and Aunt Dora—Sidney was not yet born. It was hard to remember clearly a time when someone now living was not born. He started back to the house to ask Ursa about Sid. It occurred to him that by now Sid might have returned to Tennessee. With a panicky feeling, he rushed into the house.

The first person he met was Todda, in the dining-room. He saw her apron first, bright red against a blue-dotted print dress. Her hair was combed back and up and lay in a huge pile on the crown of her head. Her face wore a deliberate, amused smile.

"Where is Sidney?" he asked.

"Now . . . you don't expect me to keep up with a Frost?"

"I expect you to tell me where he is if you know."

"Yes, master. He went thataway." She pointed through the south windows toward the Kangaroo. Lifting her chin a bit, knowing she was in complete control, she smiled teasingly, pursed her lips. "Tell me, Mr. Shannon, how did your honeymoon go?"

"I don't know as I ever slapped a woman, but you call me that again and you'll know if I have or not."

"Don't be ugly. It's a good name, though it's not quite as good as Frost. Frost is such a clean name. Don't stand there looking mad. You got what you went after. Hnnnn? That's a nice suit you're wearing. Could I feel it?"

"I'd be pleased if you'd jist answer what I asked you."

"How much did that suit cost? You want me to tell you something? You're a nice-looking man—in overalls, khakis, or most nearly anything. I've seen you in all of 'em, remember? I think you're gonna be a great success in this world—in the Hollow, anyway."

"I don't care what you think. But I want you to git something straight. I think as much of her as I ever thought of you, and that ought to be plenty."

The word struck hard, but she refused to wilt. Her endless reserve of spirit kept alive a smile tinged with mockery.

He continued, "Only difference is, one's just startin'; the other's finished."

"Listen," she countered. "I know you flying high and mighty over Sister Todda. You won; I didn't—not yet. Just be careful you don't git your wings clipped."

"By you?"

"I might manage to clip one, and that's worse'n having both clipped. Clip one wing, a goose can't fly; clip both wings, she'll sail away. Not that you're a goose, even if you do have goose pimples. Ha! Ha! Ha! You're a gander. . . . I give you credit. You got sense enough to know it's all right for a woman to marry a rich man, but it looks a little fishy when a pore man marries a rich woman. Put that in your pipe and smoke it, Mr. Shannon!"

He walked across the room and slapped her soundly. She hardly moved. Her face burned both with stubborn anger and intense joy. She felt deep-rooted victory. "Want to do it again?"

"Why don't you git out of here?"

"And stay out?"

"You decide that."

"You're a generous master, Mister. . . ." She smiled fiendishly at him while his face constricted into a spasm of muscles. ". . . Mister Frost. What a nice name. It's so much prettier than Hurley or Shannon. But don't forgit: you and me come from the same old rocky clay. . . ."

His legs shook as he wheeled, dropped his coat in a chair, and went out of the house toward the Kangaroo. He forgot Todda and Anna and Jesse and the farm; he chose to think of his own blood kin, crippled and deserted, cast off to the mercy of a boarding-house mistress who might at that minute have him sweating for the crumbs from her table. Aye god, he would be enough boss in the Shannon house to have his own brother; a prolonged stream of curses flowed through his mind as if something in the Shannon entourage had taken a whip to Sidney.

Another shock was waiting for him as he entered the Kangaroo. There at the kitchen table sat Sidney, his bandaged hand stretched out on the oilcloth, his left hand propped against his chin listening rapturously to Miss Lillie's account of her great robbery. The story was as fresh in her mind as it had been that night fifteen years ago, so her words ran unhaltingly and with full fervour while her hands kept busy at supper. Rufus burst in when the account was reaching its climax: there she sat combing her hair before the mirror when she spied the image of this man crawling from beneath her bed!

"Why'd you run off?" Rufus demanded outright, for he had already heard the end of the story.

"I didn't run off. I walked off."

"Whichever it was, how come you to?"

"I got mad."

"Who at?"

"I just got mad."

Rufus felt he had reached the limit of his good nature; he was in no mood for mystery. "You just got mad, huh? Cow kick you? Mule bite you? Or was it something I done? You gonna git mad at me like all the rest? You. . . ." Stalled, he reached out and grasped Sidney's chin, turning his face so that the childish blue eyes looked up at him with fear and aversion. "If you didn't want me to marry, why didn't you say so before now? Why'd you have to wait and run off like you was 'shamed of me?''

The fear left Sidney's eyes. With that rare discernment that sometimes falls upon the young, he understood the plight of the man towering over him. He wanted to help. "I wouldn't never be 'shamed of you, Buddy."

Rufus released his hand. He sat down on the bench beside Sidney, afraid to bring up the final, crucial point. His eyes turned toward Miss Lillie, who had remained beside the stove, her hands filled with a dish-towel and wet silverware, waiting her chance to defend Sidney and finish her story. The three waited. She thought it was time to speak. "I don't see no harm in him staying here."

Rufus searched the small face for some sign. "You ain't going back with me?"

"Not 'less I have to?"

"You ain't gonna tell me why?"

"Because I got mad at Mister Jesse. It wasn't you or Miss Anna or Todda, or nobody but him. I can't tell you why I got mad, but I ain't never been mad at you, Buddy."

Rufus knew it was finished, for the time being. He felt a deep satisfaction in that his own actions had nothing to do with Sidney's leaving. He reasoned that Sidney was an independent little rascal; and the more he thought of it, the more he admired his stubborn refusal to remain in the Shannon house. But there was no denying that the loss of Sidney was a blow, the second in less than an hour.

As he walked back to his new home, he tried to see a brighter side. Perhaps in a few weeks, when everything began to settle into a pattern, Sidney would shed his independence—or whatever grudge he had against Jesse—and rejoin the fold. Still, all of that was in the future, and a man had to live now, step by step, breath by breath. Aye god, it was no sense in popping down on your end and waiting for time to take charge. His long strides covered the ground with urgency.

A heavy dew had fallen. Dusk had drifted over the Hollow, and through it darted the sound of men going home—a few by wagon or buggy, a few on horseback or afoot. A sharp, nostalgic urge arose in him. All his life he had wanted a home of his own: a wife, a house, a brood of children. He wanted to be lord over all, the undisputed master. He wanted to be the giver of everything, and in turn the possessor, when he chose. And now he was going home to everything that was not his.

A light burned in Anna's room. He turned off the road, cut across the edge of the pasture, and hurried.

Anna was busy arranging small items in their room. He could tell that she was disturbed, though she made an effort to conceal her anxiety. He leaned against the door-facing and watched her. Their smiles reached out like hands to one another.

She glanced at his feet. "What happened to you?"

He looked down. The dew on the tall grass had wet his trousers halfway to his knees. "Looks like I fell in the creek."

"Did you?"

"No; the dew. I didn't fall into nothing. But I fell out with nearly ever'body except you." He put his arms around her, kissed her hair.

Her hands moved upward along his shirt to his collar. She unfastened his tie and threw it on to the bed; she thought he looked better without a tie. "Ursa told me Todda got mad and left." She dared not say any more.

His eyes averted her. "And before her it was Sid. I been to the Kangaroo. He wouldn't come back with me." What had been so clearly settled a few minutes before now arose as a solid doubt. "I think he's 'shamed of the way I done."

She held to his shirt, stunned, feeling the same cold silence that he felt. The immense distance between their worlds had drifted into focus again, this time with more severity. But she struggled to deny it, to prove it a mirage. To accept it would be like giving him up to the wars—no, much worse. Her hands pulled at him, embracing his powerful, immobile body. "Darling, what have I done?" she begged, hoping the fault could be laid upon her hands.

"Nothing." One arm caressed her body, while he looked down at the blowing warmth in her, the struggle in her to piece together something neither of them had torn apart. His impulse was to crush her to him and smother her doubts, and his own.

"What is it that keeps on working against us? It's something, day and night."

"Come here. . . ." He blew out the light and went to the row of south windows. Standing there, holding each other desperately, they looked out beyond the garden and the elm tree to the grey haze of fields. His hand described an arc that covered all the earth before their eyes, the trees, the hulking barn. "Fields, cattle, barn," he recited, and turning, pointed at his feet. "This house, this room, every chair, every bed, every lamp. Ain't none of it mine. Not a single handful of dirt, not a grain of corn, not a lock of cotton, not even the squeak of a rocking chair. . . ." He tried to grin.

She remained at the window, a foot away from him now, her head bowed, her hands clinging to the sill. It seemed useless to protest, to deny. She sensed the agony his pride suffered. She knew no remedy; and knowing none, she had the wisdom to keep still and silent.

He caught her chin, in the same way he had caught Sidney's a little while before, and tilted her face upward. "I don't want you to feel sorry fer me. Give me time and I'll have more'n twice what you can see outside that window. I don't know how, but I'll git it. Nothing's gonna stop me! Nothing! Not even my wife. . . ." He pulled her to him, leaned down and crushed his lips to hers. The act was somewhat brutal and wholly possessive.

PART TWO: 1917. WHITE-CROSS SLEEP

I

HE had not reckoned with the war. More especially he had never entertained any notions of helping make the world safe for democracy. He gave no thought to it, unless by chance he encountered the subject at Kingsley's gin or the store or the Kangaroo, where he went frequently to check on Sidney. His old comradeship with the men there was gone; they treated him as they would treat Jesse Shannon (all except Max Muller). He was now their superior, a stranger, not one to share in their private lives. The only question that ever came from their tongues was an impersonal, "Reckon we gonna git into the war, Rufe?"

Aye god, he didn't give a damn either way. It would do some of these fair-weather birds good to mix up with the Huns. They had pretended to be his friends, but now that he lived in the Shannon house their faces and tongues were guarded in his presence. They were too wary to ask how many bales he had made, how many loads of corn. And he was too proud to tell them. They could be on his side or against him; he would win in any case. Give him time. Some day he would control everything in that Hollow. He had a plan; unformed, but a plan nonetheless. Let them seal their lips; his conscience was clear; he had done no wrong.

He did not understand that part of their silence stemmed from respect; that sometimes they asked him about the war because they felt his new station had given him a new perception. He regarded their aloofness as closely parallel to the astute coolness of Todda, who, one day, had discarded her mask long enough to say she had almost given up on Jesse. Still, every nightfall found him driving her home, and found Howard, as the buggy stopped, lurking near a window, his nervous grey eyes set in prolonged bitterness against his sister's suitor.

The winter wore on. Rufus kept himself and most of the hands busy with terracing, fencing, ditching, and general repairing. It had been an easier winter than he expected. The agreeable nature of Jesse showed itself in every detail; he asked advice, he withdrew when possible into the background, proud to have Rufus as his vanguard. Sidney's attitude had warmed, and though he remained at the Kangaroo, he rode one of the Shannon horses to school each day: a ride of some four miles over Walker Mountain to the Woodall county school. As for Todda, she had behaved admirably; her coolness was a great help to Rufus. Occasionally, however, their truce was broken by a tigerish exchange of words. The first of these occurred late in December, when Todda, through Ursa, learned that Anna was with child.

The wild-eyed enthusiasm of Rufus infuriated Todda. He beamed, he strutted, he flaunted the matter. To him it seemed a greater miracle because it was planned; seemed more an act of magic between him and his wife than a work of Nature. He made no effort to hide his joy. Todda interpreted his extravagant elation before her as a cunning insult. Until then, she had harboured little if any malice. But, beginning with that time, she meticulously planned his downfall. Finding him alone, she struck fiercely at his promise of fatherhood. "You fixed it where she couldn't throw you out, didn't you?"

"You kiss where I can't," he answered, feeling the sting unduly heavy. He hurried out to the pasture, bit off a chew of Old Apple, and dug post-holes with a fury that sweat-drenched his clothes.

Todda went on with her plot for Rufus's undoing, which week after week remained in the same inchoate state as Rufus's plan to some day rule the Hollow. The Shannon house assumed a strange calm. Jesse withdrew farther into the shadows.

However, neither Todda's acquiescence nor the promise of parenthood held the key that submerged confusions; buried, at least temporarily, disappointments. Since the first moment that Rufus and Anna had walked into a room alone as man and wife, they had been good companions. Their natural and mutual laughter often had an intensity equal to their love-making; sometimes at night they talked for hours, without a syllable of disagreement. Though the diversity of their backgrounds promoted eruptions of misunderstanding, it also provided an endless chain of questions, of probing for secrets and dark chasms, a fascinating game of constantly discovering one another.

He learned, with pleasure, that her father and mother were uneducated people who had come from North Carolina with a surveying crew. Old Jesse had, in fact, helped survey the Hollow and by some stroke of foresight or chance grabbed for himself six hundred and forty acres, three hundred and twenty of it in the heart of the Hollow. Anna pictured her father as a slow-talking, slow-moving (with hands clasped behind his back) figure; a shrewd-faced trader, evil enough to dispel all dullness. The largest aspect of his gentlemanness was his section of land. She demonstrated with relish how he crossed his finger over his lip to keep his moustache from his drink. She criticized his unscrupulous business deals; she mocked his dry speech; yet it was clear she had adored him.

With the same harmless but biting portrayal, she drew her mother as a vigorous woman of insatiable demands; a splendid manager, frugal (an egg-seller, her neighbours had branded her, meaning she sold what should have gone into the stomachs of her husband and children), and industrious. She had demanded and pleaded and cried until that huge, high-ceilinged, ten-roomed house was completed from an old log L-building. She was a driver, a nagger; but a quick retreater when old Jesse would say, "Now, by God, Lillian, that's plenty out of you!" Often she claimed to come from superior stock, to which in the presence of company old Jesse occasionally alluded by saying, "She was barefooted when I married her, but she's made me a tol'ably good wife." In late years their arguments became bitter and cruel. Words struck with blind rage, tempers flared to madness, until the mother retreated and flew to young Jesse for affection and defence; all the while old Jesse laughed coldly and contemptuously at both son and wife.

Anna could go on endlessly, revealing their pattern of life with savage honesty; all to the complete astonishment of Rufus, who had imagined the history of that house to be filled with tranquil memories. In these astonished states, he commenced to reveal bits of his own childhood. Pride swayed his accounts, however, and gave a haziness if not a soft glow to his stingy, pelagra-ridden father; to his brittle, uncompromising sisters. Bee he pictured as a gem in the unfathomed caves. He spared no detail of their poverty—his poverty—and described with amazing eagerness the discomforts of hunger, bare-footedness, and shuck beds. His escape from fly-swarming penury was no small wonder to Anna; but his emergence whole, with the strength of a giant, was miraculous. She loved him more because of what he had endured; she would not let him make a joke of it.

When the winter evenings were not too cold or damp, they often went for long walks that usually described a triangle bounded by their house, Burke's store, and the chapel on Oak's Hill (where they attended church on the second Sunday of each month). Sometimes they walked through the church, out the back door, and across the old cemetery. These trips gave rise to their innermost confessions; they went again and again. Both sought the outdoors like a healthy animal and did not understand how Jesse could brood in a closed house, in his own room, for hours on end.

Little by little, they read each other's desires and hopes and inmost secrets; but a few places remained untouched, withheld and guarded.

The chilly winds, the driving rains lay over the Hollow week after week. Even the sawmills stopped. The flat land turned yellow with top soil from the hills; groves of pines stood needle-bare; the stock huddled, as if for protection from the acrimonious thunder; farmers raked their cribs for the last bushel of potatoes, the last bucket of peas; the butter grew pale and tasteless; children fretted all day, noses flat and white against the windows; the lean season

ruled, with its long, desolate nights. Hunters kept to their firesides
and lovers remained in their separate shelters.

Then March tore into the grey mist, swept the earth's loose
objects into a mad whirl. April burst overnight, as if the impetuous
bird-notes had been no warning. Tiny plums covered the thickets
like strings of beads; green splashed the earth like morning shadows;
cows, surfeited in the lush bottom pastures, belched the stench of
wild onions and reeled toward the dusk-covered barns; freight-train
whistles shook the night with violence that seemed strong enough
to destroy the tender peach blossoms. The sun drew out the earth
creatures, and opened the throats of frogs.

With a boyish thrill, Rufus watched the rich land break from the
wings of the ploughs; he spat golden streams of tobacco juice into
the earth and considered his plan. Nothing pushed him now.

Anna began each day with a long, pleasant walk. Dr. Fitzwanger
had prescribed it for the tiny life she carried. Often she felt a throb,
a slight quiver, that set her heart beating with pleasure. She ended
each day by telling Rufus how their child had leapt within her; she
put his hand where the miracle pulsed. "Wait. . . . Wait. . . . Do
you feel it?"

He waited a proper interval, and whispered, "There! There! I
swear I felt it then!"

The fact that he felt nothing, and she knew it, put no damper on
the joy of their game. They played it over and over as if each time
were the first one. They lived in a wonderful world.

Then the deep, dark headlines of a Memphis paper burst across
the land. Dinner-bells rang at ten o'clock in the morning; ploughs
stopped. Schools were dismissed. The sawmills closed for the day.
Azel Burke walked out of his store and stood in the sunlight for an
hour. America was at war!

Anna went to her room and cried like a child.

Rufus wondered what would happen to his plan, though he did
not yet know exactly what his plan was. But he felt the war was
going to interfere.

Todda went home and ironed all day, as if she must have Howard's
clothes ready for immediate departure.

Sidney came in from school, stopped for an unusually long visit
with Rufus and Anna, ate lunch there, reported that his teacher
considered the news wonderful: the world would now be saved for
democracy. Sidney ate ravenously. He even forgot his feud with
Jesse.

Jesse did not think of himself, nor of his own going; he could
think only of the day that Rufus would leave. It would be a great
loss; he dreaded it.

That night Rufus and Anna did not play the game with their
unborn child. They went to sleep in each other's arms.

2

THE men of the Hollow grew impatient with the slow mill of the Army. Its bunglesome series of numbers seemed ridiculous to them. When a fight was on, you got into it; waiting for numbers and classifications was like waiting for a neighbour to kill a snake that had ventured on to the church grounds or school yard. Yet they waited. And their patriotism ebbed as weeks went by and nothing happened, for some had left their land fallow, believing each day the next might find them on a troop train.

Even the baseball team had been dissolved in the face of the great emergency. Still, only two soldiers had left the Hollow by the first of June. Rufus went on with his crops; Jesse went on with his sawmills; Azel Burke sold his goods with miserly slowness. July passed. Then came the announcement of a huge October draft. On that list were Barney, Howard, Rufus, and three others.

Anna was heartsick, but calm. She took her walk each day; she attended Rufus as if each day were his last; she spoke of the war as seldom as possible. But over and over again she asked herself why Rufus must go while hundreds of others stayed—even Jesse. The thought that he might want to get away tormented her; the thought that he would die in a muddy trench was unbearable. The child leaped in earnest now, but it was small comfort, because she could not see it with her own eyes nor speak to it with her own tongue. Some days, she wished that Rufus was already gone, for the waiting was agony. Yet she was deeply thankful that he would see his child before the Government hauled him away, that he would be near her when her hour came.

Rufus looked on war as a wild, extended hunting venture. It never occurred to him that he might be killed or harmed in any way except possibly to receive a glorious wound. The romantic mystery of war surged in him. Along with other appetites, he had also a desire for intimate knowledge of death, brutality, and suffering. He expected to see it all and return unmarred from the fertile hunting ground. He was ready to board ship and sail into the heart of the struggle; give him a rifle, and the few odd things a soldier carried: all other matters were superfluous. He did not dread the war; he dreaded leaving Anna, their child, and Sidney. But the pleasure of returning would be worth all the sadness of leaving. He waited for his child and October.

The day of Anna's delivery arrived early in August, a day crisp as fall and unusually cool. Her hospital room was the same small one where Sidney had slept. But the bareness had been covered over with a new chair, a picture of the Madonna and Child, and a basket of late summer roses. Dr. Fitzwanger moved in and out of the room with amazing quickness, was overly attentive, for he had witnessed Anna's birth. This unexpected liveliness (which suggested danger) drove Rufus's nerves to a higher pitch. He had been up all night, comforted from hour to hour by Ursa, who insisted, "It ain't no need to worry. She jist like her maw, and Miss Lillian allus was easy as nothing. Hit's going to be a boy."

But the screams, with painful authority, disputed Ursa. Rufus dug his toes into his shoes; he paced in and out of the old house; huge bubbles of sweat broke on his body, drenching his clothes. A particularly sharp wail sent him outside. He saw people moving along unconcerned. He wanted to seize them, hold their ears to the cries, make them share this common burden of mankind and thus lessen it. He hurried back inside, unable to stay away from the terrible wailing; again and again he went to the door of her room. At last, the final high, piercing wail struck. He knew it was finished; life or death had arrived; he drooped across a chair. Ursa hurried out to announce the arrival of his eight-pound son. His eyes turned slowly up to her. "Aye god, I'll never have another!" It was two hours before the keen arrow of fatherhood possessed his heart. Then he had regained his strength and was undone with emotion.

At dark, as he drove home to bathe and change clothes, he reflected on his new estate. Nothing he had ever seen or felt equalled the wonders of being a father. He was glad he drove alone, for at times he laughed, or sang, or talked to himself. It was a splendid, dark night; the world was in perfect order; the war was no more than a distant skirmish between schoolboys. A man who was a father could never die in a trench.

The buggy rattled through the night. Rufus spat neat streams of tobacco juice over the wheels, as if he owned the earth. He reached down and touched the bottle of whisky which the doctor had given him. He dared not open it now for fear he might pour every parching drop of it down his throat without stopping. What would he make out of his son? Aye god, he'd have to give lots of thought to that. Never had he felt such strength in his body. The events at hand struck fire from all his senses, like the well-shod feet of the mare topping gravel. The bottle had not been opened, but he was drunk. He was happy. He had no worries. The mare knew the way home.

As he neared the house, he saw a light, which was odd, because he had left both Ursa and Jesse at the hospital. Tying the mare at the post, he went around to the back entrance, for the light was in the kitchen. He found Todda, with a towel in one hand, apparently busy. He followed his first impulse and asked, "What are you doing here?" The tone was somewhat commanding, brittle; all his senses remained at the highest pitch.

Her eyes snapped at him. "Doing Ursa's work, Mister Frost.

Maybe it's time *you* got something straight. I didn't know you was coming home. But, anyway, I been through with you fer a long ole time. I'm still through; and I'll be through this time to-marr'. If you worried about me, I'm just fixing to leave."

"Ain't nobody worried. I just wondered what you was doing, that's all."

"You don't think I stayed looking fer you, do you?" She pressed the point because she felt guilty, knowing she would have, if possible, planned it exactly this way. During all the months Jesse had driven her home and dumped her at her door like a schoolboy, during all the months Anna's body had grown larger and larger, Todda had longed for a knock-down-drag-out scene with Rufus. She was sorry; maybe she was all wrong; but her mind and soul needed the satisfaction of a cruel, bitter fight. She must be shrewd, else he might laugh at her and refuse to get angry.

"Forgit it. What do I care why you stayed. I'm a papa! You wanta know what kind?"

"You mean boy-papa or girl-papa?"

"Yeah."

She studied, not about the sex of the child, but the course she must follow in order to push his heart, at this triumphant moment, into anger and bitterness. "Why . . . in most cases, I'd say a boy. I ought to say a boy. But something tells me . . . a hunch tells me it's a little ole girl!"

"Aw, Todda, you're no good," he joked. "It's narrowed down to two things fer you. And you ain't got sense enough to pick the right one. Now, if it was a billion things instead of only two . . . well . . . you could make a mistake. But with two . . ."

She pretended to be hurt. "Are you trying to rub something in? I reckon it's no gospel fact I made a mistake between you and Jesse Shannon. Just cause you've got a son . . ."

Rufus was taken by surprise. "Look here. I was jist joking. I never said nothing about me and you. Don't go gitting your feelings hurt. I want us to be friends. Don't you want us to be friends?"

"Certainly."

"Besides, we wouldn't want to fuss at a time like this. I feel too good. Do I sound drunk?"

"No. Just strange."

"I don't mind sounding strange. Hold on! Let me show you the present I got." He hurried to the buggy and returned with the bottle of whisky. Proudly placing it on the kitchen table, he said, "There. That's what the doctor give me. See? It's got some red strength in it; not that old white stuff."

"Maybe he wants you to name your boy after him."

"Naw, naw. I couldn't do that, Todda."

"What you gonna name him? William Rufus Frost, Jr., or Jack Frost?"

"I'm going to name him Rex. Ain't that a good name? Kenneth Rex Frost. Rex means king."

"*You're* going to name him. You wouldn't know whether Rex meant king or blackberry jam. She named him. Didn't she?"

He picked up the whisky and fondled it as he might a baby's skin. His eyes were mellow, forgiving everything. "Todda, ain't you gonna never learn I'm good to womenfolks? Yes, she named him." His hands tore the seal, lifted the top. He took a deep swallow. The fiery liquid drew his face into a spasm of pain. Blowing a deep breath, he said, "Aye god, but that's good!" He took another swallow. It never occurred to him to offer whisky to Todda; their moral codes were too strictly set against it. Even his drinking in the presence of a woman was a serious breach. After another swallow, he set the bottle on the table, looked at Todda with boyish mockery. "You'll excuse my manners, won't you?"

She said nothing.

"Am I excused?"

"Long ago, Mister Frost, I excused you fer everything you done, and everything you was going to do."

He was by no means drunk, for his capacity was enormous, but even the smallest drink gave rapid assurance to his tongue. "Can I ask one other question, please? Is there any vittles in this house which has just been blessed with a son?"

"No; the hands eat it all. But since you're lord and master you can order your servant to fix some." She had searched her brain for biting, stinging words; for some vitriolic phrase to scorch his triumphant smile and set his face burning with anger. Her tongue had come up empty, or with the old weightless expressions.

He sat down, drooped his shoulders; the action emphasized the tremendous scale and strength of his body. His hands lay relaxed on the oilcloth, like two sleeping animals. He pushed at a chair with his foot. "Set down, Todda."

She sat down. The lack of food, the high pitch of his nerves let the whisky hit him with all its force, suddenly and vitally. He studied Todda; his smile was gone.

"Marriage is the most wonderful thing in the world. I've got a marriage. A good marriage. And ever since I had it," he pointed his finger, "you've toted around a axe jist waiting to chop off something; because you don't wanta see me have what I got. But, aye god, I've got it. And I'm gonna keep it; and if it hurts you I don't give a damn. You walked out. You and me coulda had the same thing. But you walked out!"

She leaped up and screamed down at him, "Walked out on what?

On six hundred acres of land and a mansion? I'll say I didn't! I walked out on a stinking little old hovel where you and your share-cropping family lived. I wouldn't live there with you or no other man and beat the flies off my children and walk through dish-water standing shoe-deep at the back door. And that's where we'd be, and you know it. I was tired of it! I'm still tired of it! But you with your rich queen . . . you're too dumb to see it!" She slapped him with a ringing explosion that shook the kitchen.

He got up and returned the same ringing slap with more force. Then, realizing the extent of his brutality, he caught her arms and pulled her to him. Her face, a nimbus of fury and hate, struggled backward. His lips moved closer and closer; he kissed her tenderly, until her eyes ceased to struggle. Like two flames, their tormented spirits merged into one last desperate effort to fulfil or to destroy the mystery between them.

Their hearts rushed with incredible violence; they seared each other with kisses; they flung themselves into the most sensual pleasure they had ever known. Their natural vigorousness and whetted nerves carried them to a terrifying satisfaction, which was more than their minds could grasp or their bodies hold. They had played the comedy furiously to the final passionate line. At last, they were like the dead.

They dared not speak, for words would pierce the darkness like fingers of light. Yet, they were not ashamed. They felt no pity, no remorse. In the shadow of such passion, they could feel nothing.

She moved to go, and in moving placed her hands tenderly on his great body. She lowered her head and whispered, "I hope. . . ." And that was all she could say.

He neither moved nor answered. He thought of hospital sheets and the tender red skin of his child.

3

FOR two weeks, the child cried day and night. Then one day he woke up laughing, and from that time forward spent his waking hours in a circus of cooing and kicking. He was clearly marked for handsomeness, with his father's nose, mouth, and chin; but his eyes were the splendid feature, and they were exactly like Anna's. He had no hair.

Todda sought every chance to care for the child: to wash his clothes or change his bed or take him up when he fretted. Ursa, feeling those rights belonged to her, withdrew with noticeable sullenness. Todda increased her attention, always in the absence of Rufus. When she held the child, a warm feeling gathered in her body and beat like a heart. She was certain she had conceived, and the feeling of certainty was a burning joy. But she would not allow her thoughts to go beyond the day when this burning joy would be proved.

From the very beginning she had earnestly hoped and had earnestly believed; now as the time drew nearer, she was sometimes seized with misgiving and fear. The heat of August faded; September arrived in bright colours. The conscripted men of the Hollow prepared for their going, as if they had one week instead of one month. Todda often blamed her uneasiness on Howard's approaching departure and his anxiety concerning it. He was not afraid, she knew, but the waiting had worn deeply into his volatile nerves.

A state of panic seized Todda. Each night she lay awake and prayed in vain against the thing she had so recently hoped for. She made excuses to stay away from the Shannon house, irritated by its aura of completeness and the calm, satisfied air of Rufus and Anna; while there, she avoided the child, never attending him, neglecting the little chores she had once assumed as her pleasant duty. His cries, even his infant cooing, annoyed her; the slightest noise set her trembling. She avoided both Rufus and Anna, and stopped her usual jokes with Ursa. Her eyes were brooding fires; she was with child.

The bright September days rolled by. The fields lay full and white with cotton and golden brown with corn. From early until late the sawmills droned. The Hollow buzzed with a smouldering urgency. Rufus stayed in his fields; Jesse stayed with his mills, driving her home each evening (on the days that she worked) as if that pattern would go on for ever.

Some nights she heard every train that passed along the edge of the cool, autumn hills. She heard, too, the restless snoring of Howard, who slept ten feet away in the same small room with her. A week remained before the men would be off to the war. Her eyes grew brighter, though they were hungry for sleep. The fangs of her secret closed about her heart. She had made a determined stand against telling Rufus. Silence now was her only chance for victory over him. Later, she might take another course.

The crucial time, she knew, was the final few days before the men would leave. She did not trust herself; she was afraid she might pour out her stubborn secret in a moment of stress and weakness. Therefore, she pretended to be sick, and stayed away from the Shannon house. Only Howard suspected something.

He had resigned himself to leaving; the first shock and reaction to it was over. It was not the war that concerned him; it was Todda. He had never felt close to anyone, had never really liked anyone except Todda. The fact they had lain together in the dark womb of their mother was the most fascinating and mysterious idea his mind had ever touched. He considered her a part of himself. He loved her as deeply as he knew how; every ounce of his narrow, twisted devotion was directed toward her. That she should fall sick on the eve of his leaving excited him, even pleased him; for he hoped she might be brooding for him.

The tension in him resurged; his nerves rekindled. He spent almost every minute of his last day at her bedside, attending, questioning, soothing. It was a prolonged, earnest scene of dark devotion. Todda was deeply moved. But she was thankful for darkness, when the house and world grew quiet, and Howard went to his own bed. She was exhausted; sleep seemed close at hand, watching her calmly, like a cat. Just as she fell asleep, a train whistle pulled at her eyes and she stared wide awake.

Then followed an hour of agonizing debate: Howard might never sleep in this house again. Her dark secret must erupt some time. What better time than now? What better person than Howard? He would not understand, but he would take her side. She must go away, of course, and now was the time to explain. Where else could she turn for help? Not to her father who read the Bible every night and prayed for the sinners of the world; not to her mother whose eyes she could not remember ever being wet with tears.

At last, chilled and trembling though the night was not cold, she crept to his bed. She shook him. He bolted upright, floundered wildly to orient himself.

"It's me," she whispered.

"What's the matter?"

"I want to tell you something."

He rubbed his eyes. Objects took shape in the thin darkness. He remembered that within a few hours, early in the morning, he would be leaving. "What is it, Todda?"

"Something bad's happened to me." Through the darkness she strained to see his movements; to see whether he understood.

He threw his feet on to the floor, preparing to get up. "What is it? You want a doctor?"

Her arm restrained him. "It's something else. I'm gonna have a baby."

His first reaction was one of terrible disappointment: her sickness was not caused by his going away. Then anger welled in him and he held her hands tighter and tighter. At last, terror gripped him, feeding the atrocious and nightmarish idea that his own body was with child. He seized her shoulders; he shook her violently. "You little fool!" he cried. "You little fool!"

She mumbled his name, pulling at him.

He thrust her hands away. "Don't talk to me. . . . Don't touch me! You little fool!" He threw himself prone on his covers, shaking as if with a malarial chill.

She backed away from him and went to her bed. She turned her face to the wall and sobbed quietly, pouring into her pillow all the desperation of the moment. She waited for him to recover and come to her; and when she decided that he would make no step in her direction, she fell into a sleep that not even the train whistles could disturb.

Howard heard every whistle. Hours went by while he lay on top of his covers and listened to her breathing. Before the first grey light appeared, he pulled his clothes from the spattering of ten-penny nails on the wall, dressed, took his ·22 rifle from the white oak forks, hidden behind winter clothes, and slipped out the window. In the sheltering darkness, he made his way to a knoll deep in the log-woods; there, overlooking the road to the sawmills, beyond Clear Creek bridge, he waited. As Jesse Shannon crossed the bridge, Howard lifted his rifle in ambush and fired. The shot was extremely accurate. Jesse slipped forward to his knees, sank, and fell backward beneath the buggy seat. The mare jumped from the sharp crack of the rifle, turned off the road, and began to graze.

Though Howard did not run; he walked at a lightning gait through the woods, around the edge of the cemetery. He dropped his rifle in an old, abandoned church well and headed for Burke's store. He was the first customer of the day. He bought two woollen undershirts and went home.

His mother and father had finished breakfast. They stood beside the kitchen stove, puzzled, waiting. Todda, pale and dishevelled in one of her father's old coats, sat at the end of the table sipping coffee. He waited for them to ask the question. But the three only stared. Ephriam stretched out his old worn hands across the stove; in another hour his son would be gone. Rachel pushed a snuff-stick into the corner of her mouth, and looking down at the cold biscuits, asked, "Where you been off to?"

He calmly shoved aside a plate smeared with molasses, placed his bundle on the table, and ripped the brown paper. He held up the woollen undershirts. "I forgot to git these yestiddy."

Todda sipped at her coffee and wondered; the old man stretched out his hands again; the old woman tested the undershirts with her fingers.

Howard ate, casting from time to time his cruel, accusing stare upon Todda. When she got up and went to her room, he knew it was a signal for him to follow her. But he would not follow. He remained near his mother. "Well, hit ain't long now," the old woman said. Her eyes were cold and hard as stones.

Howard was the first one to board the train. He found a seat and talked through the window to his mother and father. Todda had stayed at home, genuinely sick. A crowd closed in on the side of the train; he searched every face. Heavy smoke and cinders swept over the waving arms, the weeping, the ill-timed jokes. He looked at the two faces that watched him; they stood mutely, with a few cold tears on their cheeks. But he thought of Todda and her body growing larger and larger. He was glad he had not been alone when he said goodbye to her. His eyes shifted; his heart pounded. There was Rufus ready to board. One big arm reached down and hugged Sidney; the other held to Anna. If it had been this man, he thought, he would not have done the thing he had done.

"Sid-boy, you and Jesse better take care of her now."

"He meant to come," Anna said to Rufus. "He told me he'd get back in time to come with us."

Rufus kissed her briefly. They held each other for a minute, then he broke quickly for the steps. She reached down and caught Sidney's hand.

The train jerked forward. The crowd fell back and then surged closer, a patch of hysterical arms. A tremendous groan of relief erupted from Howard; a minute later he slumped in his seat and let his cheek press against the window-pane. For miles he neither moved nor opened his eyes. The other men observed him with slight curiosity, surprised that a single man should be so broken up over leaving home.

Howard could not have told what he was thinking, but his mind roared on ahead of the train. Since the brittle crack of the rifle he had expected some fit of contrition to seize him. As he felt no part of it, he grew calmer, regained his self-confidence.

Slowly he emerged from his trance and defined the sounds about him. He heard Rufus's voice and looked around to find him sitting beside Barney, a few seats away. Without their noticing, he moved to the seat behind them. It seemed necessary to be near Rufus and hear every word that came from his mouth.

"Now, you take me," Barney was saying. "It's worser on some folks than it is on me. Fellers with kids like you. Looks bad to see you going and single yearlings lagging behind."

Rufus leaned toward the cuspidor and spat a bright arc of tobacco juice. "Aw, hell. It's bad on anybody."

A news-butch came by with drinks, candy, and a stack of Memphis papers. He held a paper out to Rufus and Barney; they shook their heads.

"Here!" Howard called, as if it were the last available paper. "Right here."

He scanned the first page for a blazing headline of his crime. Then he felt foolish. Not even Rufus knew about it yet. Barney turned in his seat, his weather-hardened face screwed into a grin. "What you buyin' that thing fer, boy? You can't read."

"Trying to learn how," Howard said, and pushed the paper aside. He listened to every word that passed between Barney and Rufus. They talked of crops and lumber and fishing and the fact that Tom Phelps, at the north end of the Hollow, had a new automobile and had to pull it with mules up the ungravelled clay road to his house. The talk was soothing to Howard.

At noon he followed them to the dining-car, chose a seat near them, and continued to keep his ears on guard. The train, which had been almost empty of passengers, had now begun to fill. As more and more people boarded, passed the aisles without a glance at him, a tinge of superiority touched him: pore dumb faces didn't know what was going on in the world.

Then suddenly, like an insect sailing through the open window into his face, a misgiving grabbed him. What if Jesse Shannon was not dead? Abruptly he left the dining-car, and walked toward the rear of the train. His stares fastened on the sunken, toothless faces of old men; the malarial yellow skin of fattening women; the bright, journey-pioud eyes of children. When he came to the end of the train, the same foolish sensation passed through his mind as when he had looked for the blazing headlines. Dead or alive, Jesse Shannon could not know who had waited in ambush. He returned calmly down the aisle and took his original seat behind Barney and Rufus. Two men, shifting the back of a seat, had joined Barney and Rufus at poker. One of them was Nile Phelps, the oldest son of Tom Phelps. "Want in?" Nile asked Howard. "Hep your nerves."

Howard reddened. "I look nervous?"

"We all nervous," Nile answered. "We going to war, ain't we?"

Howard slumped near the outer edge of his seat, so that a boarding passenger might not choose to sit beside him. In mid-afternoon, another wave of doubt surged. It seemed to bloat his body, like a gaseous food. Why had he thrown the rifle away? A dumb trick. They might find it. No. Nobody would find it; but they would find it missing. He could have got it back somehow; he hadn't even tried. The minute the news broke, Todda would know everything, of course. But she would protect him. He had done it all for her.

The card game went on. The excited mumbling of the men was like a plot to trap him. A grey twilight settled on the fields outside. The car became chilly. I'm not sorry, his mind said; but drops of sweat rolled down his body like tiny gravel.

It was dark when they reached Hattiesburg. Forty or fifty draftees gathered on the cinders around three sergeants from Camp Shelby. They were divided into two squads. Howard stationed himself behind Rufus; behind the giant body, he looked like a child. "You!" the sergeant yelled, not from anger but from habit. "Move on back!" Then Howard realized the tall men led the squad; the short ones brought up the rear. He moved back, keeping his gaze constantly on Rufus until they were separated and loaded into different trucks. Howard was in a desperate mood. Surely Rufus would receive some news to-night, and he needed to be there, to read the telegram or to ask exactly what was said over the telephone. Now, separated, they might not see each other again for days. The truck rumbled on over the sandy road. Howard searched the darkness, but the other squad was not within sight.

They were fed when they reached camp. After that, they filed through a quartermaster hut for issues of clothing. Then they were carried to a barracks well heated by one pot-bellied stove and lined with cots. A dozen soldiers quipped and laughed and cat-called when the squad entered and set about the business of inspecting and fitting shoes and other gear. Howard paid no attention to the age-old horse-play. He must get to Rufus before the night was over.

Before he could form a plan, the second squad arrived, led by Nile Phelps and Rufus. In the renewed uproar and confusion, Howard could not get a good look at Rufus. He could not tell what news might have arrived. At last the barracks grew quieter. Howard went over to a cot near Rufus, watched the big hands pull on shoes, fit leggings. Somebody drawled, "I had a pair at home better'n this."

"Did you now?" another voice crowed.

Howard said to Rufus, "I thought yawl got lost from us."

"Aye god," Rufus said, looking at his shoes. "I got 'em on."

Howard remained on the cot, his back stiff and straight, his fingers probing into the blanket. He did not take his eyes from Rufus.

From two cots away, Barney called, "Howard, when you git through hepping Rufus, come over here and hep me."

Howard got up and went to his own cot near the door. He felt better. The spectacle of men climbing into khakis, as if they were dresses, became amusing. He forgot his vigil and laughed.

Then a young, thin-faced corporal entered, pushing his way through a knot of men near the door. He waved a brown envelope and called, "Frost in here?"

Howard leaped up. The corporal started toward him. "It ain't me!" Howard said, and pointed down the rows of cots. "He's over there!" He followed the corporal.

Still sitting on the edge of his cot, Rufus received the telegram. Howard's intense anxiety was drowned in the group of men that sprang up around Rufus.

"Bad news?" Nile asked before the telegram was opened.

Rufus's finger gouged into the envelope; he unfolded the yellow page and read it once. He replaced the page and tapped the envelope against his palm. "Aye god . . ." He breathed deeply. He looked up up at the men and finally let his eyes rest on Barney, excluding all the others. "Jesse was killed this morning."

"Jesse? Where 'bouts?" Barney said.

"At the sawmill?" Nile asked.

Rufus ignored the questions. He shifted his gaze to Nile, who had once travelled as far as New York City. "Can I git out of here to-night, Nile?"

Spots of confusion filled the hut. Some were interested in what had happened and some were not. Nile and Rufus went out to arrange for the trip home. When they were gone, a stranger from one corner of the barracks asked what had happened. Chet Daringhast said, "His brother-in-law got killed at a sawmill."

"Jesus," the stranger drawled sympathetically. "A man comes down here gitting ready to go git shot at and first thing somebody hands him a death message from home."

The men from the Hollow gathered to talk and share in this new tragedy. Howard sat on the edge of the group, tense and alert, watching for the return of Rufus.

"Reckon how he got killed?" Marlon Kingsley asked. "He never done much work around the mills."

"Somebody mighta knocked him in the head with a slab," Chet Daringhast said. He could not be moved by something that happened outside his own family—certainly not while he was three hundred miles away.

"Rufe never said hit was at the mill," Barney said.

Chet and Barney glared at each other, bristling, hoping the dispute would become bitter. The group was obviously divided. Tempers were ready to flare. Then Rufus returned. The men scattered. Nile informed them that Rufus had a three-day pass. Howard moved quietly to a cot near Rufus. He watched every movement; he saw the telegram put aside; he saw the fingers dig into articles of clothing. He had a frantic urge to seize the telegram. If he could read the words, he would be all right. The urge was so strong he had to turn away and go to his own cot.

The other men from the Hollow followed Rufus to the door, offering condolences and sending messages home. Howard lay stiffly on his cot and observed them with a cold, detached feeling. They would not miss him, he thought; he had never belonged to them anyway. But he felt a slight sympathy for Rufus. If it had been this man, he thought again, he would not have done the thing he had done.

The sharp blare of taps swept through the thin walls of the barracks. Darkness covered them, as if ejected from a huge spray. Men cursed, stumbling to their cots. Howard crawled under his blanket. The room grew quiet enough for a lone voice to be heard. "Ain't they got no women around here?" A stirring, mingled with laughter, rose and died away. After half an hour there was stillness.

Howard lay on his back, breathing as if in deep sleep. He was motionless except for a faint quivering of his eyelids. His mind recounted nothing of the day's events; it was obsessed only with a ragged envelope enclosing a yellow sheet of paper. When he could stand it no longer, he got up and stole softly along the aisle. The cots and sleeping forms were dimly visible. He knelt and raked his fingers quietly across Rufus's gear. Three feet away, an outline of head and shoulders raised slowly, and whispered, "What's the matter there?"

A tight core expended and burst in Howard; it was like waking from a strenuous dream. He whispered back, "I was looking fer that telegram, Nile. I can't git Jesse out of my mind."

"I can't git him out of my mind neither," Nile said.

"Did you see the telegram? What did it say?"

"I saw it. But I never looked at it."

Nile lay down again. Howard went quietly back to his cot.

4

HOWARD soon forgot the telegram and focused every nerve in his body on the return of Rufus. That would be the crucial hour. It did not occur to him that any minute, while eating or drilling or sleeping, the hand of the law might seize him. His anxieties were directed toward the minute he next faced Rufus.

He had no complaint against the gruelling hours of drills under the autumn sun. They wore at his body only enough to make him sleep at night. The spectre that should have appeared in his dreams did not appear; even in waking he could hardly remember Jesse Shannon's face. Much more clearly in his mind was the way the mare had shied and turned off the road into the woods.

Only one immediate change came over Howard; he sought out the company of the men. In the Hollow, he had spent hours alone; he would sometimes go fishing by himself while the other men were gathered in Holyoke pasture for a ball-game. Now he missed no chance to join the men in the canteen. Though he rarely joined in the banter himself, he listened eagerly and enjoyed it. The vulgar, masculine horse-play that had once annoyed him now afforded a strong sense of security. One night in the canteen, while the men were happily chaffing each other, he dared to reflect with pleasure that his crime was the only positive, straightforward thing he had ever done. All other actions had stemmed partially from another's will or direction.

But as the hour approached for the arrival of Rufus, some of his self-confidence faded. He ate less supper; in the canteen he sat on the edge of the crowd and laughed wanly. Then the electric news spread that Rufus was back in the barracks. The men left their coffee unfinished and rushed out. Howard remained; his courage had suddenly deserted him. For a moment he struggled with his powerless limbs. Let them come and carry him away.

Slowly the strength came back into his body; the fire caught in his mind. He must face Rufus some time; with the men would be better. He got up and ran to overtake them.

Rufus was lying on his cot, his back propped against the wall; his face was pale and haggard. When he saw the men he sat up straighter; his eyes brightened, but that did not erase the shadow of dissipation. The men greeted him and flocked down on his and nearby cots.

"Looks like you had a rough time of it, feller," Barney said.

"Hit was shore bad," Chet Daringhast said, as if answering for Rufus.

Rufus's eyes passed over Barney and Chet and Howard, who was kneeling at the foot of a cot, and settled on Nile. "Your daddy was mighty nice to Anna," he said. "He looked after everything. Aye god, you don't know how much it is to see after till you have a funeral in your family. He was mighty nice, Nile."

Nile nodded.

The men were impatient for details. Barney was the most restless. "What happened to him, Rufe?"

"He was shot through the heart with a ·22 rifle."

"God-dog," Chet said. "Who done that?"

Rufus grunted.

Barney glared triumphantly at Chet. "I tole you he never got killed at no sawmill."

Rufus quelled the sudden tempers. "They picked up some folks, but turned 'em all loose."

"Jist where was he?" Barney asked.

"Found him in the woods, above the bridge. And that's about all they know. Some figure it could of been a stray bullet."

"I don't know who would have it in fer Jesse," Marlon Kingsley said. "He never was hard on nobody that I knowed of."

"Yeah," Barney said. "But some time folks can have it in fer you and you don't know it. I nelly got killed that way onc't myself."

Marlon said, "I reckon your wife took it hard?"

Rufus did not answer.

"Hit's allus worser on a woman," Barney said. "And being her on'lest brother too."

"Well, what they gonna do about it?" Chet asked.

"What would you suggest?" Barney said.

"How's that big boy gittin' along?" Marlon asked, for he had been married only two months.

"Fine. He was fine."

"Didn't cry to come with his daddy, did he? He shore is a fine-looking booger."

" 'S leave Rufe alone," Barney said, having satisfied his curiosity for the moment. "He ain't been to no picnic."

The men got up, all save Howard. He remained crouched at the end of the cot, determined to meet Rufus's eyes squarely. His body surged with strength he had never felt before. Their eyes met.

"You see any of my folks, Rufe?"

"Saw your mammie and daddy. Todda was sick."

"Bad?"

"I don't know, Howard. I didn't hear nobody say."

Howard got up and went to his cot. That night he stayed awake, not from any fear or worry, but from a queer, drunken urge to enjoy his new strength and new safety. Now he could ignore Rufus. The matter was settled.

But after three or four days, the obsession returned. He could no more stay away from Rufus than he could stay away from water after the long, sweaty drills. When possible, he ate beside Rufus; he followed him to the canteen; he fed on his words until they were like a drug. He had to hear them. If he went for a day without them, he felt the agony of a dull, exhausted body and a tense, racing mind. It was not necessary for him to speak; he needed only to hear: a grunt, a laugh, an oath, a mere syllable. Each fed him, and his strength returned.

One day Howard awoke with a hunger to know what had happened at Jesse's funeral. He wanted to see the full picture, the weeping faces; he wanted to hear the songs, the words of the minister as he stood in the Chapel. For days he fought this preoccupation, he laughed at himself; yet he was impelled to ask how Jesse had looked, what clothes he had worn, where he had lain during the wake, who had dug his grave. If he could not find out these things, he felt his body would shrivel and die. One night in the canteen he found himself alone with Rufus. His mind still fired with the curious hunger, he commenced to ask. Rufus, unwary, answered casually until Howard asked, "What songs did they sing?"

Rufus was irritated by not remembering a single song that had been sung. "Aye god, what do you want to know all that fer? You never liked him no-way."

Howard felt accused; his face flared. "How come you say I didn't like him?"

"Because, dammit, you didn't!"

"Did you?"

Rufus's big grey eyes bored into Howard. "What's the matter with you? You've asked me more damned questions than the Sheriff."

"What did the Sheriff ask you?"

"You go to hell."

"If you don't wanta talk about it, say so."

"Why the hell would I wanta talk about it?" He got up and left.

From that time on, Howard felt that Rufus was laying a plot against him. The other men knew, and they were helping Rufus. When the men were cold and distant, it was a mark of their mistrust; when they were friendly, it was the false warmth of spies. His need to be near Rufus was whetted all the more. By clever manœuvring, he often succeeded in gaining the position he wanted, even a cot across the aisle from Rufus. There, as the nights grew colder and the rain increased, he slept more soundly.

Each Sunday afternoon, he lay on his cot pretending sleep until the barracks was empty. Then he stole Anna's letters to Rufus, read them hurriedly, and replaced them exactly as they were. The letters were full of news about young Rex, Sidney, the sawmills, the cotton (almost gathered), the corn (still ungathered), Ursa, Todda (who had quit the Shannon house completely and had gone—so Anna had heard—to defence work in Memphis), and the war. Jesse's death was rarely mentioned. Then one November Sunday, he came across a letter which he read twice:

"DEAR RUFUS,—Sheriff Youngblood came by yesterday afternoon and talked for a long time about Jesse. He doesn't know anything more now than he did when it happened. He came out point blank and asked if we thought Jesse could have done it himself. I said I would believe it might have happened that way if the gun could be found anywhere. They combed the woods again, but there wasn't any sign. Rufus, you know Jesse was strange. He was always unhappy and brooding and off by himself somewhere. Last week I found his diary. I found it before then, but I read it last week. The strangest, queerest things went through his mind. Some day I want you to read it. I have put it safely away where nobody else can find it. I wish the whole matter could be cleared up one way or another. Do you think he could have done it? It would not hurt me any more to know he did. I might even feel better, so long as I could *know* something. But whatever we find out, it will not help him. He was so unhappy!

"I told Sidney what you said about his going back to school. He won't listen. He is determined to help me. And you should see how he takes charge. He acts like a grown man. Since Todda left we had to quit fixing lunches for the men. They manage somehow. I guess everything else is all right at the mills.

"Do be careful, darling. We miss you so much. And take care of yourself as much as you can. Flu is all around here.

"Rex knows I am writing you. He is over there kicking like a little mule, and not a whimper. I can't leave him on the bed by himself. He puts his feet down and pushes all over the place.

He's wild about Sid. Sid can put him into a spasm of cackling where the rest of us barely get a smile. He misses his daddy a whole lot. Write us as often as you can, darling, but I know what you must be going through and that doesn't leave you much time. All the love in the world. Sid is managing the corn-gathering this week. He is so happy at it. It's his nature to be happy at most anything. I hope Rex turns out to be that way. All the love in the world again.

"ANNA."

Howard replaced the letter carefully, feeling the birth of a new security. As the cold and rain increased and winter set in, the security grew firmer and deeper. The raw wet days would at last erase everything. He slept like a child. He forgot the idea that the men were plotting against him, that someone would some time find his rifle missing. Whole days passed without any desire to be near Rufus. The halcyon season was upon him. He even derived a certain pleasure from the long drills with bayonets fixed, from the endless crawling on his belly through mud and barbed-wire entanglements. While others cursed the rain and cold that turned their fingers blue on the rifle-range, he lay prone, closed one eye and shattered target after target. It was whispered scornfully and enviously that Howard had become the best soldier from the Hollow. He enjoyed both the scorn and the envy. The only worry in his mind was for what Todda might do or say. Her failure to write had been a warning that she knew everything; knowing, she had done nothing. His feeling of safety reached such a height that he often broke into a fit of laughter merely to draw attention.

Still riding the wave of safety and boldness, he lay on the rifle-range one day beside Rufus and hit target after target. Something impelled him to speak of Jesse. He could no more stop his words than he could stop his breathing. "Rufus, did you ever think about it . . . maybe Jesse shot hisself?"

Rufus blew on his hands for warmth. "Yeah, I 'magine he did and fed his rifle to the mare."

"He coulda shot hisself," Howard pressed. "He was about half-crazy, anyway."

Rufus's eyes narrowed into a sharp stare. "He mighta been crazy, but I've seen some folks a lot crazier." He raised his rifle, fired, barely nicked the edge of his target. He chewed vigorously and spat streams of juice into the mud before them. "No; Jesse didn't shoot hisself. Somebody with mighty good aim got him. I hear you gonna git the sharp-shooter's badge."

Howard drew to his knees, crouched forward, with his rifle-butt pressed into his groins. The cold words had struck him with fury. "Lay off me, Rufus!"

Rufus remained prone, looking ahead at his target. "Are you gonna git it?"

Howard was frantic. The secure wall around him had shattered into pieces. Every nerve end was exposed to the raw wind and the needling words. His hands shook. "Lay off me!"

"I think it's fine you gonna git it. You'll git lots of Huns too. . . ."

A madness crept into Howard's eyes; a thunder exploded in his mind: Rufus knew. Something told him he must destroy what would soon destroy him, but he thought only of using his hands. His rifle fell to the ground with a flat thud. He threw himself forward, seized Rufus by the throat. Rufus, still prone when the cold hands touched his flesh, whirled and jabbed his elbow brutally into the face above him. Glaring down at Howard, stunned in a puddle of mud, he said, "You little son-of-a-bitch, you been on me fer a month like I knowed what happened to Jesse. I don't know no more'n you know. I oughta stomp your guts out."

Nile Phelps was suddenly between them, pushing them back to their posts before the sergeant should turn his eyes on them. "Take my place over there," Nile urged Howard. "Go on, if you two ain't gitting along."

Howard shrugged off Nile's hands and crawled back to his post. No anger was left in him, only a dead calm. He began to fire, splitting the target again and again. He looked up and down the line; the brief ruction had gone unnoticed in the heat of firing. A warmth came back to him; stiff surges of pleasure. Between shots, he glanced at Rufus, who frequently missed the target completely and sent up sprays of mud. He felt sorry for Rufus, particularly so now that it was clear Rufus knew nothing. It seemed to him that the big man a few feet away was the only man he had ever wronged; he must wipe his slate clean. "Rufus, I jist went crazy or something. I don't know how come me to fly off like that."

"Yeah. . . ." Rufus missed another carefully aimed shot.

"Most of yore shots going to the right, Rufus."

"Yeah. . . ."

"It's cause you pulling the trigger with yore arm instid of yore finger. Jist put the tip of yore finger on the trigger and see if it don't hep."

Rufus's good nature had almost consumed his anger; he silently followed the advice, hit the edge of the target.

"Don't it hep some?"

"Yeah. . . ." Old Noah had told him the same thing years ago, but he had forgotten. How many other things had he forgotten that old Noah had told him?

That night a rumour passed in the canteen that Company G would be shipped out within a week. Most of the men hoped it was true. They talked endlessly of Frenchwomen and wine and the valorous deeds they would perform against the enemy in order to save the world. Soon they would be free of the stinking, dish-water mud of Camp Shelby, marching with impunity against atrocious hordes. The trenches of France would be filled with sunlight and laughter; it did not occur to them there might also be mud in that far-away place. Howard sat with bruised nose and listened; he, too, saw the sunlight and laughter. Only Nile Phelps brooded. "Papa was aiming to drive down here," he told the men. "I hope he gits here before we have to leave."

A few days later Howard received his sharp-shooter's badge. He wore it boldly and proudly. Nothing had ever given him such pleasure; when he touched it, diffusive thrills covered his skin; it became a fetish against the past. Now he avoided no eyes; when possible, he moved from the fringe to the centre of the group. He avoided no eyes, for he was the first from the Hollow to be decorated.

The men, sensing the change in Howard as only a despicable arrogance, watched with more scorn and more envy. If one of them must die in the great venture before them, they hoped it would be Howard Hurley.

The firelight leaped in such a way that it appeared—like a wind—to move the various objects on the walls of the lumberjack room: the calendar hanging from a sixpenny nail, the unframed picture of a horse that came with the purchase of a box of Red Rooster salve, the year-old Christmas cards tacked in a triangular design, and the several Biblical scenes cut from Sunday school books.

Ephriam Hurley sat before the log fire with the Bible closed on his thumb. He wished to pray about this heavy matter on his heart, but what must he say? What must he ask for? Was it not both righteous and honourable to strike down that which had spoiled daughter or sister? And then, was it not written: Thou shalt not . . . ? But he did not say the word to himself.

"It's so," he said to Rachel.

"It's so," she answered.

"How can I lie fer him?"

"Have you looked ever'wheres?"

"Ever'wheres," he answered.

"He couldn't of took it with him."

The old man shook his head.

"Todda never moved it off with her," she continued. "What would she want with a gun?"

"Oh, it's so," he said. "Couldn't be nothing else."

"It's so," she said. And after a pause. "Hit was all her fault."

"Not all," Ephriam said.

"Yes; all," she said. "Hit's no good to blame the dead."

He opened the Book as if to read, and then he closed it again.

The woman squinted into the firelight. "I tole you her dress fit too tight when she left. You can't fool me. She can't hide her shame in Memphis. You mark my words. Be shore your sins will find you out. It's best she's gone. Let her bear her own shame."

The old man nodded, but he did not mean to be agreeing. He did not mean anything. "And our shame. What about our shame?"

"Ours?" the woman said.

"He's our son. But I will not lie fer him. I will not hide such a thing fer him."

"You will lie," she said. "If they ask you, you will lie. If they don't ask you, it's no lie."

He gazed into the firelight. "Silence is sometimes a lie."

"He done what you woulda done," she said. "It was her fault. I saw hit way back yonder. But a body can't always stop sich things."

"Hit's a hard thing." And he opened the Book again.

"I've washed my hands of her." She stretched out her hands to the heat of the fire, and bending over, she rubbed her shins to erase the heat.

"Washed yore hands of her? What about him?"

"That's a matter fer God."

"Yes," the old man said; "a matter fer God." He began to read.

5

ON Christmas Day they sailed out of Norfolk into a choppy and rain-covered sea. The men from the Hollow huddled together, like blizzard-struck cattle, for the last brave look at land. In the mad wilderness of dank khaki and stamping hobnails, their envy of Howard was dissipated and turned toward the hospital, where Marlon Kingsley lay with pneumonia. They had at last understood what it was to leave, and their child-sharp enthusiasm had been blunted like a toy sword driven against a brick wall. Tom Phelps had helped with the blunting.

He had arrived in Norfolk the day before the sailing, driven all the way by his brightest son, eighteen-year-old Johnny, who was the official chauffeur of the family. Tom Phelps was the owner of two farms in the Hollow, of a mule stable in Cross City; and he was considered the shrewdest politician in Woodall County, though he had been defeated in three county-wide races (once for circuit clerk and twice for county sheriff) because he was both too proud and too lazy to make the customary house-to-house campaign asking for votes. Such straightforward politics did not interest him; he preferred to meet in a dingy corner of a dingy café and plan with his cohorts devious ways of moving men into their fold. He tricked, pressured, bought and stole votes, always carrying the country precincts by huge majorities. The two large city precincts, which he ignored because deviousness was more difficult there, had each time cast the votes that defeated him. He did not mind losing, for his real interest was the campaign and not the office.

From the moment war was declared, Tom Phelps had worked diligently to keep his son Nile out of the Army. He had succeeded in delaying his call for three months, thus delaying the call of Rufus and Barney and the others. He had failed his son (and in a way his son's companions) because he had failed to manœuvre two of the members of the Woodall County Draft Board. Driving seven hundred miles, day and night, was the least he could do for his son who might never return.

When he had arrived at the bivouac area, he was told that he could not see his son. Soon, after a few telephone calls to Washington, he had not only his son but also the other men from the Hollow through the bivouac gates into a greasy, unrated café overlooking the sea. The stratagem gave him considerable pleasure. He smiled, deepening the arc of his neat moustache, showing the perfect ridge of pearly teeth, and delivered messages from the home folk. Before leaving he had gone to the homes of all the men (who knew but that he might run for sheriff again some day?) and had been loaded with food and clothes and sentimental messages—except at the Hurley house, where Howard's mother, with typical stoicism of certain hill people, said, "Jist tell him we hope he gits back all right, Mister Tom."

Nile Phelps sat at the huge table brooding, thinking of the time when his father's arm and devious brain could no longer reach out to protect him. The other men were more lighthearted, each pleased that this man of means had come to them like a rescuer. They talked endlessly, snacking on the food from home and drinking raw red whisky from a common bottle. Tom Phelps's eyes finally discovered the sharp-shooter's badge hanging from Howard's jacket. "Son, I'm ignorant of these things. What is that contraption?"

"That's a badge for marksmanship, Papa," Nile explained wearily.

"Yes . . . yes. Well, fine." His commendation was mild, seeing that neither his son nor any of the other men wore one. There were safer subjects. "By gad, Rufus, but your wife is a business-woman. She's handling those mills easy as tending to a baby. She's got lumber stacked all over the hillside and the price is going up every day. She may make you a rich man by the time you get back." And, sensing the words might sting, he added, "That boy of yours is the finest-looking baby I ever laid my eyes on. By gad, but he's fine! You should've named him Rufus; he's you all over." He studied Rufus's face, his shoulders, the rugged, awkward power ridiculously bound in tight khaki. An intriguing political idea snapped in his mind. A sudden, deep affinity was born for Rufus. "Boy, do you know what we ought to do with you when you get back? Run you for sheriff. You look like a sheriff. You're big and stout and good-looking. You could beat their ears down. We'd drive those snigger-sleeves out of office; they've infested the courthouse since I was old enough to vote. He could do it, couldn't he, Nile?"

"I b'lieve he could," Nile said loyally, from far off.

"Well, boys, let's all remember it. When you get back—and you're all coming back—we'll elect us a sheriff from Company G. We'll put in an honest man for a change."

It was well past eleven o'clock; the men had to return before midnight. The old man, still trim as a youth, got up sadly. He was over sixty years old and had never before sent a son off to war, or gone himself. He did not know exactly what one should say; that was why he preferred not to be alone with Nile. The men donned their caps and heavy trench-coats. All walked soberly through the biting wind to the bivouac gates. Tom Phelps shook hands with the men. Then he put his arm around his son, a final, tender gesture to climax his long journey. The act was too much for Nile. He seized his father's shoulder and broke into a stifled, funereal sob. "I'll be killed, Papa! I know I'll be killed."

The old man stood unconsoling as a statue, not minding the display of weakness, because he enjoyed the weakness of others, but unable to decide what to do. Then he too was struck with dejection. The men saw tears roll down his face. He wondered about the war for the first time. "Son, you'll be all right," he managed to say. "It'll be over before long."

"You didn't try to git me out," Nile cried childishly. "I wish I had pneumonia like Marlon."

The old man broke the hands from his shoulder and pushed Nile gently toward Rufus. "All you boys take care of yourselves," he said in a last effort to save the moment.

They watched him turn and blow his nose stiffly into a huge red handkerchief. He walked briskly into the wind, Johnny two steps ahead of him.

The men were ashamed for Nile that night, and still ashamed the next morning as they huddled on deck looking through seagulls in the direction where Marlon Kingsley lay in a warm hospital room. They no longer saw sunlight and laughter in the far-away trenches.

By nightfall the hog islander, wallowing in a heavy sea with sixteen other ships, had turned the men green with seasickness—all except Howard, whose cheeks were rosy from the ocean wind. The sickness had struck with insane fury: they belched and slobbered and retched, straining from scalp to toe-nail. Their eyes ached; their heads itched inside, as if insects crawled over their brains; their throats burned; their stomachs felt stuffed with dry cotton; they believed they would die. Through three days of stench and groans and prayers and blasphemy, Howard waited on them. They berated, praised, cursed, and blessed him from their bunks day and night.

"Howard," the voice pleaded gently, "bring me a towel."

"Howard, my helmet . . . ooggghh."

"Damn you, Howard! Why don't you die with us? Ooggghh . . . you're inhuman. . . ."

"Steal me an apple, Howard. I'll do anything fer you. . . . I'll slave fer you till Doomsday. . . ."

"Me too, Howard. . . . Oh, God. . . ."

He stole apples for them.

"Howard, wet this towel again, please. . . . You're a prince, you're a wonder. If a German ever touches you . . . I'll kill him. . . . Ooggghh, God . . . if I can."

"You little squeak, what have you got fer a belly? A sausage-grinder?"

"Howard! Quick!"

He loved it. He was almost sorry when the sea calmed and the retching and spewing ended. He had never been so happy in his life: about him was the vast protection of the lonely water and the voices compelled to friendliness by Fate. When he went on deck, he never looked astern, but always stationed himself on the bow and stared through the spray to the constant horizon ahead. The fear of enemy submarines, so common among the other soldiers, did not bother him. Should the ship be torpedoed, he would be one to escape—he had no doubt.

Rarely in his life had he ever wondered about anything. Now he spent hours trying to imagine how a foreign country would appear to him, how the people would be dressed, how they would walk, how they would sound. He tried to picture the trenches and the hostile faces of the enemy. As the ship moved onward, his mind responded with more clarity and more detail. He was delighted. He dreamed of the things he had tried to imagine. All his twisted, native intelligence rose from its sleeping pit; his mind was afire with impressions. A school of blue-nosed dolphins, leaping with the slow-motion grace of a rainbow, sent him into a fit of pleasure. He pounded his delight into a soldier beside him, until the soldier moved safely back into the mob of khaki. He spoke with more ease. Occasionally he wore an unconscious smile. He stole more apples for the men, though the sea had been calm for two days and they were able to steal for themselves. The display of good nature surprised himself as much as the others. He was like one miraculously saved from a fatal disease: sunlight and voices and time ticking away were as real as food. He woke in the mornings hungry to know what the day would bring. He began to wonder what went on in the minds of the other men about him; he even wondered why such things had never concerned him before.

Toward the end of the crossing he borrowed a copy of *St. Elmo* that belonged to the nineteen-year-old company clerk from Pennsylvania. With considerable effort he had read a hundred pages of it when the sight of England stirred the ship and sent men rushing topside. In the misty dawn, he knifed his way to the port rail and watched the miracle of land loom larger and larger. It was like passing into another world. The first tinge of remorse pierced him like a dull vaccination. Then it was lost in the pandemonium spreading through the sea-weary and land-starved soldiers.

All day they fretted at anchor in Southampton Harbour. That night they crossed the Channel and landed at Le Havre. By early morning they were corralled into box-cars and pulled at an ox pace out of the city into the rich pastoral country of the Seine Valley. Against the grey, hazy background, they saw cathedral spires, smoky chimney-stacks, winter-stripped apple trees, odd bridges, old châteaux and abbeys, barges ploughing along the Seine past lazy cattle, and bright-cheeked men and women who stopped their carts and bicycles or put down their straw baskets to wave. At times, above the rumble of the box-cars, they heard the strange murmuring of fresh-fish hawkers. In spite of the fine, chilling rain, some of the glory of war returned. The cries from friendly peasants urged them on.

Moving along the edge of Rouen, the young company clerk cried out his recognition of the dominant spire of the Rouen Cathedral.

"Now jist what denomination is that church? Baptist?" Barney asked.

Only the young clerk laughed.

The fine rain increased, but it did not dampen the fires kindling in the blood of the men. Soon they would be in Paris: even one night would be sufficient for a riotous season with wine and lovely young girls waiting for them in droves along the Champs-Elysées.

But long before they caught sight of the Eiffel Tower, the train stopped beside a waiting line of lorries. With angry curses, the men changed their stations, leaving in the empty box-cars their dreams of revelry. They expected to be face to face with the Huns by nightfall.

The lorries crawled along miles of precarious roads, hidden villages, and winter-quiet farms to the bivouac area. There the men marched and loafed and stood inspections and scratched and slept, tormented by filth and rain and cold and the absence of the girls they had so much expected. Some nights they got into the nearby village and shocked the old proprietor of the café by drinking his finest wines without the aid of wine-glasses. The old man kept his café open as long as they pleased, watching with the same sober, fathomless eyes as his tiger cat, thinking of his son dead in Flanders. He kept his daughter upstairs.

Howard remained a favourite. He managed to secure extra blankets from the quartermaster, extra rations from the cook. His sharp-shooter's badge was no longer visible, even when they changed from fatigue clothes to uniforms for a few hours in the café. He took long walks beyond the village, and almost always returned with a bottle of wine, somehow smuggling it past the gate guards and the guards stationed at the ends of the makeshift barracks which had once been a huge dairy barn. During his walks he often reached down and grabbed a handful of soil, kneading it into a hundred shapes, wondering if after the war he might want to stay in that strange country. He might even find a way to bring Todda there and help raise her child. But Todda was not too often in his thoughts; he was free now; he owed nothing to her or to anyone, unless it would be to her child. Sometimes he was astonished to realize that giving something created a pleasant sensation in him, like the smell of strong coffee on those cold mornings. Such thoughts led him to buy extra bottles of wine for the men. He always handed the wine to Rufus.

There were times, while he was alone in the barracks, that he considered reading Rufus's letters. He could have done so easily. But the urge always passed, and the feeling that followed was akin to the sensation of buying wine for the men. While the men cursed the stagnant hours of their life, he remained silent and calm, as if he could have lived happily in the barracks the rest of his life. He finished reading *St. Elmo*.

Every week brought a new rumour of troop movements; every week the men listened with the same credulous attention. Every week they took one long overnight hike, with full packs, through rain or snow or whatever the time offered. Every week it was reported the Germans had broken through to Paris, believable enough when the eastern sky was drowned in a shimmering glow. Every week mail arrived, giving a general view of conditions in the Hollow. Anna's letters were the most detailed; Rufus shared his news with the other men, but kept to himself the splendid, sentimental descriptions of his son, the recurring lines of his wife's devotion, the delicate statements of her passionate longing for him. Had the written word ever before carried such a burden of feeling? Not to his knowledge. Aye god, how the woman loved him!

After one such wonderful letter, Rufus left the barracks and tramped like a madman around and around the bivouac area through snow half to his knees. He spat thick tobacco juice into the gleaming snow, wishing he could spoil every inch of it, a bitter defiance of the civilized world. What a damned mess the world was in. They had left homes and children—women like Anna, if there were any others like her—to help against whatever was wrong, and for months they had sat on their back-ends in a barn, not lifting a finger except to scratch until the blood trickled through. He walked and spat, but the snow remained unsullied. It was a good damned thing the ocean lay between him and the Hollow.

When the snow melted, rain set in, incessant and torrential, a slanting sheet. They were told it was a prelude to spring. They believed it; they believed anything now other than rumours of marching orders.

The rain stopped for two days. The yellow puddles of foam gleamed in the meagre sunlight. Early one morning roar after roar went up from every quarter. A wild outburst of profanity ricocheted from the walls. Rebel yells shook the barracks, for most of the men were Southerners.

"Front!"

"Front? Hot-damn, I thought the war was over!"

"March on, you brave of heart, march on!" A Yankee voice rang clear above the others. "*Allons enfants de la patrie, le jour de gloire est arrivé!*"

"What's he saying?" Barney asked of the company clerk.

"French!" the young clerk yelled, nervous and excited.

"Yeah," Barney said, unmoved. "I wish to hell it was some way to save democracy without all this here crap." He walked over to Rufus, who stood sober enough amid all the commotion. "From here on, Rufe, ain't but one thing I'm out to save. You know what it is?"

"What?" Rufus asked gravely.

"Barney's ass."

"Yeah," Rufus said, disgusted with the childish enthusiasm about them. Only the day before he had received another wonderful letter from Anna. He had a premonition: he was afraid he was going to die.

6

THEY marched past the neat hamlets, the soft white stone houses; past long-legged sheep and patches of fir trees dotting the melancholy landscape; past beet-fields and meticulously pruned vineyards, set in strict pattern like old arms with gnarled fists.

"When this thing is over with," a teetotaller from Tennessee announced morbidly, "white crosses is going to cover this country thick as them wine sprouts."

For three days they marched. At the end of the third day they stopped on a hill at the edge of a forest. Their trenches were already dug, in a nest of poplars. They had only to dip the water with their helmets. It reminded Rufus of winter morning funerals, when the graves had stood open all night, and water had trickled in a foot deep.

In the daytime they waited and gambled and cursed and slept. At night they went out on short patrols. Some nights the sky beyond the forest was pale with artillery fire, but it was so far away they could hear none of the rumbling. They saw no sign of the enemy; there were days when they believed he had gone home. Bravery crept into them as they became familiar with every tree and gulley and meadow, and the gaping shell holes which the winter rains had aged.

They stood their watches and waited. They learned to bring back ducks and chickens from their night patrols. They felt old and experienced. The sun grew warmer; tiny buds appeared on the poplars: it was a warning. A new sergeant came to lead their patrols: it was a stronger warning.

The sergeant's name was Hamilton Littlejohn. He was quiet and stubborn; a small man with a tight, olive face, from Birmingham, Alabama. Eight years with the Army and marriage to a New Jersey girl had almost erased his Southern drawl. He had been on the front for three months. The men knew only that he knew his business; they called him Ham. Each night he borrowed a small chew of tobacco from Rufus and led the patrol deeper and deeper into the countryside. With extreme precaution, he moved, spitting his tobacco juice from tight, intense lips. He never cursed; he never talked of the battles he had seen. But he loved what he was doing.

"Ham, when's this here thing gonna bust loose?" Barney asked.

"Two weeks; maybe sooner." Tobacco juice dropped carefully through his lips. A guarded smile flickered in his eyes. It excited him to see a new man under fire. He spent grave and stimulating sessions figuring how his squad would react. A sergeant needed to know his men. The only one he felt certain of was Barney. For one reason, Barney was a little man. Howard was promising, though his eyes were sometimes a puzzle. Chet Daringhast would go with the wind. Rufus Frost was all right, he believed, but he was the type to fool a man. Nile Phelps would be all beast or all cotton; at least he was lean, which was a good sign. Well, in a few days, he expected to sight a patrol or two. He felt good. He could rest while he waited. He hoped Rufus Frost had a full stock of tobacco.

The beginning was not at all what the men expected. Early one morning they lay in a copse of bushes on the edge of a vineyard and watched a German patrol of eleven men circle around them. They lay for hours, and at mid-morning they returned to their lines at the edge of the forest. Eighteen against eleven, they had been, and not a shot was fired. What kind of war was it?

The first clash occurred near the end of a long, and apparently fruitless, patrol. They were two or three miles from their lines, marching two abreast behind Ham. The sun was just rising to their backs, casting enormous shadows of arms and legs and shouldered rifles. As they topped a small, grass-covered knoll, Ham threw himself flat on to his belly, and instinctively turned his head to see half the men still standing upright in the sunlight. "Hit it! Hit it!" he hissed through tightened lips. They buried themselves in the grass only a split-second before a volley of rifle fire tore over their heads. Ham crawled back, motioning them into a line, growling, "Don't you know nothing? You want to shoot each other in the back?" He ripped a gas-mask from Chet Daringhast's face and prodded him with the butt of his rifle. "Move up there beside Phelps!" He crawled up and down behind the men, manœuvring them, giving them orders to hold fire. A second volley from the enemy patrol dug into the grass several yards ahead of them.

Ham was pleased with the situation. Facing three or four volleys from the enemy would do his men more good than months of training; would let them know every rifle crack didn't kill a man. Something had told him there were no more than ten Germans in the ravine below them and they were already inching their way to the south. A half-dozen more volleys would be the end of it. Three sporadic volleys came in quick succession, again tearing the grass below and to the left of them. Ham could tell the Germans were moving faster now; they would soon be gone. "Fire!" he ordered.

They rained bullets in the general direction of the enemy. They shot at leaves and shadows, trees and stumps and mounds. A grey-uniformed figure suddenly rose, uttered its sharp pain and toppled backward.

Chet raised his head a foot and cried, "We got him!" But before the last syllable was out, Ham had pounced on the head and buried it with a brutal shove to the earth. "Fire!" he commanded, and the wild inundation of bullets continued. He let them fire until he was certain every German, except the dead one, was a mile away. He believed it had been a good lesson. Then they ceased firing and moved cautiously to the north. Their spirits rose to immense heights when at last they stood up and walked.

"Say, what about the one we got?" Howard asked.

"What about him?" Ham asked sternly. "You wanta go take a look at him and see how many legs and arms he's got? I can tell you, mister. It's the same number you got. In this place, we don't worry about the dead."

"We whupped the hell out of 'em, didn't we?" Barney said.

"Yeah," Ham said. "Must a' been four or five hundred."

But the men's spirits continued to soar; they had met the enemy face to face and driven him away. What more could the goddamned Army ask of its soldiers?

That night the men did not go out on patrol. They rolled into their blankets early and slept like children, all except Howard. He slept for a while and then he lay wide awake, staring up into the clear, brilliant night. Whether his eyes were closed or wide open, he saw the German rising and falling backward: surely it had been his bullet which had found the vital mark. He remembered the slow wave of grass and his careful aim. He was not sorry; he simply wanted to look at the face. What could stop him? Nothing. He entertained no debate with himself; he had known since dark that he was going.

With only his rifle, he started past the sentry, calling the night's password, "Stage-coach. . . . Stage-coach. . . ."

The sentry, remembering several complaints of the beans they had eaten that day, asked good-naturedly, "They tear you up too?"

"Yeah," Howard said, and passed on quickly.

A mile from the lines he began to run. He had no doubt of finding the way, for his mind had sketched every part of it. As he neared the ravine where the body had fallen, he approached with caution. His heart beat in powerful explosions; it seemed that he could hear in the distance wild volleys of rifle fire. He parted the grass with the butt of his rifle and moved slowly forward. Before him was a narrow path where men had crawled; a few yards away lay a dark mass from which a rifle barrel pointed like a hideous finger. He crouched and waited.

He crept forward until he was only a few feet away from the dead man's head. He dropped to his knees. What he was looking for, he did not know; but it was there, in his presence. The soldier had fallen slightly on his left side with his left arm folded beneath him. His helmet was pushed forward over his eyes and nose so that only the lower part of his mouth and chin showed. His right hand still held to his rifle; his right foot was folded back beneath a heavy thigh. His left leg jutted at an angle into the grass. These things Howard observed carefully, gathering courage to reach out and lift the helmet. He dropped his rifle, to have both hands free, leaned forward and unfastened the chin-strap. Until then, his nerves had been as steel, his every move deliberate. But the mere touching of the strap changed all his muscles into a knot: he was certain the face would be that of Jesse, though the body was fuller and stronger.

That was it: he had come, of course, to see the face of Jesse. Leaning closer and trembling, he saw the stream of dark blood caked on the twisted neck, the dark puddle covering the bruised grass like thick tobacco juice. The tip of his finger touched the cold rim of the helmet. Now for the face of Jesse! He waited a full minute, electrified, shaking, his muscles snapping like over-extended cables. With a quick thrust he shoved the helmet back. A nightmarish cry leaped from his throat. Seizing his rifle he sprang to his feet and staggered away. Scalding sweat poured down his forehead, through his eyebrows, across his closed eyelids.

He forced himself to turn. The hideous barrel-finger was pointing at him. He took the butt of his rifle and slowly, gently pushed the helmet over the face, as it had been. Then he ran, driven by panic, stumbling through the stiff grass, across the ravine, and fell exhausted at the foot of a tree a hundred yards away. It was horrible; he would go mad. He had not seen Jesse's face at all. He had seen a face as calm and beautiful as the face of Jesus. "Oh, God, why did I do it?" he pleaded, and curled himself into a violent knot with his cheek pulsing against his rifle butt.

After half an hour he sat up and drew the rifle across his knees. He had ceased to shake; a burning calm controlled him. He looked up at the brilliant sky; he guessed it must be near midnight. Strange, mysterious thoughts, like fireflies, swarmed through his mind. He thought he might be going mad. He gripped his rifle. If with one pull of his finger he could drain the last pulse from a man, why could he not rekindle life in that splendid, ashen face?

He got up and leaned against the tree. "I know I done it." He worked his lips silently. "I remember the wave of grass and closing my left eye and taking aim. But I wouldn't do it again. . . ." He wiped his sleeve across his forehead, and looked sadly toward the ravine. He wanted to leave, but the weak, rubbery feeling in his knees held him motionless. A breeze swept from some corner of the night; it was like food. He breathed deeply, and wished for some familiar sound to break his trance. There was nothing.

How could he have killed a man who had done him no wrong; not even a man, but a mere boy with thin, high cheeks and a small, half-smiling mouth? Maybe he had showered tender kisses on a lover, but surely there had been no wrong, no violation, for the face was too calm and innocent. And he lay still as Jesse, waiting for the sun to shrivel his smile. It would not take long.

Howard felt a weakness uncoiling in his stomach and spreading through his body. He slumped to the foot of the tree again. He imagined the nausea was akin to seasickness: now he understood how the men had suffered.

Almost an hour had gone by when he heard the brushing aside of grass. Below him, in the ravine, two figures moved cautiously, carrying a stretcher. A sense of danger threw strength into his body. He stood up and instinctively darted behind the tree. The two figures put down their stretcher, glanced about them, and then at their dead comrade. "Well, look," one said in excellent German, "who can doubt that God is on our side? He was so handsome this morning."

"*Ja,*" the other responded with bitterness. "*Ein feste Burg ist unser Gott.*"

The strange mumbling was a signal for Howard. He lifted the rifle and fired quickly; on the second soldier it was necessary to fire twice. Against the sharp wail of pain, his lips moved: "You two ain't no better'n he is." Then he ran like a wild man back toward his lines, gaining strength as he ran. He had never felt so much power in his body. Why shouldn't he have fired? Wasn't this a war?

From afar off he slowed to a walk, looking behind him as if the two followed. He called breathlessly, "Stage-coach! Stage-coach!" He chose to return by a different sentry, hoping there would be no questions. But he was stopped.

"Name?"

"Private Howard Hurley, Company G." And as he spoke he seemed to see himself in a mirror.

"What you so scared about, Bo? You see anything out there?"

"No."

"What you so scared about?"

"I ain't scared?"

"The hell you say. You damned fools better learn to do your business in the daytime, else you're gonna wake up with a extra hole somewhere."

He hurried on and crawled into the bough-covered trench beside Rufus and Barney. He wrapped his blanket about him and sat with his knees drawn high, looking from Barney to Rufus, hearing the adenoidal snoring up and down the trench. It was dark about him, but his eyes gradually adjusted until he could see the brown, stubbly beard covering Rufus's face. The huge body, expanding and shrinking in sleep, fascinated him. He wondered how many times it had made love to Todda, and what words had been whispered from the face behind that heavy beard. He wondered why he had ever led the way to the Hollow with the strange, bitter hope that Todda would never again look into Rufus's unrelenting eyes, or touch his enormous hands. He saw the mare shying off the road into the woods. But had it happened? It seemed so far away and alien. His mind whirled. Nothing was clear, except the face of the young German. The others did not matter: not Jesse, nor the mumbling two. Only the young face mattered. What a pity it had not escaped. It might someday have married Todda and fathered her child. . . . His thoughts stopped abruptly; he pounded his head. Was he mad? He must stop the wild buzzing in his mind, lie down and go to sleep.

He searched Rufus's face again. He believed he saw a tiny rill of tobacco juice streaking from lip to chin. Ah, a flaw! The man's mouth was usually well-wiped. Was the streak really there? Well, how could he wonder such a thing when it was before his eyes? If he could wake Rufus and tell him about the Germans, he would be all right. His mind would then lie down and go to sleep.

He put out his hands, but an instant before he touched the big body, fear seized him. He wheeled and grabbed Barney's shoulder, giving it a rough shake. "Barney! Wake up a minute. . . ."

Barney grunted and turned away from the hand.

"Barney!"

"Yeah? What the hell is it?"

"I killed two Germans a little while ago."

"Yeah. I jist killed the Kaiser." He smacked his lips and went back to sleep.

Howard lay down, pulled the blanket tight, and turned his face toward Rufus. The snoring and grinding of teeth up and down the trench was sharp and clear, but he felt better. His eyes fastened on the heavy, bearded face two yards away. Was the streak of tobacco juice really there? Ah, a flaw! He had found a flaw in the man.

7

THE next morning Howard looked closely: the streak of tobacco juice was not there.

All day the men laughed and mocked because Howard had killed two Germans during the night. Barney told the story with delight and vulgar scoffing. "Wakes me up, see? I think a earthquake's got me; and he says, 'Barney, I jist killed two Germans.' And I told him I jist killed the Kaiser! Whah . . . whah. . . . What got aholt of you, Howard?"

"Hey, Howard, what did you think you was? Dan'l Boone or something?"

"Sarge! Looney-tick case. Take him away!"

"Howard, I thought you was a good boy. I didn't know you was sich a big liar."

"Aw, lay off him, will ya? I dreamt last night I was a nightmare."

The ridicule and insulting doubts burned into Howard, but he was not angry with the men. He thought of coming engagements: he would show them. They were cowards; that was their trouble. The only answer was to overlook their disbelief. But the continual sniggering and gibing wore deeper and deeper. At last he sought out Rufus, sitting alone, oiling his rifle. "Rufus, would you b'lieve me if I swore something to you?"

Rufus pushed his tobacco carefully with his tongue and spat into a chosen spot already soaked and dyed with the rich juice. "I reckon I would."

"About last night. I swear I. . . ." He stopped. Where could he begin the story? On a hillside in the Hollow with a pale face tilted into morning light? And the sharp crack of a rifle bolting a mare?

Rufus's eyes crinkled. He spat expertly into the soaked spot of earth and rubbed the thick corners of his mouth with finger and thumb. "Did you bring their ears back?"

"I don't give a damn if you don't listen. I could tell you some things would make your backbone rattle."

Rufus smiled and spat again. A savage fury boiled in Howard, moved upward until his face was scalding red. Nobody would meet him halfway. He wished he could bash his fists against their unbelieving faces. He had held their heads and helmets while the green bile of seasickness dripped, and now they answered with infuriating smiles and laughter.

"What sort of things, Howard?"

"Things like who shot Jesse." He could no more stop the words than he could stop the saliva running under his tongue.

"Could you? I reckon you dreamed you done it from a train window. Why don't you write the Sheriff and tell him you done it through the train window." He spat again.

Howard's eyes followed the arc of juice to the chosen spot. It was like the dead blood of the young German. He parted his lips to let go with every violent curse he knew, but the grey eyes of Rufus stopped him, sobered him quickly. "What's eating at you, Howard? Don't you think we dream the same damn' things you do? I got jist as scared of them goddam bullets as you did, too."

"Did you?" Howard asked calmly, thankful that the big grey eyes had brought him to his senses.

"Hell yes. I don't want no more of it. But, aye god, we ain't seen nothing yet."

Howard warmed to the feeling of a narrow escape. "I tell you what happened last night. I went out to do my business, and I was squatting there and got so damned scared I took a couple of shots at something."

Rufus spat confidently and smiled. "That's more like it."

That night Ham chose five men for a patrol into the heart of enemy ground: Howard, Barney, Rufus, Kokonolski (a football player from Illinois who was called "Coconut"), and Bolton (a scholarly man from Far Rockaway, New York, who understood both French and German).

Night after night they went out, Howard abreast of the sergeant, Barney and Kokonolski paired, Rufus and Bolton bringing up the rear. Always at some point, Ham and Bolton left the other four and worked themselves closer to the enemy lines. Sometimes the patrol drew enemy fire, but they rarely returned it. "We're not out to shoot," Ham instructed. "All we want to do is get facts and get back." After each venture, Barney entertained the stay-at-homes, particularly Nile and Chet, with glowing tales of the night's fighting. He displayed for a bayonet wound a gash in his thigh caused from stumbling over a stump-snag. "Oh, hit's coming," he prophesied. "Hell's gonna break loose and you all setting' here like pancakes. If it's a dozen men over there, it's a million. With bayonets long as

I am. They sharpen them things with razor-straps! Ask Rufe. In fact, I didn't even feel the one that got me until the blood started running in my shoe. You better put on yore old-time religion, fellers, fer creation is gonna start shaking."

He could not know what a prophet he was: until two o'clock one morning when the whole Company was yelled to arms and rushed four miles to the south and shoved into a trench beside men whose beards made those of Company G appear as adolescent fuzz. The sky was a horrible, exploding yellow, east and west. Grey blooms of earth rose like screaming animals and settled piece by piece into and about the gaping shell-holes. A copse of trees, scarred and splintered months before, was suddenly a twisted, crumbling mass. Far down the line, a shell dug into the side of the trench and covered men alive; they screamed like horses. The men of Company G pushed their faces into the dirt; they could feel the earth tremors.

"I told you!" Barney cried. "Goddam, I tole you!"

Ham moved up and down behind his men. A fixed, demonic smile creased his face. He saw no heroes; he was pleased with himself. "All right, all right," he called, merely to let them hear the calculated calmness in his voice. There was plenty of time ahead for heroes. Right now, silence and stillness would be enough. A dull thud sounded behind him, a sharp cry spread. He wheeled and hurled himself toward Chet Daringhast, who had already drawn his knees forward and closed his eyes to die. The other men raised their heads like serpents and stared.

Ham knelt beside the first casualty; carefully he stripped the shirt back, hearing the slow, stifled groans. Just above the hip was a shrapnel scratch and a small trickle of blood. The men were crawling toward Chet, still with their serpent stares. "Get back!" Ham snarled. "There's nothing wrong with him."

Through the heavy sound of explosions and crashes and night-marish cries they moved back to their places, unconsciously feeling a tinge of disappointment. This quake of fire would be certain to claim one of them. Why not Chet? He had many faults.

The explosions came nearer. Fine dust, blown asunder to the last infinitesimal grain, settled upon them. Smoke hovered above their heads and drifted to and fro, moving the stars.

The men recovered enough to raise their heads and look about them. The veterans, down the trench to the right, sat with their backs to the earth wall, carelessly. Some of them laughed. One by one, Ham saw his men sit back; their faces were smeared with dirt. Chet Daringhast was half-sitting, squeezing in his right hand the rugged steel fragment that had scratched him.

"Feel any better?" Ham asked of all the faces.

"Better, hell," Barney said. "I feel putrefied. Ain't that where you're like a rock?"

"Petrified," Ham said gravely.

"I wisht I felt like a rock," Chet drawled.

Together, all the men broke into a laugh; it rang through the trenches like a bell, and beat back the wave of terror that had driven their faces into the earth. When the spurt of laughter had ended, they came to life. They looked at one another; the first baptism was over, and they had not strangled. From that moment they were veterans. Fear filled them as before, but always, from that moment of laughter, though fear moved in their blood, never again did it lie frozen and bind them.

They looked into the face of the enemy; they fired with accurate fingers; they crawled over the pulverized earth, through their own rusted mass of wire, past mutilated bodies of friend and foe; they crawled back again. Their fear drove them to bravery. No man believed he would die, for each hovered under the zenith of a bright rainbow: death lay at the ends.

They marked Howard for the first victim. He crawled ahead of the others; he crawled ahead of Ham. He fired first and quicker; he rarely missed. But Chet, again, was the first to feel the insane tearing of flesh; his leg was split into two dangling shreds from knee to ankle; his foot remained unfound. Faces they had never seen before carried him back.

For Howard it was, at the beginning, a game in which he set out to prove his excellence. Then it became a hunger, as if each accurate crack of his rifle was another blanket to cover the past. He would bury the old scenes so deep that not even his own mind could reach them. And he would crown it once and for all, not with steady aim, but with a brutal thrust of his tarnished bayonet into flesh and blood. He lived to hear the hideous scream that his mighty thrust would evoke. He was certain to have his chance when the real push came.

But the lines fell back: for a mile, for two miles. He was furious at the whole Allied army. The snivelling, yellow-bellied cowards. The war would go on for ever. Weeks passed. Time was measured by the length of beards.

On the first night after the long lull, Company G pushed forward a hundred yards and retreated. Nile was missing. Howard crawled alone through a heavy barrage, found Nile and dragged him back. A saucer-like dent showed in the crown of Nile's helmet. His skin was unbroken, but blood trickled from one ear and one corner of his tobacco-stained mouth. The stretcher-bearers finally came and carried him away.

Howard sat in the trench as if he had done nothing. The other men, ashamed, glared at him, eyes saturated with hate. The barrage continued. Most of the men had taken to chewing tobacco, especially at night when cigarettes were forbidden. One after another they bit off jaw-puffing quids, hardly taking their eyes from Howard.

"Have a chew, Howard."

He shook his head to say "No." His eyes swam with contempt.

"Aw, come on. It won't make *you* sick."

"Him? He's more 'fraid of a little old chew than he is of ole Long Tom."

"Him 'fraid? You aint 'fraid of nothing, are you, Howard? Here, I got it all cut off fer you. This 'bout the right size fer him, Rufus? This big enough?"

"Yeah, that's big enough, Barney."

"Now," Barney went on, "you can't 'spect to chew good as Rufe. He can beat us all. But jist try it. Not too much at first or you'll git all the goodie out. Kinda pet it along. Ain't that the correct way, Rufus?"

"Yeah; that's the correct way."

"And if it makes you curl up and die, it ain't no worse'n what happens to lots of folks around here."

"Pitch it over here," Howard said with a throbbing bitterness in his throat. He knew what they were doing to him.

Barney pitched a huge quid. Howard crammed it into his mouth, his first taste of tobacco since he and Todda as children had tasted it together and got sick together.

"Good?" Barney asked, his face drawn into a mocking grin.

"Yeah; fine. . . ."

"Like candy, ain't it?"

"Yeah; fine. . . ."

The men chewed in silence, dropping the juice between their feet. Howard, three yards away, chewed slowly and spat toward them. The barrage continued.

A week later Howard was promoted to corporal.

In midsummer, the men were given a week's furlough. They went to Paris: Barney, Rufus, Howard, Coconut, Bolton (the learned one), and Shapiro (a quiet Jewish boy from Philadelphia, who had come to the Company as a replacement). They slept three abed in a narrow, unlighted hotel pressed between two cheap apartment-houses. Five of them (all save Howard) moved as if with one mind, one aim. Each night, or early evening, they chose two girls, took them to their room, and threw high dice for the order of sexual congress. Howard looked on with disgust, thus creating an uneven number of participants and allowing the fifth man the privilege of two performances. They could have had five girls or a dozen, but they chose only two.

In the daytime, they sat at the sidewalk cafés; drank wine; thirsted for whisky; talked of the French female's astonishing comprehension of male desires, of the end of the war, of their intended hospital visit to see Chet and Nile; and listened admirably at times to Bolton's recital of history connected with the Louvre, the Eiffel Tower, and lesser-known places. They went with Bolton to Napoleon's tomb in the Invalides, which was closed; to Notre Dame Cathedral, where Barney demanded to know why Coconut, a Catholic, had "crossed his heart and split it"; to Pont Neuf, where Barney spat into the Seine and said, "That ain't no river; it ain't big enough."

Howard remained constantly with the other five, was always nervous and fidgety. Wherever they went he walked ahead, hurrying. He wore his sharp-shooter's badge and carried his head as if the extra chevrons on his sleeve supported his chin. He wanted to get back to the line and said so, in the middle of a café session while pretty girls walked by.

"For what, you crazy-ass fool?" Barney demanded.

Bolton slipped suddenly from his peacemaker role and with wine-charged eyes exploded. "You want to get back because you're bloodthirsty. You want to kill! You love to kill! Your ancestors threw the Christians to the lions. Oh, I can see it. I can read it in the miserable roots of your despicable eyes. We . . . we'll get our guts torn out before it's over, but you, you insufferable bastard, won't lose a fingernail. Not one. Not even the dirt beneath one. I consider you an incorrigible beast!" He splattered the remaining wine in his glass across Howard's nose. Each grabbed at the other's throat. It was the proprietor of the café who separated the two. A stout, red-faced man, he moved quickly between them and halted the fight so expertly that not even the fresh napkin across his left arm was wrinkled. He announced sternly, *"S'il vous plaît, messieurs, il y a en France trop de guerre déjà!"*

Bolton slumped into his chair and broke into a fit of laughter. "That's good! That's good! Do you know what he said? 'There is too much war in France already.' " And, turning to the proprietor, he got up. *"Je vous prie de m'excuser."*

"Cela ne fait rien." The proprietor shrugged.

"Au revoir, monsieur," Bolton said, and added in English, " We are beasts. The world is full of beasts."

"What did you say to him?" Barney asked.

"I asked for forgiveness."

"Did he forgive you?" Barney asked earnestly.

"Oh, yes. The French always forgive."

Barney shook his head in wonder. "Unnnhnnn. If I could talk that stuff like you can, I'd git me a womern all to myself."

An hour later, the six walked peacefully toward the Arc de Triomphe and spat huge splatters of tobacco juice on the Amazonian sidewalk of the Champs-Elysées.

On the last day of their leave they went to the hospital. Chet, with his leg amputated just above his knee, had been transferred.

They found Nile propped up on a cot, his eyes staring from a skeleton body. He recognized them immediately and grinned, but the old friendliness in his voice was gone. His talk and questions had no more ardour than a child's spelling of an incomprehensible word. He noticed that Howard was a corporal; he stared at the chevrons, but made no comment.

Soon they made excuses to Nile that they must leave in order to catch their train. Nile nodded his understanding. Apparently he was not sorry to see them go. Nile's vacant, listless stares did not bother them so much as the mutilated rows of unknown Allied soldiers, grotesque patterns of the living dead. The British lay quieter than the French and the French lay quieter than the Americans.

In the train station they watched the unloading of a box-car of wounded British. Nearby, a young Frenchman, barely old enough to shave, gazed through the thick lenses of his spectacles and spoke in slow, precise English, "The English make wars with the breasts of other peoples." His three companions glanced at him uneasily. "With the breasts of other peoples," he repeated clearly.

Before anyone could know what was happening, Bolton stepped forward and unbuttoned the youth's shirt. "Show us the scars!"

The youth, stunned and awed, fumbled to rebutton his clothes while his companions, ashamed and embarrassed, stood like statues; then two of them broke into a flood of laughter. One cried in French, "A lesson for your tongue, my dear!"

The accuser turned and fled. The three companions remained; the laughter of the two ceased as quickly as it had commenced. The one who had kept silent and grave spoke to Bolton in English, "It will please you to understand my friend has lost in the war his father and two brothers."

The three followed after their friend.

"If I was you," Howard said to Bolton, "I'd catch up with that boy and button his shirt."

"You go to hell, Corporal," Bolton answered. "No doubt you are exceedingly happy now. We're on our way back."

The front was quiet. The six took their place in the trenches, and recounted to each other what had happened to them. The recollection seemed more real than the living had been. When they fell asleep, they slept better than they had slept during the whole short week.

Almost a month went by, with no more than occasional skirmishes. Then they moved forward against a light barrage and sporadic rifle fire to their old position, where they had first entered the trenches. They hardly recognized the landscape, for the forest was levelled except for a few poplars, each standing bare as a chimney above house-ashes.

A week later they moved forward again. Within the same hour, Ham and Kokonolski died, both with neat, silent wounds. Ham fell forward and lay still, hiding the blood that poured from his forehead into a mat of grass. Kokonolski fell forward too, clawing at his heart; he moved once on to his back and set his eyes skyward. The line moved on.

Howard became a sergeant.

The nights grew colder. The leaves faded. Signs of frost hung in the air. Autumn had arrived with a dull splendour. Rufus and Barney shared their blankets, and through filthy beards cursed the sight of Howard. They believed he was insanely bent on destroying them before the war could end.

"Rufus, that crazy-ass fool, is itching fer me to drive a bullet in the back of his brain. We'll never see the end of this thing if I don't."

"I reckon I ain't got the guts to," Rufus said.

"It ain't gonna take no guts," Barney said. "I'm jist gonna let my finger slip."

In the cold, dark hours they considered the scheme. It knocked endlessly at the doors of their minds. But the doors would not open, for both Rufus and Barney still remained beneath the zenith of the magic rainbow, and death remained at the ends. Exhausted and drained, they did not fully believe the fleshless face would breathe on them, no matter where Howard led (it had passed them by too many times). The end of the war was in sight. They heard rumours of it; they felt it; they believed it. And, more, Howard was always ahead of them, always a few steps nearer than they, crawling relentlessly toward the face that belched everlasting nothingness.

Howard, too, knew the end was in sight. He had one last hunger: to drive his tarnished bayonet into living flesh and blood. The desire was not prompted by malice, nor by anger, nor by bitterness. It rose from the old well-spring of fear: the need to cover the past with a new blot. He had long since lost sight of any detail of his crime; he did not remember Jesse's face, nor did he remember the beautiful face of the young German. Framed in his mind, above all else, was the picture of a child, whose face, he imagined, was a replica of his own.

Soon after the Paris furlough, he had received a letter (forwarded several times) from Todda; a short, blunt letter telling of her son. She was not in need of anything, she wrote; her letter was primarily to tell him that her son's name was Howard Aberdeen: she called him Dean, a name Howard had carried in his early childhood. He destroyed the letter immediately, for fear that someone (particularly Rufus) might read it. He kept the envelope. Later he drew all the money accumulated to his account and sent it to Todda. He saw the future clearly; he planned. He would devote his life, like a husband, to Todda and her child. Had not the pieces come together at last into one unbroken pattern? Only a few more conquests, and who could say the past had ever existed? If he forgot it, then it would die, like all the enemy faces on whom he had drawn his accurate bead.

With his sergeant's stripes had come new power, and with the power the new mad bravery. He loathed the uninspired actions of Rufus and Barney and Bolton and the others. He cursed their cowardice; he knew when the doors of their minds shook with the scheme for his destruction. But he was not afraid. He needed one last thrust, the thrust of his bayonet into an onrushing belly. Then the final death rattle would sound in the throat of the past.

But no bellies rushed toward him. They moved back and back, lighting a fury in him that burned day and night. He cursed the enemy for dirty, cringing cowards. He looked at Rufus and Barney and Bolton and the quiet Jew and yelled his madness. "The sneaking bastards won't fight! We can't win when they won't fight!"

"That's right, Sergeant," Bolton said with all the contempt he could muster. "Those obsequious little rascals ought not to keep the whole world at bay for four years. They ought to beat hell out of it so we could go home."

Barney, not understanding Bolton's remark, but accepting it as good, added, "I tell you something, Sergeant Hurley. You gonna wake up some morning hanging from a limb, and I'll be goddamed if I'm gonna cut you down."

Howard got up, pacing nervously about them. "You'd better git some sleep if you can. Patrol at four o'clock."

"How come it's our time?" Barney asked.

"Because the Captain ordered it. I don't ask the Captain questions."

The quiet Jew listened. Howard was the first man he had ever hated.

Rufus rested his head on his knees and let sweet tobacco juice leak through his lips. He was too tired and too cold to say anything. His hate was old and wearing thin.

It was early October.

But the next morning they did not go out. The Captain had changed his mind. They waited.

The glorious end was certain. Men thought sadly of the bonds soon to be broken. The affinity between Bolton and Rufus was strong. They made rash, and sincere, promises of visiting each other in the years ahead. After all the weeks and months of fighting and waiting and sleeping side by side, it came to light that Bolton was a high school history teacher, that young Shapiro worked for a wholesale paper company. For the first time it came to the attention of Barney and Rufus that Shapiro was a Jew. He mentioned it himself one night while recounting, with sudden ardour, a light, pleasant story of his childhood in his grandmother's house. He was pleased when he saw they had not bothered to question his heritage; the bond between them was strengthened. Bit by bit, all their histories unfolded. Sometimes they even felt a tinge of discontent that the war was dying.

All of them, except Howard, became superstitious. When they started on patrol, Rufus always shifted his quid of tobacco to his left jaw; Barney would sleep only on the right side of Rufus; Shapiro held the strap of his helmet between his teeth for five seconds before slipping it under his chin; Bolton carried a shell fragment in his pocket. During the quietest lulls they huddled in the trenches. The bravest of the brave moved forward with the utmost reluctance. Familiar ground always seemed the safest.

Howard fell on a bright afternoon, while the enemy with the sun in its face moved in a half-hearted counter-attack. For no sane reason, he leaped over the top and inched forward, the shadow of his bayonet clinging to the earth like a serpent. Rifle fire cut into his belly three times. He rolled in the dust, clenched himself into a knot, and cried.

The men looked at each other. The crying, writhing form lay thirty yards away. None moved to drag it back. To the left and right of them the tempo of fire increased. Barney and Rufus and Bolton pressed their bodies against the wall of earth; sweat popped from their faces and rolled in sheets. The writhing knot of flesh began to scream. Rufus let his rifle slip down between his legs; with a brutal thrust of his tongue, he shifted his wad of tobacco from right cheek to left. His hands clawed the dry earth; he raised himself a foot. Then he sank back as if struck. Shapiro was already over the top. With one thin hand clutching above an ankle, he uncoiled the body and dragged it back. Nearer, a spasm of hands reached out to help him.

They laid Howard gently into the trench. Shapiro slumped against the back wall. Through his livid and immobile face a victory shone. Bolton and Rufus and Barney looked at him with hate and admiration. Then they knelt beside Howard. The firing became spasmodic; the counter-attack had stalled.

Howard opened his eyes. Volcanic stares poured out. "You stinking . . . stinking . . . stinking . . . cowards. . . ."

"Give him something," Bolton said.

"Don't give me nothing. You stinking . . . stinking . . . cowards." Weak and strong, the words alternated.

He beat the palm of one hand against the trench wall. He locked every draining energy about the last narrow thread of life. His eyes fastened on Rufus. The big, bearded face—so old now—brought back his own and Todda's childhood. Out of nothing the pieces flew together into a new pattern. With the astonishing clarity of the dying, he understood everything. He felt almost no pain, only a creeping numbness.

"Rufus, I allus liked you . . . even when I didn't want to. . . . I'm gonna tell you something. If it'd been you instid of Jesse . . . I wouldn't have . . ."

Rufus was hardly listening; he was too tired and too old to listen now. But he heard without listening.

"Give him something," Bolton said.

"Don't give me nothing. Rufus knows what I mean. Don't you, Rufus? I shot him because he ruined Todda. . . . If you don't believe . . . believe me . . . the rifle's in the well by the graveyard. It was me. Early. Before we left. . . ."

They waited for him to continue, or to close his eyes, or to scream again. But his eyes remained clear, and blinked as if to allow the escape of tiny birds.

"God won't burn me fer shooting a man that ruined my sister. . . . Will he, Rufus . . . ?"

Rufus could say nothing. He could hear the words falling like over-ripe fruit. He knew; he remembered; but he was a stone with a stone's cold tongue.

"Will he, Barney?"

"No."

"I rather He'd burn me fer all the Germans. . . . Will he, Bolt? You ought to know."

Bolton only stared at the mouth that spoke such wild things.

"Will He . . . ?" His eyes strained for Shapiro. "But you don't know. Jews don't b'lieve in God, do they?"

"Give him something," Bolton said.

"Why? I don't hurt. I don't feel nothing. Rufus . . . Todda's got a boy. . . . She named him after me. If she was to need . . . you'd help. . . ."

Rufus let his head nod. Or rather, he let it fall a few inches, which counted for a nod. He was a stone, and he was tired and old.

"Lemme tell you where she is. It's . . ." He tried to reach his pocket and could not. Barney drew out the empty envelope and handed it to Rufus, who took it without looking.

Howard struggled to move; water-beads stood on his forehead like bright nail-heads. "Who come . . . after me . . . ?" He closed his eyes. The tiny birds beat against his eyelids. The faint life-flame dimmed, and a minute later struggled to the surface again. The lips trembled. "A Jew . . . a Jew. . . ." He continued to repeat the words for a long time.

Shapiro moved down the trench and turned his back on the men, who would not look at each other. Finally, the Captain came and knelt at Howard's feet. "My God!" he whispered. "Is it over? He was brave. He was the bravest boy I ever had."

The Captain got up and went for the stretcher-bearers. They came at dark.

Though the night was not terribly cold, Rufus and Barney slept close together. Each could feel the other's body, could smell the male odours. The closeness was a great comfort.

Birds flew against the eyelids of Rufus; he would not let them out. So the heart of the trouble was Todda. Had she lied for his sake? To save him? Howard was dead and Jesse, and Todda had a boy. And the war was not over and the night was cold and Barney was warm. And how would you summarize it for Anna?

Anna, it was Howard. Early. Before we left on the train, and that's why he never come to see me off. You know I always got along all right with Jesse.

Howard Hurley? What did he have against Jesse, Rufus?

Jesse got Todda . . .

That couldn't be. Jesse never touched a woman that way in his life.

Far away was the weary sound of artillery, smothered by distance and the night. Death creeping nearer, and what could one do? It will happen to me, Rufus thought. I will be next. Jesse paid for me for a while, but not for always. Or did he really pay for himself?

Men coughed up and down the trench, and when the stillness and quietness came again, death walked by and Rufus moved closer to Barney. What a pity it was to say strange words in death, almost the greatest pity of all. One should say things that would sound like old Noah on the steps of his house, carving a piece of cedar in the last rays of the sun. What will I say? Rufus thought. I will lie still and ashen. Never again will the sweet-bitter juice burn faintly on my tongue, never again will my face touch the face of Anna, never again will my hands hold my son. Which son? In a flood of self-pity he understood that death, to-morrow or one day next week, was meant for him, for Barney, for all men. With brisk, autumnal vision he understood and was terrified.

"Barney?"

"Yeah."

"Reckon we gonna git through it?"

"I swear I don't know, Rufe. We the on'lest ones left from home. Somebody ought to git back." He did not mind the closeness of Rufus.

Rufus grunted. The autumnal vision faded into a bleak winteriness. Home, and rain over the Hollow. Rex crawling across his knees and pulling at his chin. And Sidney. And Anna.

Howard Hurley? What was his reason, Rufus?

I don't know. Men don't have reasons when it comes to such things.

What things?

"Barney, what we gonna do about what Howard told us?"

"Does folks have to find out?"

"Aye god, I don't know."

"He paid, and if he didn't, they shore God ain't nothing the law can do now."

"They shore God ain't."

Bright October night, smothered artillery and white-cross sleep for Sergeant Howard Hurley. White-cross sleep for all the world, the murderers and liars, the rich and the poor, the strong and the weak, the faithful and the unfaithful: to-morrow or one day next week.

PART THREE: 1918. THE PIGEONS

I

THE golden crusade had come to an end. But the crying and howling, the insane bells, the laughing and praying, belonged to the un-uniformed mobs who had never stared into the face that belched everlasting nothingness. It did not belong to Company G. They withdrew to their old dairy-barn bivouac, scrubbed their bodies until they bled; shaved; and could not help but feel it would soon begin again.

Some sought the crosses of fallen comrades; some drank until their eyes burned; some searched the villages and countryside, swearing at the rain and cold and dearth of girls; some found warm billets with generous peasant families. Sleep and rest which had once appeared as divine blessings were now avoided and scorned. They must move and eat and drink and swear (and love, if possible): the end of the golden crusade did not heal their snarling, bitter nerves.

"Ain't this a wonderful world?"

"Yes, friend. We've made a wonderful damned world."

> "I'm gonna git married,
>   Git a kid . . . or two;
>   I'll send them back,
>   If this don't do."

Snow fell in swirling heaps. They were loaded into lorries. They dug graves all day, laughing and swearing, joshing the teetotaller from Tennessee:

> "I'll work and fight
>   From dawn till night;
>   I'll shun no job that's risky.
>   Write on my stone
>   When I am gone:
>   'These lips have never touched whisky.'"

"Drink all you can, gentlemen," Bolton said. 'The pleasure of the grape will have vanished, the art of distillation will be extinct when we return. America has made the world safe for democracy and now wishes to make it safe for women and children."

The heavens opened and the rain came down in torrents. It blew through the shutters and seeped through the roof. The men wore their knees raw around dice games, but the tedious boredom hung like cheap perfume. Packages came for Christmas. More graves were dug. Beards grew long again.

Rufus stood erect and neat, rain-sprinkled, freshly shaven, bleeding at the chin and neck. He looked down at the Major.

"Corporal William Rufus Frost?"

"Yessir."

"Captain Holleman tells me you're from the home town of Sergeant Howard Hurley."

"Yessir."

"What do you do there, Corporal?"

"Farm, sir."

"You know Sergeant Hurley's people?"

"Yessir."

"Are they friends of yours?"

"Why, yessir. I reckon they are."

"At least"—the Major smiled—"you hope they are."

"Yessir."

"Sergeant Hurley has been posthumously awarded the Legion of Merit. We want you to personally deliver the award." He pushed a small package toward Rufus. "Extend our heartfelt sympathy, and tell them what a fine job their son did. This is small remuneration for such courage and devotion—for the supreme sacrifice; yet it's a splendid thing for his parents. The Legion of Merit is rare, Corporal. You know that?"

"Yessir."

"It's as rare as honest-to-God bravery. That's the way we look at it. I don't think we're wrong. Do you?"

"Nossir."

"Captain Holleman will write a letter ahead of you. This will be your last official assignment for the United States Army. You don't object to it, do you?"

"Nossir."

"In case you do, I want to point out that this small duty enables us to send you home two or three months ahead of the others— maybe six months ahead. I don't know. Does that shed a different light on the matter?"

"Yessir."

"We considered Corporal Stovall for this, but you're a married man. You want to get home. Any children, Corporal?"

"Yessir."

"How many?"

"One."

"Good. You see, the Army isn't always wrong. Sometimes we pick the right man for the job. In fact, Corporal, there's a fashion of logic behind the most obscure detail in the Army; unfortunately, there isn't always justice. If there were, Sergeant Hurley would be here to receive his own reward, and his appointment with Destiny would have been filled by—vulgarly speaking—a man with less guts. Do you agree?"

"I don't know, sir."

"Do you disagree?"

"I don't know. I'm not a good judge of bravery."

"But who is?"

"Whoever give him the medal, I reckon . . . sir."

The Major was neither dull nor slow. He felt the trap and wished to break it quickly. "But the point is: who can see behind the bravery? Isn't that the point?"

"Yessir."

"Of course. We see these things. We reward them. But who can know what fountain of strength feeds a man and gives the will, the courage to . . . to actually die?" Ah, now he had rescued his point from confusion and contradiction. It was time to quit. He stood and placed the package in Rufus's hand. "That child of yours, Corporal. Is it a boy?"

"Yessir."

"Good. I hope he'll never face what you've faced. The sergeant has your orders; you'll sail from Cherbourg as soon as possible. You've been a fine soldier. Good luck."

"Thank you, sir." He saluted and turned.

"Oh, Corporal?"

"Yessir."

"Of course, you'll wear your uniform when you deliver the medal. It . . . well, it adds dignity to the occasion."

"Yessir."

Three days he had, and he spent them at the barracks, because he knew that he would be lost without Barney and Bolton and the others; without the mad, unwholesome life that had charged so deeply into their blood. Goodbye, you bastards. Bring your wife and all your children. We'll make a pallet. Goodbye, you gutted land; bring your trees and flowers and come to see us: we'll make a fire and a bouquet. Bring all the things I'm leaving: curses and fear and sleepless nights, sweet-bitter tobacco juice, and noise and wonder and strange peace. Oh, damn you, and come to see us, and bring it back to me.

He left alone, and it was hard, sad going.

In the middle of the Atlantic the male faces, the contour of the embattled ground began to fade. He looked ahead to Anna and Rex and Sidney and Ursa. Their faces rose from the mist into solid reality. And there was Todda too. He stood long hours at the rail and spat and wondered how the tangled threads would unravel.

In New York the sergeant, wearing khakis creased to knife-edge sharpness, asked, "You want to go out early in the morning or catch another movement four days from now?"

"In the morning."

"Okay. Here's one T.R. to Memphis, and another from there to Kangaroo Hollow." He wanted to ask if there were any Kangaroos in Kangaroo Hollow, but thought better of it, for the man looked fractious and impatient.

"Do I have to go by Memphis?"

"You don't *have* to go nowhere."

"I mean, couldn't you route me another way?"

"What do you want us to do, Corporal? Build a railroad to your back doorstep?"

"Skip it."

"Jesus, you guys what think you're Mr. Vanderbilt because you got a taste of French wine and heard a howitzer."

"I said skip it, didn't I?"

He got a cheap room in a cheap hotel. Up and down the dim, worn hall was the crude noise of soldiers and sailors and the giggling of painted women. If Barney or Bolton was there, they could get a woman or two; but to get one alone would be too much of a sin against Anna. After an hour, he took his duffle-bag and left.

The lights were coming on along the broad avenues. It was bitter cold. He stopped before the huge glass windows to look at suits and hats. He pushed on, into the aimless, thickening crowd. Where could they all be going? The war was over. On a street corner he stopped and waited like a sentry. In the grinning, garrulous tide, no face like Barney's, no voice like Bolton's. Oh, damn you, come to see us and bring all your children. Me and Anna will sleep on the pallet and give you the bed. But it won't be any need to. Three bedrooms downstairs and two upstairs, and they all belong to her. But my wife likes company. She likes what I like, or used to.

He bought a pint of red whisky. How it burned and warmed. Barney would have had no trouble finding it. Have a drink, Barney, you old bastard. I bet you never come back to the Hollow to stay.

He went to the station. It was better there, for the faces hurried by with intense direction. The close, foul air was like a barracks. Stealthily he slipped the last third of his red whisky into a porter's hand and cautioned him, "If I go to sleep, you wake me up at four o'clock." He went to sleep and got a crick in his neck from the straight, pew-like bench. At four-thirty he awoke, hungry and cursing. The train left at five.

He climbed into the troop car filled with snoring men and crowded with trench-coats and khakis hanging from the rows of three-decker canvas bunks. He learned that he could have boarded at midnight. Old, stupid Rufus, he thought. Aye god, I'm gonna have to git smart or the world's gonna leave me hatching on my hind end. It seemed to him that the men saw through their sleep and laughed at him for being a hick. Let them laugh. He'd bet, aye god, he was going back to more than any one of them: the heart of the Hollow was good black land.

The hillsides of Tennessee were motionless with blue cold. Even the smoke above the unpainted and weather-beaten houses hung still as the grey rock chimneys. He thought of his father: If you asked him where I've been, he'd say, "Across the waters," not knowing whether it was England or France or Germany, not really knowing where the war was fought. But that was all right, because he was old, and war was for the young. Sometime, maybe before the crops got started, he would take Sidney and go back for a few days; Bee would be home by then. Her husband had escaped the war and had gone to the shipyards in Norfolk. And she had gone with him, she wrote. If Bee was all right, he didn't worry about the others. But he had never known, never considered before how barren, how cold and lifeless that country was. He would be there yet, except for Todda. No; except for Howard. It was odd. Ah, maybe it was the train window, for nothing was the same through a train window. The trip was a long one.

Late afternoon of the second day, the train jolted to a halt and backed into the Memphis station. In the midst of a throng of crying mothers, aunts, sisters, and quiet-eyed fathers welcoming returned warriors, he stood alone and thought: Where to now? He told himself that he must make a decision. But that was not true; the decision was already made, and he stalled because he knew it.

In the men's room, he shaved and changed his shirt. The mirror proved the war had left no scars: the same big eyes, strong teeth, straight nose, broad chin. A little leaner, that was all. Just a little leaner and wiser.

The address was clear in his mind. He checked his baggage and hired a Negro hack.

"You know where it is?"

"Yessuh, I sho . . ." He stopped. There was no need to tell this fine gentleman it was not far from where he lived.

The hack rolled past the Wentworth Machinery Company, past grey, corner grocery stores covered with signs of cure-alls and grand elixirs, and into a narrow, muddy lane. A fine, cold mist was falling. It was late January. As he climbed from the hack, he heard the healthy wail of a child.

"You wants me to wait, suh?"

"No; you n'en to wait."

It was a long, shoe-box house with a narrow porch. A tall Negro woman, wearing glasses, peered through a slight crack in the door. Before he could ask anything, she announced, "I'm Lizzie. Miss Todda ain't heah."

"Where is she?"

"She works."

"Could I come in?"

"Is you related to the lady?"

"Well . . . I'm . . . Yes. . . ."

The door opened. He entered a small room, surprisingly neat and warm. A coal fire glowed, casting soft light on the bed and two cane-bottomed chairs draped with drying diapers. To the left of the hearth was a cradle-crib. The child had stopped crying and was lying on its belly staring up at the intruder.

"You Miss Todda's brother . . . ?"

"No. I'm somebody else."

"You not? She allus talking 'bout her brother in the Army. I thought you was her brother."

He went to the crib, picked up the child, and awkwardly pressed him to his face. For a minute the child was pleased; then he puckered his face to cry and reached for the Negro woman. She took him. "He jist sleepy. He frets when he sleepy." She shook him gently and his face relaxed into a smile.

She removed the diapers from the chairs so that Rufus could sit down. "I thought you was her brother. She's been looking fer him."

He said bluntly, "Her brother is dead."

"Aw. . . ." Sudden, familiar grief registered through her thin face. "Ain't the war ovah?"

"He was killed before it was over. Didn't she know it?"

"Nossuh. The Gov'mint nevah told her."

"What time will she be here?"

" 'Bout dark, most usually." As if her answer was a reminder, she put the child back into the crib and lit the small coal-oil lamp on the mantel. Rufus went to the crib, knelt, and poked one finger between the bars, teasing the child. Occasionally the child seized his finger with a firm grasp. The light grew brighter in the room. He remained kneeling, feeling the curious, relentless eyes of the Negro woman. He was studiously comparing the tiny face with his own.

The door opened and Todda burst across the threshold. She did not see Rufus. Quickly she shook a torn black umbrella and stood it outside the door. She took off an old coat—one Rufus had seen many times—revealing the blue uniform of a waitress.

"Lizzie," she cried, "I got my feet soaked. Look!"

"Miss Todda . . ." Lizzie cautioned with a nod toward the crib.

Rufus stood, holding one hand on a crib post. Lizzie disappeared toward the back of the house.

Stunned, almost frightened, Todda finally said, "Lord how mercy! When did you blow in? Is Howard with you?"

"No. . . ."

Her face clouded. "He wouldn't write if he knowed when the

world was coming to an end. I thought you-all was in France."
She came toward the fire, leaving wet tracks on the plain floor.
"It started to pour when I was halfway home. I got good and
soaked." Placing one hand on the mantel, she held one foot, then
the other near the glowing coals. She turned her face to Rufus; but
her bright, intense eyes were fastened on her child. Slowly, shadows
of fear clouded her face. "How did you know where to find me?"

"Howard give me your address."

"Where is he?"

"Todda, don't you ever hear from home?"

No fear had yet shown on her face. "I don't want to hear from
home. They don't know where I am, unless Howard told them, or
you." Her voice was accusing. Then it rose in a wave of fear.
"Where is Howard? Is he in trouble?"

"What kind of trouble, Todda?"

"Oh, you know what he done! How could folks be so blind?"

"Maybe they thought it was you."

"Me? Who . . . who thought it? Have they got Howard?"

"No. He was killed . . . and the war was almost over. . . ."

The glow of lamplight and fire exaggerated the slight trembling
in her face. "And that's what you come to tell me," she said softly.

"I didn't come to tell you. I thought you'd already know."

She sat down in a cane-bottomed chair, her hand pressed to her
lips, her eyes dry. Steam rose from her soaked shoes. Rufus stood
behind her chair. Now that she was hurt, she might as well be hurt
all the way and have it finished; yet, he did not say the words to
hurt her. "Todda, why did you tell Howard it was Jesse?"

She continued to stare in a dull, fixed manner. Her head moved
slightly, gnawing at her finger. The child began to cry, but she
would not look at him. "I didn't tell him. . . ."

The child began to scream. Then turning her head slowly toward
him she said, "Oh, hush!" The tears gushed down her face. All her
body shook with quiet sobbing. She went to the window, and
keeping her back to Rufus, she asked, "Do I have to cause everything?"

He was sorry for the way he had broken the news. "It's no need
to blame yourself. If . . ."

"Well, who's to blame? Somebody's to blame. Somebody's
always to blame for everything." She seized her child and held him
tight against her, smothering him with hot kisses. Again she turned
her back to Rufus. Her tears dropped on the child's bald head, on
his cheeks and nose. It pleased him. He kicked and laughed. She
was at once smiling and crying. "Look what Mother done to you!"
The spell was broken. She stopped crying, cleared her eyes, and put
the child back into his crib.

"Tell me how it was."

"There's not much to tell you, Todda. It was rifle fire, and it was over right away. He got the Legion of Merit for bravery. Here it is. That's nearly as high as you can git."

She took the package and looked carefully, as if she could see the award through the neat wrapping. Stooping over the crib, she said, "Mother will save this for you."

"You can't. It don't belong to you."

"Why don't it belong to me?"

"It belongs to your father and mother."

"For them? Why? They never loved him. Nobody ever loved him but me." She moved behind the crib, grasping the package. Her eyes blazed; they were rimmed with red. "You won't git it back."

"I have to git it back."

"What did you come here for? To git him too?" She touched the child.

"I come to help."

"How?"

"I'll send you whatever you need."

"I don't want your help. I want him to be all mine."

"Be reasonable, Todda."

"Yes . . . be reasonable . . . and take Anna Shannon's money!"

"My money!"

"But where does *your* money come from?"

He made a wild gesture toward everything in the room. "Where did all this come from?"

"I'll tell you! It come from Lizzie. She owns it. The house and all. We cooked together in a restaurant. She took me in. She lives in the back and I live in the front. That's where it comes from! All but the crib. I bought the crib."

A vacant, defeated stare filled his eyes. "What do you want me to do, Todda?"

"Nothing. I don't aim to hang on to you. I never did before he was born, and I don't aim to now. You don't owe me nothing, except to let me have him all by myself."

"That don't leave much fer me to say."

She looked closely at the big face for the first time; it had grown older, like her own. A wave of pity filled her. She looked down at her child. "Hold him, if you want to."

"I helt him once and made him squall."

They looked at each other. The old, old fire flickered in their eyes. "I'm ready to go. Give me the medal."

She moved forward and placed it in his outstretched hand. "You can see him whenever you want to. Is that fair?"

"Yes. . . . That's fair."

He put on his trench-coat and went out.

For a minute she looked after him. Then she dropped into a chair and continued to gaze into the glowing coals.

Lizzie came quietly into the room. "Is he the one?" she asked with secret breath.

"Yes; he's the one," Todda answered.

2

OUTSIDE his room, the switching freight cars joined in violent smashes. The rain poured down. The room was cold as a barracks. When he got up to spread the trench coat over his feet he saw the trainmen, in black slickers, swinging their lanterns in crazy arcs. That was all they had to think about: coupling and uncoupling the cars. Maybe they thought about the rain, too. While he had a hundred decisions, standing in line like hungry soldiers with empty mess-kits.

Todda had been right. Whose money, Rufus? Send me whose money? Aye god, a man was clever who could tie his own feet and own hands. Cleverer still, if he could undo them by himself. I don't know what I'm gonna do, he told himself, but I'm gonna find a way to stand on my own feet. But he did know what he was going to do. He was going to Tom Phelps and remind him of all they had said that night in Norfolk. If it blew up like a bubble, then he would think of something else.

The clashing of box-cars went on, the rain poured, and the ghost questions walked through the windows.

Howard did it. Why, Rufus? What could he have had against Jesse?

I don't know, Anna.

He touched the brass head-rails of the bed. They were like green icicles. The trench-coat was heavy on his feet. A few moments of ease passed over him like warm air. This would be the last night he would sleep alone.

What did you say, Barney?

I said I don't see no need to go telling everybody Howard done it. If it leaks out, let it leak.

I didn't mean to tell everybody, Barney. But Anna's there beside me, and me knowing. What do I do? (And there's something you don't know, too.)

He got up long before daylight and went to the station. He ate breakfast, read a newspaper, and finally went to the men's room and shaved. His eyes were bloodshot from cold and lack of sleep. It had been a miserable night, but at least he had made one decision: he would deliver Howard's medal first thing and have that off his hands.

As the train moved along through the early-morning haze his

spirits lifted. The old anxieties, the old ghost questions flew away; if they returned like homing pigeons, he would deal with them when the time came.

A man in clean, faded overalls and a leather jacket boarded at one of the country stations. He took a seat near the front of the car, and later, spying the khaki uniform, came to sit beside Rufus. His face still held the deep brown of last year's sun, his hands were chapped and rough, his shoes smelled of tallow. He asked about the war in vague, innocent terms, and marked Rufus for a hero. Rufus was sorry when he got off the train. "Jist going to spend the day with my daughter," he said. And he made it sound like a great adventure.

Rufus's heart was lifted. That's my kind of people, he thought. Anna would like him. Bring your wife and come to see us. When he looked from the train window down into the Hollow, his heart was bubbling over.

He was glad no one knew he was coming, because he wanted to walk from the station down by Ephriam Hurley's place and every step of the way home. He left his baggage in the station, and, holding the Legion of Merit securely in one hand, started down the hill. Every step was sheer joy; he wanted to run. Not since he was the age of Sidney had he felt that way.

Rachel Hurley, who was a constant watcher of roads, saw him when he turned into the yard. She threw her black gum snuff-stick into the fire and wiped hurriedly at her mouth. She ran to the door, and pulling it wide open, said, "You come in out of that cold, boy."

"Who is it?" Ephriam called from his bed, which had been pushed close to the hearth for warmth.

Rufus filled the narrow doorway. The bright wood fire, the iron bedstead, the churn on the hearth, and Rachel Hurley smiling at him reminded him of his childhood.

"Now I don't see no harm in you jist hugging me," she said.

Rufus put his arms affectionately about the thin, tall body. He turned to Ephriam, waiting impatiently, and shook hands. It was a warmer welcome than Howard would have received (not because they had found the rifle missing, and knew; but because such people were like that with those not of their own blood). "I didn't expect to find you in bed, Mister Eph."

"Hit's my back," Ephriam said, and with a grimace propped himself higher against the head-rails.

"Why, he ain't hit a lick at a snake in nigh on to three weeks," Rachel said. "Tell him what happened to you, Eph."

"Hit was me. I done it myself. Them back steps was nearly rotted down and I knowed somebody was aiming to ketch a fall. I comes in from slopping the hog one night and thinks I'll jist tear it down, and did. And I puts the slop-bucket rat there so's to remind Rachel them steps is gone. After supper I goes out to . . . to . . .''

"His reg'lar night call, Rufus," Rachel helped.

"I walked square-dab over that blasted slop-bucket!"

"And hit landed rat under him on the ground," she said. They were all laughing. Their laughter died away, leaving only the crackling sound of the fire.

"We got a letter saying you was coming by. But we knowed you'd come by anyways," Rachel said. "I'm proud you got back all right. It was so many that didn't. But you have to learn to give your folks up. It's fer the best. . . ." She looked at the old man.

Rufus wondered how much they knew.

"I like to think the Lord does ever'thing fer the best," she added. Then, as if to stop something Rufus might have said about Howard, she said, "You know, Todda run off and left us. I reckon she couldn't stand hit here without Howard." Her voice did not accuse. It was monotonous; an apathetic statement of facts. "Ain't you gonna set down?"

"I ought to go on. I've not been home yet." He held out the small package; she took it cautiously. "Here's Howard's medal. The Legion of Merit is a mighty high honour, Miss Rachel."

She opened the tiny brown carton, then handed it to Ephriam. "Ain't it pretty?"

Ephriam nodded. "Tell him what we thought about."

She took the medal and looked at it again. "You was with Howard. You saw hit all. We want you to have this."

He backed away as if she held out a serpent to him. "No'am. I couldn't do that atall, Miss Rachel. Captain Holleman said Howard was the bravest soldier he ever seen."

"We wisht you'd take hit," she said.

"No'am. It wouldn't be right. It's fer you and Mister Eph. I'd better go, I reckon. You know I ain't been home. I'll come back to see you. Is it anything you need?"

"I reckon not," Rachel said, withdrawing her outstretched hand. "Miss Anna sent us the biggest cord of wood you ever seen, and paid Eph jist like he was working. If we need you, we'll shore holler."

"Yes'am, you do that."

"I'm gittin' lots better," Ephriam said. "Your wife's been awful good to us. You married yourself a fine woman, Rufus."

"I reckon I did, Mister Eph." Rufus went toward the door. "Now if you-all need me, you holler."

Rachel, ready to latch the door behind him, called, "I hope them Army clothes is good and heavy. Hit's cold out there!"

He made long, hungry steps. Never had the Hollow seemed so much like home: the churn; the old iron bedstead; the hard, unvanquished faces; the offer of a dead son's medal. He would take care of them; he would never let them leave the Hollow. He drank in the cold, damp air and hurried on. My people, he thought again; they are my kind of people. Nothing can destroy us.

The sun shone through patches of clouds; the wind pinched uncovered flesh. The deepest dead of winter spread in every direction. But it might as well have been filled with peach blossoms and wild dogwood blooms and long rows of knee-high cotton. A few nights and a few days and winter would be gone with the war.

Ursa was the first to see him, and with a scream that seemed to carry from one side of the Hollow to another she flew at him like a grotesque angel. He was almost annoyed when she threw her arms around him and cried, "Lawd, Lawd, Mista Rufe!" Belatedly he returned her embrace. She had only recently taken Rufus into her heart; it was necessary to take someone to fill the void Jesse had left. Rufus was the most logical one, and the fact that he was away had heightened the endearment.

In the living-room she put up a warning hand. "Miss Anna is gone to the mills. Her and Mista Sid. Now you wait till I put a clean suit on yo' baby. You ain't gonna know the chile. Oh, he the finest baby! I have him down heah 'fore you git yo' feet warm." Panting, totally disorganized, she ran into the hall and up the stairs.

Rufus stood on the hearth and warmed his feet, though he felt no cold. His eyes searched every detail of the room, as if he had never entered it before. It was bright and cosy; the fire crackled faintly, like far-off music. Aye god, but Anna could fix a room. He turned to the huge mirror over the mantel and studied his face. His eyes had cleared; the wind and the walking had brought thick red patches to his cheeks. A brief grin wrinkled his face: he was lord and master.

Ursa's hurried steps sounded on the stairs. She burst through the hall doorway and stood Rex at her feet. He was dressed in neat white shoes, red socks, and blue rompers. Bewildered by the sudden commotion, he turned his brown eyes to Ursa and clung to her skirt. "There, honey! Lookey there!" She pulled his fingers away from her skirt and pointed to Rufus.

In a burst of energy, Rex ran toward the front door. Rufus ran after him and scooped him up. Being an agreeable child, he remained totally still and stared at his captor.

"Ain't he fine? Ain't he fine?" Ursa cried.

Rufus went to the centre of the room, knelt, and stood Rex before him. They continued to survey each other. Rex sat down, relaxed as a drunken man, and grasped a ball of mud from Rufus's shoe. He inspected it and held it up for Ursa to see.

"Ain't he fine?" Ursa cried.

"Want some more?" Rufus asked. He raked his forefinger around the edge of his soles, rolled the contents into a marble and put it into Rex's hand. The child looked up and laughed.

"That enough? If that ain't enough, we'll git some more."

"It ain't enough," Ursa said. "He won't nevah git enough of nothing, Mista Rufe. He won't."

Rufus looked up as if he heard a mysterious prophecy. "How come?"

"I can jist tell. Ain't he fine?"

Rufus ran his fingers through the shock of golden hair. Rex continued to inspect his mud.

"An' he takes his favour from you. 'Scusing them eyes, he ain't nothing but a little you."

"Come here!" Rufus said. He grabbed the child and held him near the mantel mirror. With possessive affection, he blinded the face with kisses. Then he let the child slip to the floor and toddle wildly about the room.

They heard the sound of a buggy. Through the window they saw the mare dashing frantically up the driveway. The buggy stopped; Anna leaped from one side, Sidney from the other. Anna cried, "That's not fair, you little rascal! You can outrun me!" He was through the door, and with a violent jump he landed astraddle of Rufus. "I beat her!" he panted, and reluctantly slipped aside for Anna. With his face buried in her hair, Rufus said, "I b'lieve you-all are glad to see me!"

Sidney, still fired with emotion, seized Rex and showered him with kisses. Ursa, who had no one to kiss, remained near the hall door and cried quietly. Goings and comings were the holidays of her life.

"We come by Mister Eph's, and he told us," Sidney explained, hoping for more attention in the midst of the heart-flaring spectacle.

At last Ursa went back to her kitchen, Peter Cat and Jim came in for their greetings, and the house assumed an air of order and peacefulness. In the afternoon, Rufus and Sidney pottered about the barn, took a long trek through the muddy fields, while Sidney pictured a virtual famine in last year's crops compared to the ones Rufus had raised. Late in the afternoon they drove to the sawmills. The old misgivings did not strike Rufus until that night, after an enormous homecoming supper, when he and Anna were alone in their room upstairs surrounded by the peaceful sleep of Rex. Then it settled upon him: no foot of land, no board of timber, not even the squeak of a rocker was his. They moved around in the light of the dying fire and in the soft glow of an Aladdin lamp, unable to stay so far apart as across the room.

They stood at the edge of the hearth. They needed to talk, to laugh, to look; they sensed the need not to touch too quickly. It was important that the night should stand in their memory like a pyramid. All day they had built the foundation, slowly, sometimes awkwardly, waiting for darkness, and nearness, and the silent golden pinnacle. How strange it was that this night was more awkward than the first night they had lived together as man and wife. He was uneasy, not because there were things he dared not tell her, but because his mind was filled with things that should not matter: a broken poplar, a dented helmet, sullied snow, and water pouring into a trench. She was not far away—it was not the distance—but he was afraid, just as he had been afraid to move when Howard lay writhing a few yards beyond them.

They did not talk of Jesse. They talked of Nile and Chet and Howard's medal. They talked of the mills and the Kangaroo and of Max Muller, who had left the Hollow, and of many things that did not matter. It was a foundation, but it was not enough.

The time had come to measure himself, to weigh himself. And she stood like something he had no right to touch: soft, sun-golden, complete.

"Have you done all right with the sawmills?" And why should he ask that of all things? But it was a part of the measuring, the weighing.

"Real well," she said, and she, too, was afraid, for now she understood that he had not only to bear the old wound of having nothing but the weight of a war as well. It might be better if she could say, "Not well at all. I have buried the talents."

He remained silent, resting his hands and face against the mantel. If I could only be ploughing, he thought; or stacking lumber, or pulling corn, with the sweet-bitter juice on my tongue.

Fear gripped at her heart with brutal fingers. Why must the war keep its men, even when they returned? "What are you trying to tell me?"

"Oh, I don't know." And his hands fell away from the mantel as if he had lost his grip.

"Is it something you went through over there?"

"No."

"I know I could understand if you'd help me."

"People who've got things don't understand people who've got nothing, no matter how much they love."

"No, Rufus, that's wrong."

He drew a sharp, furious breath. His hands curled into tight knots. "Well, do you understand I've got to have something of my own? Something I can give to you? To Rex? To Sid? To anybody I want to give to? I've got to have it, Anna. I've got to, no matter what it takes to git it. Just so I git it myself. Will you stand by me . . . whatever it is?"

"Yes . . . whatever it is . . . so long as you don't hurt people."

"But if I was to hurt somebody . . . somehow?"

"I don't know. I might not stand by you . . . but I'd love you. . . . I'll always love you."

The single thread of doubt, of reservation, worked far more magic than a total promise; it fed his senses with something stronger than wine. The night would have its golden pinnacle.

3

RUFUS chose late afternoon to visit Tom Phelps. He put the best saddle on the best mare (Tom Phelps was a lover of good horses) and paced up the muddy road to the brown house wedged in a cove of giant cedars.

The house was a twin-gabled log building with a narrow porch all the way across the front and a wide hall that separated the vast high-ceilinged rooms. The twin hall doors and tall windows on either side were filled with stained glass. The house, in years gone by, had been a splendid tavern, a renowned stage-coach stop for passengers travelling to and from Memphis. In those days, it was known as the Kangaroo (from which the Hollow had got its name), and many trees along the east-west route bore signs: STOP AT THE KANGAROO, ONE GOOD HOP FROM MEMPHIS. As the mode of transportation changed, the tavern changed from owner to owner, along with a three-hundred-acre tract of land. At last the title came to rest in the hands of Dixon Phelps, horse and mule trader, who owned a farm over the ridge from the Kangaroo. His wife, Pamela, known as the most-educated woman in Woodall County, fell in love with the tavern and moved there with her husband and only son, Tom. It was she who covered the logs with boards from virgin pine timber and crowned each gable with lightning rods that rose like thin silver augers.

When Tom Phelps came to the throne, he carried on the horse and mule trading and left most of the farm affairs to the mismanagement of his sons. Each morning he was driven in his automobile to his stables by Johnny and each afternoon he was driven home (or as near home as the roads would allow), always with the latest Memphis paper tucked securely under one arm. A few minutes before supper-time, he would seat himself in the "front room" (that is, the room which was used to entertain company) beside the library table and read the paper thoroughly while his wife's voice would roll across the wide hall, "Now, Tom, you come on here to supper!" The meal would go on without him, and near the end of it, the paper finished, he would take his place at the head of the table. The meal finished, he would go back to his paper as if he had not looked at it; and, occasionally rubbing his pearly teeth with a black gum stick and a touch of snuff, he would design political plans for weeks and months ahead.

On Sunday mornings, he rose at his usual early hour, casually inspected the fields and barns, and returned to the home to prepare for Sunday School: he was the presiding officer. Ministers flocked to his house, to his huge table overloaded with food, where they were generously given the chairs while the children crowded closer together on the bench that had supported so many tavern guests in the old days.

He would not lie about a horse; he would give one away before he would lie. But the corrupt designs of his politics fed his mind as air fed his lungs. He forgot nothing: no stutter, no blink of the eye, no promise. Clear in his mind was the night in Norfolk and the fire he had kindled in Rufus Frost. But men must come to him, so that later the blame would rest on their shoulders as well as his own. There was no cleverness in pushing an honest man into corruption; the sport came through subtle leading. He was anxiously waiting for the arrival of Rufus. He knew he would come.

He had not lit his lamp on the library table in the front room, partly because of the roaring log fire and partly because he was not yet ready to delve into his newspaper.

Rufus dropped the mare's reins into a horseshoe nailed to one of the cedars and strode forward with high hopes. At the first knock, Tom Phelps was on his feet and answering. Smiling and flashing his shining teeth, he ushered Rufus into the front room. He was a cordial host to all guests: ministers and itinerant peddlers alike. "The boys told me you came in yesterday. You're all right, I reckon?"

"I'm fine, Mister Tom. Nile here?"

"No, The boy's run off somewhere in the car." He drawled a long laugh and stretched his feet toward the hearth. "By gad, but my boys like to ride. They'd ride a sapling if they didn't have anything else. Always riding and nowhere to go. Your folks well?" No man could be more considerate of illness than Tom Phelps. He did more than ask; he visited the sick, often carrying tall cans of tomato juice, for that was his favourite non-alcoholic beverage.

"Yessir; my folks are all well."

"I'm just getting over a cold. I got stove up at Christmas and, by gad, I thought I'd never shake it loose. Worrisome."

The talk ran in that vein for a while, until Rufus said, "Mister Tom, I might as well git down to my business here. I want to run for sheriff."

The seed had sprouted. "You didn't forget what I said to you, did you?"

"Nossir. I thought about it a lot. I want you to tell me if I've got a chance."

"Wait a minute, son. Wait a minute. You tell me whether it's gonna rain to-morrow and I'll tell you whether you'll be sheriff."

"I didn't ask you if I was gonna win, Mister Tom."

He studied a minute, jerked his eyes from the flames to Rufus's face. "No, by gad, you didn't! You didn't even ask if you had a *good* chance. Most folks ask: Will I win? I had my mind set that's what you'd ask. Yessir; I can answer you. You've got a chance. More than that, you've got a good chance. Here's why: first, you're big as a bull; a gun on your hip wouldn't look like it was overloading you. Second, you've got a good face; that gets men and women both—and the women help, even if they can't mark you an X. Third, you've got no political scars. Fourth, you've been to war. Fifth, you've not got too much education. Now son, I wouldn't offend you for my right arm. But if you'd been to the University, it would cost you votes in this county. I reckon they figure a University man would throw them in jail if they spit on the courthouse steps. And, by gad, the people in this county are going to spit where they want to, come hell or high water. What's the next question?" (Whatever it might be, he had already figured out an answer.)

"I don't know. You talk, and I'll listen."

"To my knowledge, no man has ever been Sheriff of Woodall County without spending a nice little bit of money. First of all, you've got expenses for cards and posters and general advertising. Second, there are fourteen political picnics—one for each precinct— which means you'll have to buy half the kids in Woodall County fourteen ice-cream cones and fourteen cold drinks—that's the minimum. Next will come poll taxes; they'll say, 'I'm fer you, but I ain't paid my poll tax.' Which leaves you to say, 'I'll take care of that.' It's the custom. You can't buck custom. Let me see. Then comes the borrowing stage. Five and ten dollars at a whack. That's an old custom, too. A man who won't befriend before he's elected certainly wouldn't after he was safe in office. You remember this: people in this county vote for you because you buy 'em, in one way or another; or they vote for you because they think you'll help 'em out in a tight. That's the beginning. It gets deeper and deeper. There's not much choice of what to do. The office is too good; too many people are after it. A sheriff gets two to five per cent. of every tax dollar collected. If he knew he could win, he could afford to spend. Had you thought about the money?"

"No."

"Oh, you might win without doing all these things. But, again, you might wake up in the morning with a pair of wings. One is about as likely as the other. Too many folks with patched overalls . . . too many hungry faces."

"Did you spend your own money?"

"No. My first rule is never spend your own money in a political race. There are enough fools in the world without adding another."

"What did you do?"

"By gad, I like the way you get down to business!" His sharp eyes twinkled. "You may not be sheriff, but you're going to run the britches off of somebody." He got up and stood at the end of the mantel, glancing at the six pictures of his children scattered along the shelf, three boys and three girls. "I'll tell you what I've always done in my races, one for circuit clerk and two for sheriff. Folks love to gamble—always have, always will. They put up the money: free if I lose; I repay double if I win. We'll get the money. I'll see that you get the money, and I'll tell you where I always placed it, the key spots. My men will get in it for you. I'll tell you all I know and do all I can." His hand came to rest on Dora's picture. She was his favourite child. "Anything else you want to ask?"

"The fact that I wasn't born in this county. . . ."

"Oh, we'll fix that. You can say, 'Folks, I didn't have the good fortune to be born in Woodall County, but I did have the good sense to move here.' They'll take that. Anything else we ought to go into at this stage?"

"I don't know enough right now to ask much." Rufus got up.

"One thing I ought to tell you. An old politician, with the scars I've got, is like a millstone around the neck of a newcomer. Don't ever talk to me in crowds; don't even speak to me. And when you come here, come after dark. Politics is like cotton; it grows best at night. You already know folks will tell you things in the dark they'd never dare to mention in broad, open sunlight." They laughed, both conscious of the unlit lamp.

Rufus started to go and hesitated. "Shouldn't we come to some understanding as to what I'm gonna owe you?"

Anger pinched the old man's cheeks like a vice, but the innocent, straightforward look of Rufus replaced the anger with a delicious burning. What a curious pleasure it was to watch that face absorb the devious designs. The old man smiled. "Son, you're so new in this game you hurt my heart. I've bought a thousand good men, but you couldn't buy me with a kingdom. I'm for you because I want to be for you."

"I didn't mean to be trying to buy you. I couldn't buy you if I already had you, could I?"

"That's right, by gad. You've cleared yourself." He was immensely pleased. Twice to-night this young turk—his protégé—had clipped the master's wings. What a season of pleasure this young disciple would bring to him before the elections were over in August. And, by gad, he had the face and manners to win. He bubbled inside. "Way back in 1900, Rufus"—his first use that night of his disciple's given name—"I dabbled in politics for the first time. I remember that year I kept thinking how wonderful it would be to live until 2000. I tried my utmost to imagine what the world would be like a hundred years later. "I tried . . .""

A strong voice rolled across the hall, "Now, Tom, you come on here to supper!"

"I tried to design in my own mind fantastic devices, far ahead of the aeroplane and radio and automobile. But I was no designer, and, anyway, I wasn't going to live until 2000. Then one day I said to myself: 'It's foolish to worry about the end of the century when I don't know what's happening under my nose right now.' I had been to the University, but I didn't know where a grand jury came from, and right on down the list. Well, I got into things. I don't know what this century will produce, but whatever it is, it can't be more fascinating than politics. Politics is a drug. A dangerous drug. It grabs a man like whisky grabs a drunkard; it clings to your system like a narcotic; it's cancerous. Of course, you can't believe it now, for you stand on reasonably innocent ground. When you get in the middle of the stream, it wouldn't do any good to believe. You can go upstream or downstream, but you never touch holy land again."

Rufus grinned. And Tom Phelps grinned too, believing his warnings would whet his protégé's appetite rather than dull it.

The voice rolled across the hall again, "Now, Tom, you come on here to supper!"

Rufus started out. As the two reached the hall, they were met by Dora, a plump, quiet child of fourteen. She had beautiful white skin and coal-black hair. "Papa, Mama said to please excuse her. She didn't know you had company."

"All right, honey." He put his arm around her. She paused for the brief affection and retraced her steps. As he opened the front door for Rufus, he thought in unworded terms: She sends my favourite child to smooth a breach of manners. Why not one of the others? Is that politics? Is the whole world mad?

"You let me know what happens, Rufus. We'll get this circus rigged and rolling."

"Yessir. I'll let you know everything."

"Fine." He watched the husky shoulders rise above the saddle; with one flick of the reins, the restless animal broke into a snappy pace. After a quick appraisal of the mare, he returned to the front room and looked about for his paper and a match to light the lamp.

As Rufus turned into the road, he bit a huge corner from a fresh plug of tobacco and chewed with high spirits. The quid was just softening and becoming juicy when he reached his own driveway. He kicked the mare into a faster pace and rode by, across the Hollow, and all the way to Burke's store. What could he buy? He must buy something. A couple of work shirts. He wiped his mouth neatly, entered, and made his selections.

"Cash or charge?" Azel Burke said.

"Whatever you want," Rufus answered.

"Well, as the feller says, I always like cash on cold days." His high, nasal laugh dribbled through the store.

Rufus put down two dollars and left. The mare's gentle pace, the creak of the leather beneath him, the smell of new clothes and horse-flesh, the sweet-bitter juice on his tongue, set his senses afire. He rode back slowly; each arc of juice he spat was a keen pleasure, the beginning of a triumph. Aye god, he was on the way some-where.

Sidney was sitting on the lot gate waiting for Rufus, the bill of his cap pulled deep over his forehead. Rufus reined the mare abruptly and drew his imaginary gun from his hip. "All right, you! Don't you move. This is the high sheriff. I've got a warrant fer your arrest. In the name of the law, put 'em up. We know you stole old man Do-funny's horses. Where are they?"

Sidney, a bit puzzled, but ready for the game, raised his hands. "Don't shoot, sheriff. I'll tell you where they are."

"Start talking."

"I sold them."

Rufus dismounted and moved toward the gate, his shirts tucked under one arm, his finger-gun aimed at the heart of the criminal. "Who to?"

"Mister Tom Phelps."

"Where's the money you got?"

"Ain't much left. I spent it. I bought some clothes and shoes for my wife and children. And groceries, a whole passel of groceries. You wouldn't put me in jail for that, would you, sheriff?"

Rufus spat a huge stream. "You mighty right I would. It's my duty to maintain law and order around here."

Sidney lowered one hand slowly.

"Keep that hand up, mister! I don't want to make orphans out of your kids."

"I was just reaching for the money, sheriff. Couldn't you take the money and let me go?"

"Bribe, huh? This high sheriff is honest, mister. You couldn't buy me with a kingdom."

"Look out behind you, sheriff!"

"That's an old trick, mister. You can't get away with. . . ."

"What on earth are you two doing?" Anna said. "Supper's been ready for thirty minutes."

Rufus wheeled, his finger-gun drawn. "Lady, don't never slip up behind the sheriff when he's making an arrest. I come in a spat of shootin' you!"

"You look like a sheriff."

"Do I? That's what some other folks said."

"I'm going to shoot you and Sid and Mister Tom all if you don't come on to supper."

"Hey, mister. Put my mare up and I'll let you go free."

Sidney leaped from the gate. "Thanks, sheriff."

Rufus put his arm around Anna and headed for supper. She stood in the bathroom door while he washed. His face and hands fresh and clean, he leaned over and kissed her. "You wouldn't mind your husband being sheriff, would you?" he whispered.

"I bet I know where all that came from."

"Well?"

"He's been running for something almost as long as I can remember, and he's never won anything yet."

"But he doesn't look like a sheriff, honey. I do. You said so yourself."

"Rufus, you're not really serious about running for sheriff?"

"I'm already running. I started an hour ago. Well, don't look like that. You act like I'd shot somebody. It's not that bad. It won't cost me nothing but my time and hard work. If I lose I just lose."

"But you might win. . . ."

"I hope so. Else I wouldn't be running. What's the matter? You afraid somebody might shoot me?"

"Not that. I don't know what I'm afraid of. But I'm afraid."

"You said you'd stand by me. But if you're dead set against it, if you're dead set, I don't do it. Tell me you're dead set."

"Maybe I'm wrong. A woman might be wrong about these things. You wouldn't let them ruin you. I don't believe you'd let anything ruin you."

Ursa opened the kitchen door and looked across the hall where Rufus and Anna stood in a quiet embrace. "I reckon it ain't nobody ever gits hungry around heah but me."

In the middle of the night, Rufus raised his head a few inches and looked at the dead ashes in the fireplace. The room was cold, but his body was in a fever. His pillow was wet with sweat. Anna lay peacefully on his arm. Little by little he freed himself, hoping he would not wake her.

He slipped from the covers and stood by the window. Across the Hollow, no higher than a man's head, was a thick layer of fog. Over the fog was a crisp blanket of moonlight. It seemed like an endless stretch of evil. He was wrong and Anna was right. That was why he could not sleep. He searched the fog, as if he might see old Noah stumbling along, waving a walking-stick he had carved from dried hickory, pointing the tip accusingly toward the window. He could smell the old man's room: tobacco and shucks and rich cedar; and he could hear the voice like tender green crops sprouting through the earth, but not the words—the words were too far away.

He must turn now while he could still hear the warnings; and he remembered how the first day at the sawmills was always the loudest—after a week you could hardly hear the saws.

He moved around the foot of the bed toward Rex's crib. He stumbled over a toy.

Instantly, Anna stirred the covers. Her hand touched the wet pillow. "Rufus? Are you sick?"

He towered in the room like an overstuffed ghost. "No. . . . I was awake. I was worried. . . ." He went to the bed, and, kneeling, he buried his face against her throat.

"You'd better get under the covers," she whispered. "You're damp. You'll take cold."

He moved under the covers and pressed her to him.

"Couldn't you sleep? What was the matter?" she whispered.

"I was thinking about what I was gitting into. Tell me I'm wrong. . . . Tell me I can't do it. . . ."

But she remembered the hotel bill at the Loyola House and the way he had slumped in his train seat. Her hands moved over his face. She kissed his lips, light, tender-kissed. "Darling, I love you so much. You know it, don't you?"

"Yes. . . ."

"I'm not afraid now."

"But Anna. . . ."

They held to each other, breathing as one. His lips relaxed against her throat. He went to sleep.

4

THE HONOURABLE LABE YOUNGBLOOD, high sheriff of Woodall County, was not permitted by law to succeed himself in office. However, he was very much in the race with his hand-picked candidate, Hoxy Weatherall, the present circuit court clerk. Hoxy went to the posts as a favourite. Next was Blain Maclin, a former sheriff. The wary old experts gave Rufus Frost the third position: he was a veteran and fine-looking. Bringing up the rear was old Bill Crumby, perennial candidate, who held a steady four hundred (mostly relatives) of the five thousand voters of Woodall County.

Each Thursday, the weekly *Woodall County Journal* carried a list of all county candidates, beginning with sheriff and ending with the justices of the peace in each of the five beats or districts. Occasionally the state candidates were listed. But no gubernatorial race could create the stir caused by a county contest.

Every four years, from the first of April until the end of the second primary in August, farmers left their crops and congregated on court square in Cross City to hear the latest scandals, deals, line-ups and quips regarding the mad scramble "to serve the good people of Woodall County" as sheriff, or circuit clerk, or chancery clerk, or supervisor, or justice of the peace, or whatever. Sawmills closed down, hay ruined, fruit rotted in the orchards, cows went unmilked, corn curled from lack of thinning, and the grass grew higher than the cotton. Bets were made; spies kept their eyes squinted, their ears tuned; hard-liquor jugs passed from mouth to mouth.

Early in the spring the trek began. Candidates, afoot, on horse-back, in buggies, explored every road and trail and path that led to a house. Confident, smiling, burning with the desire "to serve," they talked and laughed, hugged and kissed the children, and gave thousands of cards printed with their names, offices sought, and the line that had long ago lost its magic: *Your vote and influence will be appreciated.*

"What a hell of a mess," Rufus told Anna. But he kept to the long trek, faithful as a hound. He had the mare shod four times.

At the end of May, the signs began to appear, nailed to fence-posts, trees, country stores, wagons, or wherever the notion struck.

Vote For

HOXY WEATHERALL

for

Sheriff and Tax Collector of Woodall County

Weatherall will make Woodall safe for all

Blain Maclin gave a twelve-year-old a dime for each time he wrote beneath a Weatherall poster: "Hoxy is foxy." The boy kept his own count.

Maclin, beaming proudly over his malignant term as sheriff some years before, designed his posters to read:

Vote For

BLAIN MACLIN

for

Sheriff and Tax-collector of Woodall County

With Blain we can do it again

To which a Weatherall fan added in pencil: "With gin, anybody can do it agin." Within a week, all the Maclin posters bore the new pencilled addition.

Old Bill Crumby advertised with: "Fill the bill with Wild Bill," but nobody bothered his posters, for they had been reading his slogan for sixteen years.

Rufus's posters were designed by Anna.

RUFUS FROST
Candidate for
Sheriff and Tax Collector of Woodall County
World War Veteran   Farmer

It was inevitable that "Rufus" should be scratched and replaced with "Jack." But the scrawling that caught on was made by a friend: "If Frost don't win in August, he'll kill something in October!"

In June, Rufus met Uncle Sweetheart, the key to Tom Phelps's political underworld. He was a short, dumpy man whose enormous shoulders, dark skin, short neck and missing front teeth made him look very much like a groundhog. "What's the name?" Rufus asked.

"Just Uncle Sweetheart, son. That's all you n-n-need to know."

"Mr. Harpole is a scientist," Tom Phelps said. "A political scientist."

"That's right. The s-s-science I practise is greenback. You c-c-can mix it with anything and get an explosion."

The three stood in the corner of a stable in the middle of Tom Phelps's trading barn. In the trough before them was a smoky-globed lantern. Julian Harpole pulled out two rolls of bills and pitched them into the trough. "If you'd b-b-blow out that lantern, we might c-c-could see."

"He sleeps in the daytime," Tom said to Rufus.

"You c-c-can count it," Uncle Sweetheart said. "But it's there. Folks are gonna start b-b-borrowing beginning with the first p-p-picnic on the Fourth. Half the folks you loan to will vote for s-s-somebody else. But you can't help that. We're t-t-trying not to lose the other half. The secret to p-p-politics is knowing who is your f-f-friend and who is your enemy. But nobody's ever found the s-s-secret. There's two hundred f-f-fives and a hundred ones. That'll get you s-s-started. The ones are for the k-k-kids. Buy 'em ice-cream and soda-pop till their little b-b-bellies burst. If we c-c-can get you in the second primary, you gonna w-win."

"We all understand," Tom said, "it's pay double if you win. Forget everything if you lose."

"You might t-t-tell him, Tom, I've had to forget three times. I hope I'm riding a h-horse this go-round instead of a mule."

"You can stand it," Tom said. "You can stand it, man."

Rufus took the rolls of bills and stuffed them into his front pockets.

"That's money my p-p-pore old grandmother left me. I had a d-d-dream about her the other night."

"Did she say we'd win?" Tom asked.

"She d-didn't say much of anything. But she always believed in helping the y-young. Why don't you c-c-clean up this barn, Tom? It s-s-stinks."

"It just smells like horses. I like the smell of horses, Harp."

"It d-don't smell like horses. It smells like d-d-damned ole plug mules. What about the money at the p-precincts? Have you two decided on that?

"We haven't talked about that yet," Tom said. "We got to decide on his speeches first."

"You don't need to d-d-decide on a speech. Be for law enforcement, f-f-fair weather, and Red Rooster salve. Be against the b-b-boll weevil, the nigger, and sin. Tell the folks you were raised on molasses, c-c-cornbread, and sawmill gravy. That's what they w-want to hear. Tom couldn't tell them that, R-Rufus. That's why they t-trimmed his ears. How do you f-feel about your race? You've seen lots of people by now."

"If I git in the second primary, I think I'll win."

"The b-b-best I can figure, there are nine hundred and f-forty folks that sell. If we could h-hook five hundred I know you'd get in the second."

"You mean there ain't no chance for me unless. . . ." He had put off the issue as long as he could, as if some miracle would settle it. One hand fingered the roll of fives. He withdrew the hand and rubbed at his face and neck. The musty smell of manure rose like steam.

Tom Phelps was quick to see the struggle. "Why don't we go into that later? When we can tell more about what's happening? Main thing now is to keep gaining a little bit every day."

"You're p-p-picking up, all right. You can tell a lot more after the F-Fourth. Maybe Hoxy and Blain will try to b-beat each other's brains out. If they do, we'll s-s-sneak in."

"That's right," Tom Phelps said. He picked up the lantern.

"Wait a minute," Uncle Sweetheart said. "I'll roll you two h-high man for a dollar. P-Pull out your ice-cream money, Rufus." He laid a pair of dice in the trough. "T-Throw according to age."

Tom Phelps threw a four. Uncle Sweetheart threw an eight. "Eighter from Decatur! See what you can do, Mister Rufus. See if you can climb over that big eight." He did not usually stutter when he was gambling and when he was angry.

Rufus threw a nine.

"Niner is a winning liner. We're riding a real horse this time, Tom. I rather have luck in this world than an education. If it suits you g-gentlemen, let's bring this conference to a c-close."

Rufus pocketed his three dollars.

It was midnight when young Johnny stopped the car and let Rufus out in front of his house. When the car was gone, Rufus walked toward the garden and looked out across the fields. The night was hot and oppressive, for July was only three days away. In such weather, the cotton would shoot up like a mushroom. He grinned. Sidney had been the boss of the fields. Rufus saw the boyish, innocent face sweating in the midst of the hands, beaming at breakfast over what he had done and what he was going to do. It was a fine crop. There was something so clean and good about cotton and corn and new hay. His hands closed about the bills in his pockets; he gripped tighter and tighter. He wished that to-morrow morning he would be going to the fields with Sid. He had a sudden, keen desire to kiss Anna. She was asleep upstairs, heavy with child.

He leaned against a post and looked toward the lighted living-room. Anna always left the light burning when she thought he would be home late.

If I don't, he said to himself, I'm going to get beat. And if I do. . . .

The figure of a man moved from the living-room on to the front porch. At first sight Rufus was startled. Something might be wrong with Anna. Then Barney, in his uniform, stepped off the end of the porch. Rufus hurried forward and grabbed Barney as if he would choke him. "Aye god! I never was so proud to see nobody in my life."

"You shore took your time gittin' here. You politicians lay out worse'n a man courtin'."

"You looking good. I swear you are! When you git here?"

"This morning. Been to see you three times already." And he continued an account of landing in New York with Bolton, and the week they had spent there together. And he told of the last few weeks in France, how Rufus had left much too soon for the real fun. He added to everything, including the amount of money he had won in a four-day poker game on the ship back. Then he inspected Rufus more closely, actually feeling his thighs and his arms, proving the man was all there. They sat down on the end of the porch.

"So you running fer sheriff, damn yore old time. Are you gonna git it?"

"I don't know, Barney. I'm in a mess. I don't know what to do.

"I know what you're gonna tell me."

"I swear to God I hate to buy folks. Buy a man just like you'd buy a slab of fatback. I'll be damned if I can see it. But I want to win.

Aye god, you work your end off and if you don't pitch in with some greenback you git it bought right out from under you. That ain't funny either. I'm gonna git a good vote. Lots of things in my favour. Still, Tom Phelps and Harpole—I know you know him—swears I won't git to first base if I don't git in the market. It's their money—Harpole's. They ain't lying to me."

"No, they ain't lying to you. Didn't you know what you was gittin' into?"

Rufus got up. "Why, hell yes! I was told as plain as any man on God's green earth could be told anything. I didn't have to be told. Any fool would know it. I jist shoved it aside and pushed on. I'll be damned if I know why."

"I know why. You wanted to be sheriff."

"I still want to be sheriff."

"I been in this county a long time, Rufus. Let me ease yore mind on one thing. You ain't gonna buy nobody that ain't been bought before—'less it's somebody voting for the first time."

Rufus rammed his hand into his pocket and peeled off ten five-dollar bills. "Listen, Barney. I want you to take this and hep me however you can. Folks expect drinks and dinners and. . . . You know how it is."

"Put that back where it come from. I don't want your money."

"It's not my money."

"It'll be yours if you win. Ever' dollar will be worth two. I know how Uncle Sweetheart works. You keep it. I don't want it. I've got some money. When folks want a dinner on you, I'll buy it. Don't worry about that."

"Now look, dammit. I want you to take this money. I want you in this thing with me. I don't care what you do with it. Burn it. Tear it up. Give it away. Throw it in the creek. But take the damn' stuff." He shoved the bills into Barney's hand.

Barney shook his head slowly. He crumpled the bills into his palm. A curious contraction covered his face. "They shore put you between a rock and a hard place, ain't they, buddy?"

Rufus was looking out across the fields. "I crawled into it myself. Ain't nobody else to blame."

"When you make your first speech?"

"The Fourth. At the picnic."

"Know what you're gonna say?"

"No telling."

"If I don't see you before then, I'll see you there."

Rufus wheeled. "You're not leaving?"

"Man, you got to git some sleep."

"No! You're not going. You're gonna stay all night with me."

"I got to git back. My things are all at the Kangaroo."

"Your things'll be all right." Rufus stepped on to the porch. "Come on."

Barney looked up at the commanding grey eyes. He had seen the same tired, frightened look in them after a long bombardment or a close call on patrol. And he remembered how the big frame, lying under the same blanket with him, had been like a protection, like an extended helmet. "Shore I'm gonna stay." He held up his hand that gripped the five-dollar bills. "I wanta tell you something though. Ain't another man under the sun could put this kind of money in my hand."

Rufus's eyes had relaxed. "I figured that, else your taking it wouldn't mean nothing."

They went into the living-room.

"Lemme tell you one other thing, Rufus, and then you got to git some sleep. You're the type feller folks will vote fer. I wouldn't be surprised if they was to pick you up and give you as good a vote as they ever give any man, money or not. If they do, you gonna feel right porely in your heart."

"But will they?"

"That's right: will they? I reckon it ain't no way of telling till the night of the first Tuesday in August."

When the front-room bed was fixed for Barney, Rufus turned out the lights and climbed the stairs quietly. He felt a momentary sense of relief, like a lull between skirmishes. At the top of the stairs he stood for fully a minute; he wished he had talked longer with Barney, listening to his voice in the dark. It would not be the same in the morning, in the daylight, just as old Noah's voice was best when he sat on the steps of his house, in the dusk, pushing the bright blade of his knife across the rich grains of cedar.

As on many other nights, Rufus opened the door and peeped into the east bedroom where Sidney slept. The slim, lean body was curled on its side in a square of moonlight, stark naked. Was I ever that young? Rufus thought. Was there ever a time when I slept that still? (Yes, he had been that way, in the days when he dogged the shadow of old Noah.) Sometimes he wanted to lie down beside Sidney and go to sleep.

In his own room, he undressed slowly and stood beside Rex's crib. Wasn't it all for them: for Sidney and Rex and Anna? If it was for them, how could anything be so wrong?

He stood beside the bed, pushing his hands over his muscles. With meticulous care he lay down, trying not to wake Anna. Her pregnant body made an awkward, gentle turn toward him. He moved so that her hand would not touch him. Why didn't you stop me? You could have and you didn't! He sat up in bed. An accusing, angry wave swept over him. He imagined that she was

smiling at him, a curious, superior smile. He looked down at her
outstretched hand, the long, slender fingers, now a shade fuller
than usual. Despite their pale taper, they were stronger than his;
her hands were stronger than his; and she had not stopped him.
She had never got angry; she had never stopped him from anything! It was too late now. He seized the fingers in his hand. She
stirred.

"Rufus?"

"You been feeling all right to-day?" he asked.

"Unnhnn. Is it late?"

"Nearly one."

"Did you see Barney? He was dying to see you."

He lay down and moved his arm across her. "He's staying all
night with us."

Her hand searched gently around his shoulders and neck. "You're
worn out, aren't you?"

"Kiss me," he whispered.

She moved her face to him.

5

IN the shimmering, stifling heat of July the crowds gathered in
Oak Grove south of Cross City. Early in the morning the
crusade began: cars and trucks, wagons and buggies, prancing
horses and poking mules. The clouds of dust settled on the sheltering
leaves in the grove and dropped noiselessly into the boiling pots of
Brunswick stew. Stacked between the trees, neat as cord-wood,
were a thousand cases of soft drinks; and in the refreshment pen,
framed by strips and a quadrangle of giant oaks, were two hundred
gallons of ice-cream. By nightfall many a child would pat his
swollen belly, boast of twenty bottles, half a gallon of ice-cream, and
jolt home in a wagon for a night of delicious misery. "Ole man
Maclin bought me three pops and four cones, and the last time he
said, 'Ain't I bought you one before, sonny?' And I said, 'Naw, sir.
That musta been my brother.'"

Later picnics would be like harmless pimples around an enormous
sore. The Fourth set the incomparable pattern. By one o'clock, flies
were swarming in the grove. Toothless old men blew them away and
sipped their stew with pasteboard spoons.

"Listen at him talk. You can't beat a feller when he makes
the womenfolks cry and little acorns fall. Can't he talk,
now?"

All day long their voices blared above the milling crowd and
the babies who cried even while ice-cream was pressed against
tender noses. "That's all right, lady. No need for you to move. If I
couldn't out-talk a pore little squalling young 'un I'd never stand

a chance in the Legislature against that Delta mob who've tried to rob these sun-kissed hills ever since your brave old grandfather fell at Shiloh. I promise you good people . . ."

The woman retained her seat. She didn't know whether her grandfather or great-grandfather or great-great had been at Shiloh or not. But John A. Metcalfe had been to the Legislature: he ought to know.

The sheriffs spoke last. It was the custom.

Old Bill Crumby fiddled.

Hoxy Weatherall quoted poetry. Life was real and earnest and the grave was most certainly not the goal. . . . "If you elect me—and I know you're going to—I promise you. . . ."

Blain Maclin raised his stentorian voice to its maximum. ". . . I was born and reared in the golden hills of Hatchie, on the very bank of that crooked little stream that rises out of the clear blue water of Rockwell spring. . . ."

Beat three it was; usually known as the "bloody third," from which so many clever men and clever schemes had come: the place might have been called the "mother of sheriffs."

". . . I am thankful to every one of you because in any other county or any other state my name might have been written in dust. Not so here, my good friends! Not so! Eight years ago you chose to place a trust in me that lifted me to a higher ground of public service. There is but one greater call, my friends, and that is when the Master on High places in your heart the burden to deliver His undying gospel throughout the length and breadth of this noble land. When you called me to serve you eight years ago, I accepted the challenge with humility . . ."

"The old bastard got rich. But Lord, can't he talk! If I could talk like that I'd run fer Guv'ner."

". . . and I served you good people faithfully and honestly, despite the fact that bootleggers and gamblers and men of ill repute hung around me like Grant hanging around Vicksburg. This is my last time to come to you and ask to serve in public office. If you elect me—and I know you're going to—I promise you that . . ."

Rufus felt the light push of Barney's hand. He mounted the platform as if he climbed up the wall of a trench.

"This is the first time I ever made a speech. There's no telling what I'm liable to say. The fact is, there's not much left for me to say. You've been promised everything already. And, anyway, a man scared like this is liable to promise you something now and forgit about it when the time comes to take office.

"A lot of you don't know me. I was born in Sparton, Tennessee, and raised on a farm. I came to this county a year before the war broke out. I got married and then I went to France a year or more later. I want to say to you as sincerely as I know how that I'm not running on a you-owe-me-something platform. You don't owe me anything for going to war. I'm glad I went, and I'm certainly glad I got back all right. A lot of people from this county didn't get back all right, or didn't get back at all.

"I don't know much about politics, this is my first race. I don't think any man is completely honest or completely fair, because we'rc all human. But I think I'm reasonable in both cases, and I've always believed that using common sense was the best way to handle anything.

"I want you to vote like you please, but naturally I hope it pleases a lot of you to vote for me."

He had not meant to end it there, but he was suddenly finished and knew it. He had spoken with sincerity and warmth and with a correctness that amazed himself. He felt rather good about it and was (even before he stepped down from the platform) already looking forward to the next time, when he would do better.

The crowd surged in upon him, partly because they liked his looks and manners, and partly because he was the final speaker. The women stood in line like converts at a protracted meeting, though they could not vote. But the effect was strong enough that the wise old experts stretched their necks and wondered.

"Yore wife ain't here, they tell me. I'd shore like to meet yore wife." The woman spoke in a sing-song voice.

"No'am; she didn't come. She's not very well."

"She's expecting, they tell me."

Rufus's face flashed red. "Yes, ma'am."

"Well, I hope she gits along all right. Hope you win. Sam's gonna vote fer you. That's my husband. He ain't agin nobody; jist wants a new face in the courthouse, and you're a soldier-boy."

The line pushed her on. There were three women to every man. After the handshaking spree was finished, the crowd dispersed. Within a few minutes the grove was deserted, leaving only the fly-covered rubbish and a few politicians huddled with their cronies in the deep shadows. When darkness settled and only Rufus and Barney remained, Tom Phelps and Uncle Sweetheart came like thieves from a thicket of saplings and grape-vines.

"Best day's work you ever done," Tom said.

"You downright a-astonished me," Uncle Sweetheart said. "I said to Tom, 'L-Listen to them Abe Lincoln rhythms. That m-m-man's put himself in the race.'"

"Just keep talking it," Tom said. "By gad, just keep talking it. You've got one month and thirteen more speeches. We're getting in better shape all the time."

Uncle Sweetheart nodded. "It's a g-great pity the women can't vote."

By six o'clock on the morning of election day, the machinery which Tom Phelps had designed was set into motion. It was quite simple. In the seven boxes where his team was scheduled to buy votes, he had managed to buy at least one of the election-holders; he had also managed to steal a few blank ballots and had voted them for Rufus Frost and for certain other candidates with whom he had been able to deal. When a seller was cornered and the price was finally agreed upon by the set of buyers, he was given a voted ballot which he carried to the proper election-holder. Returning with a blank ballot, the seller was given an initialled, sealed envelope, which he carried to Tom Phelps's stables in Cross City. If the voter had sold for five dollars, the envelope contained a whippoorwill pea; a white grain of corn designated seven-dollar votes and a yellow grain designated ten-dollar ones. At the stables, the sellers were paid immediately by Tom Phelps or Uncle Sweetheart.

The system of paying at the stables rather than on the spot at the precincts served two purposes. It provided a check on the team of buyers; it got the seven- and ten-dollar sellers away from the polls before they spread word of the price they had received.

Two hours after the polls closed, Tom Phelps made a summary of the day's activities, which he was preparing to submit to Rufus. In his small, neat printing, it appeared on the page:

Election holder	(RJM) .	.	.	.	$35.00	
,,	,,	(PO) .	.	.	.	40.00
,,	,,	(ER) .	.	.	.	30.00
,,	,,	(ABB) .	.	.	.	45.00
,,	,,	(LP) .	.	.	.	50.00
,,	,,	(CF) .	.	.	.	30.00
,,	,,	(LF) .	.	.	.	30.00
,,	,,	(TS) .	.	.	.	40.00

Total	.	$300.00
Spotters (SM, TR, FO, LP, LO, CE, LE, JR, BA, PC, FT, BT, LL, RA) . .	$20.00 *each*	
Total	. .	$280.00
Votes: 138 at 5	$690.00	
202 at 7	1414.00	
52 at 10	520.00	
Total	. .	$2624.00
Advance: (total)	. .	$1100.00
GRAND TOTAL	. .	$4304.00

Note: You check these figures, Rufus. If you're left
out in the rain you know it's $0. Otherwise 2 x 4304.00=
$8608.00. Harp says if you get in the second the sky is the limit.
I say, if you're not in the second there's not a rattlesnake in
Georgia.

He folded the note neatly and sent it by a Negro stable-
boy to Rufus, who waited at the courthouse for the first
returns. Then he passed along the alley, running his hand over
stall doors and patting the noses of his horses. He ignored the
mules. Win or lose, he had had a splendid six months of
corruption.

An hour later, Nile hurried into the stables and announced with
a wild, vacant stare, "Papa! Rufus is leading the ticket!"

From the Confederate monument to the corner of Court Square,
blackboards stretched covered with names and small yellow
figures. With each new return, sweating, red-faced candidates,
women with children straddling their hips, old men with
canes, pushed and clawed their way forward for a glance at the
figures. One woman, whose husband was running far behind in
the three-man race for supervisor of the Fifth District, sat down
in the middle of the square, hugging her one-year-old child,
and wept. "He sold the last cow we had," she said. Old Bill
Crumby with eighty-one votes out of almost two thousand reported,
appeared on the courthouse balcony and began to fiddle. As the
crowd jelled to silence for an instant, he yelled down, "I'll git
'em four year from now, folks!" The screaking of his instrument
went on. Steve Folsom, already conceding defeat in his race for
clerk of the circuit court, climbed to the highest step of the courthouse and waved his arms and yelled for attention. "Folks, I'm
going home and git me some sleep. I know I'm out of this here
thing, but I just wanta tell all of you: I ain't mad at
nobody."

"That's real noble of you, feller!"

"What you gonna do now, Steve?"

"Go back to share-croppin'," Steve answered.

"I wouldn't," a voice leaped from the crowd. "I'd git me a gun
and shoot some of them lying scoundrels!"

Rufus and Barney huddled near a clump of shrubbery.
"Let's git away from here fer a while, Rufus, before yore
enemies start givin' you the glad hand. If the Cross City
box comes in like it ort to, you can't hep but win in the first
primary."

"Well, where's Sid?"

"Aw, he'll be all right."

They went to the railway café. It was deserted except for the usual

railroad men, laughing, and slapping each other good-naturedly
with their gloves. "They tell me ole Hoxy's in the hospital with
a stroke."

"Aw!"

"Yeah. What I heard. Clean passed out when the first count
come in."

Barney and Rufus sipped their coffee in a corner booth and
looked at each other. They had passed within a few feet of Hoxy on
their way to the café.

Rufus put his arms on the corner of the table, dropped his face
and went to sleep.

From a deep, grey chasm, where cool water bubbled, his mind
spiralled to the surface. He heard the excited voice of Sidney,
"Buddy! Buddy! You're leading all three of 'em by two hundred
votes! You're gonna win in the first!"

"What time is it?"

"Two o'clock," Barney said. "I knowed you'd win!"

Rufus rubbed his face. "No; you didn't!"

"That's right," Barney said. "I didn't know. Ain't nobody can
tell who a woman will marry and who a man'll vote fer."

The three went back to the courthouse.

An hour later the fiddling had stopped, the shouting had died
away, the last yellow figure was printed on the blackboard. Rufus
had a total of 2,936; his opponents had a combined total of 2,112.
Rufus was stunned; his followers were stunned; his enemies were
stunned. Hoxy came over and shook his hand. "The good Lord
was with you, boy."

"Yeah," a strange voice put in. "The good Lord and nelly three
thousand voters."

Blain Maclin went home cursing his buyers, who, he said, had
"stuck the damned money in their pockets."

Old Bill Crumby waved his fiddle case in a moronic frenzy and
went off gaily, already thinking of four years hence.

Old, defeated politicians gathered in knots with their few faithful
cronies and bitterly debated their various mistakes.

Sidney dashed off to carry the news to Anna.

Rufus and Barney stood alone under the naked, glaring light in
the courthouse lobby. "I wanta show you something," Rufus said.
He unfolded the sheet which Tom Phelps had sent to him early in
the night.

"Bought three hundred and ninety-two," Barney said. "You
didn't need a one of 'em. Makes you feel kinda porely in the heart,
don't it?"

Rufus took the sheet, tore it into shreds, and dropped the pieces
into a spittoon.

"Well, I'm tired, sheriff. I'm headin' fer the Kangaroo.

Besides, I don't want to be around when they come after you."

"Who?"

"The dealers. They'll git to you before daylight."

"Aye god, they's no end to it. Is there, Barney?"

"None at all."

"What would you do?"

"I've asked myself that lots of times lately. I was allus scared to answer. I got a confession to make. I was hoping you wouldn't win."

"Honest?"

"I'm thirty-five years old. I can remember twenty-eight years of sheriffs. Ever' last one of 'em had to face the same thing; and ever' last one of 'em sooner or later got around to the same answer. If you don't know now, you'll know by daylight. Ain't no man borned of woman ort to have to face what you'll be facing."

"I asked you what would you do." His eyes were fixed on Barney.

"Why, I reckon I'd jist go cut my throat. That'd be the easiest way out." He gave Rufus a friendly punch, a quick laugh, and left.

Rufus remained under the naked, glaring light, as if it afforded some strange protection. His shadow was an ugly botch around his feet. He could feel eyes gouging at him—merciless, burning eyes. It was not long before steps sounded around him. Of course, he thought, they had waited until Barney was gone: Barney was part of his strength; they had fought together, hadn't they? He was tired; he wanted to go home and lie down beside Anna. Put his arm around her and hear her say she was all right. The sound of steps grated on his ears.

"Rufus?"

Tom Phelps's pearly teeth were shining. His face was green and pale.

"By gad, son, you took the britches off of everybody."

"Fooled me worse than anybody," Rufus said quietly.

"Let's go into the supervisors' room. There's a party that wants to discuss a few things with you."

They entered the room which had been used all day as a polling place. The floor was littered with soiled posters, cards, handbills; and splattered in spots with tobacco juice. At the end of the shining mahogany table appeared the profile of a young man in a dark blue suit. He turned in the swivel chair and got up as Rufus reached the table. Uncle Sweetheart remained seated in his chair, with one foot propped on the table.

"Mr. Jefferson," Tom Phelps said. "Meet Mr. Frost. The new sheriff of Woodall County."

The young man nodded. He was too far away to shake hands. He leaned forward waiting for Rufus to advance; but Rufus remained still. "You from this county?" Rufus asked, wasting no time.

"Yes. I was born here. My father and I left eight years ago. We . . . we found better business opportunities elsewhere."

"He means," Uncle Sweetheart said, "the p-powers in control didn't exactly s-s-smile on his vocation here."

"What do you want?" Rufus asked.

"Wait a minute," Tom said. "Aren't we being a bit hasty. I trust we're all among friends."

"All right," Rufus said, settling himself on the edge of the table. "I'll listen . . . but if I'd had as much faith in the voters as they had in me, I wouldn't owe eight thousand, six hundred and eight dollars. I'm going to pay every penny of it, and I'm going to run the sheriff's office to suit me. I don't figure to do anything that hurts the people." His eyes turned towards Tom Phelps. "Not for a kingdom, Mister Tom."

"You're jumping the gun, Rufus," Tom said.

"All right. We'll start over."

The slightest relief showed in Tom Phelps's eyes. "Do you know what's going to give you more trouble than anything else?"

"Yessir. I think I know."

"You mean bootlegging?"

"Yessir."

"Do you believe you or any man can stop it? I don't mean control it. I know you can control it. But can you stop it?"

"Nossir. Not altogether."

"Exactly. If you keep good whisky out of this county—which you can do—folks will drink Holyoke rot-gut or some other man's stuff. Any of it would drive a monkey wild. Any kid with money in his hand can buy it. These are just simple facts, Rufus. Mr. Jefferson wants to operate two clubs. He personally runs one; his father runs the other. They sell only first-class goods; they close on Sunday; they absolutely do not sell to minors. It's nothing in my pocket whether you do it or don't do it. The only thing I get out of it is the chance to have a decent drink instead of lye-water. That's the situation. Unless, Mr. Jefferson wants to add something."

"I'll add that we don't ask this for nothing. We ran two places here when Joiner Cartwright was sheriff. You can ask him if we lived up the agreement to the last letter. I'm prepared to tell you our offer right now."

Rufus got up. He looked at Uncle Sweetheart. "This is the fastest company I ever been with. I've been elected three hours."

"Rufus, we m-m-meant to be getting here fustest with the mostest." Nodding at Jefferson, he said, "Make your offer and let's m-move on. This man's tired and w-w-worn out."

Jefferson took his pen and on the back of a handbill wrote without hesitation. He shoved the handbill down the table toward Rufus. The big hand covered it slowly. He waited a few seconds. Then he picked it up and read: "$4,000 cash, delivered in denominations you prefer the last of each month. The last of December, $6,000. Total for each year: $50,000. You guarantee one-hour notice before any raid, otherwise agreement for that month is void."

Rufus folded the sheet, creased it with his fingernails, and slowly tore it into small pieces.

Jefferson said, "I'm glad to see you take proper precautions to prevent that from falling into the hands of a grand jury."

Uncle Sweetheart gave a coarse, nasal laugh. "You won't f-f-forget what was on it, will you, Rufus?"

"If you do, I can write it again," Jefferson said.

"That won't be necessary, Mr. Jefferson," Rufus said.

Uncle Sweetheart got up. "Let's m-m-move on out of here. This man's w-w-worn out and wants to go home."

The three went out.

Rufus went to the swivel chair at the head of the table and sat down. Slowly his head bowed to his arm on the table. His temples thumped with pounding blood. It seemed to him that flies swarmed through unscreened windows and doors; that he could smell the body odours from old quilts too long exposed to naked flesh, and feel the lumpy hardness of shuck beds; that he could hear the voice of his father rising weakly but harshly from a pellagrous stomach. He could see that stooped, gaunt figure standing nightly at the end of a rotting porch; he could hear the splatter of urine which left mild odours at Christmas time, but on August nights like these. . . . He saw the vast stretch of rocky earth where corn sprouts leaped through cow droppings into the March wind and died with the first sunlight of April. The land seemed so far away. We'll go up there, he thought, me and Sid, before cotton-picking time.

The grey light was flooding through the tall windows. He raised his head and rubbed his face. I'm tired, he thought. I wonder if Anna is all right. A minute later he heard scratching in the lobby outside the room. He knew the sweepers had come to clear away the wild day's rubbish.

He went outside and stood on the landing at the top of the courthouse steps. Grey light was rushing from the east to cover the empty streets. A drove of pigeons possessed the square; they moved with tender steps across the still, dew-damp handbills. It seemed to him they read the silly promises on every coloured page and jerked their necks in silent laughter.

From the plug he held in his left hand, he bit off an enormous hunk of tobacco. Slowly he chewed until his mouth was flooded with the sweet-bitter liquid. Then, in one violent explosion, he sent the juice hurdling down the steps. The sudden splatter frightened the pigeons; they lost possession of the square.

BOOK TWO

PART ONE: 1931. THE HOUSE OF FROST

I

ANY stranger on the train could tell the four boys belonged to the man. Not by their eyes, for one pair was grey, another was blue, a third was fiery black, and the fourth was deep brown; nor by their hair, for one head was black and the other three were blond as clear oak. But all four carried the unmistakable impression of their father's face, a replica quality so common among certain hill people that even the closest neighbours confused the identity of brothers.

"I'm gonna sit by Papa."

There was some commotion, some elbowing, and a few objections, "You don't. I'm going to. Can't I, Papa?"

"All you little babies want to set in my lap? That what you want?" the man asked, his huge face mocking them.

"I don't," Morris said. He was seven and the youngest of the four.

Rufus gave each one his ticket and sat down beside the window.

"I've got a whole ticket," Rex said. "I get to sit by Papa. You can't put a half-fare in the seat with a whole fare."

"Push that seat back," Rufus said. "If you all gonna act like babies, we'll crowd in here together."

Rex pushed the seat back and sat down facing Rufus. Morris climbed into the seat beside his father; Wayne sat beside Rex. Bayard sat in the seat across the aisle, conscious of a noble self-sacrifice. "I'll sit here," he announced. He was eleven.

Rex turned his deep brown eyes on Bayard. "Look at Papa's little man. Ain't he pretty?"

"I tell you what I'm gonna do," Rufus said. "When the conductor comes along, I'm gonna have him put all of you in the calaboose."

"That's a jail," Morris said, his grey eyes suddenly dilated.

"Is it, funny-face?" Rex asked.

With a stout, healthy leg Morris kicked out and struck Rex a solid blow on the shin. Rex let out a yell.

"Git over there and sit by Bayard!" Rufus blazed out against Rex. "Wayne's the only one not acting like a bronco."

Wayne squirmed in his seat and lowered his eyes. He was nine, the third son, and usually quiet. He had Rufus's straight nose, but Anna's fierce black eyes. His hair was black and he was of slighter build than the others, with narrow shoulders and long thin arms. His work in school did not compare with the work of Rex or Bayard. He had a passion for honesty.

"He's such a sweet child," Rex said, with a special face contortion aimed at Wayne, which might have been mockery or a secret sign of understanding. Rex loved attention and affection, and when he failed to get either, he changed instantly from a child of sunshine to a subtle demon. He knew he was the most handsome of a handsome lot. There was no question. It was as simple as the fact that twelve times twelve was more than eleven times eleven. Bayard was not handsome; he was pretty. He was as pretty as a girl. Morris was a little too chubby, Wayne a little too thin. Jarvis. Now there was competition, but Jarvis was the baby and didn't count in things, yet.

As Rex sat down beside Bayard, his mind searched frantically for a plan by which he could quickly reclaim the good graces of his father. He was always alert, usually to the point of nervousness. During times of disfavour, he measured himself from many angles, sometimes with severity, gradually admitting that Bayard's mind was mighty keen, almost equal to his own; that in athletics he had neither the swiftness of Wayne nor the natural power of Morris; but in the great over-all, in the grand totals, he could sit back and smile: the oldest one, the chosen one, the leader, the crown prince. He sought the admiration of all his brothers; his favourite changed from day to day, from hour to hour.

"We don't want to sit with them, anyhow, do we Bay-bay?" Rex said.

"No," Bayard said, rekindling the flame which had flickered such a short while ago.

"When we get to Memphis we'll run off and leave the young 'uns, won't we?"

Bayard nodded, pleased to be in a conspiracy.

"You won't run off," Morris said. "Papa won't let you. Will you, Papa?"

"Don't talk to 'em," Rex said to Bayard. He fingered an imaginary cigar, leaned back and blew imaginary smoke toward the ceiling of the coach. "I'm just running up to Memphis for a few days. I need to sell about a million feet of lumber to old man Whatcha-may-call-it. What kind of business you in, mister?" Another huge draught of smoke toward the ceiling.

"I'm . . . I'm a well-digger," Bayard said.

"Yeah? You know, I need some wells dug, mister. About how deep can you bore?"

"We don't bore. We use a shovel."

"Oh, well, we couldn't trade. My wells have to be bored through solid rock. Wish we could make a deal. Too bad." Another cloud of smoke.

Rufus turned his face toward the window and pretended not to listen. Wayne and Morris drank in every silly syllable. Morris thought it was wonderful. His laughter rang above the noise of the train. Remembering his vicious attack of ten minutes ago, he climbed down from his seat and stood penitently at the arm of Rex.

"Rex?" He tugged at his brother's sleeve.

Rex flicked imaginary ashes at the tugging hand. "Run along, sonny. I'm on a business deal with the gentleman here."

"I want to buy a million feet of lumber," Morris cried with all the enthusiasm he could muster.

"Sorry." Rex brushed the tugging hand from his sleeve. "I don't sell my lumber to people who kick me."

"I'll give you a hundred dollars a foot!"

"No!" And he blew smoke in the penitent's face.

Morris turned to Rufus. Tears had formed in his eyes. "He won't sell me any lumber."

Rufus pulled Morris into the seat beside him and began to whisper in his ear. The tears dried suddenly and his big grey eyes began to shine. He looked at Rex and laughed; his arms and legs relaxed: they were extremely well developed for a seven-year-old.

Rex, wisely guessing that his father merely pretended to be telling a secret, went on with his game, delighted that Morris had been properly humbled.

"Son," Rufus finally said to Rex, "would you mind throwin' that cigar away. The smoke bothers me."

Rex knew it was time to quit. He reached for a magazine which Bayard had brought along.

Morris leaned against his father and went into a fit of laughter. He giggled until the conductor appeared.

From far down the aisle the conductor waved at Rufus, obviously pleased to have five more passengers to add to his scanty load. He had a bright, red face that beamed above his black alpaca coat. His big square mouth was set in a half-smile, as if to prove the Depression could not get him down. "My God, Rufus! Is this crew all yours? Now, how do you feed 'em all?"

"Plenty of milk and cornbread. A little fat-back."

"They look like they gittin' plenty. I didn't know you had four boys."

"Five."

"Where's the fifth one?"

"Home with his mother."

"Jarvis is too little to go," Morris said.

Rufus looked down at Morris, who knew the signal was a stern reminder he had spoken out of turn. "Boys, this is Mr. George Daringhast. Chet's uncle. This is Rex, George, my oldest boy; Bayard; Wayne." He tousled Morris's hair. "And Morris, the meanest one."

The conductor punched each ticket with extreme care. He too, tousled Morris's hair. "How old are you?"

"Seven."

"Can you plough?"

"I can. But I have to carry water."

"Great Scots! A boy like you carrying water! I bet you could plough the britchen off a pair of mules." He surveyed the other three. "No trouble seeing they're all your, Rufus."

"Yeah," Rufus said. "I reckon they're a pretty good bunch when they're asleep."

"How's the land working out?" He referred to three hundred acres Rufus had bought from his brother Charlie.

"That's good land, George. A little cold-natured, but it's all right. I got lots of it in pasture right now."

"I used to walk myself raw between the legs down some of them old long rows—when I was about the size of this boy." He put his hand on Wayne's head. "Ain't no better place for a gang of boys than a farm. You string this crew out and they'd make you a hundred bales of cotton. All you have to do is lay up in the shade. Course, you don't git nothing for it right now. But you don't need nothing. You got plenty stacked away to live till the first of January, then you'll be sheriff again. What you doing? Going to Memphis to celebrate your election?"

"Going so the boys can celebrate it."

"How'd you do it, Rufus? You know you're one of the few men ever been elected sheriff a second time in this county. What's the secret?"

"Aw, luck mostly."

"That's a hunk of luck."

Rufus looked sharply at the big, square mouth. The remark was harmless, but it seemed to lift every window in the coach and draw in all the shadows of the past twelve years, especially the four years of being sheriff: the endless web of deals. Did any man ever come to me for help and git a cold shoulder? The small, voiceless voice: Ah, no, but you sold your soul. I never intentionally hurt any man. Ah, no, but the law is the law and you took the thirty pieces of silver. Thirty? You're wrong: it was several thousand. Several. Sometimes I'd like to start walking, over the hill and into the blue space beyond. . . .

Still looking at the square mouth, the bright, red face, Rufus wondered why all the years of walking down a sunless aisle had not left its pale mark.

"Not long till January," George said.

"No," Rufus grinned.

"Which one of these boys is gonna be a politician?"

"None of 'em, if I can help it."

"About ten more years and it'll be a different story, Rufus. Just about ten-twelve more years. . . ." He moved along the aisle, and, turning, asked, "What ever happened to your brother?"

"He's farming. He bought the Basil Strickland old home place."

"Who'd he ever marry?"

"Amy Knight. Joe Knight's girl. I don't know whether you ever got acquainted with Joe or not."

"Did he live on the Arcutt place?"

"Naw. I think that was his half-brother, Cy. Joe lived down on Polk Levee."

"Shore a fine-looking bunch of boys, Rufus."

"I reckon they take it after their mother."

Liar! Liar!

"Ten-twelve year from now—when you git ready to send one of 'em to Congress—I'll donate one X." He hurried along as if an overflowing coach of passengers awaited him.

"I'm gonna run for Congress," Morris said.

"You're gonna"—Rex whispered a shocking word—"and fall back in it. Water-boy! That's how come Wayne to swallow a lizard. You wouldn't bring any water to the field, and he had to drink out of the creek."

"He didn't swallow a lizard!"

"Well, ask him."

Morris jumped out of his seat and stood before Wayne, eying him suspiciously. "Did you, Wayne?"

Wayne thrust his tongue out quickly. Morris jumped back, and leaned against his father's knee, without friends.

Rex and Bayard were doubled in insane laughter. "He thinks it was his tongue!" Rex cried.

Wayne, smiling in his dull, inhibited manner, motioned Morris beside him. Morris accepted. Wayne put his arm around him and said, "They wouldn't know a lizard from a redworm, would they?"

Morris shook his head. He felt better with the arm gently about him.

"When we git to Memphis," Rufus said. "I'm gonna lock all four of you up in a room and make you stay there till we start home. I'm not gonna take you to no ball-game to-morrow."

Rex, envious of the harmony between Wayne and Morris, suddenly shifted to the seat facing Bayard. He winked at Morris.

"Come here, Punkin. I got something to tell you." His voice and manner charmed.

Morris was torn two ways. Only yesterday Rex (who was always bestowing gifts and performing handiworks to soothe ruffled feelings) had made him a splendid pea-gun.

"Come here." Rex winked again.

Morris slid slowly from his seat and crossed the aisle to Rex, who pulled him close and whispered, "If they lock me and you in a room, we'll tie some sheets together and climb out. Won't we?"

Morris nodded. His face was lighted with certain, daring adventure.

"We got things to talk about they don't need to hear."

The two moved toward the end of the coach and sat down close together.

Rufus turned his eyes from all the empty seats in the coach and gazed out the window. The coach was like the Hollow, now that the sawmills and all the itinerant workers were gone. The Kangaroo was filled with hay now, and the lumberjack houses had gone into the making of new cow-stalls or the repairing of tenant houses. Ephriam and Rachel Hurley had gone back to Tennessee. So many things had gone, so many faces (Tom Phelps was dead; his father was dead), so many voices; all as if to make way for his sons. He could not help it if his spirits were suddenly dampened.

It was a bright still afternoon, the first of September. The city lay sullen and quiet, bound by the approach of winter and the heavy shadow of Depression. Rufus, shoulders straight and square in his expensive suit, his hat angled slightly, led the way through the vast lobby of the Peabody Hotel. Behind him, Morris and Wayne trotted to catch up, after they had stopped to gaze at the lobby fountain. Rex and Bayard, having seen it all before, took little notice.

A few minutes later, Rufus left them in front of a theatre. He gave Rex a twenty-dollar bill. "I've got something to tend to," he said. "When the show's over, you go straight back to the hotel. Eat supper there and go to your room. I'll be back by then."

Rex nodded. Morris caught Rufus's hand. "I'm going with you."

"You can't go with me, Punkin."

Morris hesitated, then trotted after the others. Rufus watched them until they were inside. He had a strong urge to rush after them. For a few minutes he stood on the edge of the kerb; then he walked south. Almost without decision, he retraced his steps, crossed the street, and entered the lobby of the Loyola House. He had not been there since his honeymoon, yet he had a faint notion he would find everything as he had left it that day, fifteen years earlier: the flushed, agreeable faces of the planters—though now, they would be talking about five-cent cotton instead of the Kaiser. The lobby was deserted, except for the counter girls and an old lady, deep in a plush chair, working feverishly with her crochet needle. Not to be completely outdone, Rufus bought a cigar, and as he half-heartedly smoked he read Todda's letter:

"DEAR MR. FROST,—I need your help and advice. The next time you are in Memphis I would appreciate it if you would come by to see me.

"Sincerely,
"MRS. T. TEMPLE."

It amused him that Todda had taken the name of Temple because Sterling Temple had carried her baggage to the train the day she had left the Hollow.

Outside the hotel he threw away his cigar and bit a chew from his plug, for cigars sometimes made him slightly dizzy. The drawn, silent faces he met reminded him of the poverty of the times. No doubt Todda had been pushed into the ring with all the other hungry faces. Automatically his hand sought the roll of bills in his front pocket. He felt a certain pleasure in knowing that her fierce pride had at last been broken. Twice since his first trip to her house he had gone to offer her money, and each time she had coolly rejected his offer. Not so now. At last he would win: whatever she asked, he would give twice as much, and never miss it. The Cross City banks had not caught him napping: he had placed his money in the Post Office, in two Memphis banks, and kept plenty in crisp new bills in safety deposit boxes. Nobody in the Hollow was hungry, white or black. No one could say he had not—or could not—take care of his own.

He walked all the way to Todda's house, chewing with regularity and spitting with satisfaction if not precision, for a fever blister was giving him trouble. Dusk had settled when he knocked on her door. The sound of steps and Todda faced him.

He had not seen her for four years and he was astonished that she should seem so young, much younger than Anna. There were patches of freckles on her face that he had never before noticed. Her hair was bobbed and fell in natural waves. Only around her eyes was there any sign of tension. She wore a fresh blue linen dress. Everything about her and about the house seemed arranged for company. "Well, look!" she cried. "I didn't expect you so soon."

"Now, Todda," he chided. "You was looking for me."

"Looking, yes. But not expecting you."

They sat down, he in a new solid red Morris chair, she in a

rocker. He noticed with a mild shock there was no crib in the room. Of course, there had been no crib the last time, nor the time before, but it had not registered strongly on him then.

For a minute the old magic flowed between them, the old magic without its burning passion. As if to ward off something Todda said, "Is it still five or have you got another one?"

"Five. That's enough, ain't it?"

"Some folks have more. Looks like you'd had one girl, anyway."

"I just took what the good Lord sent me. I'm not kicking."

"I'd like to see them. Are they spoiled?"

"No. But I'm gonna give them everything, Todda. Everything you and me didn't have."

"You'll ruin them."

"If it ruins them, I can't help it. They take my money. Some folks won't."

"Folks like me?"

"For one."

"They don't know where it come from."

Their meeting, which had been almost a love scene, was quickly charged with bitterness; old wounds gaped; they recoiled from one another. He thought she was telling him to forget the old world, set in its playhouse atmosphere, and wake up to the present where men scratched in garbage cans for worm-eaten apples and moulded bread. "If you've gone hungry, it's your own fault," he snapped.

"I haven't gone hungry."

"You wanted me to come here . . . for what? To look at me?"

"If you're fishing for a compliment, I can say you still look all right. You know, Rufus, the best thing ever happened to us was not gittin' married to each other. You got a wife that thinks the sun rises and sets in you. She thinks it twenty-four hours a day. Sometimes I can't help it: I just take a notion it ain't so. That's when the trouble starts. Other times, I can see the sun all right. Here lately, I can see it better when I'm thinking about you rather than looking at you . . . your picture. Like as not, I get mad because you got what you went after. I didn't. I figured out something else not long ago. A railroad man wanted to marry me. He'd been eating at the café for seven or eight years. I remember one night I was laying awake trying to decide what to do. All at once I was thinking: I can't marry Luther. Rufus could wash his hands of me; I don't want him to wash his hands of me. I didn't give a flip how you got your money. That's not why I didn't take it. If I took your money, you'd be free. If I didn't take it, you wouldn't be."

Rufus had turned so that he could look directly at her. "Todda, sometimes you can be awful honest. I reckon now you're gonna take it."

"No. But if I did, you wouldn't be free. That was only a notion. You'll never be free of me . . . will you?"

To shake her. That would be pleasant . . . to shake her: at least then he would have his hands on her. You could lie with your lips, but there were things inside a man that would not lie.

"You're not hurting me."

"Maybe not. The truth don't always hurt. That's just another notion."

His hands gripped his thighs. He was going to show her. He would not touch her for all the world. "What did you want?"

"I wanted you to come here because of Dean."

"You fin'ly decided he's part mine. After you kept him here in a nigger house, and God knows what he's had to eat and wear; after all that, you fin'ly decided he's part mine."

"Oh, I always knew he was part yours; that's why I kept him to myself. You needn't start blaming me. What else did I have? I want you to know he's had plenty to eat and enough to wear. I sent him to school . . . when he would go. I never had a minute's real trouble with him till I told him about you."

"What possessed you to do that?" He was trying to deny the sharp knot of pleasure that rose in him.

"He's thirteen years old! That's what possessed me! I was a fool. I know I was. I've been one all my life. I don't know what happened to him. He changed overnight. I had told him his daddy was killed in the war—like Howard." She got up and went to the mantel. With her back to Rufus, she continued. "He's a little thief. I know. I caught him! He came in with too much money. Ten times more'n he'd ever make on a paper route. I followed him one morning, three mornings. I watched him steal four or five bundles from one of the trucks. He don't even have a morning route." She turned to face Rufus. Her face blazed with emotion and tears. "I don't want your money! I just want to know what to do!"

Rufus got up. He started to put his arm around her, then in a feeble, helpless way, his arms dropped at his sides. "What can I tell you?"

"Tell me something . . . even if it's wrong."

"Did you . . . say anything to him?"

"Yes. I said everything. I threatened to tell the police. He laughed. He just laughed at me. He told me to go ahead, he knew more on me than I knew on him. He accused me of carrying on with Luther Whitmore. He . . ."

"Was it true?" His voice penetrated all other matters at hand and fastened on this new concern.

"Yes; it was true! I'm a woman, Rufus! The least you could understand is that."

"I understand it," he said, almost whispering, wishing he could sit down and hear nothing for a while. "But what . . . ?"

"I don't know what. Don't ask me questions. I didn't know a child had to have a father, a man. Maybe if I'd married Luther . . . I didn't know these things, Rufus. How could I know? There was nobody to tell me."

"Maybe they didn't know either."

"Lizzie saw it. She tried to tell me. But a woman won't listen to a woman, unless it's gossip. I want you to tell me what to do. I want you to do something. You're not like me. You ought to know where to start."

"But I don't know."

"You're a man. You got a house full of boys. They don't go out and steal things. Why does mine. . . ?" But she knew it was finished; there was no need to go on. She looked at his body. If she could only take her hands and uproot some of the strength in this man and thrust it, graft it on to her son. Strength, and something else too.

The silence was as real as snow.

They were both aware of the darkness. Todda casually lit a lamp, and the soft glow was like a rising hope. Her face lost some of its dark distress. "Oh, well, he's not the first mean young 'un in the world. There's really nothing you can do. The only help you can give me is in knowing about it. He'll be home in a little while. I guess it'd be just as well if he didn't find you here."

"I'll go or stay, Todda. Whichever you want." You see, he thought, I'm not free.

"If it gets much worse . . . really serious . . . you'd come back?"

"You know I would. It's my place to do what I can." One hand had inched downward into his pocket; his fingers touched the roll of bills. But her face told him it was no use; he would not win this time either. "When you want me . . . you know what to do." He turned to go.

"There's one thing I want. I want to see your boys some time. Did they come with you?"

"Yes."

"Would you bring them to the Union Café? Maybe for breakfast in the morning. They wouldn't know me, but I could see them. Would you do that?"

"Yes. . . ." He answered slowly. "I'll do that."

He went out.

At the hotel he telephoned the room, but the boys were not there. He went to the coffee-shop and watched for them while he ate. By chance he encountered Forrest Lowry, a stout, jovial lumberman from Cross City, whom Rufus had known during his years as sheriff. He insisted that Rufus join him, and a few friends, in his room for a poker session.

"I will later on," Rufus said, "when I git my boys bedded down for the night."

A few minutes later, Rufus saw the four enter the coffee-shop; innocent, healthy faces with eyes shining like sun rays through a window. Not until then did he understand the anxiety that had brought the tears to Todda's eyes. Not until then did he realize he would hardly recognize Dean if he should meet the boy face to face. He felt a pang of regret and shame that he had been of so little help to Todda. He got up to go toward the four, but, sensing that he preferred to watch them, he sat down again behind a column where he might go unnoticed.

The four sat at a large round table, glancing at menus that hid their faces. When the waitress came for the orders, Rex spoke with exaggerated dignity and authority. "We shall have four shrimp cocktails."

"I want a hamburger," Morris interrupted.

"Quiet!" Rex continued. "You shall have exactly what I order for you. This is not a hamburger stand. But, waitress, make his order . . . uh . . . mild, please. No, I tell you . . . bring him fruit cocktail instead. He's really very young to his age, you know. . . . I mean, very young to his size."

"Stop acting crazy," Bayard said.

"He can afford to act crazy," Wayne said. "He's got the money."

Rex looked from Wayne to the waitress. "Ah, at least he said something sensible. You know, we thought for years the lad couldn't talk." Rex stuffed his napkin into the front of his shirt. "Now I'll have roast leg of lamb, and if you don't mind, a double order of mint jelly. I'm terribly fond of mint jelly."

"Me too," Morris said, afire with laughter. "I'm terribly fond of milk jelly too."

"Mint jelly!" Bayard corrected, and promptly received a kick from Morris.

Rex, still in full role, demanded, "What do you say, Bay-bay? Lamb and jelly for you?"

"Yes, Uncle Rex."

"I want fried chicken," Wayne said. "I'll pay for it myself."

"He has no sense of the exotic," Rex said. "To come to the Peabody and eat fried chicken is simply unforgivable. Well . . . milk for all. I usually drink black coffee, no sugar, no cream; but to-night I believe I shall have milk. . . ."

Morris's eyes dilated as if a ghost had risen in the centre of the table; for at that moment, Rufus towered above them. "Bring two black coffees," Rufus said, and pulled up a chair.

Rex's face looked as if blood popped from every pore. Stealthily he pulled his napkin down across his lap.

"You like the show?" Rufus asked, lightly.

"We couldn't get Morris out," Bayard said. "He wanted to see it twice."

Rufus said, "You wanted to git your money's worth, didn't you, Punkin?" He remembered Todda, the concern in her eyes, and something inside him began to well over, as when he saw cotton stalks drooping under the weight of too many bolls, or corn bending with too many ears, or trees breaking with too many apples.

The waitress brought milk and coffee. Rufus took one glass of milk and placed both cups of coffee before Rex. Rex, thinking it might be safe to joke, said, "You can have one cup."

"No," Rufus said. One nod made it clear to Rex what he had to do. By the time the meal was finished, he had managed to get down every bitter drop from both cups.

Rufus left them in their room. "I'm going down to Mr. Lowry's room for a while. It's 611. You can stay up long as you want to, but I better not hear a lot of noise out of you all."

When he was gone and the door safely locked, Bayard and Morris led a dance in the room, with a chorus of mockery:

"I'm terribly fond of mint jelly."

"Are you terribly fond of mint jelly?"

"Oh, yes, I'm terribly fond of mint jelly!"

"I usually drink black coffee, no sugar, no cream; but to-night I believe I shall have milk."

"Are you terribly fond of black coffee, Mister Rex?"

At last, as Wayne failed to respond, Bayard turned on him. "Oh, you have no sense of the exotic!"

"I'm sick," Rex said. He curled on the bed, his face contorted, his eyes walling, and let out long, smothered groans. Bayard and Morris laughed and laughed. Then their laughter ceased when they saw the tears rolling from Rex's eyes. He tumbled and drew himself into a knot. His lips trembled. His body shook. "Oh, me . . ." he cried. "Papa knows I never drank coffee. Ohhhh, me. . . . Coffee and mint jelly will kill you." The tears rolled all the way down his face and across his trembling lips.

Morris's face turned pale with horror. There lay his brother in the last throes of death.

"Ohhh, me! Papa caused it . . ." Rex cried.

Morris dashed for the door, fumbled with the lock, and was all the way down the hall, near the elevators, when Rex caught him to bring him back. "You little fool! There's nothing the matter with me!"

Morris sat against the headboard of one bed, his feet drawn under him, and stared at Rex sprawled across the other bed. His big grey eyes licked out tongues of anger and hurt. "I hate you," he said.

"Aw, Punkin. . . ." Rex was not yet over his laughing spell. "You don't hate me. I was just fooling. Come over here."

"I hate you," he stubbornly insisted. Occasionally his mouth puckered as if to cry.

Wayne sat quietly in a chair.

Bayard leaned against the dresser, watching the master of reconciliation.

Rex winked and coaxed. "See? Punkin was the only one cared anything about me. Rest of you would just let me die. I guess I know now who likes me. Come here, Punkin. I wanta whisper something in your ear. We'll play a trick on Papa. Come over here." The jerk of his head was magnetic. Morris climbed down and made his way to the other bed like an automaton. Rex put his arms around him and kissed his neck and nibbled at his ear.

Peace reigned for a few minutes. Wayne went to the mirror and picked at his face. Bayard curled up in a chair with a book he had bought at a news-stand. Rex continued to soothe Morris's hurt feelings.

Wayne turned from the mirror, and with a blank face astonished the three by observing, "I bet Papa's got a girl down there."

"Call him and ask him!" Bayard cried, thrilled from head to foot with the idea.

"You call him," Wayne said, and went back to the inspection of his face.

"I'll call him," Morris offered.

"Call him," Bayard egged.

"You better not," Wayne warned, suddenly afraid of his idea.

Morris looked at Rex: he was the final authority. Rex nodded. "Say, 'Room 611, please.' "

Morris obeyed.

A husky, masculine voice answered, "Hullo. . . ."

"Papa?" Morris quivered.

"Who you want?"

"Papa. . . ."

"Just a minute. Rufus. Telephone."

Rex grabbed Morris's arm. "Tell him I got a girl up here. Tell him!"

"Yeah?" Rufus said.

"Papa. . . . Rex's got a girl up here."

"He has?"

"Tell him you're afraid," Rex whispered.

"I'm afraid. . . ."

"Tell him she's pinching you."

"She's pinching me, Papa."

"Can't you pinch back?"

"I could. . . ."

"I'm coming up there and pinch some tails . . . with a belt." The telephone clicked.

"What'd he say?"

"Said he was coming up here and pinch some tails."

"Now you've done it!" Rex said.

There was a mad scramble to undress and get into bed. When the key turned in the lock, the room was dark. Morris lay quietly beside Rex; Bayard beside Wayne. Rufus switched on the light and took out his belt. "Turn over, Rex. You're first."

Rex turned over.

"Pull them drawers down."

Rex pushed his underwear down. Three moderate strokes sounded against the naked flesh.

"Wayne? You tell him to call?"

"Nossir."

"Bayard?"

"Yessir."

"Stick it out here."

He turned and slipped his underwear down. Two strokes.

In the meantime, Morris had turned on his face and exposed his naked rear above the covers. He waited. Rufus went back to the door. Morris peeped under his armpit, the top of his head flat against the sheet. "I was the one that called," he said.

"Yeah," Rufus said. "A whupping wouldn't do you no good. I'm gonna let you stay in here tomorr' while we go to the ball-game. If I hear any more racket up here, we're all going home early in the morning."

Morris's naked end slowly revolved and buried itself beneath the covers. "Can I sleep with you to-night, Papa?"

"I don't know. I may just sleep on the floor when I come back." He closed the door, locking it after him.

There was a minute of silence.

"He ain't such a bad guy," Rex said, and, remembering his first few lessons in Latin, added, "But sometimes you have to take him *cum grano salis.*"

2

RUFUS stood before the basin, his face covered with thick lather, shaving his left cheek. Morris stood on the end of the bathtub, held to the basin, and with his forefinger wrote his initials in the lather on his father's right cheek. Rex bathed. Bayard sat on the commode.

"Wayne!" Rufus yelled. "Come 'ere!"

Wayne appeared in the bathroom doorway. Rufus went on with his shaving. "What did you want, Papa?"

"Aye god, I wanted you in here with all these others. Something might git you out there by yourself." Turning to Morris, he said, "Son, I'm fixing to shave this side." He patted his right cheek. "Better stop writin' or you gonna git your pencil cut off."

Morris shed his underwear, kicked them toward Wayne, and leaped into the tub with Rex.

"Look at him, Papa!" Rex cried. "The little idiot."

Water splashed from the tub and crawled under Bayard's feet. "Idiot," Bayard repeated.

"He don't want a suit," Rufus said. "I can tell when a boy don't want a new suit."

Morris leaped from the tub and began to dress.

Outside the hotel, Rufus, as if an idea bright as the morning sunshine had struck him, asked, "What you say we walk down to the railway café for breakfast? Then we'll all be hungry."

"I'm already hungry," Morris said. "I been hungry since last night."

"Well, you just got a worm in you," Rufus answered, letting Morris catch his hand. "That's why you can't git full."

"Will it kill me?"

"Naw. Just make you mean."

"I can feel it," Morris said, punching his navel. "It's right there. It's two feet and nine inches long. It's bigger than a lizard. His name is Raymond."

"Make him stop, Papa," Wayne said, registering one of his rare complaints. "He's giving me innergestion."

Bayard caught up with Morris and said, "I bet Raymond is terribly fond of black coffee, no sugar, no cream."

"He don't like coffee," Morris said.

The Union Café was a long hall, filled in the centre with marble-topped tables, lined on one side with booths and on the other side with the counter, cigar-stand, and the cashier's niche. They sat at one of the tables. Todda, neat as a nurse in her blue uniform and red-checked apron, came from the cashier's niche to serve them. "Don't tell me all these boys belong to you," she said deceptively.

"Well, the good ones are mine and the mean ones belong to my wife," Rufus answered with the air of a stranger.

"Which is which?"

"You guess."

"Let me see." Her hand passed affectionately over Morris. "I'd say this one is the best one."

"Oh, ho!" Rufus roared. "She missed that a country mile,

didn't she? Why this boy is so mean he pulls up little green corn when it's too late to plant over. In fact, they're all mean."

"I don't believe it. Tell me what you want to eat. I'll bring just heaps of everything you want."

"Rex is terribly fond of black coffee," Bayard mocked.

"No. Coffee will turn him yellow."

"He's terribly fond of it," Bayard insisted. "No cream, no sugar."

One look from Rufus brought silence. "Bring a half-bushel of corn-flakes, about a gallon of milk, scrambled eggs and bacon. One cup of coffee."

Todda brought everything with pleasant efficiency. It seemed a miracle to the boys that she could carry so much, as if every finger were a hand. Was that all, Mr. Frost? Did they want anything else? Just hollo, she would be at the cash register; a customer waited to pay his check.

"She's very nice," Bayard said. "I bet she owns this place."

"She knows Papa," Rex observed. His sharp, adolescent eyes missed nothing.

"How do you know?" Rufus snapped. A defensive question he had meant to be offensive.

"Unnhnn," Rex smiled. "She called you Mr. Frost."

Rufus quickly changed his approach. "Now don't you-all go back home telling your mother about your daddy's girls. She wouldn't never let us come back to Memphis, would she, Punkin?"

Morris shook his head. His mouth was too full to utter a syllable.

Todda returned to their table, and, noticing Morris's empty glass, brought him more milk. "You're a hungry little boy."

"You know why he eats so much?" Bayard asked. "He's got a worm in him."

Morris stopped eating and trained his big eyes upward. "I have too." He held out his hands to measure. "He's that long. His name is Raymond. I have to feed him good. If he was to die I'd die."

The topic was terribly unpleasant to her, but she quickly recovered herself and said, nodding to Wayne, "You're mighty quiet."

"He's got a lizard in him," Bayard explained.

"What's in you?" she asked.

"A chatterbox," Rex answered. "If you put tape over his mouth, he talks through his ears."

Bayard, properly offended, dropped his gaze.

"Oh, I didn't mean it, Bay-bay," Rex petted. "Here." He put a slice of his bacon into Bayard's plate.

"And to think," Rufus said to Todda, "I've got another one."

Todda went back to the cashier's stand, but she kept her eyes on the five. She had a warm feeling for the young faces, as if they belonged to her, and she wondered whether she would be called on to mother them if something should happen to Anna. Did they like their mother as much as they liked Rufus? Would he spoil them by giving them everything? One after another a covey of questions flew through her mind. They were not like her own child: Had the mere presence of Rufus fired each youthful body with something her son would never have? She must touch each one of them before they left. And, coming from behind the counter, she fulfilled her desire as they filed out on to the street.

Rufus paid the check and waited for a comment. Todda was slow returning the change, feeling an old sadness and wishing she had not asked him to bring the boys there. Overanxious about her quietness, Rufus said, "Well, I've got to take them now and git 'em all a suit. I promised them."

"Take them where?" she asked, knowing it did not matter.

"Starhart's, I reckon."

"Oh," she said. Starhart's was expensive. A silence fell between them that seemed to reach all the way back to their childhood. Her face sprang alive, out of shadows. "They're so fine, Rufus!"

His lips moved to answer, but stalled as if her hand had been placed over them. He quickly put down a fifty-dollar bill and whispered, "Git him something." Almost before she knew what he had done or said, he was on the street leading his flock. She went to the door and watched them all the way to the corner, where they turned north.

Their fingers pulled eagerly at rows of limp sleeves. Their faces were red with the thrill of buying. Their bodies could not remain still for the deft measurements. Envious eyes were cast toward Rex, the crown prince no less, walking about in full-length trousers. Ties? Yes, of course. Socks? Oh, a half-dozen pair each. Underwear. Shoes. Shirts. My lord, how long have we been here? Better let me count my money again. A sly smile from the clerk. I know you: a pocketful, I'll bet. From the Delta? You know, folks from the Delta spend like hell when prices go down or they have a crop failure. You're not from the Delta? But it's sort of on the edge of the Delta, isn't it? Don't know my geography, do I? Bet this boy knows *his* geography: George eat old grey rat at Pa's house yesterday. Oh, yes. We'll have everything ready this afternoon. Seven years old? Well, I can tell you that suit ordinarily sells to a twelve-year-old. Now come on, boys, you're not going to let your daddy buy all these fine suits for you and not get one for himself. You'll feel bad if he does that, won't you, boys?

Rufus was finally fitted. Then they went to The Four Sisters and each bought a present for Anna: hose, handkerchiefs, scarf, gloves, and an expensive brooch. After that it was time to eat; and after eating, it was time to start for the ball-park.

Near the park was a small carnival. The crowds, early for the ball-game, stopped off for a few minutes at one of the various devices, the most popular one being the game of baseball: a monkey sat on a stool inside a cage; on either side of the cage was a round, six-inch target; hit the target and the stool collapsed beneath the monkey; three baseballs for a quarter. Shining new knives, bright-coloured dolls, bronze horses, watches, clocks, silver belt buckles, hats and walking canes. "Bring the boys right on up here, mister. Who's the pitcher? Dump the monkey good and hard. Dump the monkey for one big point. Two points wins a knife, five wins a clock. Twelve points wins any prize in the house. Step up. Who's the pitcher?"

Men with holes in their socks threw ball after ball.

A small boy, with hungry eyes set on the row of shining knives, threw while his black-haired, gangling companion urged, "Let's go, Hershel. You not gonna have enough left to git in the ball-game."

Women watched, waiting for their heroes to win them bright-coloured dolls.

"I tipped it! I tipped it!"

"That's not enough, sonny. You have to dump the monkey. Step up folks. Dump the monkey."

"Throw, Papa."

"You boys go on. I can't hit that thing."

They threw. Wild, angry, hopeless pitches; they threw again and again. Rufus shelled out quarter after quarter, all the while swinging his right arm, warming his shoulder muscles.

"You throw, Papa."

"Come on, mister. Get the boys a knife. Dump that crazy rascal from the stool! Don't let him make a monkey out of you!" He placed three balls in Rufus' hand.

"Give me six. I got to warm up first."

He threw six pitches, not aiming at the target. "Mind if I warm up a little more?"

"Warm up all you want to, mister. Quarter for three balls is all I ask."

He threw six more. Then he studied the distance. "I got to hit it eight times for four knives. Right?"

"Right."

"Give me nine balls." He put six in his coat pockets, held three. "Pick out your knife, Punkin. You git the first one."

Bang. Bang. Bang. Bang. The monkey fell four times and leaped back to his stool. The crowd watched with amazement. "That's half of 'em." He moved a few feet. "Lemme try the other side. I'll curve him this time." The ball shot from his hand, obviously a foot off the target. For the fraction of a breath the crowd froze, knowing their hero had failed. Then the ball broke sharply and smashed the centre of the target. He repeated with three more curves. "That's eight, ain't it?"

"All right! All right! Step right up. Who's the next pitcher?"

"Wait a minute, feller. I ain't through yet." His glance had caught the starving, envious eyes of the frail boy named Hershel. "Gimme some more balls."

Rufus rubbed the scarred leather in his palms; the barker distributed four knives, asking, "What your daddy do? Pitch for Memphis?" The boys laughed proudly and inspected their prizes. The monkey fell again and again. He was slower each time in returning to his stool. At last he had to be coaxed. While that process was going on and while the crowd roared with laughter, Rufus gave his latest trophy to Hershel. The small boy could hardly believe the miracle. He clutched the knife and feasted on its shining jaws. His tongue was paralysed, but his eyes spoke well enough.

"Where's your buddy?" Rufus whispered. "I'll git him one."

The boy pointed to the edge of the crowd. "There. Dean!" he called. "He'll git you one too."

Rufus felt a sudden knot in his stomach, as if one of the balls had fallen down his throat. "What's his name?" But there was no need to ask.

"Dean Temple," the boy answered quietly.

Dean appeared at Hershel's side. He was tall and thin, with extremely black hair and eyes that accentuated his pale complexion. The prospect of a knife did not excite him. His cool, steady eyes focused on Rufus. "You don't have to throw for me. I'd just bring you bad luck."

They gazed at each other, while a single question rained about Rufus: Does he recognize me? Rufus could feel his face glowing red. His hand poured sweat and left his fingerprints on the ball.

"You don't want me to throw for you?"

"Sure. Go ahead. But you'll miss. Here's a quarter."

"I've got a quarter." He clinched the ball. He wiped his hand dry. As if getting his pitching signal, he studied the narrow, pale face. It was older than its years.

He threw a fast ball; it missed by inches. Before the crowd had finished its groan, he fired another fast ball. At the last split second it took a hop and sailed over the target into the netting. "Un huh!" Dean cried. "See what I told you!" He broke through the curious onlookers.

Rufus instinctively followed him, rushing through the crowd. "Say, say," he called. One hand grasped the tan mackinaw jacket whose sleeves were too short. Dean stopped.

"Do you know whom I am?" Rufus whispered.

"Sure. You're Dizzy Dean. Only Dizzy wouldn't a' missed."

Laughing, he broke away from the big hand and slithered into the crowd, headed for the ball-game. Hershel, grateful but bewildered, followed after his companion.

"Hey you! Hey!" the barker was yelling. "Bring them balls back!"

Rufus turned toward the frenzied barker. "Aw, shet up! I'm not going nowhere with your damned old balls." He let go with a fast pitch that sailed into the centre of the target. The other balls he dropped into the trough, and motioned to his sons to follow him. Disappointed by their father's two misses, puzzled by his sudden disappearance and strange manner, they followed; only the knives reminded them of his amazing feats.

Clear of the carnival and on the sidewalk, Morris asked, "How come you to miss, Papa?"

"I got *you* a knife, didn't I?" he snapped.

As they climbed into the grandstand, the Memphis Indians were taking the field. The loudspeakers poured out the first strains of "The Star-spangled Banner"; a few thousand people rose. Even as the music played, Rufus's eyes continually searched for a narrow, pale face. Then he chose a seat, high and at the east end of the grandstand. Always, on entering a ball-park, he had felt a great surge of strength, had felt himself on the mound ready to deliver tremendous curves and blinding fast balls. Now he felt weak; his right arm and shoulder ached a little. He sat down wearily. The continual argument of who should occupy the seat beside him began. Usually the argument pleased him. Now it irritated him. "Sit down!" he commanded sharply. A woman, two seats below, looked up and marked him for a grouchy husband. He stared straight over her head at the playing field. The boys sat down and looked at each other and kept silent.

The game bored them; they felt none of the usual excitement, because their father sat speechless, in a dull trance. Morris, occupying the favourite seat, leaned against the big thigh ; but there was no response. Sometimes they saw that their father watched the crowd instead of the game. A young vendor passed with popcorn, peanuts, and cold drinks. Their father made no move to buy for them; they remained silent. Once Rufus got up, and without explanation, went down several rows and across two sections of the grandstand. He returned without a word: the shining black head of hair was not the one he sought.

The pitcher threw high and far outside. "He nearly threw that one away!" Bayard said.

"Oh, he didn't. It was a pitch-out. They thought the man on first was gonna steal," Rex explained. "Didn't they, Papa?"

"That's right." He melted a little.

The pitcher struck out the batter. The crowd roared.

"Now they'll have a pinch hitter," Rex said. "A left-handed pinch hitter."

"How do you know?" Bayard was taking issue with all Rex's explanations, envious of such knowledge.

"Because the Memphis pitcher is right-handed, and because a left-hander can hit behind the runner easier, and because a left-hander is two steps nearer first when he hits. You don't know nothing. They'll use a left-hander if they got one good enough, won't they, Papa?"

Rufus nodded, pleased with the diagnosis. The loudspeaker announced the pinch hitter. He was left-handed.

"I bet they bunt," Bayard said.

"I bet the hit-an-run is on," Rex said.

"I do too." Wayne made his first prediction of the game.

Morris leaned heavily against the big thigh. "Did you hurt your arm, Papa? Is that why you're mad?"

Rufus looked down at Morris. "I ain't mad." Then he whispered, "Bet it's a pitch-out."

"I bet it's a pitch-out," Morris cried.

"That's not fair! Papa told you!" they chorused.

The pitch-out came. Morris stood up and yelled. "I won!"

"I won, too," Rex said.

"You didn't!" Morris said. "It was a pitch-out. You didn't win."

"Yes, he did, Punkin." Rufus warmed to his own analysis. "He's partly right. The hit-and-run was on, but they changed it at the last second. See, the runner barely got back to first. Dangerous. If the sign had stayed on, Mister 24 down there would be a cooked goose."

"Number 24 is Hobson," Bayard said, salvaging something.

Rex propped his feet on the back of a seat and looked at the confused Morris. "Sonny, you can't fool Uncle Rex."

Rufus had come to life. He bit a chew from his plug of Old Apple and worked it gingerly into his jaw. Between each diagnosis he spat a neat stream of juice over the edge of the grandstand into the creek that flowed by the park. The game took on a dazzling tempo. He yelled to the young vendor to bring food and drink to his charges. While they ate and drank, he called each pitch, explained each obscure move. He watched their eager, vibrant faces, lined in a profiled, ascending row from Morris to Rex. His heart surged with extra force. He wished Anna could be there. When he turned his head to spit, he still saw clearly in his mind the bright faces. The juice was sweet on his tongue, a faint bitterness, but no taste of staleness. He forgot the narrow, pale face.

Morris was the first into the house. Clutching his suit-box and packages, he flew up the steps and across the porch, a bare two steps ahead of Bayard. Rex and Rufus, loaded down with all kinds of packages, were next; Wayne, in his usual, unexcited manner, was last. Anna had the door open, expecting them, for she had sent Peter Cat to the station in the car.

"Mother! We got you some presents too!"

"Did you, darling?" She went through a delightful siege of hugs and kisses and a medley of enthusiastic cries about presents and suits and knives and the great, wonderful journey. Wayne, undisturbed, unemotional, entered the doorway. Anna looked at Rufus. "My goodness, you didn't leave Wayne in Memphis, did you?"

A faint grin broke across Wayne's face. Without a word he kissed his mother and turned to Jarvis, who had by then passed through two pairs of petting hands.

"He's been watching the road all day," Anna said. "He's been real blue."

Jarvis was passed to Rufus's arms, as if he were four months instead of four years old. He was large and stout, built like Morris; but he had the facial perfection of Rex, with the same dark brown eyes. Almost every night there was a general bidding among Rex and Wayne and Bayard (each of whom had a downstairs room of his own) to have Jarvis as a bedfellow. One or the other had been slipping Jarvis (who shared with Morris the east room upstairs) downstairs since he was two. In the beginning it was a question of who could steal him first. But when he turned four, he chose his own bedfellow for the night and the competition for affection grew keener. Rex won more often than not. Bayard, feeling sorry for the deserted Morris, often left his own room and spent the night in the east room upstairs. Of late, Rex had won so consistently that a pattern seemed established; but the competition did not lessen. Now, as Jarvis slid down his father's body to the floor, he was instantly surrounded by four pairs of gift-bearing hands and four faces demanding, "Whose Sugar Baby are you?" Each had bought his gift as secretly as possible, but each knew what the others had.

"Don't do him that way," Anna said.

Rufus snatched him from the competitors, and after a few rough bites at his neck fastened about his arm a watch that actually ticked. "Tell 'em you're Mother's and Papa's."

"I'm Mother's and Papa's." He spoke distinctly, but he was clearly impatient to have all that belonged to him.

Morris held out a red fire-truck, Bayard a pistol, Wayne a cowboy hat. Rex, deliberately choosing to be last, broke open a box and shoved a football into the overloaded arms. Then, with the irrefutable gesture of triumph, he drew from his pocket the carnival knife, seized Jarvis and ran into his room.

"You want to see my suit, Mother?" Morris asked.

"Yes, darling. But let's wait till in the morning, when you can get all dressed up in it. And I'll dream all night about the pretty presents I'm going to get."

"Aye god," Rufus began, as if announcing the official end of the journey. "I wanta see some A's on some report cards this fall."

There was general commotion of preparing for bed. Rufus and Anna went upstairs together to their room. He slouched wearily into a chair while she prepared for bed. In the soft light of one lamp he studied her, approved of every line of her body. It seemed amazing, at that moment, she should have borne five children. But more amazing was the fact that she never fussed at him about anything. "Come over here." He prepared his lap to receive her.

She went immediately and sat down and put her arm around his neck.

"Am I getting old?" he asked.

"Why?"

"I don't want to git old till you do. You look like a girl. I know how you do it." He kissed her cheek. "You never fuss about nothing." He drew her tight against him. Her skin was fresh and smooth; she smelled pure and clean, with no trace of perfume. "Have I told you lately how much I love you?"

"No; you haven't."

"It's a whole lot." His nose brushed about her cheek and ear. "Why don't you ever fuss at me?"

"I will if you want me to."

"Go ahead." Somehow, he meant it.

She took his ear between her teeth and bit it. "That hard enough?"

"That what you call fussing?"

"Yes."

"What if I told you I saw a very pretty girl in Memphis . . . and I stayed with her?"

"Well, if you told me, I'd have to believe it."

"And if you believed it, what would you do?"

"You'll have to tell me first. Did you?"

"I saw more than one pretty girl . . . but I didn't. . . ."

"What did you do? Tell me everything you did."

"We went to a ball-game, and to a carnival, and we spent this morning in the stores. We eat last night in the hotel and I played poker for a while. When I come in I had to move Morris in bed with Wayne and Bayard. So he woke up mad. We went to breakfast at a place where a pretty girl flirted with us. . . ."

"Us?"

"Well . . . the boys said they'd tell you. But I'm telling you first. When we got there Friday night, the boys went to a show, but I didn't go. I . . . you're not checking up on me, are you?"

"Sort of."

A frown covered his face.

"What's the matter?"

"Oh, I pitched a lot of baseball at the carnival, gitting the boys a knife. My shoulder's sorta stiff; it hurts a little."

"You want something on it? Some liniment?"

"Naw. Then you wouldn't sleep close to me. I'll let you keep it warm."

They got into bed. Footsteps sounded on the stairs.

"Who's that?" Rufus mumbled, not really caring unless it was someone coming to their room.

"Bayard, I guess. Going to sleep with Morris. I wish they wouldn't do that. They sleep better by themselves."

"I don't know," Rufus said, drawing her closer. "I'd hate to have to sleep by myself."

Bayard opened the door to Morris's room and went quietly to bed. As he stretched out and pulled the covers about him, a sudden, terrifying void told him he was alone. He lay for a few minutes unable to move. Then climbing slowly out of bed, he went stealthily down the stairs. Opening the door to the middle bedroom, he saw in the darkness Morris's arm curved along the covers across Wayne's body. He returned to his own room and sat chilled in the centre of the bed. It seemed totally unfair that he should be left alone. He switched on his bed light, and, finding his newest *Tom Swift* book, he read to the last page. Still, in open and bitter rebellion against some force that had cheated him, he would not put the book aside. He held it open across his stomach until he dropped off to sleep with the light burning brightly above his face.

While he washed for breakfast he looked up into the mirror and saw that his eyes were red and swollen. He did not care. It was secret revenge.

In the hall he came face to face with Anna. She stared at his eyes, and calmly reprimanded him. "If you stayed in your own room you'd sleep a lot better. And Morris would too. Is he up?"

"I don't know," he answered. He stared back at her as if she were the force that had treated him so unjustly.

She went down the hall and knocked sharply on Wayne's room. Pushing the door ajar, she saw Morris and Wayne sleeping soundly in each other's arms. Turning, she paused to say something to Bayard; but he disappeared into his own room and closed the door, leaving her with a puzzled look.

On the Monday a letter came addressed to Rufus. He recognized the small, neat handwriting as belonging to Todda. It read:

"DEAR MR. FROST,—Enclosing fifty-dollar bill overpayment.
We hear you won lots of knives at the carnival.

"Yours very truly,

"Starheart & Company."

The narrow, pale face came sharply to his mind again.

3

THERE was more than the usual commotion on the Court
Square of Cross City. It was Saturday before the first Monday
in January, the day set by law when new county officials
took office. Hoxy Weatherall, who had been a reasonably good
sheriff for four years, moved among the men on the square and
joked pleasantly, as if it had not occurred to him that his reign would
end two days later. His round, agreeable face drank in the mild
winter sunshine; the silver badge glinted from his tall, rawbone
body. He was standing with his hand on a farmer's shoulder when
one of his deputies brought word of a cold-blooded murder in the
south end of Cross City.

A dozen people saw it happen. They saw Joe Lee Hutter, one of
a clan that lived in the heart of Walker Mountain, climb down
from his unshod horse and enter the small grocery store. When he
got drunk on his own home-made corn whisky, he wanted cheese.
He had to have cheese; his system craved it with the same gnawing
urgency that he would crave another drink the minute he began to
feel sober. Old Austin Goings had the best hoop cheese in town.

When Joe Lee entered the store, Austin Goings was waiting on a
Negro woman, a steady customer who was buying a twenty-four-
pound sack of self-rising flour.

"Gimme a pound a' nigger cheese and a box of crackers," Joe
Lee demanded.

"Jist a minute," Austin answered, recognizing his customer, with
whom, a month ago, he had had a few bitter words concerning an
old debt. During almost forty years of selling groceries, he had
grown somewhat crabbed, but he had never left one customer for
another. It was true the Negro woman was slow in choosing the
sack she wanted, for the cloth of each had a different design, from
which she made bright aprons and dresses.

Joe Lee took an old owl head pistol from his jumper pocket. "I said
I want some cheese, I want 'em now, and I ain't going to wait."

"I guess, by damn, you will!"

No one can say whether it was pride or courage or stubbornness
that ruled the old man in that moment, for in the space of another
breath he lay on the floor with a bullet through his head.

As Joe Lee walked out the door toward his horse, he told the frozen-eyed witnesses, "Send the sheriff atter me. I'll git him too."

The newspapers carried Sunday headlines of the crime. Hoxy Weatherall went out with his deputies. Late Sunday afternoon, while waiting below the Hutter barn, one of the deputies felt a bullet take off his hat. Hoxy was no more of a coward than the ordinary man, but he did not wish to die—nor have one of his men die—as a last official act of his tenure in office. He withdrew with his men to Cross City and considered the idea of asking help from the National Guard. The Monday morning headlines carried the news that Joe Lee Hutter was still at large.

The inauguration of county officials occurred on schedule at ten o'clock in the court-room. A few minutes later, in the sheriff's private office, Rufus Frost and Hoxy Weatherall faced each other. Hoxy did not know what to say. He felt somewhat like a person who refuses to wring the neck of a chicken, but gladly sits at the table and devours the crisp-fried meat. His face burned. He stared across the desk at the huge shoulders, the square jaws, sun-hardened face, and cool grey eyes of a man who was neither his friend nor his enemy. At that moment, the idea of the National Guard seemed childish. He handed over the rings of keys, the silver badge. The big hands, hard as rocks, reached out for them casually, as if Joe Lee Hutter were safe behind bars.

Hoxy wanted to walk out without a word. Let the accusing grey eyes settle the matter. After all, Rufus Frost had been sheriff once before. He needed no advice; he could do whatever he pleased. But Hoxy did not move. "I swear, Rufe, I hate to leave you with this Hutter mess."

"Just tell me all you know so far," Rufus said coldly. His voice admitted clearly that he had no stomach for being ambushed either.

"What I know ain't much."

"Did you see his mammie or daddy? Any of his folks?"

The burning in Hoxy's face turned to anger. "Look here, Rufe, let's git something straight. I was sheriff till ten o'clock this morning. I won't take no insinuations about what went on before then."

"I just asked who you seen."

"Nobody. If you want to go roarin' up there with your pistol cocked and your badge shining, that's your business. I tell you one thing, though, if you don't git a belly full of rifle fire going, you'll git a back full leaving. I tried to lay a trap. That's what you better do, if you want to live and stay healthy."

"You know he's still up there?"

"Course to hell he is. He's right there in that big two-storey log house or in the barn. At every upstairs window there's his brothers, or their wives, or old Stu Hutter hisself, all with a rifle in their hands. You go storming up with one man or fifty, and somebody's gonna git killed."

"Maybe. What sort of trap did you have in mind?"

"He'll mosey out some time."

"Yeah. That might be next week or next year."

"Okay. I'm not trying to tell you how to run your office. You're the sheriff now. You've been sheriff before. But you damn' well better bear in mind what you're up against. I know the Hutters. They're wild as goats. Joe Lee, Piney, Abe, the girls, old Stu, all of 'em. I'm just giving you a warning. I'd bet a fat yearling one of that crew killed Jesse Shannon, accidentally or on purpose."

The look he got from Rufus was so strange that he decided to skip the point. "Don't expect them to act like human beings. Maybe it won't be you. Maybe it'll be a deputy, or two deputies, or three. Whatever it is, the sheriff's running the show. He's responsible."

"I'm just like you. I'm not itching to go up there, Hoxy. I didn't sleep much last night for hoping I'd wake up this morning and find out you'd got him. But since I figured you wouldn't, I spent the time working on a plan. I'll have Joe Lee here by sundown. Make it midnight to be safe. Won't be no killings neither."

Hoxy leaned forward and rested one hand on the desk. He believed the big man was laughing at him. His eyes shot burning beams toward the square jaws. "I don't know whether you're making light of what I done or didn't do. But before this day's over, you'll find it ain't no joke. I know lots more about the Hutters than you do. I got a hundred dollars says you can't do it. You want to cover it?"

"Who'd the Hutter boys marry?"

Hoxy softened his feelings and straightened up. "Piney and Abe? They married two Holyoke girls. Sisters. They're wild as the Hutters, if not wilder."

"Got any children?"

"House full. All ages, all sizes, and most of 'em big enough to carry a gun, since they usually learn to shoot before they can walk."

"I'll cover your hundred. What's the old woman's name?"

"Aunt Belle, all I ever heard. I reckon her name's Isabelle."

Rufus studied a ring of keys as if one of them would answer something for him. Looking up slowly, he said, "Much obliged."

Hoxy went to the door, and, holding it ajar, he looked back at the huge shoulders, the solid, brown face. He could not help liking the man. As he closed the door behind him, he had the uncomfortable feeling that he had lost his bet.

Rufus toyed with the keys a few seconds, then opened the door to the larger office and called in Barney.

"I hope you got that gentleman told," Barney said. "When we going up to the Hutters? I might be scared, but I be damned if I'd set around two days and leave a job like this fer somebody else to do."

"I know you wouldn't. Here's what I want you to do. Take Wes and Charlie and meet me at Clear Creek bridge about a hour by sun."

"You mean we ain't going up there till to-night?"

"You not going at all. Your job is to meet me like I say. I'll have Joe Lee with me."

"This is not time fer a stunt, Rufus. You go up there by yourself and Miss Anna won't have a husband and five little boys I know won't have a daddy."

"I'm not going by myself. I don't want no questions. You do exactly like I say. If I don't meet you by sundown, then you can come after me." Grinning at the tremors that crawled across Barney's brown, stunned face, Rufus buckled on his gun, pinned the silver badge to his lapel. For a few seconds he held a pair of handcuffs, pushed them aside and went out.

As he drove toward the Woodall Grammar and High School, he felt the first misgivings about his plans. But he shook off the doubts, and bit off a moderate chew from his plug of tobacco to steady himself. So maybe Hoxy was right, but there were things about hill people that Hoxy didn't know. Lots of ways to kill a cat without choking him with butter. The years of his childhood, in the rocky hills of Sparton, rushed upon him like the wind against his windshield. He remembered old men with pipes, the blue, hazy winters, gum-boots that never wore out and never got warm even when thrust out before a roaring log fire; he remembered the sudden springs, the scattered patches of cotton and tobacco and sorghum: the wine-ripe sorghum tops in late August, the slow turn of the mill, the steady stream of green juice pouring into the sectioned, boiling pan, the skimming, and the miracle of golden hot molasses. And winter again. He slowed to spit a rich arc of bitter-sweet juice clear of his window. He was not wrong, he thought. He could not be wrong about the Hutters or anybody else who lived in the hills.

The day was warm and unusually bright for January. Low-flying clouds passed with polite briefness across the sun. The few remaining leaves fluttered in the wind as if to prove they could outlast the winter. Rufus looked at his watch. It was after twelve—time for the noon recess. They would be waiting for him.

He passed by the lone filling station, the two corner stores, and parked his car behind Robby's eating-place, where children with as much as a dime came at noon for a hamburger and a soft drink. He entered the low shoebox building through the back door. Still holding the knob in one hand, he spotted the four faces that belonged to him. One by one they slipped from their stools and came toward him, all dressed in dungarees and brown leather jackets. Which one would he choose? They followed him to the car.

He placed one foot on the running board of the car and looked at them, as if he did not know already every colour of eye, every turn of mouth, every freckle. Which one?

Morris stood closest to him. "Where we going, Papa?"

"Wait a minute," he answered, like one doing a long row of figures in his mind. His eyes passed over Rex, Bayard, Wayne, and back to Morris. Then quietly he said, "Bayard." After he had spoken, he continued to study them. They remained still, puzzled before this strange scrutiny, not knowing what was happening but sensing it was something to remember. Rufus opened the car door and nodded to Bayard, the pretty face. "Jump in."

The other three moved back, disappointed that they had not been chosen for the mysterious journey. A flutter of questions rolled out of them.

"We're just going on a short trip," Rufus said. "I want you-all to stay here after school. You can play ball in the gym. Peter Cat will come after you a little before sundown." He left them gazing after the car.

Bayard sat forward in his seat, his fingers spread against the dashboard. He was afraid to ask anything, afraid his father might suddenly change his mind and go back for one of the others. But deep down he knew: he knew it had something to do with a man who had killed a man. Stealthily he turned his eyes down to his father's pistol; then, lest he should be caught looking, he shifted his eyes quickly to the road ahead.

Peter Cat was waiting with two horses at Clear Creek bridge. His steady black hand gave Bayard a leg into the saddle, and then he turned to Rufus for instructions.

"Anna see you leave with the horses?" Rufus asked.

"Nossuh. I slipped 'em down through the pasture, like you said."

"Tell her the boys won't be home till late. They're playing ball. You go to the schoolhouse after 'em about a hour by sun. Don't tell her nothing else. No matter what she asks, don't tell her nothing else. You got that straight?"

"I got it, if I can jist keep it. She asks things so natchel, it seem natchel to answer. I reckon I can keep it."

"Aye god, you better keep it." He reined his horse off the road into the shortest trail that led up to Walker Mountain.

For the first mile there was not room enough for the horses to walk abreast. Rufus glanced frequently over his shoulder to watch the bright, innocent face that bobbed up and down behind him. He had the feeling that he had chosen well. Though he did not put the thought into words, he knew there was a certain lack of boyishness, a certain beauty in the face behind him that made it different from the others. A tenderness, it might be called. A mysterious quality that must have come from Anna. The next minute he was fighting a wave of guilt. Had he chosen for this act his least favourite son? He flicked the horse with the rein. Of course not. He had no favourites. A son was a son. But the flick of the rein did not destroy the small, voiceless voice: So a son was a son? Dean was a son. Why didn't you choose Rex or Morris, even Wayne, who were all no doubt more eager to go?

He flicked the horse again, and almost in the same motion reined him back and waited for Bayard to pull alongside. The trail had widened.

"You not afraid, are you?"

"Nossir."

"You know why I picked you?"

"Nossir."

"Well . . ." For the briefest second the reason had been clear in his mind. Now it had gone like a shooting star. He thought of other things. The trail grew steeper, broken by small gullies and rock ridges. The horses slowed. Occasionally one stirrup brushed against another.

"What're you thinking?" Rufus asked.

"I was thinking I'll miss my music lesson this afternoon."

"Can't you make it up?"

"Yessir; but she doesn't like for us to miss."

"I didn't know you had a lesson on Mondays."

"Yessir; I've always had a lesson on Monday."

Rufus flicked the horse again and rode ahead. It was too late to turn back.

The horses began to sweat. The wind grew stiffer, bending tall saplings as if a weight hung in the tops. From bare ridges they looked down into a valley of blue space. Far below a school of blackbirds moved like ants across smoked glass. When I get back, Bayard said to himself, I'm going to write a poem about falling out of a mountain. He looked with anxiety toward his father's big neck, afraid that his thoughts might travel like whispered words.

Half a mile farther on, they came across small patches of last year's cornstalks, the snaggy roots of sorghum. The yelp of a hound travelled on the wind like an arrow. A minute later they came to the edge of a wide clearing and stopped. Two hundred yards ahead of them was a long, two-storey log house. At either end of the house smoke rose from rock chimneys, the only sign of life. They dismounted; Rufus tied the horses to a low limb of a water oak. "Just stay close to me," Rufus whispered. "Won't nothing happen."

They walked slowly up the path. Rufus glanced at the face beside him. If it had grown paler, he could not tell it. The yelping of the hound had ceased. The only sound was their footfalls. The wide, open hall straight ahead was empty, except for an armchair

made entirely from finger-willows. At the west end of the porch
two bright patchwork quilts swayed from a line. They reached the
clean-swept yard and stopped. From the right centre of the hall,
the slight creak of hinges broke the stillness. Bayard moved nervously. Then a vertical row of young heads was thrust out from the
facing; there were four, two boys and two girls. The four pairs of
dark eyes, stacked six inches apart, looked quietly and waited.
They demanded nothing.

"Could I see Aunt Belle?" Rufus asked.

There was no answer, but the tallest head disappeared. The other
three remained. Not an eye nor a lip moved. Rufus moved forward
and placed one foot on the lowest porch step. The tallest head
returned to its position, silent and immobile.

"Did you tell her?" Rufus asked.

The tallest head nodded the full measure of an inch.

Through the hall Rufus saw the well in the back-yard, the rope
coiled neatly beside the pulley. Beyond the well was a strip of
garden covered with bright turnip greens. Beyond the garden was
the barn, where a few cows lay with their faces turned toward the
winter sun. Rufus was about to say something to the children when
Aunt Belle walked past them into the hall.

She was a tall, straight figure. Though her face was lean and her
arms and hands were thin, her body appeared to be huge. A scarf
covered her head; a small afghan was thrown loosely about her
shoulders. "You a Govermint man?" Her voice was deep, hiding
its anxiety.

Rufus took off his hat and nodded. "I'm Rufus Frost, Mrs.
Hutter."

She cleared her throat. Her eyes noted the silver badge, the pistol,
and then rested on Bayard.

Rufus put his hand on Bayard. "This is one of my boys, Aunt
Belle."

She cleared her throat again. Her old eyes remained fixed, their
fierce light feeding on a time long since gone. Her cheeks leaped
with tiny quivers, as if something flew around inside her mouth.
With a birdlike jerk of her head, she turned to the vertical row of
faces. "Don't stand there like a bunch of guineas! Come out an'
say howdy to this here child." The four poured into the hall. They
said nothing, but the old woman seemed not to notice. She sat
down in the willow chair. The sharp black toes of her shoes showed
beneath the hem of her dress. It was obvious that she intended the
next action to come from someone else.

Rufus looked through the hall to the garden. "I been looking at
that patch of sallet. . . . I wish I'd come after a mess of it, and
nothing else. . . ." His eyes turned to her; he rested one hand on
Bayard's shoulder. Before he could go on, she waved the four

children into the room from which they had come. She waited. "You know why I'm here," he added.

She cleared her throat again. She waited, as if she heard a sermon and so had neither right nor intention of answering.

"Sometimes . . . a sheriff has to do things that he wisht to the good Lord he didn't have to do. I can't promise much. But I know this ain't easy for you. I know, because I got five boys of my own. I can promise just one thing for your boy. He'll be treated all right as long as he's in this county, and I'll see that the State gives him a good lawyer. If he goes now, without no trouble, that'll help him some."

The long silence began again. She sat so still and breathed so quietly that it seemed as if she would remain there all winter before she would part her lips for one syllable. Then suddenly her eyes let go of distance and rested on Bayard. "What's yore name?"

"Bayard." The word was jolted out of him.

"What did you come fer, child?"

He looked hopelessly at his father. A tinge of red crept up his cheeks, around the blue eyes, and into the mass of short blond hair.

"I brought him, Aunt Belle, to show you that I wanted all this business to be peaceable."

She cleared her throat again; this time with a prolonged, resigned cough. "Marlene!"

The girl's head popped out beside the door facing.

"Tell yore Uncle Joe Lee that Ma wants him on the front porch."

The girl leaped out of the hall and ran past the garden toward the barn. Rufus heard the first sound of steps upstairs. Looking up, he saw the faces of a man and woman pressed against a clouded window pane; he also saw two rifles.

Joe Lee rode a few yards ahead of Rufus and Bayard, who doubled on one horse. His shoulders were rounded and his neck was bent stiffly forward. Across the back of his wrinkled jumper a few pieces of hay clung like beggar-lice. Once Rufus rode alongside Joe Lee, and having cut a quid of tobacco for himself, he offered the plug to his prisoner. But Joe Lee shook his head. They went on at a slow pace, the stillness broken only by the sound of hoofs and Rufus warning Bayard of low-hanging limbs. For Bayard, the trip seemed more dangerous and wonderful with each step that brought them nearer home. He locked his arms around his father's waist, not so much because the trail was rough, but because he felt he was as strong and brave as the big man he held.

From a narrow opening they looked down again on vast blue space. Bayard felt as if he could leap off the horse and sail for miles to a harmless landing. He drew his legs tense to keep from kicking the horse's flanks. His father spat a mouthful of juice into a cross-wind; he felt part of it splatter across his wrist. Leaning forward, his head pressed against the side of the huge back, he stared at the golden drops. He made no effort to shake them off. They turned cold and dried. Before this day, he might have been offended at his father; but now he understood and did not mind. He was rather proud of the golden marks.

"I'm glad you took me with you," he whispered.

"We won't tell nobody what happened up there," Rufus said. "We'll just let 'em guess."

When they turned into the road above Clear Creek bridge, they saw two cars waiting. The three deputies stood by one; Hoxy Weatherall sat on the fender of the other. Joe Lee looked back at Rufus, for the first time during the long ride down. They stopped a few yards in front of the cars. Joe Lee slid out of the saddle. Barney motioned him into the deputy's car. "Ain't you going with me all the way?" Joe Lee asked.

"They'll treat you all right," Rufus answered, and, turning to Charlie, who held a pair of handcuffs, he said, "You don't need them. He's all right." The four got into the car and drove off.

Hoxy had not moved from the fender. He looked up with a half-squint. "Rufus, how'd you do it?"

"Telling no secrets," Rufus said, shaking his head.

Hoxy stood up. "I come prepared to pay, but I figure it goes to this young feller instead of you. Still, you're due some credit fer knowing that even a Hutter wouldn't shoot a man down with his kid beside him." He stepped forward and stuffed five bills into Bayard's jacket pocket.

Rufus took Bayard's arm and helped him transfer to the other horse. "Where'd you think I was born, Hoxy? In the Delta?" They left Hoxy standing beside his car, his shadow long and crooked in the last pale rays of the winter sun.

They rode abreast at a smooth pace. Rufus felt a great burden lifted from his shoulders, and it seemed that the burden had nothing to do with the Hutters.

"What's this money for, Papa?" Bayard asked.

"Just a bet I made."

"Did he think they'd shoot at us?"

"Yeah; he did."

"Did you?"

"I didn't know, son."

"Are they different from us?"

"Not much different." After a while he added, "But some. Ever'body likes different things. Like maybe Rex wants to play football and Wayne basketball and Morris baseball, and you want to read a book or play the piano."

"But why would anybody like to kill?"

"I don't know about that."

Bayard rode close and held out the five bills. "Here's your money."

"You can keep it. If you save your money, you could buy the piano you want." Both of them noticed he was speaking of a piano with the same natural ease he would speak of a horse.

Bayard laughed. "You don't know how much a piano costs."

As they rode up to the house, Rex and Wayne and Morris and Jarvis came running to meet them. Rufus dismounted and handed his reins to Bayard. "You boys take the horses on to the barn. I've got to go make peace with your mother. I'm afraid it's gonna be a big job."

"She's mad at everybody," Rex said.

The four looked up at Bayard with awe and envy. A medley of cries rang out. "Did they shoot at you, Bay-bay? Did they shoot at you?"

He grinned down at them, holding his secret though it fluttered inside him with wild wings. When they laughed at him about his music lessons and stole his poems and teased about his pretty face, he would not have to do anything. He would merely keep silent and they would remember this day. They would marvel at all the things they did not know, would never know. But he would know and his father would know and the bird inside him would never die. He had a great belief it would some day sing.

Supper was over, but peace had not been established between Anna and Rufus. They sat uneasily before the small fire in their room, she working on a doily, he fussing with the paper though not reading a word of it.

"Why don't you say something? Dammit all, cuss me out and git it over with!"

"That wouldn't get it over with."

"What're you gonna do? Hold it against me all the rest of my life?"

"I won't; but Bayard might."

"Him? He wouldn't take a million dollars for going, and I'm glad I took him."

"You see! You're still not sorry."

"No; I'm not."

"Risk a child's life, and you're not sorry. How can you explain that to me?"

"You don't understand maybe." Now, Todda would get his point; she understood hill people.

"There's a lot about it I don't understand. Suppose they had shot? Just suppose that?"

"If they had you'd be a widow to-night. It woulda been at me and they wouldn't a' missed. You'd still had your five sons."

Silence caught the room again. Anna's fingers worked more rapidly.

"But they didn't!" he burst out. "And they didn't because Bayard was there." Yes, Todda would get that, easily.

"All right; they didn't. I know that."

"You're just mad," Rufus said.

"I reckon I am."

"But you'll git over it."

"I reckon I will. But will Bayard?"

"My God! You're mad at me because I went. The others are mad at me because they couldn't go. Bayard's the only friend I got left in this house." He got up and went to the door.

"Where are you going?"

"Going to see me friend. If he turns against me, I'll go stay with the Hutters."

He went downstairs, entered Bayard's room, and began to pull off his clothes in the darkness. Bayard raised up to discover what was happening. "Papa? That you?"

"Scoot over, son. I'm in deep trouble with your mother."

Bayard moved toward the wall; Rufus slipped under the covers.

"Did I git your warm place?" He put his arm around Bayard. "I'll git you warm."

"Is Mother that mad?"

"Yeah." He pulled the small body close to him, rubbed his face against the boyish throat.

"We could take that money and buy her a present."

"Naw; it'll be all right. She'll git cold up there by herself. She'll change her tune in the morning."

Bayard thought it was all rather wonderful.

But Rufus was beginning to doubt, and once he admitted the doubt he began to sink in a quicksand of misgivings and humiliation. Dethroned, defeated, his arm unconsciously closed tighter and tighter about Bayard.

"You're hurting me, Papa."

The huge arm relaxed. "That all right?"

"Now it is," Bayard said.

They went to sleep like lovers.

4

IT is October and the leaves flutter down on Court Square. When you are in office, Rufus thinks, the years go by quicker. It is like crawling round and round on a huge, inflated inner tube, patching one lead after another until even the patches have to be patched.

Rufus, I've got to have twenty-five dollars. My wife's sick. You hand over two tens and a five, and after the man is gone you put his name down in the Book. He may repay, he may not; but you put his name down in the Book under the R's, and notice the full pages. There are a few pages completely filled, though often a line is drawn through a name and you know that man has paid.

Under the Q's you notice the name of Gary Queen; not once, but three times, listed for odd amounts: seven dollars, nine dollars, three dollars. He is a small man with dried yellow skin. All day he stands on Court Square with his hands in his overall pockets, wearing the same grey coat, khaki shirt, and a green tie tucked inside the bib of his overalls. Where does he go at night? Not far, because he is there again in the morning.

The name that appears most often is under the K's. This man sits on the green benches all day and whittles. Once each month he comes to the door of the sheriff's private office; he pulls his trouser leg up and shows a right leg purple from ankle to knee. You think: if he does not move carefully, the flesh will fall off the bone. About two dollars, he says. He goes away with the two bills in his hand; you have never seen him put them into his pocket.

A woman comes to the office and asks for twenty dollars. Every spark of life in her face and eyes seems to flow downward through her swollen body to her unborn child. You think of labour-ridden women of your childhood. Caught in a moment of remembering, you hesitate. She believes she will be refused. Hit's a lot to ask, she says, but Dr. Kemp's got to where he won't hardly come 'less you show him the money first. I don't hardly know what we'll do. Hit's twenty dollars he charges. You take three ten-dollar bills and hold them out to her. For a minute she is puzzled. Hit's twenty dollars he charges, she repeats. She leaves one of the bills on the desk and goes out. You put the bill in the corner of the desk drawer; it stays there for a week.

The months go by. She returns. Hit's twenty dollars he charges, she says. You hand her three tens, but she will take only two.

Two years pass. She returns a third time, her head tied in a plain scarf, her body too large for the neat print dress. Hit's twenty-five dollars he charges now, she says. You give her three tens. Ain't you got a five? she asks. No, you answer. Ain't you got five ones? Nothing but tens, you lie, taking a curious pleasure in forcing something upon her. She leaves. You sit down and prop your feet on the desk, a rare gesture for you, and feel a wonderful contentment because you have won. The woman returns through the private door, lays five dollars at your feet, and leaves. You take out the Book and make a third entry under the X's, because you do not know her name. You hope you will never know her name. She is Mrs. X; that is all. But there are days when her face comes to you like a flash;

you think of her children: boys or girls? You wonder what names she has chosen. You count the months and know that her time cannot come again while you are in office; you feel a loss. More than once you have wished that you could sleep with her. Why you do not know, but the desire is sharp and clear and sets you on edge for hours.

A woman comes into your office. She is grey-haired, sixtyish, and meek, until the doors are closed and you two are alone. Her finger shakes madly. You're ruining my boy, she says, you and none other. Any fool knows folks that want to drink are going to drink. You drive out all the whisky, and what's Lester going to do? I can tell you: drink mouth-wash! It drives him wild! Her steady eyes kill the anger in you. You answer: There's plenty of good whisky at The Golden Circle and the North End Club. If Lester had been to church, he'd know it. It's been announced from ever' pulpit in the county, except the Catholic. Are you Catholic? she asks. No, ma'am. You don't think I'd be sheriff if I was? She confides as she reaches the door: I'm a Methodist, but Lester don't belong anywhere. The door closes, and you wonder if it could be some half-baked temperance union trap—not that it matters.

But one day you meet her again, face to face crossing the street; she nods and smiles. You tip your hat and wait until she is well past before you spit the full mouth of tobacco juice toward the kerb.

The trial of Joe Lee Hutter is drawn out through two sessions of court. You see that the State gives him a good lawyer. The sentence is ninety-nine years. One night Anna asks you if the Hutters could have killed Jesse. Certainly not, you say. She is a bit puzzled at the certainty.

Gray Leeven, Manager of the Farmer's Feed Co-operative, comes to your office to swear out a warrant against one of his clerks, who has made false bills and entries and done away with $2,882.25. The State auditor has uncovered the fraud. Before you can serve the warrant, the clerk appears in your office. He is dressed in clean overalls, clean-shaven, and hollow-eyed from lack of sleep. I know ain't nobody going to believe me, Mr. Frost, but I never stole a penny in my life. I made out a lot of bills, but I never wrote nothing except what Gray Leeven told me to. I had to work. I got seven kids. I done whatever I was told. I didn't know it was anything wrong.

You believe him. Something about his overalls and the leather band running to his dollar watch and the clean cut of his face. You believe him, too, because you know Gray Leeven is a swindler: you saw him crowd about tired, bewildered schoolteachers, cash their warrants for 60 cents on a dollar; smile and click his little false teeth and make them feel it was a real service, for the banker had said State funds had not arrived. But when the day's business was finished, Gray Leeven walked down an alley, entered the back door of the bank and split his 40 per cent. profit with the banker, who died a year later and was buried in a solid copper casket, and was wept over by teachers who remembered all the wonderful things the 6 per cent. man had done for them. So you believe the man in his overalls. You talk to the supervisors. The jury is fixed. The man in overalls is free. And when you pass him you wonder if he knows what you have done. You hope he does not, for you have done it before for those not innocent. Under the G's you list his name and the fifty dollars you have paid for his lawyer; and a cold chill catches your shoulders when you wonder what would have happened to the man in overalls if you had not believed him.

You make a mental note to see that Gray Leeven is billed before the next Grand Jury. It will do no good, of course, except that you will have the pleasure of seeing him click his little false teeth faster than ever, spend $2,000 to clear himself, and have $882.25 left over.

Sidney comes into your office. You are glad, because he does not come often. He is always at home, fencing, terracing, painting his barn, pruning his orchard, wading through a flock of white leghorns, feeding his stock. Instead of the old yellow Strickland house, he has a small white bungalow with green shutters. Sidney and Amy do all their own work; not even a Negro woman to help with the washing. Yet they never look tired. They are the happiest people you know. But sometimes you are sorry for them: they have had two stillborn children, a girl and a boy. Sometimes you send Jarvis to spend the night with them. In June you send all the boys to help with the hoeing. They like it. They would rather work there than at home.

Sidney sits beside the desk, silent as a prisoner, waits for you to talk. He is hard and lean; you think of him as a son. Finally he says: I'm gonna buy a new pick-up, Buddy. I can't hardly afford it, but I need it. I want you to go look at it. You go. You are glad he asks you about such things.

A letter comes from Todda. Though she does not say so, you know it has something to do with Dean. You take Sidney with you. He is like a young boy. He blushes when you tease him about a waitress. You ask if he has ever made love to anyone except his wife. He answers No. After supper you go alone to Todda's. She had moved to a new place. She had not seen Dean for a month. What is to be done? Nothing. The old magic burns fiercely; there are no unkind words. You make love to her, never once kissing her lips. When it is over you ask intimate questions about her life with Luther, the railroad man. Before you leave, you handle his picture on the small round table. At the hotel, you wonder what you will tell Sidney. But he is asleep. You take a careful bath and get into bed beside him. You do not feel clean or unclean. You think of the old magic; there is a strong urge to dress and return to her.

Driving home, you talk of land and cattle and a murder case set for the next session of court. Sidney asks nothing of the night before. There are so many things you would like to tell him; but the winter sunlight shines through the car windows and makes everything unreal. Everything except the old magic: the sunlight cannot touch it; it is deep inside you. You offer Sidney a chew of Old Apple. He takes it and you are surprised. You feel: he is with me; no matter what I have done or will do as sheriff, he is with me. Occasionally he rolls down the window to spit. You drive more slowly to prolong the pleasure of the trip.

You do not care much about football, but you move a family to your place so the son can play right halfback for Woodall County High. He's a good boy, the coach tells you, but he runs too high and he can't cut inside. If I had another runner to go with Rex, we could git some place. The line's all right. You see, Mister Fross (he never pronounces the "t"), you got to have two good runners to fool a defence. Like it is, they know it's going to Rex or ain't going nowhere no-way. I heard they was a boy at Roots we might could git, if we could rig up something for his daddy. You try, but the daddy doesn't want it rigged. Woodall settles for five won and four lost and waits until the next year.

The boys come home with questions. Papa, what's the capital of Oregon? I don't know. Ask your mother. Salem, darling. Papa, when was the Louisiana Purchase negotiated? Ask your mother. 1803, she says. Is this right, Papa? $A^2 - 5AB + 6B^2 = (A - 2B)(A - 3B)$. Ask your mother. Yes, that's right, she says. Jarvis looks up from a watch he is taking apart: Mother knows everything and Papa don't know nothing. There is nothing to do but laugh; still, the laugh hurts your throat. Anna knows. She gets up and punches at the fire. Aye god, you think, at least you are learning to talk better.

Wayne sits one night crying not to go back to school. I'm not smart like Rex and Bayard, he cries. He cries until you stand him between your legs. What got that in your head? you ask roughly. Miss Hooper said so; she told me. You cannot answer. You look for Anna, but she is upstairs. You want to go somewhere alone with Wayne.

Morris never worries one way or another. He comes home with long rows of C's. He likes baseball and is trying to learn how to throw a slider. Sometimes he trades with Bayard to fill out his workbook; you pretend not to notice. You overlook many things.

You watch Rex shave. He is suddenly a man, a senior, a star. He is gone from the bathroom, and you stand before the basin, lathering your face, seeing patches of grey in your hair.

It is an early fall afternoon. Through an upstairs window you see Rex returning from football practice, flanked by Wayne and Morris. On his left cheek is a bright red abrasion. You hear him downstairs talking to Bayard, who is writing something. He has not had enough on the field; he wants to practise a pass play and has need of another player. The commotion shakes the house. They drag Bayard to the front yard while he squalls: Papa! Papa! You prefer not to judge in this matter. If you are quiet, they will think you are still at the barn. Where is Anna, anyway? These matters are for her. A minute later Bayard is back in the house. He storms into your room, face wet with anger. You look surprised, as if you have heard nothing. What's the matter? you ask. I'm going to move upstairs and put a lock on the door! he cries stoutly. Morris stays with Wayne all the time, anyway. Can I do it? You'd better ask your mother, you say. In time, the transfer is made; the lock is installed.

Bayard is mad at Rex and will not go see him play in the season's first game. His light is burning upstairs when you and the others return from the night game. The boys crowd at the foot of the stairs and call: Bay-bay, don't you want to know who won? Not particularly, he answers. But they tell him, anyway. Rex scored three touchdowns, passed for two, and made two extra points and quick-kicked for seventy yards. Did the coach use anybody except Rex? he asks. Rex says to the others: Aw, leave that foggy-headed monk alone. He thinks a quick-kick is what Coach gives a player when he makes an error.

Morris and Wayne are hurt because Bayard is spoiling everything. He is spoiling something for you too, for you feel good: you have promised to take them fishing to King Lake to-morrow. You go up the stairs and turn the door-knob without knocking. The door is locked. You pound. The voice inside says: Grease your belly and slide under. You shout: Open this damn' door!

The door is quickly opened. I thought you were Rex, he says. That does not stem the anger that crawls over your body like a school of ants. You're not going with us to-morrow, you hear? Long as you act like this you're not going with me nowhere. First thing in the morning you git a cotton sack and you go to the field with Peter Cat and you stay with Peter Cat. That means all day. How does that suit you? Silence spreads to every corner of the room. He answers slowly: I don't want to go anywhere with anybody when I'm not wanted.

The anger is still crawling, but you close the door and go to your own room. You get into bed and wait for Anna to say something. She lies beside you and acts as if nothing has happened. You know you have lost because you were wrong . . . no, because you asked one question too many. Why would I raise a boy like that? you demand angrily of Anna. You climb out of bed and stomp toward the mantel. You are raging. The ants are gnawing through every pore of your body. The words spill: I'm goddamned tired of having my whole family tell me I'm dumb. I know I'm a hill-billy and never learned nothing but my ABC's, but aye god, I've worked and I've got things, honest or not. I got it for you and for them. I do everything I can for my family. I plan something like to-morrow, and one of them comes along and spoils it and makes me look like a clumsy-ass clown. Then you take sides against me!

She is out of bed with the furious grace of an animal; her eyes shine like those of a cornered cat. You have never seen this before in Anna. You wait a minute, Rufus Frost! I've never taken sides against you but once. Whatever you've done or said, I never have. And that ought to be very clear in your mind. If your family thinks you're dumb, it's something I haven't seen. We're all under your thumb, from bread-tray to horse-trough. If you looked like a clown to-night, you did it yourself. You acted the Great Judge without benefit of trial or jury. It didn't concern you or me either. It concerned Rex and Bayard. They're jealous of each other. I've seen it for a long time. But they'll have to get over it themselves. You might help matters a little by making Rex stay at home to-morrow and pick cotton for tearing up Bayard's papers.

The ants crawl off into the darkness. You have been defeated twice in the space of minutes. You sit uneasily on the side of the bed. Finally you crawl under the covers and know that she is there too. What kind of papers? you ask. Oh, I don't know. Something he was writing, she says. You consider for a while. If Rex started it, why didn't you tend to him? you ask. She answers quietly: I thought Bayard's way was all right. It satisfied him, and Rex felt it.

You think about baseball. You think: They ought to play baseball, and stuff like this wouldn't happen; they wouldn't be jealous of each other. You feel as if you are waiting foolishly for something, as if you have hurried from field to barn to avoid a downpour, while the rain-cloud passes without a drop falling. You turn to Anna and whisper. The love you make together is alive and warm and tender for the first time in two years.

The morning is bright and crisp, with the clear sky of September. As you go toward the barn you see Bayard behind the crib adjusting the strap of a cotton sack to fit his shoulders. You go forward to lift the sentence, remembering something Barney overheard in the courthouse: You can't send a man to the pen if Rufus Frost don't want him to go. You call out cheerfully to Bayard; your tone is in keeping with the bright morning. The sentence is changed. All you ask is help in shucking a bushel of corn for the hogs. Bayard gladly returns his sack to the cotton shed and climbs into the corn crib. Shucking corn is the most satisfying thing you have ever done with your hands; it is to your fingers what good tobacco juice is to your tongue. You notice the slow way Bayard's long fingers work into the shucks. He does not feel what you feel. You know he does not feel it at all. You wonder if he feels it when his fingers rip over piano keys. You wonder if it is the same thing.

How many touchdowns did Rex score? Bayard asks. Three and passed for two, you answer, knowing all is well once again. But Bayard adds: It'll give him the big-head sure enough now. You simply spit and find out there is no juice in your mouth. You remember Morris's long row of C's. You wonder how it would be to have a houseful of girls instead of boys.

In the Thanksgiving game with Cross City, the Roman holiday of Woodall County, Rex drives off tackle from the four-yard line to score the winning touchdown. He is kicked in the face and trots off the field wiping his bleeding mouth, but happy. You drive the boys home. They are feeling the frenzy of victory. Rex nurses a punctured lip and the broken corner of a lower tooth. He looks over his shoulder to the back seat. Did the blood scare you, Bay-bay? Bayard answers: A tooth for a touchdown. From the side of his bruised mouth, Rex whispers to Jarvis, who stands up in the seat and faces Bayard: Rex said you'd trade your p—p for a poem. You want me to lock you up in jail? you ask Jarvis. He sits down.

Men who have been famous tackles and half-backs a decade or two ago come to your office. They want to sign up Rex. One handsome old half-back offers four years of education, spending money, and a new automobile—when he is a sophomore. You think it is some kind of joke, until the other offers come. Colonial University is wiser. They send a pleasant little man with dark glasses. He hardly mentions football. He talks of Rex's high scholastic record.

Two weeks before graduation Rex becomes a magic diplomat: he gets Bayard to help him write his valedictory address. The night arrives. You and Anna are ushered to front row seats. Off-stage to the right, Bayard is at the piano. He plays something you have heard a hundred times within the last week. You listen to Rex speak. When he pauses, your heart leaps for fear he is forgetting. You do not remember a word, but you think it is the most splendid thing you have ever heard. When Rex stands to receive his diploma, the Principal pauses. Then he adds: May I say that Rex Frost is not only the first All-state football player in the history of this school, but he has also set a new scholastic record with an average of 96·1. There is a great ovation, and you wonder if it is in order for you to cheer too. As you wonder, you glance at Bayard, who sits motionless with head slightly bowed. You feel sorry for him; you think he has been conquered at last.

The summer passes and Rex is gone. You feel as if he had died.

There are few arguments, no fights in the house now. There is more laughter at the breakfast table. Anna is nervous these days: she is passing through the change of life. You are pleased that nothing is changing in you, except you must fasten your belt another notch nearer the end.

It is quiet work in the office. There are no murders, no rapes, only a burglary now and then, a few drunks, and a fist fight in the south end of town. Barney can handle everything.

You go to Memphis alone. You stay with Todda. Her new place is fresh and bright and sparkles with red curtains. In the night, Dean telephones her from somewhere in Mississippi. You wonder what the trouble is. Nothing, she says; he just called. It is not exactly the old magic, but it is magic none the less. Not a cross word passes between you. In the morning you leave with the autumn sun pouring through the windows.

It is October again and the leaves are falling on Court Square. You count the time until your reign is over: two months and nineteen days. You feel everything is ending. Through the office window you look at the falling leaves. They remind you of the bright curtains in Todda's place. You will not go there again, you think. But you know the falling leaves and autumn sunlight are playing tricks with you. Barney! you call urgently. You want to talk to him, though you have nothing to say. You thumb through the Book and listen for Barney's approach.

5

REX streaked up the steps of the dormitory to his second-floor room, and after thirty seconds of frantic searching found his book of *Great Short Stories* under the radio. Remembering it was chilly outside, he jerked a sweater (adorned with a football, four stripes, W for Woodall, and a star for All-state honours) from his closet and struggled into it on his way downstairs. He had no intentions of being late for Old Krit's class. While he did not seriously consider the tales of how Old Krit bashed skulls with his walking cane, he was halfway afraid of the bespectacled little fossil. So he ran, took his seat on the second row near the window and opened the book to the selection: "The Apple Tree." But he did not read. His eyes shifted two seats to his right and settled on the legs of Peggy Featherstone. He mused on the cruel twist of Fate that had made her name Featherstone instead of Forrest and shoved her two seats away from him. He was about to speak to her across the big fat-boy barrier named Forrest when Professor Kritemier tapped the door facing with his cane to announce his arrival. The class stood, and remained standing until the little man had placed cane, notes, and books on the shining desk and seated himself.

With hardly a second's glance across the room, the professor announced, "I find Mr. Hauser and Miss Kane absent. Splendid. Perhaps they are under some apple tree watching for the bogle. Mr. Porter, you do not understand my pleasantry, do you?"

"Nossir."

"Obviously, you have not read your lesson, Mr. Porter. But don't worry. The custom of reading assignments was obsolescent with the arrival of the Monroe Doctrine. It is now obsolete. And you are—shall we say?—*à la mode*. You have heard of the Monroe Doctrine, Mr. Porter? It has nothing to do with the Baptists." He adjusted his books to the centre of the desk. He always brought several books to class; he never opened one of them. Nor did he refer to his notes, though they were placed carefully before him.

"To-day we are studying the singing and the gold: which is, first of all, the sad music of what might have been. A proposition that has brushed the minds of the common herd and stirred the minds of the sensitive throughout the ages. But that is only the beginning. It is through the minute that the universal is most ably expressed. Mr. Porter does not follow me. Mr. Porter has not read his lesson. I presume that Mr. Porter sat in the Grill last night, preferring jazz to the still, sad music of humanity. It is the business of Art, of fiction, to create. . . ." He spoke for forty minutes. Then he pulled his books and notes a few inches toward him to signal the end. "And when you come to the Great Judgment, Mr. Porter, kindly refer to one or two of the points I have mentioned. By Great Judgment I mean the examination, a word that derives from the latin *exigere*: to weigh accurately."

Eugene Shook, an end on the freshman football team, leaned forward ready to break for the door.

"Retain your composure, Mr. Shook. There are nine minutes remaining. Nineteen years ago I had a student rise too early, and I admit without remorse I cracked his skull with this very cane—it's quite durable. This mad disease of rushing baffles me. In my youth, if one missed a stage coach, he simply said, 'That's all right, Father. I'll go next week.' To-day, if one misses one section of a revolving door, a fit of anger transpires that verges on apoplexy. Perhaps you'd understand me better, Mr. Shook, if I said: Hold your potato if it ain't too hot. Mr. Frost!"

"Yessir."

"Are you staring at those . . . those shapely devices by which Miss Featherstone commutes to class? No; don't answer. It was merely a rhetorical question. Would you stand up, Mr. Frost?"

"Yessir."

"Stand near the window, please. Let the autumn light bathe those splendid shoulders. Would you take off that jacket, please?"

Rex shed his jacket and draped it across the back of his chair.

"Class, observe this young man closely. Straight shoulders, a neck with exquisite power, a face off Olympia, wind-blow golden hair, narrow hips. Would you kindly lift one trouser leg, Mr. Frost? Go ahead. Go ahead. We know you're properly embarrassed. A little higher, please. Thank you. Note the classic beauty of that calf. Mr. Frost, why are you for ever staring at Miss Featherstone? It would be much simpler to look down and raise your own trouser legs, and would save Miss Featherstone a world of embarrassment."

"May I sit down now, sir?"

"Oh, no, Mr. Frost, if you please. Now, class, don't you agree with me: isn't there something about Mr. Frost that reminds you of the singing and the gold? That is, if you take him without his jacket. Do you have another jacket, Mr. Frost?"

"Yessir."

"Then be so good as never to darken the door of my classroom again with that alphabetical monstrosity drooped over the back of your chair. Come in your shirt-sleeves, your pyjamas, your football togs; come naked if you choose. But not in that ghoulish garment. Give us a chance to see the singing and the gold."

"Professor Kritemier, would you mind if I sit down?"

"Mr. Frost, why should you object to being made a spectacle before twenty-seven people while on the gridiron you occupy a similar role for thousands, with those splendid calves showing? It has come to my attention that you are the great cleated hope of this University. Is that true?"

"I couldn't say right now, sir. I'll ask Coach Kellogg this afternoon and give you an answer at the next meeting."

"Would you do that? It would be a great service. I'm an old man, but, to coin a phrase, I try to keep up with the times. Of late I have heard the name of Frost on so many tongues I do believe the fickle mob has forgotten the days when Goethe and Dostoevski and Dante and Homer played for this University. Goethe was a tower of strength in the middle of the line. And Dostoevski! Oh, he was great! Of course, the other schools accused us of going up into Pennsylvania and giving him a horse and buggy in addition to his tuition and books and board and fifteen dollars spending money each month. Jealousy. Green-eyed jealousy it was. But that didn't stop Dossy. I remember one game, the last of the season. A cold, murky day in December. Even had snow. If you think he was afraid to pass in the shadows of his own goal, you don't know Dossy. He had guts! But no tricky end-around stuff for him. He loved best of all to go right up the middle, busting through arms and lungs and hearts and loins. Oh, he got inside you and then exploded. I think he was probably the greatest of them all. Old Homer couldn't see good, you know—a great handicap. And Dante fell in love with some girl. A mad affair. It got to the point that he wouldn't touch those juicy steaks on the training table. Coach Kellogg knows how to hand such things now, but in those days we had a dumb coach. I don't recall his name, but he was slightly—shall we say?—cracked. He'd gather the boys under a tree and just sit there and talk to them. Finally killed himself. Took poison: no more worry about winning on Saturday afternoons. Mr. Frost, you're too young; you never saw Dostoevski play, did you?"

"Nossir."

"A great pity." He frowned. "You've heard of him?"

"Oh, yessir. My brother saw him play."

"Really? Where?"

"Karamazov Stadium."

"Splendid! Mr. Frost, you are flirting with an A."

The buzzer sounded. As the classroom emptied, the professor hunched his shoulders forward and frowned as if struck in the small of the back with an arrow. When he knew that he was alone he closed his eyes and weighed the hour as satisfactory, but not exceptionally so. Nowadays, his mind could measure future time almost with the same clarity it measured the past. They will not love me, he thought, but they will remember me.

It was dry October, and leaves were burning. The spirit of Woodall High had subsided somewhat, for its great line and star halfback were gone. There was nothing left to do but write themes, read poems, memorize dates of battles, factor $A^2 - B^2$, and chase butterflies for biology. That was not much worse than watching your team get beaten by six touchdowns. Miss Whitlan, the English teacher, felt the dullness too. She did not know very much about football, but she knew the crowds this year were slim, and there was little of last year's frantic fever which had made the long weeks of butchered poems and unreadable themes more bearable. A few weeks before it had occurred to her that she would not put her eyes out this year deciphering the work of children who had never learned to write a legible hand, much less to think. Standing before the class, stumbling through their own hastily devised pieces, might help them to understand the cruel red marks of her pencil.

She entered the sixth period junior class in time to see a spit-ball bounce off the head of Willie Smithers. She promptly ignored the shot, having no doubt that Willie had started it, and opened the text to *The Cask of Amontillado*. She drew a deep breath and remembered that to-morrow was Saturday: she was going to Cross City for a pair of new shoes. She asked a few questions about the day's lesson, got fewer answers, and as she talked about the story she found herself wondering whether John Honeycutt, history teacher and assistant coach, was ever going to marry her. If and when he asked, her decision was ready, for nothing could be worse than this hopeless task of flinging knowledge at empty heads thirty hours a week. "Now," she said, closing the text as if she too helped seal the wall against poor Fortunato. "Who's scheduled to read for us to-day?" She opened her small black grade book and read down the list of names. "Bayard, I've got you marked for to-day. Are you prepared?"

"Yes, ma'am."

Bayard stood before the class and gave a hasty glance toward Willie Smithers. He felt a slight misgiving. When Willie had read, two weeks before, he had included in his philosophy an attack on crooked politicians. This he had taken from his father, Willie Smithers, Sen., who was openly an enemy of the Frost régime, and had been an enemy since the day Rufus Frost stopped young Willie from shooting firecrackers on Court Square. Bayard felt the misgiving because young Willie was hefty and tough enough to play first string tackle, now that last year's great line had departed. He sensed that Willie was expecting a rebuttal.

"Now, class," Miss Whitland said, "get out your pencils and paper and be prepared to give a grade to this paper. We're assuming that all words are spelled correctly and all punctuation is in order. I'll check that later myself. Make a note of any words or sentences you question. And watch for unity and coherence."

"What's coherence, Miss Whitlan?"

"Now, Ralph, you know very well what coherence is."

"Yes, ma'am. I know. But I forgot."

"All right, Bayard. Let's hear your philosophy."

Bayard began to read:

My Philosophy of Life

The literal meaning of *philosophy* is the love of wisdom. The Greek word *philos*, meaning *loving*, is combined with *sophos*, meaning *wise*. If I should hold to the radical meaning of the word, my theme would therefore be: My love of the Wisdom of Life. But words, through usage, lose their radical meanings and take on new shadings. Philosophy in this case, then, will mean a body of principles underlying a major discipline.

A philosophy should not have form; it should not be listed one, two, three with subtitles *a, b, c*. The best part of any philosophy should be its infiniteness and not its finiteness. If it must be defined, then its best parts must be destroyed, for you can not define the infinite. A perfect example of this is Christianity. Men have spent almost two thousand years trying to define a few simple truths. The more they have defined the more they have destroyed. Now Christianity is represented by a conglomerate mass of humanity, one ready to bury his nails into another's throat for daring to teach that Christ was sprinkled instead of submerged. Another example is man's futile efforts to define God. He will not let God rest in peace, wherever He is or whatever He is. Man is much more concerned with reducing God to his own level and image than with attaining the higher degree for himself. I believe that man is subconsciously angry because, first of all, he does not know whether there is a God. Next, if there is a God, he does not know what He is. Is He an eagle? Is He a group of clouds? Is He a bearded patriarch who sits somewhere in the sky, in a golden city, on a golden throne? Or is he sunlight and thunder, rain and dry wind, a trillion-fingered creature pushing the grass through in April and picking the leaves in October. You do not know. I do not know. And we are angry and do not even know that.

Good and Evil are the two major forces in the world. They belong to the universe and are a part of it, just as the trees or the oceans or the deserts are parts. Neither can be defined except in their relationship to one another—that is, they oppose each other. In the most general terms, one is creative, the other is destructive; one gives and adds to the wellbeing of life; the other destroys and hinders the wellbeing of life. Since all things die, it must be concluded that all things are involved to some degree with evil. The same with good. Inanimate objects have no life and so have no intrinsic relationship to good and evil.

It is the struggle between good and evil that gives meaning to life. A totally good world would be dull and uninteresting. A totally good person would be dull and uninteresting. I prefer people who have enough evil in their lives to make the good they do seem significant. Like most people in politics, my father has been accused of doing wrong things. Whether these accusations are true or not, they are far less significant than the fact that he screens and paints all of the white and Negro tenant houses on the land he owns. And each house has a good garden, well fenced. Mr. X^2 (I call him that because he is very thick and very wide and looks square to me) criticized my father publicly. When I think of what he said, I remember that Mr. X^2's tenant houses have no screens on the doors or windows, no paint on a single board; and his tenants are not permitted enough land for a garden, nor are their children permitted to attend school in late spring and early fall. But it should be pointed out that Mr. X^2 is Superintendent of the Sunday School and spends much time defining God. Perhaps he does not have time to inspect his tenant houses or his philosophy. To inspect is one thing, to define is another. Rather than death-bed confessions that wipe away the sins of seventy years, my philosophy would include a nocturnal inspection of oneself: Have I stolen bread from the mouth of a hungry child? Have I, because I own eight team of mules and a herd of cattle and a section of land and a painted house, taken advantage of any man, white or black? Have my actions been aimed at making others happy? And would I be afraid if I knew the sun would not rise to-morrow?

I cannot define my philosophy of life. It is a state of mind. It is like lightning or wind or a rainbow or the trillion-fingered creature pushing the grass through in April and picking the leaves in October, the splendid leaves.

He sat down quickly. For a minute Miss Whitlan had stopped thinking of where she would buy her shoes to-morrow and had even pushed John Honeycutt to the back of her mind. "Well," she said, and nodded her head slowly. "Write down your grades and any comments you might have. Remember to initial your paper."

Bayard sat with his head bowed, hearing a rustle of papers and Miss Whitlan walking about making her collection. Then she sat at her desk reading, "A, A, A, I guess, but I don't believe God has a trillion fingers; A, no comment; A. . . ." She stopped and frowned for several seconds. She put the paper aside, picked it up again and read, "This theme is as splendid as the leaves, but the grade should go to his mother. She wrote it."

Bayard saw red creep up the neck of Willie Smithers.

"What do you mean, Willie?" Miss Whitlan asked, and her mind wandered to John Honeycutt, and back to what seemed more and more something she herself could not have written. She was ripe for doubt.

"Skip it," Willie said. "I don't know whether she did or not, but she said something about it to my mother."

She looked at Bayard; the whole class looked at Bayard, who had begun to tremble, an obvious sign of guilt. This was worse, he thought, than all the times Rex had teased him about poems or torn up his work. He would like to kill Willie Smithers.

"Bayard," she asked, "did your mother write that for you?"

He would not answer.

"I'm simply asking you, Bayard. Are you going to answer?"

"No!"

"No; she didn't do it? Or No; you're not going to answer?"

"No; I'm not going to answer!"

"Don't you think that gives me room to doubt?"

"You don't have to be given room; you can take it."

"You want me to send you to the Principal?"

Willie said: "You can't whip him, Miss Whitlan. His daddy will put somebody in jail."

"That's enough out of you, Willie. All you have to do, Bayard, is tell me you did it yourself."

He sulked.

"Are you going to tell me, Bayard?"

"I'm not going to tell you anything."

"I'll have to give you an F."

"You can give me whatever you please."

"I think you're being very ugly."

"I think you're being very stupid. You don't even know who Mr. X² is."

"Who is Mr. X², Bayard?"

"You find out."

"Go to the Principal, Bayard! Immediately!"

As he reached the door, a wave of fear struck Willie. He could not back up his accusation, and all sorts of things might happen: he might be kicked off the football team. "Miss Whitlan, I think I made a mistake. I might have misunderstood."

She motioned for Bayard to wait. "What do you mean, Willie?"

"You see, Bayard is in Mother's Sunday School class. He wasn't there Sunday. His mother said something to my mother. I guess I misunderstood."

"Willie! You told a story on Bayard, didn't you?"

"Nome. Not a story. Just a sort of joke."

"Willie Smithers! Don't you ever . . . ever . . ." She was still saying "ever" and Bayard was still standing in the doorway when the bell rang. She dropped her face into her hands and tried to think about shoes and John Honeycutt. Anyway, the day had ended; the week was finished.

Bayard waited at the school bus. He was afraid of Willie, but he was not going to tuck his tail, any more than he would tuck his tail for Rex. When he saw Willie coming, he said, "It wasn't a joke. It was a barefaced lie!"

"You had no business writing about my daddy!"

"You wrote about mine!"

Then they were behind the bus. For every lick Bayard landed, he was taking five over the eyes and across the nose and on the chin. Children were running from all directions toward the buses, panicky with freedom, paying no attention to the fight in the background. Except Morris. His left arm was loaded with books, his right hand gripped his baseball. As he reached the front of the bus he saw the struggle and the brutal force drawing blood from his own brother. He dropped his books and let go with his fast ball. It caught Willie above the left ear and crumpled him cold to the ground. The ball rolled into the grass and hid itself. Lest he be caught that instant as a murderer, Morris grabbed his books and assumed the air of an innocent bystander. No other, not even Bayard, knew what had happened. The crowd was suddenly there, reviving poor Willie, while Bayard wiped blood from his own face and hands. Some lifted Willie to his feet and others lifted Bayard's miracle fists into the air, shouting, and swearing they saw every magnificent blow. They herded both contestants into the bus before the Principal could arrive.

"I saw it," Ralph said. "It was a right upper-cut to the jaw and pore Willie was out like a light. Sick 'em! Sick 'em! Let's do it all over agin."

Janie Dixon sat beside Bayard and held his books. Her heart beat a song of love. She began to believe that she too had seen every stroke of the great battle. Bayard asked Morris for his handkerchief, but before Morris could get to it (for he was still in a state of mild shock), Jarvis proudly produced his. Janie had the pleasure of putting the soft white cloth into Bayard's hand. Someone pulled back the neck of Bayard's jacket and read the trade-mark, "It ain't no wonder," the voice screeched. "He's wearing a *Samson* jacket." Some of the students found the quip exceedingly funny.

The oldest student on the bus, a twenty-eight-year-old married woman who got up every morning at three o'clock to do her house-work and cook her husband's noon meal before leaving for the long ride to school, looked at the blood seeping from Bayard's face and said, "Willie, you ought to be ashamed."

"Me?" Willie cried. "Me ought to be 'shamed? He cold-cocks me and lays me out in the gravel and you yell shame on me!" He was beginning to take everything as a joke, even the knot above his left ear. Surely everybody knew that Bayard could not repeat his performance if they fought for a million years.

The bus began to move. Morris looked longingly toward the grass and his baseball. Maybe he could find it there Monday. He crawled across a seat, and, scrounging between Janie and Bayard, whispered, "I hit old Willie with my baseball, but I won't tell nobody. Keep him thinking it was you."

Bayard was relieved to have the mystery clarified. Maybe the blood would stop now. Already two handkerchiefs were soaked.

When they reached home, no one was there. While the others raided the kitchen for food, Bayard remained in the bathroom applying hot cloths to his face and hand. In his room, he inspected himself more closely in the mirror: the cut over his eye, the skinned spots on his cheek and nose and chin, the raw knuckles of his right hand. He propped himself comfortably in bed and began to read. Occasionally he stretched his right hand along the covers and went through the motion of several notes from the *Pathétique*. There was something futile about his gesture. It reminded him of trying to kill a wasp in the open air with a Sunday School book.

He heard steps on the stairs and his mother calling. He put his book away and went to her room. She had been told by Morris about the fight, but she was not prepared for the bruised spectacle before her. "Bayard! What on earth did he hit you with?"

"His fist, Mother. Both of them."

"Lie down on the bed there and let me find something to put on it."

He obeyed while she rushed to the closet for iodine. With each rake of the applicator, he flinched and she matched his flinches with tightening frowns. "Don't paint my whole face, Mother."

"Your whole face needs it. There." She finished and sat down beside the bed to observe her patient. "You're the last one I expected to get in a fight like this."

"Why?" He did not want an answer. He wanted to lie there and understand his mother. She was getting old—already past forty—and might die with many things a mystery between them. How could she be satisfied to stay at home and work the way she did for them? Always cooking and ironing (now that Ursa was old and slow) and sorting clothes and cleaning house and working the garden and helping with lessons. Still finding time to carry things to Lady Striplan, who was dying with cancer and didn't know it. How could she be satisfied with all those things that never got her name even into a county newspaper? Now she was here beside him and the others were somewhere else; they had forgotten him.

"Because I didn't think you liked to fight."

"I don't."

"What started it?"

"I guess it started over Papa." He was surprised that she did not look surprised. "Willie read his theme in class two weeks ago, and he wrote something about Papa. So I read mine to-day and I wrote something about his. That was the main reason. Mother, what would you do if somebody said Papa wasn't honest?"

"I don't know what I'd do."

"Don't you think Papa is honest?"

"Well, nobody is perfect, Bayard."

"I know that. But I can tell he's honest because of the way he treats the Negroes. He wouldn't treat them the way Mr. Smithers does. I don't care what else anybody says about Papa. Mother, you can tell whether anybody around here is good by the way they treat Negroes. You can tell more by that than anything. Negroes love Papa. Did you know that?"

"Yes. I think they like him."

"They know people, and they like people that are good, but not too good. That's why they like Papa. I wish I was like Papa, but I'm not. I know why you said you didn't expect me to get in a fight. It's because I'm different. Mother, why am I different?"

"Who said you were different?"

"People say it all the time, even when they don't say anything. I know, Mother, but I don't guess you understand. All the others are like Papa, and I'm not. I never will be. I'm like. . . ." But he would not dare say it. Both of them were relieved that he had broken off sharply and got up.

Anna stood in the doorway, listening to steps rather than watching a bruised figure disappear across the hall into the other room. Her body burned with a sudden, oppressive warmth. It seemed that something was going out of her life for ever, like a dream, like a shooting star, like the robed dead sealed in a marble tomb. Strange words passed through her mind: I had a boy once; he was kind and quiet and sweet. I loved him as much as all the others, no more, no less. God will bear me witness I have measured my love out the best I could. If it has not been enough. . . . The words faded into falling snow. She could feel her body cooling.

She sat down and thought about Rufus. She hoped he would come home early.

I

THE house was dark green. The people who lived along the small street rarely saw anyone enter or leave the green house, which sat an unusual distance back from the street. When they passed to and from work or the grocery store or the cleaners, something about the house drew their attention. They looked, saw nothing more than an empty porch and drawn shades, and passed on with the feeling that black crepe hung on the door. At night they sometimes saw light behind the shades and heard hill-billy music low and clear.

Dean walked by the house and down the street for several blocks before he turned and retraced his steps. Cleve had told him to come at dark; and it was not quite dark yet. He went into a corner grocery, drank a Coca-Cola, and watched the face of a thin, black-haired boy as he placed groceries in tall bags and followed fat, powdered ladies to the parking space outside. Probably works from the time school is out until eight o'clock for 50 cents, Dean thought, and wondered if the boy had sense enough to make off with a few bars of candy and suchlike. Once when he had worked in a grocery he had taken a large safety-pin and fastened a choice steak inside his shirt, had cooked it himself before his mother got home, and then could not eat it for remembering how it had brushed against his naked chest. Anyway, the fun had come in getting it safely outside the store. He put the bottle into the wire rack and started back toward the green house.

There was a light behind the drawn shades, the sound of low music. He smiled at the thought of Cleve listening to music, even hill-billy stuff. He took the key which Cleve had given him and opened the front door without a knock. In the narrow hall, he heard the crackle of a magazine; the next second he was looking into the living-room at a woman instead of Cleve. She sat straight-backed on the couch with her feet tucked beneath her, smiling at the shock on his face. He knew her. He had been knowing her for two or three years, but he expected her to be at the Moon Harvest Café on the water-front rather than in Cleve's living-room.

"You made a mistake, chum."

"Yeah? How's that?" he asked.

"Cleve's playmates come through the back door. Didn't he tell you that?"

"He didn't tell me either way. But the key fits the front door."

"Sure. It fits the back door too. I got one just like it. He was trying you out to see how smart you are. There's a convenient little alley back there and a break in the fence behind the garage. The next time, you better remember it; that is, if you want to make a good impression. That's not a warning; just a helpful hint. Personally, I'd be glad to see you if you came down the chimney. Where you been lately?"

"Around."

"Where'd you bump into Cleve?"

"I forget. Some place around."

"Accidental, huh? Small world."

"Sometimes."

She snapped her head back and pushed at her long golden hair. There was a flicker of mockery in her deep black eyes. "You don't have to be stingy with me. You met him last night at the Hilltop between nine and ten."

"How come you're so sure?"

"I sent him there, you little jerk. But I think I made a mistake."

"I come through the front door and I'm a jerk. Is that it?"

"No. That's got nothing to do with it. I'm thinking about something else."

"You seem to keep up with everybody. Where's Cleve?"

"He's been delayed a couple of hours." She got up and went to the table where a small radio sat. Her thin body, which appeared taller than it was, moved easily as a shadow. He noticed that she was in her stockinged feet. Her shoes lay by the couch. "You don't like this kind of music, do you?"

"I don't like no kind of music."

She turned off the radio and stood on the rug between the table and the window. "Do you remember that night at my place and you swore you couldn't dance? I want to know if you told the truth?"

"I want to know something too. I want to know about that mistake you made."

"The mistake was in telling Cleve about you. You don't want to mix up with him. You ought to pull out. Tell him it's off."

"What's the matter with Cleve?"

"Oh, he's all right. You've been in a few boy scout deals. More fun than anything else. You might even grow out of it. But Cleve . . . his is not boy scout stuff. Not big time either, but it's rougher than the Army." She went to the hearth and held one foot out toward the screen. He was aware of the fire for the first time.

"What else, Jenny?"

"Did I say there was anything else?"

"You meant to. Don't hold out on me."

"I wasn't holding out. I sort of like you, that's all. We had good fun together a few times, didn't we?"

He remembered the times he had been to her place, the small, bright place with flowers, over a second-hand furniture store. From her bed you could look out on the river. If you leaned far enough, until your nose touched the window screen, you could see the bridge like a huge dark mark on the sky.

She turned from the firelight to face him. "Well, did we?"

"Sure we did. But what does that spell?"

"Maybe nothing for you."

He went across the room, pushed her shoes beneath the couch, and turned out the light. "Come and find out."

She went to him.

Dean sat alone on the couch and waited for the sound of steps at the back. He got up and punched at the dying fire, though the room was already too warm. He thought of the radio, but it would be his luck to find nothing more than music or some silly cops-and-robbers story. He wished Jenny had not been there in the first place, and in the second place she should have stayed until Cleve arrived. The magazine was there, but reading was for women who had nothing better to do. He leaned back, closed his eyes, and felt the blood ticking in his temples like a watch. The sound of steps in the back brought him quickly to his feet. Cleve came briskly into the room, moving himself at a gait that seemed unnatural to a rather large and clumsy-looking body. He appeared quite different from the man Dean had met at the Hilltop the night before. Then he wore a large leather jacket, a soft-collared maroon shirt with no tie, and a light brown hat. Now he was dressed in a grey suit, a light grey top coat, an orange, soft-collared shirt with bow tie, a dark green hat with a tiny red feather in the band. His square, clean-shaven face was pleasant enough, but he observed Dean as if he were a stranger. "How long you been waiting?"

"A good while."

"I don't measure time by whiles. I measure it by minutes and hours. Haven't you got a watch?"

"No."

He went to a small table in the corner of the room, opened a drawer and drew out a gold watch with a long gold chain. He pitched it halfway across the room, the chain dangling after it like a kite tail in a heavy wind. Dean succeeded in catching the watch in one hand and the chain in the other.

"Where's Jenny?"

"She's gone to work."

"Couldn't wait, huh?"

"She left a message." He fingered the watch nervously, feeling that Cleve was reading him. He had been foolish, of course; and Jenny should have stayed. He should have had more sense than put his neck in a noose the first day. The silence bothered him. His fingers twisted the watch stem and it seemed that he was winding something inside himself tighter and tighter.

"You need a hat," Cleve said. "I might have one would fit you." He turned back into the hall and toward a bedroom, motioning to be followed.

Dean followed. The tightness went out with a long breath. He looked into a closet, where twenty or twenty-five hats lay crown down. Cleve made a quick survey, selected one, adjusted crown and brim and placed it on Dean.

"Heah; that'll do," Cleve judged. He exchanged his own hat for a darker, featherless green.

They returned to the living-room. Dean looked into the small, cheap mirror over the mantel. He felt himself a totally different person with the dark tan felt drawn a little to one side of his head.

"Okay?"

"Sure."

"What was the message from Miss Jenny?"

"She said if the right customer came in she'd call."

"Nothing else."

"No."

"How long you been knowing Jenny?"

"Two or three years."

"Two? Or three?"

"Two."

"She's all right, don't you think?"

"Sure. Why not?"

He nodded for Dean to follow him. They went to the garage. Cleve took a screwdriver and a pair of pliers and quickly replaced the Tennessee licence plate on his car with one from Alabama. He put the discarded one into a toolbox with several others and snapped the lock. The whole manœuvre was completed in the darkness within a matter of seconds.

In the living-room again, Dean began to notice the pictures and furnishings. Jenny might not have selected them, but he was certain she had arranged them. He loitered about the room, casually inspecting pictures, ash-trays and vases, while Cleve fixed himself bourbon and water. "You don't drink anything but beer, Jenny said."

'That's right."

"Plenty of beer in the ice-box."

"I don't want anything."

"Okay. Every man knows his own thirst."

Dean picked up a small framed snapshot of Jenny standing between Cleve and another man, who, he thought, must be Bill. Gathering courage, he turned toward the fireplace. "What happened to Bill, Cleve?"

"Didn't Jenny tell you?"

"I didn't ask her."

Cleve got up and turned his back to the fire. He was in his shirt-sleeves now; above each elbow was a white rubber band, which pulled his sleeves high on his wrists. Dean noticed that he had thick, hairy forearms and pale, thin hands. "Bill went to California."

"Why?"

"You ask lots of questions."

"I got a right to ask a few."

"Don't race your motor. Bill is greedy. He wants to be a big fish and splash a lot of water. That's the kind that ends up in hot grease. And the minnows—like you—get hooked for bait. If you're smart, you'll play it in the middle: somewhere between a whale and a minnow. You don't wiggle on top of the water and you don't send up a geyser. Bill's all right. But he's thinking too big. The Hounds will get him. They always get that kind. It's like this stuff." He held out his glass. "It's all right till you get to wanting too much of it. Now you've got Bill's case. What kind of notion did you have? You think maybe I painted his wagon?"

"No. I didn't think that. I could've thought of a lot of things."

"Like what?"

He would be bold, take the offensive. "Like maybe there was trouble between you and him and Jenny."

"So women is your worry, huh?"

"Not specially."

"Well, it happens to be mine, in a certain way. But Jenny didn't cause any trouble between me and Bill. You didn't know he was Jenny's brother?"

"No."

"Sit down, and let's settle another matter or two."

Dean sat down in an armchair and waited for a declaration of rights concerning Jenny. He had brought it on himself, he thought; but it might as well come now as later. "Okay. What is it?" he asked, hoping to show that the matter was of no concern to him.

Cleve sat down and stretched his legs out comfortably, not at all like a man anxious about a woman. "This business to-night won't amount to anything: just a little excursion to break you in. But we've got some others lined up. Not big, but big enough. You get a quarter, Jenny gets a quarter, I get a half and foot the bills. House, eats, drinks, car: that's expenses, and on me. If that's not square, don't talk to yourself—or Jenny; talk to me. Start right now if you want to."

"That's plenty fair."

"Like I told you, I'm not in the big time. Maybe I'm not smart enough; maybe it's no guts. I like three. No more. Three's lucky. With the right kind of plans, that's all you need. We plan everything, no matter how little it is. This business to-night we started working on about two months ago. Every ten days the guy comes in to the Moon Harvest for two or three nights in a row; always pays from a thick wallet. Last night he pays with a twenty. He goes back to the Loyola House through the alley. Okay. Maybe he goes that way to-night; maybe he don't. Maybe he's got a pocketful of ones, or nothing. Maybe he don't come in at all to-night. All right. That's a little job. The next big job is six or seven months away. About next November. We started working on it last fall. It's a neat little piece. Full hive and no bees. Down across the state line at Colonial University. We checked every football game last fall. They quit selling tickets when the second half begins. Two sellers take the bag from all six windows, walk a quarter of a mile across the campus into the Administration Building, where not even a janitor is left. We figure to work the University-Tech game next November. Is that a full hive with no bees?"

Dean grinned. He was beginning to have a good deal of respect for this square-faced man who, in spite of his big shoulders and stout forearms, looked somewhat like a college professor.

"Only thing is," Cleve continued, "I nearly get the jitters wondering why somebody don't beat us to it. It's the most natural set-up I ever saw. You ever been to the University?"

"No."

"In the first place, the north fence is a hundred yards from the stadium. The only place you can buy a ticket is at one of those six telephone-booth affairs. The selling's over; they got to take the stuff some place. Everybody with a voice is raising hell and you couldn't attract a Hound's attention with a cannon. So there's four roads out and seven to eight thousand cars. They gonna put up a road block and search two thousand cars in every direction? Maybe. We stay right in the middle of everything. Look at this." He took a pencil and drew hurriedly.

"We relieve the gentlemen at point X. Shove the goods into a suitcase covered with Colonial stickers. You break for the car. I herd the gentlemen to the closet under the stairs. We checked that closet four times last fall. It was never locked, but it's got outside lock-harness stout enough to hold any two for a few minutes. I wait at circle X until you return to the west door. We got four or five minutes to get back to the game, leave overcoats and hats in a certain men's room. I've checked all that too. From that spot we'll take new coats and hats, and join Jenny at a new seat. Let them find the coats in a certain stall behind a certain concrete pillow—that's okay. So we move out with thirty thousand other people and eight thousand cars. Suppose they put up a road block. That's where you fit real nice. You're a college student, complete with identification card, a bright Colonial sweater with a big red letter, and a few stickers on the windshield. We're going home for the week-end. If the Hounds see that and still put their finger on the half-trap in the gas tank, then we better give up, anyway." He talked with animation, but with a strange softness. His brown speckled eyes waited for admiration. "What do you say?"

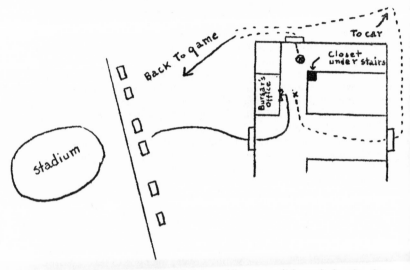

"I say it's terrific." He felt he could not possibly wait for the time to come. "How come you know every detail this far ahead?"

"We had it set for last November, when they played Alabama, but it was pouring rain and the crowd was mainly folks that had already bought tickets beforehand. Why spoil a good deal for four or five G's when you can cool your heels and pick up thirty? Plus the chance to make two or three more checks on everything." He crumpled the sheet of paper with the drawing and threw it into the fire. "Jenny wanted to cut you in on it last fall."

"But you had to look me over for a while?"

"Partly. And then I don't like four. I like three. Three's lucky. Not many times I overrule Jenny. She's bright, and square all the way."

Dean did not want to talk about Jenny. "What do we do between now. . . ."

The telephone rang sharply. Cleve pounced on it like a cat. Dean got up and paced nervously at the edge of the hearth, wishing he could hear.

"Hello. Dorothy?"

"That's right."

"I was calling to tell you . . . just walked in . . . about the curtains. Looks okay. Go on over there. Bye."

Cleve jerked on his coat and straightened his hat before the small mirror over the mantel. His right hand automatically checked his pocket. "All aboard," he said, almost as innocently as a child leaving for a picnic. Dean followed and closed the back door quietly.

The brown Buick moved quietly down the driveway with only the park lights on. Near the kerb, they waited until a passing car was out of sight. Then Cleve turned on the headlights and moved into an empty street.

They parked three blocks from the Moon Harvest and waited like sentries in the alley that led to the Loyola House. It did not occur to Dean that anything might go wrong. He watched Cleve from the corner of his eye and felt the cold seep through his shoes. The thin black gloves on his hands seemed heavy as mitts. Cleve motioned for him to put his hands in his pockets.

Then the figure moved into the alley, passed a few yards away. Cleve nodded.

It was over and Dean was pulling the car door closed before he felt his heart quicken. He reviewed the scene in triumphant safety. The man had not even looked around at them, had said nothing; and he had kept walking slowly down the alley toward Main. By now he would have reached the street and turned left, toward the hotel. Instinctively, Dean handed the wallet to Cleve. The car rolled smoothly south, turned at the proper time and came back along the river, then up the hill on to an avenue where the traffic was thicker.

With lights off, the car moved quietly into the driveway beside the green house. In another few seconds Cleve had replaced the Tennessee licence plate, and led the way into the house. They stood silently before the hearth. Dean did not like the silence.

"That was sorta neat," he said.

Cleve added coal to the fire. "Who built the fire?" he asked.

"I don't know. Jenny, I guess. It was built when I got here."

"Which door did you come through?"

Dean's eyes flashed with suspicion. He remembered Jenny's warning. "The back, why?"

"Back, huh? Always come through the back. It's safer." He took out the wallet and went through it casually, looking at the driver's licence, a post office receipt, a laundry ticket . . . dropping each item one by one in the fire. "Not bad. Could've been worse. Two hundred and sixty-four. That gives you sixty-six. Right?"

Dean did not bother to count. "That's right."

"The same for Jenny. One thirty-two for me and the house."
He handed one share to Dean and tossed the wallet with the
remainder into a chair. "What went on between you and Jenny?"

Now it had come, just when he thought it was over. "When?"

"Think hard and see if you can figure out when."

"Nothing."

"Nothing at all?"

"I said nothing!"

Cleve moved forward a half-step and slapped him squarely across
the face. Dean did not move. A few bills dropped from his hand;
the blood ran down his nose and dripped on to the edge of the
hearth.

"Why do you have to lie to me? The key you've got won't fit
the back door." He seized the wallet and began counting the
money. "Take a good look! It's three hundred and sixty-four.
What kind of partnership is it when you lie to each other? I don't
give a damn what goes on between you and Jenny. She's just
a partner to me. Just like you. Why did you have to start off
crooking?"

"I was afraid."

"Of what?"

"Afraid you'd think I was dumb for coming in the front door.
And afraid . . . Jenny was your girl."

"Wipe your nose. I like neat people."

"I don't have a handkerchief."

Cleve pulled a handkerchief from his pocket and pushed it
roughly into the outstretched hand. "You can forget or you can
pull out. I don't much give a damn either way. But I sort of liked
you."

"I'd like to forget, if you'll forget I crooked on you."

Cleve turned and looked into the fire. Then he spat. "Okay.
That sounds okay."

Silence filled the room for a minute. Cleve looked up. "You
hungry?"

"I could eat something."

"There's plenty in the kitchen. We'll fix something."

Dean looked at the stained handkerchief. "I guess I ruined it."

"Throw it in the fire and forget it. We ruined it together."

He pitched the handkerchief into the fire. The strange blaze
brought back his strange new world.

2

THE editorial room of *Voices*, the Woodall High newspaper, was long and spacious and well equipped with five typewriters and eight desks. The large desk on the north wall belonged to Miss Cossitt, faculty adviser. At the other end of the room was a large desk which belonged that year solely to Bayard Frost, Editor-in-Chief. To his right sat Juanita Oldham, associate editor. She was a large, attractive girl who weighed everything carefully and wanted, above all else, to be a registered nurse.

"Is it finished?" she whispered.

"Nearly," Bayard answered. He was making a clean copy of the editorial.

"She won't let it go through," Juanita said, meaning Miss Cossitt, who was seated with her back to them.

He did not have to answer. He knew that Juanita was always with him: they thought alike. They had made the paper into something respectable. (Why be modest about it?) Had set off a few bombshells, and this one was the biggest yet. He liked the way Juanita sometimes leaned over toward him and whispered with the proper mocking tone, "You and me—we're geniuses." She was the cleverest girl he had ever seen, and if there were not so many things for him to do in this world he would think about marrying her. He finished the new copy of the editorial and pushed it across her desk. She read slowly:

"A student is dead. Not one who marched in and out our doors, up and down our concrete steps, because he was not of our colour. But he was of us: a fellow student is dead. The tragedy came in a strange and terrible way, and those who looked on must have felt as one would feel watching a sunset in the east.

"The front steps of Clear Creek School were made of two log butts and one cross-piece of bridge timber held in place by twenty-penny spikes, which the sun and rain had loosened. As the three o'clock bell rang last Tuesday afternoon, nine-year-old Charles Decatur Wilson clutched his tablet and reader and rushed toward freedom. His foot landed on the front step, too far to the right. The cross-piece turned. And Charles fell on his back with a rusty twenty-penny spike piercing the base of his skull.

"He was buried Thursday afternoon at Mount Olive. As they watched the small pine coffin lowered, his playmates and teacher, his brothers and sisters, his mother and father, must have been asking *Why?* in their hearts.

"We are asking *Why?* too.

"We went to the School this morning, across the rocky playground, past the single basketball goal, and looked at the fatal spot. He died still holding his reader and his tablet, on which was scribbled several times the exercise: *I love the trees.*

"As we left, we looked back at the grey, two-room building where one teacher and thirty-eight dark faces sat mute and stricken. The morning sunlight shone against the windows, leaving dark spots that marked broken and missing panes.

"We returned to our school, marched safely up our concrete steps to class. The teacher demanded, *Why*—why we were late? It was a reasonable question. We answered her.

"But who is going to answer us? We want to know *why*?"

Juanita read a second time. "It's wonderful," she whispered, " 'rushed toward freedom.' Look what that means. Did you do it intentionally?"

"No. I never thought what it really meant."

"Give it to her and see what she says."

Miss Cossitt not only knew her bookkeeping and shorthand and typing thoroughly, but also knew how to impart the techniques to students. She was well liked, partially because she took the middle of the road on almost every issue. He placed the two sheets on her desk and waited.

She read, moving her pencil across each word. She turned, lifting her puzzled, tiny face. "I don't think so, Bayard. I don't think we'd better run this."

"What's wrong with it?"

"It could stir up a lot of ill-will. It's not our business to deal with the race issue. Matters like this belong in other hands."

"Apparently the other hands are not very capable."

"Bayard, think what this would do to your father if he ever ran for office again."

"That's not a consideration. He doesn't care what I write, and even if he did care it still wouldn't matter."

"But what good would this do? The child is dead. What's your purpose?"

"What is any editorial for?"

"Bayard, you know very well I would do anything I could to help Negro children. But I can see no point. . . ."

"But there is a point. And I think it's very clear."

"Juanita. Call Mr. Lott in here."

Mr. Lott was a short, smooth-faced man of fifty-five. He was always immaculately dressed in a grey suit and shining black shoes; his miracle lay in keeping the campus as neat as his clothes. He had a quiet, acute sense of right and wrong. While *Voices* was not rated as highly as his pet project of beautifying the campus with flowers and shrubs, it nevertheless rated well above the football team. It took him two minutes to read the editorial and make his decision.

"Miss Cossitt, you're the faculty adviser. This is entirely your responsibility." And he left the room.

Miss Cossitt was somewhat angered. He had given her no indication of what she must do. She chose the safest route. Standing, in order to emphasize her decision as final, she said, "I'm sorry, Bayard. It's very well done. But it's out."

"You'll have to get a new editor then. I refuse to edit a paper that prints nothing but 'Agnes is making goo-goo eyes at Herbie,' and 'Willie broke through and smeared the runner for a four-yard loss.' "

"Bayard, I don't understand you."

"That's all right. I've been around myself longer than you have, and I don't understand either."

She refused to show anger. "But you're every bit as smart as Rex. He was a model student; he never gave anyone a minute's trouble."

"He never had any ideas. When he begins to have ideas, he'll make trouble for somebody too."

"You're a rebel, Bayard. A deliberate rebel."

"Without a flag."

"But why, Bayard?"

"I don't know, Miss Cossitt. Just another *Why?* that can't be answered. I'll clear my desk now, if it's all right."

"Certainly it's all right. It's perfectly all right with me."

That night Bayard started his notebook. He wrote every day, even if it were no more than a single sentence. His journal was entitled: *The Trouble is.*

November 9, 1936.

I know that I was right to do what I did. I wish that I had not had to do it. But Mother said I was right, and what is more, Papa said it too. I don't know whether I made him say it or whether he really thought it. I have learned how to handle him. All you have to do is go to the barn at feeding time and help him shuck corn. In the crib he will say Yes to anything. I kept shucking while he read my editorial; I told him how everything was. I caught him at high tide. I said: Mr. Lott won't care, but Miss Cossitt will be mad at me. He said: I wouldn't give a s——. That is a word I don't like from other people, but he can do anything with it. I know that everything is all right. I have decided something: I am never afraid of Papa, because I know he has committed his share of sin. When he goes to Memphis, I wonder what he does. I have noticed that he is quieter now, and sad. It is hard to imagine Papa being sad. But he is. I am sure of it. Maybe it is because he is no longer in office. I have decided something else: I am more afraid of Mother than of Papa. She is always here. She is always doing the right thing. I try to think of something wrong she had ever done. I can think of nothing. Mother does not make errors. And silence . . . silence . . . how she uses it. I have not said a word, but she knew I was not going to the University to-morrow to see Rex play. Tuesday she asked why I didn't do an extra hour at the piano for three days, and that would make up for Saturday. She had said nothing else. I have decided to go. But not for Rex. I am going for her and Papa. Before I showed him the editorial, I asked him what time we were leaving in the morning. That was smart. He was pleased. I know, because of the way he spat out the crib door. I know he wishes I could be a star like Rex. Papa is a lot more interesting now that he is sad.

November 10, 1936.

I swear I will never go see Rex play again. He is too much of a star. He showed off on the football field, at the College Inn during supper, and later in his room. He knows he is the golden boy. In the first place, he should have let Davidson score the third touchdown. If I were playing guard, I would let a tackle come through and bust him once or twice. Anyway, he had no business playing with his sleeves rolled to his elbows. All he talked about at supper was cross-bucks and laterals and mousetraps and spinners. He knew I was sufficiently lost. He said: You understand it was a spinner, Bay-bay, not a spinet? That was unnecessary. Wayne and Morris and Jarvis think he is wonderful. He would be if he didn't know it. How he makes straight A's with nothing on his mind but mousetraps and spinners is a worthy puzzle. Of course, he has got a brain. But I will show him. It may take a long time, but I will show the golden boy a thing or two.

November 19, 1936.

I did not go to the funeral. But just before dark I went to Mr. George's house. He was drawing water, alone, in the back yard and filling the chicken troughs. I thought that must have been something that she always did. I stood and watched him and thought I was going to call out her name: Lady Striplan. She was sixty-four. He is sixty-nine and stooped and does not quite fill his overalls. He said: Howdy, son. I went to the well beside him. He said: The chickens never had no water all day. Then he asked me if I wanted something. I said: No, I just came to see him. His son is in the Army in Panama; his daughter is in Louisiana and could not come home because she had given birth to a baby girl the night Lady Striplan died. There he was alone. The crowd had gone. He built a fire in the stove and I helped him wash a lot of dishes. I said: Why don't you come to our house to-night, Mr. George? He said: Well, son, what would I do to-morrow night? We went to the barn together. I helped him feed. The calves took care of the milking. He told me he had never stayed away from her one single night for thirty-eight years. Once he was on a jury and did not get home until four o'clock in the morning. But it was January court and still dark, and that night did not count. As we walked to the house he carried a small basket of eggs on his left arm; his right hand was lightly on my shoulder. I think that was to show me he was glad I had come. He never said so. When I was leaving he said: Tell your mother she's been mighty nice and we're much obliged. We? I thought. It was dark and I kept thinking, We? I looked back, but I did not see a light in the house. Rex stayed in my mind. I will tell the truth: if he should die it would be more terrible than if I should die. I do not believe he loves anybody. He wants the whole world to love him. I guess it does. I hope nothing happens to him.

November 21, 1936.

I helped Mother wash the dishes to-night. She sent Ursa home because she knew that Ursa was tired and almost sick. Then I went to my room and began to read. After a few pages I knew that Papa and Mama were having a real quarrel. It was not the thing to do, but I opened my door and listened. Rex must have hurt Papa's feelings at the game. I remember now that somebody asked Papa if he was a graduate of the University, and Rex said: He never went to school, but he's got two degrees from the sheriff's office. I cannot remember all the quarrel, but it went something like this:

That's not what he meant.

It is what he meant.

All right. You can look at it that way if you want to. You can blame yourself, but it's not your family blaming you.

I'm not talking about blame. I'm talking about respect. Do you mean to tell me they respect me the way they respect you?

If you could line them up and make them make a choice between us, you'd see what I'm talking about. They are devoted (that was not the word: I can't remember the exact word) to you. Every last one of them.

You see. We're off the point again.

What is the point? A college degree?

The point is where I come from and where I got to and how. They're growing up. They're looking at the steps on the ladder.

Are you accusing me of pointing out the steps?

You know I'm not accusing you.

You said I could have stopped you.

You could have. But I'm not accusing you. I'm accusing myself. I don't know where to go to now.

You could give what you have to the poor. That's what Christ said to the rich young ruler.

And what would I give to them?

Whatever you have left.

Oh, Anna. . . .

It was a strange, hopeless sound. A kind of uttering I could not imagine coming from Papa.

I have felt all right about Rex since the night I came back from Mr. George's. Now I am changing my mind again. I don't know what I would like to do to him, but I would like to do something. Men who wash dishes do not hurt other people's feelings. I will go to the Thanksgiving game for Papa's sake, but I hope Rex gets every punt blocked and does not complete a single pass and does not gain a single yard from scrimmage. No. I will take that back. I hope he is a star. That's what Papa wants him to be. Anyway, that's what he will be, unless he breaks his neck.

November 25, 1936.

It seems that something terrible is going to happen to our family. The most terrible thing I can think of is a death, but there are other things more terrible. I am trying to think of exactly what I mean. I cannot put my finger on anything. I think of Lady Striplan and what if Mother went through that same thing. We are not happy now. We are like the whole world. Maybe it's the falling leaves and the sight of winter. Poor Wayne comes in with some more F's. He cannot understand. I cannot understand either, and I have all A's. It seems that I would like to have a strong steel bar in my hands all the time and have it fastened to something permanent. Even Mother worries. She will be glad when the Thanksgiving game is over. There are so many cars on the road and so much drunken driving. And she has God. She believes. Papa has only us. I went to the crib to-night and helped him shuck corn. I wonder why that is the only place he seems to be completely happy. There are two other times almost like being in the crib: when he is around the Negroes, and when he is showing Morris something with a baseball. But, still, they are not like the crib. To-night I said: If you had a tractor, you wouldn't have to shuck all this corn for the mules. I wonder if he could tell I was kidding him. He just looked at me and frowned and then spat a big stream of juice out the door. It almost hit Jarvis squarely, but he dodged and caught only a part of it on his leg. Papa never said he was sorry or anything, but when he went over to Uncle Sid's for a while, he asked Jarvis to go with him. One evening I am going to watch and turn the corner of the crib at the right second and let him hit me squarely with a mouthful. I want to see what he will do. There is a note about something I wanted to put down. Why can't I remember? Rex would not forget like that.

November 28, 1936.

It is two o'clock in the morning. I am not sleepy. I had fun at the game and on the way back too. Barney is a clown. And Rex outdid himself to-day. He made the Tech men look like sand-lot players. I admit he is clever. Almost as clever as whoever pulled the robbery. That is the neatest thing I ever heard of. They made the cops and patrolmen look silly. Cars lined up bumper to bumper for ten or fifteen miles. All the proud, uniformed figures must have felt they had made a marvellous check. They threw their flashlights in Papa's face and then took a peek at the rest of us. Barney said: It's back in the trunk, fellers. One of the patrolmen got mad. He was so stupid, I believe he would have looked in the trunk if he hadn't recognized Rex. But once he saw Rex, he would have waved us on if the money had been piled up before his eyes. Rex was good, picturing poor old Fortenberry breaking out of that closet and running from the Ad building to the stadium to tell the President first that he'd been robbed. The poor man is afraid he will lose his job as cashier. I don't believe he urged the President to have the Tech crowd investigated first. If the man is that stupid, somebody should have robbed him. Anyway, he will be more famous on the campus now than Rex. It is all so funny I almost hope they get away with it. Another note to prove that people are stupid: When the robbery was announced over the public address system, there must have been five thousand people who left the stadium immediately. Maybe they went to check cars they had left unlocked. I think I will copy my new poem here and then read a few pages of Dostoevski. What do you think of this bright, splendid world, Mr. Dostoevski? Isn't it a lovely thing?

Courthouse

The Courthouse is a lovely thing,
With all the pigeons wing to wing
Above the Doric columns
Lately cleaned with sand.

The solemn chamber has a shine,
An ancient smell of turpentine,
A new-framed one
Of Washington
To catch the eye and hold it:
Never let the people know
The jury's stacked for So-and-so.

The walls have no tobacco juice
Where certain people turn it loose,
Miss the spittoon half a mile
And smile, above the blots,
At one another:
Good paint will cover
Many spots.

The Courthouse is a lovely thing,
With all the pigeons wing to wing
Above the Doric columns
Lately cleaned with sand.

Good night, sweet prince, high scoreman, triple-threat, golden one, wearer of the coat of many colours, Adonis (whom no wild tackle has yet slain). May the deep night rest softly on thy famous brow. Dream sweet dreams and remember: I will make ten thousand hearts to leap when thou no longer wear a single cleat. Good night. I have a date with Dostoevski.

January 4, 1937.

Christmas is over, and I am glad. I want to feel time pouring through my fingers like the wind. Lighted trees and crepe and silver bells make me sad. They are sham beside the dying, golden hickories of October or the surging dogwood of April. But Mother was happy. I am glad of that. And Papa was happy for a while. He enjoyed Fred. Fred is wonderful. Maybe his presence in Rex's room will work a miracle. If the University is forced upon me this fall and I must crawl in the hallowed shadow of the golden one, at least Fred will be there. He is touched with sadness too: his mind is too keen not to be burdened. Papa enjoyed him more than anybody who ever came here. I wonder if he thought: He does not know what my sons know? Now Papa is back in the mully grubs again. It gets worse and worse. That is partly because it is bad weather now and not much work can be done outside. Not the real reason, of course, but the reason it shows so clearly. I have heard no more quarrels, but he still thinks we hold against him every questionable thing he did in the sheriff's office. He picks up the slightest implication. Or, rather, he picks up the slightest word and makes it an implication against his official record. It would not change my feelings if he had burned down the Courthouse. But I know that my opinion does not count with him as those of R. and W. and M. and J. I am different. None of us are alike. Poor Wayne was born under a good star, but not a very bright one. Probably his life will be more satisfactory than any of the rest. He will marry early and be a farmer and have a dozen kids and live for ever. Morris has his heart set on baseball.

Jarvis will end up in some kind of business. Rex will end up in the Governor's mansion, and I will end up different. When Rex gets into law school this fall, I suppose he will talk to us in terms of *nolle prosequi* and *sub judice*. Rex, little king, drive your golden chariot. I learned something during the holidays. You will be a Cæsar or nothing: *aut Cæsar aut nihil.*

April 14, 1937.

If she could have heard it, that would be all I would ask. Fig-face Cossitt. What do I care if she has given me nothing but 90's since our unhappy altercation? I had made nothing but 98's in typing and 97's in bookkeeping before my departure from *Voices.* 90's, you fig-face. No, it is not really a fig-face at all; none the less, that is exactly what I see. I thought I would break his record, anyway, for honest Lott kept giving me his consistent 96 in Latin and Miss Whitlan did not vary, nor did Miss Coats. I will not break King Rex's record, and Juanita will be valedictorian. I say figs to you, Miss C. Figs and sour cream and a long life without children. I could not wish on any tender spirit the task of calling you Mother. Figs and fig leaves and mice hair and pepper and sour cream. Do you think it matters to me? You should have heard Papa. That is all I would ask. I caught him in the crib all right and shucked corn with him and told him while he shifted a big wad of Old Apple from one jaw to the other. He spat on you. The biggest stream I ever saw. Right out the crib door and on your little cat feet. He is too much of a gentleman to spit on you any place else. He said: I wouldn't give a s——. Figs to you, Miss C., and fly specks and dandruff and burnt motor oil and red ink and another fly speck and tobacco juice and more sour cream and a rusty spoon. Do you think I care? I will write in your yearbook: *varium et mutabile semper femina.* And you will not know what it means until you run on your little cat feet to Mr. Lott. He will clear his throat and say: Why, Miss C., I believe that means: Woman is ever a fickle and changeable thing. No. I will write something else. I will write: *Nous sommes toujours dans le moyen âge. Mais n'ayez pas peur, vous avez la majorité.* Quick! Quick! To Miss Coats. She will say: Florence, it means, We are yet in the Middle Ages. But have no fear, you are in the majority. Tiger! Tiger! burning bright, in the forest of the night. What poor mortal human eye can see the dagger in my heart? I am laughing at you, Miss C. And stirring and stirring: mice hair and fly specks and sour cream and pepper and all. Let the record stand. *Vive le record! Vive le bon roi* Rex! Rest in peace, sweet prince. Your record will stand for ever. I have failed.

June 20, 1937.

Why Rex had to sit in on the conference, I don't know. That

was why I acted smart. He had no business being there. I suppose his perennial glory gives him the key to any door. There he was in the middle of us. Not only there, but master of ceremonies.

Rex: In the first place, you wouldn't find another school in the state equal to the University.

Bayard: Not so far as football teams go. No; I wouldn't.

Rex: Don't act smart. You'd better be making up your mind what you want to be.

Bayard: I want to be great. Like you. Except, I'd use my fingers where you used your feet. A certain delicate difference there so far as. . . .

Rex: Aw, hush.

Mother: You two stop arguing.

Rex: I'm not arguing. I don't care whether he goes to the University or not. But that's the place for him. He doesn't know what he wants to be.

Papa: What do you want to study, Bayard?

Bayard: I want to study music.

Papa: What's the matter with the University?

Bayard: At the University I'd be a satellite to this athletic planet. (Record here a grave mistake on Bayard's part. Papa registers a considerable frown. No doubt he thinks B. is mocking him to some extent, or being disrespectful. His big jaws puff and red runs up his cheeks.)

Papa: Aye god, I don't give a damn if you never stick your foot in another classroom. What's the matter with my family? If you had to work like niggers from daylight to dark there wouldn't be so much of this goddamn nonsense around here!

Bayard (his cucumber is sufficiently cooled. After a lengthy pause, when the red fades somewhat in the master's cheeks, he speaks with the utmost calm to Mother): Why does Rex have to sit in on something that concerns you and Papa and me? I don't see why you and Papa need any extra help. (He hopes this will show that any sting in his "satellite" remark was aimed solely at Rex, who promptly leaves the room and is heard outside calling to Jarvis. He believes Papa sees the point, or maybe even feels that B. is not against him, could never be. B. continues slowly) I'll do whatever you and Mother say. Besides, you're paying my way. You ought to tell me what to do and not to do. But it's not Rex's place to tell me, as if he wanted me down there to shine his shoes and clean up his room. (Papa likes this. Something is placed on his shoulders, and he likes things on his shoulders.)

Mother: You wouldn't room with Rex.

Bayard: I know I wouldn't.

Mother: Bayard, you must get over whatever this fight is between you and Rex. It will grow on you. You're ill as hornets with one another.

Papa: What's the matter with you two, anyway? (He asks as if it is the first time he has noticed the friction.)

Bayard: I'm jealous of him. He's everything and I'm nothing. I'm not Bayard Frost, I'm Rex's brother. I'll be Rex's brother at the University. But it would be the same anywhere else, almost. (That scores again with Papa, who is for the underdog. But B. is not fooling himself: Rex still wears the invisible coat of many colours.) I'll make out my application to-night. Papa, would you write me a cheque for fifteen dollars? I have to send in a room reservation fee.

Papa: Yeah. I'll write you one. (He almost smiles.)

Note: The cheque pleased Papa more than anything. He was doing something for one of his own. Mother could write the cheque as well as Papa. I wonder what he would have done if I had asked her to write it? I remember two or three times I have heard Rex— just before leaving for the University—ask Mother for a cheque. She always said: Where's your daddy? He'll write you one. It all came out of the same account. But she knew exactly what she was doing. Mother sees what goes on beneath the surface. She can see Papa wrestling with his angel. She is willing to help, but the angel will not wrestle against two. Papa does like things on his shoulders, so long as they belong to other people. But what he is carrying now is something he put there himself. He does not know what to do with it. If he knew Latin he could say: *inopem me copia fecit.* Maybe that would help him to laugh. I have not heard him laugh in a long time.

3

A PALE mist of smoke hung over the river. A long barge pulled under the bridge and slowly upstream like an overstuffed caterpillar. It was dry September and the water was low. Dean leaned into the window until his nose touched the screen. Jenny's golden hair brushed over his shoulder.

"It looks like a good place to go swimming down there."

"That! That's filthy," she said.

"I know it's filthy. But it doesn't look filthy."

"I wouldn't swim in that if it was pure as peroxide. I'm afraid of water."

"Why?"

"I can't swim. You know I can't swim," she said.

"I don't know any such thing. What I know about you I could write on a cheque blank. You won't talk."

"I talk all the time."

"Not about yourself. Do you ever go home?"

"Not if I can help it. I haven't been home since my mother died."

"When we came up from Jackson, Cleve showed me where you lived," he said.

"Isn't it awful country?"

"No. It's pretty country."

"It might be pretty from a car window, but it's not if you're out there with a hoe in your hands or a pick-sack."

He took her hand and rubbed her long soft fingers. "Did you ever pick cotton?"

"Bales and bales. I was the best cotton-picker in the family. I could pick as much as Bill and Perry put together. Bill was lazy and Perry was slow. I didn't mind working."

"What was it you minded?"

"The cold winters, when I had to sleep by myself and freeze and move my bed when it rained and stuff old quilts in the broken windows. Things like that. I used to sleep between Bill and Perry till I got too big."

"How big?"

"Oh, fifteen or sixteen."

He remained silent. She had expected some sudden exclamation from him, but then he did not know the things she knew.

Finally he said, "You came to Memphis to get a bedfellow?"

She slapped him gently and pulled his hair. "Not the kind you're thinking about. I lived with three girls. They were all right and a lot of fun. They're married now."

"When are you going to marry me, Jenny?"

"One day next Tuesday."

"You don't really believe I like you as much as I say."

"Yes; I do."

"No; you don't. You laugh at me when I talk about it."

"I don't."

"You kid me, then."

"I kid you because you're a kid."

He looked out the window at the river and was quiet. Because she was afraid she had hurt him, she began to rub his neck gently.

"I don't know whether I love anybody, Jenny. But if I do, it's you. I thought about you all the time we were in Jackson. I thought about getting back. And now I'm back. And I feel like I don't want to leave again."

"I'm a lot older than you, Dean. A lot older."

"Seven years. When you're seventy, I'll be sixty-three." He kept his eyes on the river.

"But I wouldn't marry anybody as long as I'm mixed up in . . . all this."

"We could get out," he said.

"For a while, yes. But not for long."

"I expect to get out some time. Don't you?"

"I've quit expecting anything, Dean. Maybe if I don't expect to, I will. We're in this business because we feel cheated. Somewhere we didn't get what we think we should have had. Cleve is in it because he likes to plan and then watch his plans work. That's the main thing to him. He could get out easier than we could. We want something for nothing because we once got nothing for something. Agreed?"

"Agreed. Why don't you quit work, Jenny?"

"I like to work. Work is healthy. And I've got a notion I helped build the Moon Harvest into something."

"Sure. For somebody else."

"That's true. But still, it's something I did. And Greeky's good to me. I work when I want to, mostly. I get paid enough."

"Have you ever thought about a place of your own?"

"I might think about it, some time."

"We could go in together. I've still got every penny of last year's haul from the University and most of the Water Valley rake."

"I can go better than that. I've got every penny I ever made in this business."

"Have you really?"

"Every one. And you'd be surprised how many too. I've never wanted to spend it. You remember about two years ago when I went to the hospital? I got panicky. I thought I was going to have to spend some of it."

"That's silly. What're you saving it for? To give it back?"

"I wouldn't know where to give it back, most of it. The only Moon Harvest customer we ever worked was the first time you went with Cleve. We got that old toad because he insulted me."

"How?"

"Every time he came in he'd ask something about Greeky. If he was a good bedfellow and stuff."

Dean laughed. "So you rigged him. You ever see him now?"

"Sometimes. Let me tell you what I did. If you tell Cleve, I'll cut your ears off with a pair of dull scissors. Don't you breathe a word of this to him. One night, about a week after the University, old toad-frog came in reading the paper, and I waited on him. That was about the time they thought a couple of students had pulled the University job. He was reading the story and talking to me about it. He asked if I thought they did it. I'll never know why I said what I did. I said, 'No, it was probably the same crew that got you.' "

"That was bright!"

"Well, listen. He looked real wild and said, 'Me?' I knew I'd stuck my boot in big. I could feel the roof breaking around me like a plate. I could have sworn he had told me about getting stripped. But when he looked real wild at me, I remembered he hadn't told me at all. He had told me he lost over three hundred dollars in a crap game. How I could have forgot that, I don't pretend to know. I thinks, Lord, what will I do now? He said, 'Did I tell you about that?' My brains spin a few times and I think, if I say, 'No' he'll think, 'Yes.' 'You didn't tell me,' I said, 'It's the gipsy in me. I got a way of seeing things.' 'A gipsy with golden hair,' he said. 'You ought to appreciate me. I tell you things I don't even tell my wife.' "

"You're giving me goose-pimples," Dean said.

"You! I had a quick case of the measles."

"Did he ever mention it again?"

"No. Do you know why I'm telling you about it?"

"Not exactly."

"I'm just showing you we're going to slip up. Maybe not to-morrow. Maybe not next year. But sooner or later, no matter if you plan every breath. Cleve is clever: like making us put that money in the bank a little at a time each week. But it's not so much whether you're clever or right or wrong. It's against Nature. If you violate Nature enough times, you're going to trip up. Don't you believe that?"

"Maybe."

"It reminds me of something at home once. I could outjump Bill or Perry either. There was a real deep creek between the corn-field and the sorghum patch. I never could quite get up enough courage to try to jump it. But one day I thought I'm gonna try it if I break my neck. I made it. So from then on I wouldn't go to the bridge. I guess I thought if I could do it once I could do it a million times. Until one day I didn't make it. I ran just as hard and jumped just as hard, but for some reason I landed in the creek and nearly broke my neck. We'll end up in the creek, sooner or later."

He turned to her and kissed her throat. "You know, Jenny," he whispered. "You're okay."

"Sure. We're all okay, if we had sense enough to know it."

Silence crouched in the room like a cat. After a few minutes they got up and went for a paper. The night was clear and cool, the first brittle night of autumn. The thin layer of smoke, from forest fires to the south, hovered over the buildings like a cloud that had lost its way. Returning, they stopped to watch a train moving west-ward across the bridge.

"I wish we were on it," he said.

"Where would we get off?"

He did not answer. The sound of the whistle reminded him of an old Negro man he had seen that afternoon, two blocks from the green house, raking leaves and piling them in a wheelbarrow. He bore a brown pair of woollen pants, a vest, blue shirt and a pair of rubber gum boots. When he knelt to gather the small pile of leaves into his arms, he could not rise. Finally, he staggered backward and to his feet; the leaves, all but a half dozen clutched in his fingers, scattered into the wind. He dropped the few leaves where the neat pile had been and turned to his rake, leaning against a light pole. He must have been a hundred, Dean thought.

They climbed the steps side by side and forgot the train. Jenny lay curled on the bed reading the front page. Dean stretched out beside her reading the sports section. There was a huge picture of a football player set for the snapback, and below, the caption read: "ALL-AMERICA CANDIDATE, Rex Frost will be sending Indian arrows against the powerful White Elephants from Alabama at Hemingsted Field. Last Saturday, in the season's opener, he routed the Texas State Punchers with three touchdowns and a field goal. He weighs in at 168." He read the accompanying story of a column and a half. After that he was through with the sports page and began to look out the window. He wondered what Jenny would say if he should show her the picture and say, "That's my brother. He raked it in last year, and we raked it out." She would laugh, of course. It would be like telling her that he loved her. His mind played with a tricky thought: He is kin to me, but he is no kin to Mother, nor to old railroading Luther with his pipe. Looking more closely at the river, he tried to decide whether he could tell, if he did not already know, which way the water was running.

"We've been cheated," he said, trying to mock her and bring a shadow of hurt to her face.

"What?" Jenny mumbled, half her mind still reading advice to the love-lorn.

"I said I don't mind the weather if the wind don't blow."

Smoke drifted down over the Hollow, for somewhere in the hills the dry September leaves were burning. Rufus had left the fields and the cotton-pickers at his usual time, walked to the barn to start feeding. He hated the idea of gouging his finger into a cotton-boll; it was nothing like the feel of his fingers tearing through shucks to the hard kernels, ripping deftly, twisting, turning out an ear every five seconds. He could do it much quicker, but that would spoil the pleasure. After all, there were only five bushels to shuck: two for the mules, horses and the mare; two for the hogs; and one for the calves, shoats, and chickens.

When he reached the barn he saw several piles of droppings scattered about. He scooped them up into the manure pen, mildly annoyed that he could not go straight to the corn crib. Once finished with the scoop, he saw a long strip of weather boarding that had been knocked loose; then he was disturbed. By the time he had hammer and nails and found out he could not slip the board into its proper place, hold it, and nail it by himself, he was angry. He saw Wayne come through the gate and he yelled, "Aye god, I want some of you to come out here and help me now!"

Wayne quickened his pace, seeing the red face and hearing the familiar intonation. He had hoped to catch his father in a good humour, for he had a grave problem to present: he had come home with another row of F's, and he wanted to quit school. If he hurried now and was helpful, and if the wind blew just right, there might still be some hope. He picked up the board, grunted unnecessarily in slipping it into place—all this to make certain he did not give the impression that it was a one-man job.

Rufus wet a nail; drove it home. Wet another, rolling it in his mouth; drove it home. His strokes were rapid, waspish. After four nails the tension eased. Another two and the job was done. Casually he dropped the hammer into the loop of his overalls, cleared his throat, spat a stream of tobacco juice.

Wayne pulled at the board, testing it. He thought it safe to say, "That'll hold it, Mister Rufe."

The big eyes lighted briefly, almost into a grin; but the face was not yet totally relaxed. They went toward the crib, which sat high off the ground on cypress blocks, wrapped with tin so that mice and rats could not climb up. Rufus made a ceremony of opening the door, scraping out a few shucks, pushing the basket to one side, and sitting down in a position favourable for spitting. Wayne climbed past him, careful not to step on the corn with his feet; it was all right to lean back against it, though. He watched his father work with the gentleness and reverence with which an ardent neophyte counts his beads. He mimicked each movement. He knew not to shuck too fast or too slow, not to get any shucks behind him, not to pitch the corn into the basket in such a way that it shelled off; in short, he knew he must be more careful around his father in the crib than around his mother at the table. He eyed the big hands ripping into the shucks, the slow and deliberate manner of spitting all the way through the doorway; he felt the obliviousness of the big man. He had never tried to figure out his father; he liked him well enough. The ears were falling into the basket at the right interval now. Another breath and he began, "Papa, I failed nearly everything this month."

"Huh," the voice said, and a stream of juice went through the doorway. The voice was neither pleasant nor unpleasant; simply unconcerned.

Wayne was disappointed; there was no opening to make his point. He pitched three or four ears with a little too much force. The face glanced around; that was all. He avoided the eyes, shucked steadily again, raked a pile of corn closer to his father. When he felt that everything was mended, he tried again. "I just keep failing, Papa."

Rufus spat, rubbed at his lips, using exactly the length of time it would take to shuck one ear of corn. He answered nothing.

"I . . ." Wayne began, but at that moment his father spat again. Wayne was disgusted. Here he was trying to get over the most important thing in his life and all his father could do was pull at a damned ear of corn and chew Old Apple and spit through the doorway. It was too much. The ease and naturalness of it was too much. He decided to explode. "I don't give a damn if they kick me out of. . . ." He stopped, for the face had turned, was staring. A wave of panic struck him: such ice, such fire, he had not seen in those big grey eyes in a long time. He swallowed, felt corn husk stinging all over him. His fingers began to pull at one shuck after another; he was working too fast. Everything about the man beside him was still. The silence bore down, hovered like a thousand blackbirds. Then the face turned and spat. It was as if the thousand birds took sudden flight. A relief rushed through him, down his body, into his bowels.

"You can go on to the house," the face said.

He climbed out of the crib, leaving an ear half-shucked. At the lot gate he paused and looked back. He saw juice splatter outside the crib. Another F, he thought. Wasn't it a damned shame? He could hear the crack of Jarvis's mitt, catching Morris's pitches. He would try again, to-morrow or the next day or next week. It was not a design, not a plan—for he never planned anything; but a vague understanding that though the barn was the place, to-day was not the time.

Rufus moved back a foot, nearer the corn, wondering why in the hell every boy he had hated to mix his hands with shucks. Well, they had really got away from him: that was the core of it. They did not need him now. Suddenly irritated, he began to work faster, doing an ear every three seconds. The basket filled quickly.

After supper, Rufus left without explanation and went to Sid's house. He had no special reason for seeing Sid and Amy, except that was the direction he turned when he was feeling low. He liked to sit in that small house and remember the days when he felt toward Anna as Sid felt toward Amy. Something there was like walking through an orchard in April.

When he stooped to go through the bottom pasture fence, he felt the sharp pain in his back again. He had done a foolish thing that morning, lifting at a bale of cotton by himself. Time was when he could have lifted it clear light. This morning he had simply thrown his shoulder into the bagging and up-ended the bale, and it was as if a wire had snapped in his back. He had been aggravated by something; now he could not recall what it was. He rubbed at his back and found himself thinking how much easier life would be if five girls had been born to him instead of five boys.

They did not need him now: he could keep walking over the hill and beyond, out of sight and never get tired. Walk the pain out of his back. Find a nook somewhere, even if it was off-bearing at a sawmill—the thing he was doing when he first saw Anna. How strange it was that any mention of that in his house—her house—drew nothing but silence, as if to deny it, as if it was a thing he had done one rainy day and not an everyday business to keep a jumper on his back and something in his belly. Aye god, at least he could talk about it in Sid's house. What was getting into him, into all his house, all the world, causing him to wake up in the morning and not even look out the window for sunshine?

He knocked on the door. No answer. He knocked harder, for there was a light in the house.

"Just hold your horses!"

He laughed quietly. Sometimes she reminded him of Todda. A bit of hellcat, he thought; flies off the handle quicker'n me. He liked that.

Amy opened the door. In her mouth was a small gold safety pin; in one hand was a belt, in the other was a brush. Evidently she had been brushing her hair. She laughed at her remark and motioned him inside.

He sat down. She turned her back to him, faced the full-length mirror on the closet door, and continued to dress herself. He studied her. She did not have good legs, but he had never paid much attention to legs, anyway. She was tall, not too thin, but not too straight either. Still, she had the finest face he had ever seen on a woman. Perhaps it was her hair that did it: a mound of coal black hair, combed straight back and rolled into a huge bun. Every angle of her face was sharp and clear, and the few uneven places in her teeth made her mouth delicate. Her eyes simply did what everything else did not do. They were dark.

She finished before the mirror, sighed in a way that made him want to do something for her. Kiss her gently, perhaps, if Sid was there. "You tired?"

"I just got up too early this morning."

"Where's Sid?"

"Gone fox-hunting. How can a man work all day and then go traipsing off on a fox-hunt?"

"Who with?"

"Chet and Nile. I don't know who else. Why didn't you bring me a cigarette?"

"I never thought about it." He grinned. Three or four years ago he might have been jolted by the way Amy talked, might have disliked it. Now, however, it brought them to the same level: made her older, made him younger. Her quirk of occasionally smoking a cigarette on the sly amused him.

"Did you want something specially?" she asked.

"Nothing more'n to pay you a visit." He felt somewhat foolish, and started to say something else, but she sat down and he forgot what he was going to say. She was a good bit like Todda.

Suddenly she got up and ran into the bedroom. He heard a drawer open and close. She returned with a package in her hand. "I forgot about these. They're the ones you brought a month ago." She took a cigarette from the pack and handed it to him. Within a few seconds she had returned from the kitchen with a match. They smoked together.

His hand was unsteady, his lips awkward, very much like a ten-year-old. Smoking was not part of his make-up: the number of times he had been drunk in his life was more than the number of cigarettes he had smoked. After a few draws he breathed long and laboriously, realized that she was like a child too. If Sid should come in, he thought, he would feel exactly as if he had been caught in the act of making love. His heart beat with tearing thumps. Quickly he stubbed out the cigarette in a small clay tray, and got up.

"You're not leaving?"

"You're tired," he said. "You need to git to bed early."

He could not stand it there any longer, but he tried not to show anything. Still, he jerked at the door, and closed it a second too quickly. At the edge of the yard he took out his plug and bit into it furiously. As the taste rolled on his tongue and the brisk air struck his face, he felt better. He walked toward Clear Creek bridge.

The sound of the foxhounds stopped him near the bridge. They were coming closer and closer, hot now, sending up their seesaw cries. He sprang across a gulley, climbed to the highest point near him, squatted, and waited. The sounds were muffled for a while: red fox, all right, leading them down the creek. He stared straight ahead. Actually, he saw nothing more than the glint of moonlight on a new strand of barbed wire, but his body was tense, excited, guilty, as if he spied on an innocent young woman. The sound grew faint, turned, swayed back toward him. He dropped on one knee and chewed slowly.

For almost an hour he remained there, squatting, resting on one knee, spitting at regular intervals. Occasionally a horn sounded, but the chase went on. Something about the yelping was like mad cries in a love scene. The night grew eerie and cold. He thought of the times he had squatted with other men on a barren slope listening to the hounds. Something about it was unmistakably like making love, yet he had never heard such a notion mentioned before. But they had known too. They must have known. Why else would a man work all day long and sit on a cold clay ridge at night? Sid might have asked him to go along, he thought, Yes, he might at least have asked him. "Hell fire!" he said, remembering how foolish he had felt sitting there with Amy, smoking, thinking how much she was like Todda. The word was flung out, but not with disgust; rather, his lips let it go with the same concern and carefulness with which he spat a sweet mouthful of juice.

The chase moved on, so far away that he could hear nothing, not even a horn. He got to his feet. The pain in his back started again, like the rapping of a tack-hammer. He had a strange feeling that it would stop if he could hear the hounds again. But they were gone, like something between him and Anna. If this thing came to an issue, between him and Anna, where would the boys be? Where would every damned one of them be, even Jarvis? And don't think they didn't see it. He hadn't successfully hid anything from any one of them since they'd found out about Santa Claus.

He started back toward the house. At the driveway he stopped. There were no lights in the house. He spat into the road ditch, feeling his body cold and full, and the hammer beating as regularly as his heart. A few clouds had quickly cast a thin layer of darkness and gloomy shadows. There might be rain to-morrow, a long week of rain with all the cotton hanging heavy in the fields. He cleared his throat and began to urinate fiercely on to the edge of the gravelled road. He enjoyed the sound of it. It carried him into time far back, when he could have worried about rain coming with cotton in the fields.

He entered the house and climbed the stairs quietly. Anna was asleep. Without thinking, he closed the door and went to Bayard's room. He looked around and began taking off his clothes. For no reason he rummaged through the few books and papers on Bayard's desk. He opened a notebook and read: "The sun has no choice of whether it shines upon us: it is the clouds and fogs and mists and rain in between which determine that." Taking a pencil, he wrote beneath the paragraph. "A man does not know where he is going until he gets there." Where the idea came from, he did not know for the moment—it might have been Barney's or Tom Phelps's or something he had heard, or another of those strange notions that he found in his head lately, as curiously out of place as a new egg on the front porch. And why should he write it down? He did not know. Then he remembered where it came from: he had not thought of old Noah for a long time.

He picked up a small book whose cover was labelled at the top with NOTES FROM UNDERGROUND and at the bottom with DOSTOEVSKI. By chance he opened to page nine and read through page twelve.

With a curse he abruptly closed the book and switched off the light. He slipped under the covers, wondering what went on in the mind of his strangest son that would make him read a book like that.

The pressure of his back against the mattress stopped the hammering pain. He listened for the hounds. Almost half an hour went by before he heard them, far away and lost. He felt that all the world was dead; his was the last unwinding heart.

Sleep took him and carried him to Memphis, to Todda's bed, where he raised up in the darkness and pushed a picture crashing to the floor and said, "Train whistles might sound like hounds, but Luther's never been on a fox-hunt." Then he was back in his son's room, curled on his side, the hammer eating into his back. Anna could fix a hot salt poultice quickly, and that would stop it, but he owed her too much already.

He turned on his back. After a while sleep took him again, this time down a long ladder of years to lean days filled with stunted tobacco and knee-high cotton, to cold nights where his urine splattered and smoked on rocky earth.

4

"MR. FROST, would you stand up, please?"

Mr. Frost stood up.

Professor Lucius Cincinnatus Bowman tapped his great fat forefinger on the desk. The day's work concerned the Norman Conquest of 1066, but the professor was concerned with more recent history. It was his private opinion, often publicly expressed, that A.D. 1861 in American history corresponded exactly to A.D. 476 in Roman history. It was his deepest conviction that America had reached the height of its glory in 1835, the year that Briarcliff was finished, a six-column mansion in Natchez that rested securely in his possession. He had motored to Natchez during the week-end, spent two luxurious nights under his high ceilings, attended constantly by servants who, he announced with pride, were the blackest below the Mason-Dixon Line. He had returned to the campus, wonderfully refreshed and in a jolly good humour, only to have it all ruined by a nasty little article appearing in the *Wigwam*, the University newspaper. Newspapers, at best, irked him immeasurably; history usually proved them insignificant.

"Where's your home, Mr. Frost?"

"Cross City. Near there."

"Sho' now." That explained everything, of course. Hill-billy country. A hill-billy was not supposed to know anything except how to milk a goat. Woodall County had been full of Union sympathizers during the war. "Sho' now," he repeated in his exaggerated drawl, which always carried a touch of contempt for the English language, even when he prayed to the Almighty in the First Presbyterian Church. "You a sophomore, Mr. Frost?"

"Yessir."

"You know the meaning of sophomore?" He thrust his flabby jaws forward in the familiar way that had earned him the name of Bully, ole Bully Bowman.

"Yessir. You want the Greek meaning or the American meaning?"

"In this case, the Greek."

"It comes from *sophos* meaning wise and *moros* meaning fool."

The professor grunted. "You stand right there. I want to read the class something from page two of the *Wigwam*. Evidently, class, our distinguished editor of the *Wigwam* asked several students to write their opinions of Religious Emphasis Week which was held on our campus last week. Mr. Frost was one of the chosen. Here is his Appraisal." He read in his usual exaggerated drawl:

"LEONIDAS AT THERMOPYLÆ

"Those with eyes inclined to see and ears inclined to hear must have observed during the programs of Religious Emphasis Week that stupidity is ubiquitous and selfishness the law of the land. The theme for discussion was racial tolerance, and the key question that kept cropping up again and again was: Should Negroes be admitted to the University? If anything was accomplished it was a clarification of who is in what camp. Surely nobody doubted that the walking hickory nuts were in the overwhelming majority, but it was a bit surprising to see them backed up and egged on by the walking walnuts: that is, slightly larger nuts clothed in polysyllabic doubletalk, holding professorships, admitting every liberal proposition advanced by the guest speakers and then quickly adding a negative suffix. The question was clear, or should have been clear, to all animals who consider justice a virtue. While debate on any issue is always admissible, twisting and clouding and doubletalking is unforgivable. At least one faculty member is to be commended for his outright statement, 'Hell, when the nigguhs come, I go.' He is not to be classified as a walking walnut; he is not hiding behind a green shell.

"The several professors who stood their ground quietly and honestly and registered an unequivocal 'Yes' when the key question was put should be given the rating of men of goodwill. But one professor should be cited for bravery above and beyond the call of duty. Small in stature, he stood like Leonidas at the Battle of Thermopylæ. Brilliantly and deftly, he turned the spotlight on the little brown shells and exposed the holes where the worms of prejudice had bored through to spoil the kernels—in such cases where kernels had ever existed. To watch that one mind in action was worth struggling along with the guest lecturers and discussion leaders who, careful of the wind's direction, hid their convictions diplomatically behind a maze of evasions and pop-lolly, 'What I mean is. . . .'

"A final observation deals with the religiouses who sponsor the groups who sponsor the week's activities. If their spirits are so lame and their convictions so weak that they must pay a speaker two hundred and fifty dollars to answer such a simple question, I want no part of their creed. I thought the program was planned to convince the heretics. It would have been a great success if it could have convinced just half of those who sponsored it.

"BAYARD FROST."

"Mr. Frost, you did write this?"

"Yessir."

The professor grunted and his second chin shook like a turkey's nib. "I was hoping they might have forged your name to this piece of sophistry. Where'd you get 'walking walnuts'?"

"I just happened to think of it."

"Tell the class the name of this outspoken professor who is not to be classified as a 'walking walnut.' "

"I prefer not to call any names."

"You want me to do the name calling, Mr. Frost?"

"That's none of my business, sir."

"Well . . . we don't want to keep the class in the dark, do we?" There was no answer.

"Class, Mr. Frost was referring to a certain history professor whose name I will not call but whose initials are L. C. B. Now, Mr. Frost, how about a small apology?"

"Are you suggesting that I misquoted you?"

"I am suggesting that you are a lame-brained sprout magnificiently unqualified to speak on the racial issue. Do you know anything about nigguhs, Mr. Frost? Anything at all?"

"I'm sure my knowledge is a mere drop compared to your oceanic storehouse."

"Don't lose your temper, Mr. Frost, and I'll try not to lose mine. Now how about a small apology—not a big one—and we'll call it quits?"

Bayard remained silent; the professor's second chin grew redder and redder. "Then how about making an exit, Mr. Frost? As quietly as possible."

He went to his room and lay on his bunk. Just before lunch time, when his room-mate entered, he turned his face toward the wall and appeared to be asleep. After a few minutes he was alone again. At one o'clock there was a note from the Dean's office: report immediately.

He sat for a while in the ante-room, watching the prim, grey-haired secretary, while the Dean of Men conferred with the four officers of a fraternity that had set up a still in its cellar.

"You Rex's brother?" the secretary asked.

"Yes, ma'am."

"He's a mighty fine boy. I noticed where *Gridiron* listed him on their All-American team. Did you see it?"

"Yes, ma'am."

"They say if we beat Tech Saturday, we're going to the Sugar Bowl. Wouldn't that be wonderful? But they'll beat us. You wait and see; they'll beat us. They'll come up with something. They can play like a high school against everybody else, but against us they'll play like Old Sewanee. The only advantage we've got is the open date last week. Maybe all our boys will be good and rested." The buzzer sounded. "The Colonel will see you now," she said.

The walls of the inner office were lined with bookcases, a safe, filing cabinets and military trophies. Colonel W. B. Haverton, a World War I officer, had for many years been commander of the local Reserve Officer Training Corps before assuming the duties of Dean of Men. He was a huge man without a pound of excessive fat, though he was fifty-two years old. Usually he was quite pleasant, and even while announcing stiff penalties would pucker his mouth into a halfway grin. At fifty he had married a second wife, the director of the University Beauty Shoppe; three months ago she had presented him with his first son. Some of the Colonel's good humour had escaped him for the moment, because he had observed during lunch that his son was covered with a rash. He did not yet know that the rash was merely the result of too much orange juice.

"Sit down, Frost. What's your trouble?"

"I don't know exactly."

The Colonel glanced at a note on his desk, then let his eyes fall on a copy of the *Wigwam*. "I'll begin by telling you that the brother of the greatest football player this University has ever had—and the second greatest player I've ever seen—is in trouble. Bad trouble, Frost. How's that for a beginning?"

"It's all right."

"All right, huh? Frost, have you got any notion what it's like trying to keep two thousand young hellions in harness? Huh?" He puckered his mouth into a grin, but Bayard, watching the eyes, did not mistake it as being friendly.

"Nossir."

"It's my conviction that a university should be tolerant. But we can not and should not condone open ridicule of our professors. Should we, Frost?"

"I should think that would depend on whether the professor made himself ridiculous."

"In your opinion, Professor Bowman made himself ridiculous last week?"

"In my opinion, Professor Bowman has made himself ridiculous every week I've been on this campus."

"You consider him intolerant?"

"Yes; I do."

"Well, I notice here—as an example of his intolerance—that of five grades so far this semester, in World History, your lowest is ninety-three. Does that smell like intolerance and unfairness?"

Bayard opened his mouth and felt that he had walked directly into a wall; his forehead and nose and knees, everything, had struck at once. The face of the Colonel, which had looked as just as a pair of scales, was now a hideous mask.

"That has nothing to do with it!" Bayard protested, astonished at his anger, for he had made up his mind not to get angry. "That's exactly what happened last week. They deliberately refused to face the issue. What have my grades got to do with. . . ."

The inner office speaker screeched and the secretary's voice announced, "Rex Frost, Colonel. . . ."

"Send him in," the Colonel answered.

Rex entered, his face shining like polished oak. He was the epitome of poise and stability. "I'm sorry to be a few minutes late. I didn't get your message until. . . ." He saw Bayard and stopped short.

The Colonel motioned for Rex to sit down. He did so, keeping his eyes turned on Bayard, his forehead knit into a frown.

"Your brother has run afoul, and I thought you might help us straighten him out. What time are you due on the football field?"

"Two o'clock."

"If you're two or three minutes late, I'll give you a note to Coach Kellogg. Have you read your brother's riposte in this week's *Wigwam*?"

"Yessir."

"I was explaining that regardless of how we feel about any question, we cannot allow students to publicly ridicule faculty members. Do you agree with that?"

"Yessir."

"I think we can overlook everything if uh . . . uh . . . Bayard will apologize to Professor Bowman. Do you think that's fair enough?"

"Yessir."

"What do you think, Bayard?"

"Since Rex is making my decision for me, I think he ought to make my apology."

The Colonel shoved his chair backward and puckered his mouth as if preparing to inflate a balloon. "Look here, Frost! I'll be damned if I'll play wet nurse for you. You'll apologize to Professor Bowman or face the Faculty Council to-morrow afternoon with my recommendation for expulsion. That's all, Rex. You wait a minute." He nodded to Bayard. "I'm not finished with you."

Rex went out. The Colonel realized that he had not handled the matter very well. In fact, he felt that he had made an ass of himself. To be honest (he thought again of the rash on young William's body), he had considered the piece clever the first time he had read it. Bowman was decidedly unmilitary, really a bit of an old maid, and hallowed on these grounds because his mother had given half the money to construct Bowman Hall. "Frost, if you want to think this thing over until nine o'clock in the morning, that's all right with me."

"Colonel Haverton, exactly what would you have me say to Professor Bowman?"

"Say . . . I don't care what you say, so long as it's acceptable to him. We can't have sophomores referring to professors as walnuts."

"But I didn't call him one! I said he was to be commended for *not* being one."

The Colonel's first impulse was to reach for the paper and prove himself right. But before his hand had moved six inches he realized his blunder. Three furies burst inside him: one against this insolent student, one against Bowman, and one against the rash on young William. Behind the three was a shadow: he felt as if he were in an argument with his first wife. "I won't quibble with you another second, Frost! Are you going to apologize?"

"No." Bayard stood up. "In the first place, I wouldn't know why I was apologizing. In the second place, I wouldn't apologize, anyway, to anybody who called me a lame-brained sprout. I am neither lame-brained nor a sprout. And the University can do whatever it likes about it."

The Colonel stood up. He was no longer in an argument with his first wife; now he was soldier facing soldier; and the sudden transition threw him off balance. "Goddamn you, Frost. You report to the Faculty Council to-morrow afternoon. . . ." And, catching himself, he added more calmly, "To-morrow afternoon at two o'clock."

Bayard went out. The Colonel sat down. He had been expecting to give a student a cussing for years, and now, at last, he had done it. The three furies, still working in him, fused into one against the men (the walnuts, he thought briefly) who had planned Religious Emphasis Week in the first place. Even a sophomore could see it was a crock full of . . .

He took a form and made out his report to the Faculty Council:

Name . . .	Bayard Frost
Classification . .	Sophomore
Major . . .	English and music
Charges . . .	Insubordination
Appearance . .	First
Recommend expulsion	No
Remarks . . .	Give him a good scare. Brother of Rex Frost.

He put down his pen and looked at the opposite wall. He felt like a young lieutenant in France (How many years ago?) with his company pushed back and shot to ribbons. Lost for a few seconds, he lifted the telephone to call his wife and ask about young William's rash.

Bayard refused to debate with himself about the sentence hanging over him. Like any other day, he took a stack of music from his closet and started for the music-practice hall. At the head of the stairs, on the second floor, he stopped five minutes, listening to a student working on Haydn's Sonata in G major. Suddenly he burst out laughing and ran on to his assigned room.

He leafed through his music, and, coming across a Ravel fantasy, he thought: I'll work on this; ole Bully would not like Ravel. As he worked, he became angry: angry at Rex and the Colonel and the walnuts and at Bully most of all. Every ivory key was a sharp pin with which he tortured ole Bully, who had become Gaspard de la Nuit, personification of the Devil. After an hour, he put the music away and began to play from memory. His anger had cooled, but there was a trace of fury left. He was transported and knew it; never had he felt so absolutely certain of what he was doing. The door opened; Madam Sartoff entered. He stopped.

Around her enormous body was a green afghan, pulled high on her neck, hiding a pile of yellow hair. The pince-nez rested as securely on her face as a wart. It was not often that she came out of her spacious den, made small by a grand piano, a recorder, reams of music, studio couch, pictures and two canary cages. Outside that sanctuary, she lost some of her effusive power. She was a Russian who had come to the University soon after the World War, but her English was exactly as it was the day she arrived on the campus. "Dahling! Iss fust time in long time you have played music for me! I come the long stairs because you touch me here." She laid a long yellow hand over her heart. "You see vot I tell you? Music is delicious madness. Not horses' feet, not bird vings. Iss something else. Now you know vot it is. Iss the vay I played ven I vas girl. Ah, *mon enfant*, music is music. *Les autres etudiants:* they play and they play and they play. *C'est toujours perdrix. Tu comprends?* How do you say it? Play, play, play. . . . Alvays partridge; too much of a good thing. Iss not music! Music iss vot you have done just now. *Continuez, mon enfant! Continuez!*" And, pulling the afghan tighter about her throat, she disappeared down the stairs.

When the smell of her perfume had faded he turned to the "Pathétique," which he had worked on years before. He did not wish to try to repeat what he had done with old Gaspard de la Nuit, because he was afraid he might fail and she would hear him. Leave old Gaspard to die in the historic remains of Gothic Dijon. He worked on the Beethoven until the room was dark. The door opened a second time, and there was Rex, still shining like polished oak after three hours on the football field. He came all the way across the room and stood between the window and the piano. "Will you stop those contortions one minute and listen to me?"

"Yes. What could I do for you, Frost?"

"You don't know how close you are to being kicked out of here. The Dean won't fool with you. When you mess with him, you're not messing with Mr. Lott."

"So?"

"Did you apologize to Professor Bowman?"

"No. I don't believe I did."

"Why do you have to be so stubborn?"

"I didn't do anything to ole Bully Bowman. He can go bite a fat hog in the ham."

"Yes; you did something to him. Why did you have to write that idiotic thing, anyway?"

"It's not idiotic. And I wrote it because I was asked to write what I thought. It's exactly what I thought. This is a University, not a kindergarten. Just what's wrong with what I wrote?"

"Maybe nothing's wrong. That's not the point."

"If it isn't, there isn't any point."

"It's a matter of give and take. Maybe you're right, but if Bowman don't like it, you ought to go up and tell him you're sorry. That's not asking very much. I've had people kick me in the face and I'd still shake hands with them after the game."

"You might consider that admirable, but I don't. You've practically said there was nothing wrong with what I wrote."

"Well, I didn't see much of anything wrong. I thought it was good."

"Then you let me down. You couldn't say anything but 'Yessir.' Why didn't you say you didn't see anything wrong with it? That would have cooked the old Colonel's goose."

Rex was pleased to think that he might have scotched the Dean. His mind, whirling like a gyro to find direction, considered briefly the proposition of rising even now to the defence of his brother: *Sir, I have reconsidered this article. I find absolutely nothing wrong. If he goes, I go too.* That would stop the old rooster from laying eggs.

Then his mind recoiled from the proposition and fastened on to the easy, the certain way. "I guess I should have said that," he admitted. "But it's too late now. You'll have to apologize. He'll send you to the Faculty Council, and you know what that means."

"I'm not afraid of the Faculty Council. He's already sent me. I'm going to the guillotine to-morrow afternoon. At two."

"You're deliberately trying to make trouble."

"If you choose to think so. . . ."

"If you choose. . . . If you hell. . . . Can't you think of somebody beside yourself?" Rex was angry now. If Bayard was banished, he would leave not only his own record for ever soiled, but a large scar on the brilliant record of Rex Frost, honour student and All-American. "How would I feel running around here with everybody knowing my kid brother had been kicked out. You're not a nobody, you know."

"I know! I'm the brother of King Rex!" He began to play a few notes of the sonata with his right hand.

"Stop that!" Rex seized the left hand, his powerful grip closing like a vice on the second and third fingers. "You're gonna telephone the Dean right now and tell him you'll apologize. Say 'Yes.' Say you're going to."

"Say 'Yes.' Say you're going to," he mocked, leaning back from the painful pressure.

"I'll break your damned hand."

"Break it!" he cried, and spat a sudden mouthful of saliva into the handsome face.

Wild with rage, Rex applied a final powerful twist. He felt the fingers give way like two thin strands of wire. Bayard tumbled backward on to the floor into an ugly heap, still and white as a fallen snowman. Sweat rose on his face like bits of oil on water. Rex stood over him frantically whispering, "Bay-bay! Bay-bay! I didn . . . I didn't mean . . ."

He opened his eyes and saw the terrified face above him. His right hand clawed weakly; his left felt no pain, only a tingling numbness. "Leave me alone, you heroic son-of-a-bitch. I hate you. I hate every drop of blood in your body." He burst into sobs; the water ran from his eyes into his ears.

Rex pulled gently at his shoulders.

"Leave me alone," he yelled. The tears ran faster.

Rex moved to touch the injured hand. "Is it broken?"

Bayard recoiled and staggered to his feet. He went out the door toward the stairs. Rex caught up with him, offering to help and mumbling, "Bay-bay . . . Bay-bay. . . ."

"Will you please just leave me alone? I'm not dying."

Rex stopped at the head of the stairs. He saw Bayard grip his left wrist and descend slowly. Then he rushed to the window and followed the figure as it crossed the campus, walking as if nothing had happened, except for the strange way he gripped his wrist. He turned into the street toward the infirmary. Rex dropped his head on the window-sill and wished that he could cry, but his eyes and throat were filled with dust. His mind crawled down the stairs and on to the campus and back along the years.

This was his first defeat, bitter and sharp and burning. He had come a long way without one. He looked down on a dozen students, chiefly freshmen—judging by their short-cropped hair—playing touch football near the Ad. building. It was getting too dark to see the ball and yet they were reluctant to leave the field. He remembered the days when football had been a game to him, when it was fun to play with Wayne and Morris and Jarvis. He felt old. Without thought, he returned to the practice-room and gathered up Bayard's music. He was still holding it when he sat down at the training table.

The team was in a happy mood. Along the long table juvenile chanting mingled with the rattle of silverware: Pass me the Sugar. They ain't no Sugar. Where is the Sugar? Way down south in New Awleans. . . . A tackle was telling the story of Buddy Johnson, third string tailback with two bad knees: Buddy had hurt one knee the night before while jitter-bugging in the Grill and had hurt the second knee that afternoon while trying to explain to the trainer how he had hurt the other one. A quarterback from the piney woods country was giving an account of his mother, who adored funerals and dragged him, as a child, to everyone within ten miles of their home. A guard was yelling, "We gonna egg the Engineers?"

"Yea man!"

"I say, we gonna egg the Engineers?"

"Yea man!"

Finally noticing the strange cloud over their star, somebody asked, "What's the matter with Rex-all?"

Word had spread. "Lay off," one whispered. "His bud's about to get the axe."

"Yeah? What for?"

"Caught him in the Laundry boiler-room with a co-ed, I heard."

"Ain't they gittin' snoopy nowdays? Ain't no place safe."

Rex ate a few bites of his steak and went out. The eyes of the team followed him. He walked past the infirmary, around the block, and back again. When he entered the lobby, Mrs. Simpson, the night nurse, came over to meet him, a ring of keys jingling at the side of her uniform.

"I want to see Bayard."

"Bayard?" The connection dawned on her. "Is he your brother?"

"Yes, ma'am."

"He's asleep now. He had two breaks, but Dr. Spence got a good set and put him to sleep. They ought to stop touch football around here. We get more injuries from that than we do from you boys who play on the team. Somebody is going to get his neck broken. They don't have equipment and they don't know how to take care of themselves, the way you boys do."

"Touch football?"

"He fell on these two fingers," she said. "And I guess there was a dozen on top of him. He's all right, but a finger, you know—oh, it'll be a little crooked."

He felt as if someone had hit him head-on in a jarring tackle. He sat down in the nearest chair. "When can I see him?"

"I wouldn't wake him up to-night. Why don't you come back in the morning? Say around eleven. He'll be all right. He won't miss but one or two classes."

"Could . . . could I use your telephone?"

"Of course. . . ."

As he dialled the Dean's number, he was ready to tell him a few things; tell him in certain terms: If Bayard goes, I go too. "Colonel Haverton?"

"Speaking."

"This is Rex Frost. I'm calling about my brother. . . ."

"Oh, don't worry about him, Rex. The boy's all right. We're not going to do anything. Just scare him a little."

"But . . ." He was lost. Where to now?

The voice said: "You take care of Tech. We'll take care of . . . of Bayard. Got to scare him a little, you know. . . ."

"He don't scare very easy. . . ." Abruptly, he replaced the receiver. He was not satisfied. He had not done what he wanted to do. Outside, on the walk again, he wondered whether Mrs. Simpson had followed his conversation.

He thought of calling home, but what would he say? He went to the Law Library to prepare for his Property class at nine o'clock the next morning. After a few minutes he returned to his room, glad to find Fred gone. He put a sheet in his typewriter and started a letter. Then he remembered that his father and Wayne and Morris and Jarvis would be there Saturday morning for the game. He crumpled the paper and went to bed. His mind began to crawl again, down the stairs, down the University avenue, and down the years. He could hear a hundred thousand voices cheering him on; add to them the thirty thousand who would come Saturday, for the grand finale, and that was the end of it. He remembered a night in New Orleans when he had scored four touchdowns to give the University its first win over Louisiana A. & M. in eleven years. He had escaped, alone, and had lain in his hotel bed and cried. For nothing? For the joy and sadness of being a great star and knowing it would not last for ever. He could see the end now, more clearly. Jumbled lines from *Othello* came back to him: he had played the title role last spring for the Blackfriars. *Soft you, a word or two before you go. I have done the University some service and they know it. . . .* Where are the hundred thousand voices? The cheers? Why are they not gathered about me now, to tell me it is only a play? To tell me it will be finished when the curtain is drawn? *In Aleppo once. . . .*

In Hemingsted once, when a malicious and charging tackle gave me the elbow and got my breath, I took my knee and flattened the dog. . . . But the crowds cheered.

In Hemingsted once, when a malicious and a towering end grabbed my ankle and rolled in the dirt, I took my toe and cracked his chin. . . . But the crowds cheered.

Where are the voices? Where are the cheers?

Not poppy nor mandragora nor all the drowsy syrups of the world shall ever medicine thee to that sweet sleep which thou ow'dst yesterday. . . .

Touch football, with a dozen piled on top of him. Ah, yes, that was the way it had happened. It would be clear when the play was over and the curtain was drawn.

Fred entered, switched on the light, was startled to see his roommate in bed so early. He quickly switched off the light and undressed in the dark. After a few minutes he was snoring peacefully. Rex turned to look at him. *Not poppy nor mandragora. . . .*

The nine o'clock sun came through the window and laid a bright square on Professor McCullar's desk. "Mr. Frost, will you begin the discussion by explaining the principle involved in Dixon *v.* Barnes?"

"I'm not prepared, sir."

"Class, can you imagine Mr. Frost being unprepared? I suppose we'll have to excuse you, with one proviso: that you're fully prepared Saturday. If not, we'll be in for a miserable afternoon. Mr. Williams, will you explain the principle involved in Dixon *v.* Barnes?"

When the class was over, Rex rushed to the infirmary. It was ten-twenty when he got the attention of a student nurse. She informed him that Bayard had left early that morning. He found Bayard's room locked. Not knowing where else to look at the moment, he returned to his own room. In his typewriter there was a letter addressed to him. He read:

"Dear Rex, What happened was as much my fault as yours. For the sake of the record, I told Dr. Spence I got hurt playing touch football. And that's the way it happened so far as I'm concerned. I'm going to Memphis, where I'll find something to do and have the chance of getting some things out of my system. I am a writer, not a musician. I am glad the matter is settled. You will see Papa Saturday. You can tell him simply that I left before I was kicked out. I am sorry on his account. But the truth is that I don't want a degree from this institution, not when I have to sit at the feet of men who have about as much compassion for humanity as a swarm of fleas.

"I wouldn't stay if the Colonel himself got up in assembly and made a public *apology* to me.

"I might as well make a few confessions now, too, so I can start with a clean page. I am sorry that I have so often envied and belittled your fame. I am sorry that I provoked you to last night's incident. I am sorry for one thing: Last spring I acted as if I did not see the Blackfriars' production of *Othello*. I went each of the four nights. You are a good actor. I would have told you then, but I wished too much to see myself in your clothes. I have at last forgiven Nature for giving you so much.

"B."

Rex did not practise that afternoon. He reported to the infirmary with a slight fever. Coach Kellogg growled his way through the last rough work before the big game. The Colonel checked the failure of Bayard to appear before the Faculty Council and found that he was no longer on the campus. He went to the infirmary and was told that Coach Kellogg had given strict orders no one could see Rex. At six o'clock the wire services broke the story that Rex Frost was in the hospital. The New Orleans bookmakers quickly changed the odds on the Colonial-Tech game.

In a cheap hotel, overlooking the water front, Bayard read his brother's name in headlines across the sports page and went to bed. At midnight he was awakened by an army of bed-bugs. His left hand was aching.

5

THERE was a scattering of cotton in the fields and acres of corn that had not been pulled. Water stood in the furrows, and all gathering had come to a halt. Rufus walked across the fields, feeling the mud cake on to his shoes, cursing beneath his breath. It was the damned weather, he thought, and yet he knew it was not the weather that bothered him. Rain would not hurt the corn, and if every lock of cotton remaining should rot, it would be no more than two bales. He sweated profusely and the wind dried it on his face. Why he walked in the fields he did not know. Certainly it was not necessary. He knew exactly what was there and what was not.

Across the Hollow, smoke rose from chimneys and was lapped up by the wind like a hungry tongue. Winter was coming, or winter was here. The idea struck him like a hundred typhoid needles. He felt the vaccine spread through his flesh. A violent nervousness seized him. He squatted in a hedge and relieved his bowels. His body said that he was sick; his mind rejected the obvious proof. Standing, he looked down at his own waste with curious fascination. Aye god, he thought, and set out across the pasture as if his first step would be a hundred miles away. At the creek he stooped to wash his hands; and looking about him to see whether anyone watched, he dried his hands on the bib of his overalls. He caught sight of the smoking chimneys again and they carried him back to the land of rocks. He was a child who wanted to go home.

He tried to see Sidney's house from the creek bottom, but a clump of trees cut off the view. Was it possible that Sidney could ever feel as lost in this land as he himself felt? Unable to pursue his questioning to a logical conclusion, or to prove any point, he washed and dried his hands again.

All fall he had felt that once the crops were gathered he was going somewhere. Not home, but somewhere. Over the hills and beyond, walking. Or take the train to Memphis. Not exactly to Todda, not to anybody. But away from the Hollow, which looked now as if it had seen no peace since the day he had arrived. It was not Anna's fault. All the same, in her quiet, stand-offish way, she had allowed things to happen. She knew ahead of time, and he knew afterwards. That was the difference.

He climbed up the bank and walked along the edge of the creek. His fingers tore the cellophane wrapper of a new plug of tobacco; his stout teeth bit off a chunk. But it was like chewing old hay. Sometimes tobacco was like that, and an hour later, from the same plug, the juice would have the pure, sweet-bitter taste. He knew it, yet he cursed Azel Burke for selling him something that was old and stale; and he spat unpleasant streams ahead of his feet.

Halfway to Clear Creek bridge he turned through the woods toward the chapel. He approached the graveyard as if he were on patrol with Barney and Bolton and Howard. Turning once again, he crept slowly up to the old well. The well-box had long since rotted away, and the well was covered with small white oak poles, worm-eaten and barkless. He laid one pole aside and leaned down to look. There was nothing but a circle of darkness and a few spider webs. He knelt for a few minutes wondering how he could fish the rifle out. Something inside him wanted desperately to see the rusty barrel and what might be left of the stock. It was one of the things that lay between him and Anna. Suddenly rising, he spat the tasteless chew of tobacco into the dark circle, kicked the pole back into place and walked off, feeling as if he had opened a grave.

He entered Burke's store through the back door. Last night there had been a fuss between Jarvis and Morris about pencils. He picked up two dozen. The small figure of Azel Burke came toward him, his round, bald head shining. Quickly searching his pocket, Rufus pitched the plug of tobacco on to the counter. "That tastes exactly like a goddamned cake of sedge grass," he said.

Azel was stunned. He had been on the friendliest of terms with Rufus, had voted for him twice, had publicly defended his official acts, had always enjoyed his trips to the store because he bought and paid cash and never complained of anything. Now one little plug of tobacco with one corner chewed off lay like a black cloud over all those days. With a bitter twist of his mouth, not in keeping with his placid nature, he demanded, "What do you want, Rufe, a nickel?"

"Hell, no. I want two fresh cuts."

Azel picked up two plugs and slid them along the counter toward the other. Rufus picked up all three and counted out change for the tobacco and pencils. His cold, arrogant counting caused Azel to say something he had never before said to a customer. "I don't handle nothing ain't fresh, and I don't give a damn whether you trade here or not."

"I know you don't," Rufus said. "But I'll be back, anyway." He went out, leaving Azel feeling better and wondering what kind of joke Rufus had tried to pull.

Rufus did not pretend to himself it was a joke. The words simply spilled out of him like water from a poisonous spring. Nowadays he felt that if his arms were long enough he would reach up with his pocket-knife and whack the sky to pieces. Only last night Jarvis had come home from school and asked, "Papa, when you was sheriff, did you let the bootleggers sell whisky?" "Why?" he had asked, thinking of nothing else to say at the moment. "Dennis said you did," Jarvis had said. "Who's Dennis?" "Dennis Kingsley. Mister Marlon's boy." He had wanted to answer, "You ask Dennis if his daddy killed any Germans in the war." But he had managed to say nothing, and had managed, also, to realize that the Germans had nothing to do with it.

They could go to hell. All of them: the Kingsleys and all the whoevers that poisoned the minds of his boys. Hadn't he personally seen that Marlon Kingsley got a job driving a road-grader, which had kept him off the W.P.A.? But they had forgotten. They had forgotten everything except the land he had bought, his bank account, and the new bills stacked in his safety deposit boxes. When he left the Hollow, Anna would have the keys and he would have one bright bill, one only, with a picture of Benjamin Franklin. Who were the ones that talked? The same damned ones that had lapped one favour after another from his hands. The only human being you could loan money to—interest free—and not get burnt, was a woman. A woman understood money. A man wouldn't pay and wouldn't speak. If you gave it to him, he still held it against you. Heavy, heavy hangs over your head; fine or superfine? Always hanging there, reminding him that you was smart and he was dumb. A man cannot stand to receive; receiving is a woman's role.

Having momentarily satisfied himself with such thoughts, he left the gravelled street and took to the fields again. Near the creek he sat down on a stump to dislodge some gravel from his shoe. One thing he could say: he took particular pride in his shoes. Every night he cleaned them carefully, dried them, put powder on the inside, and rubbed the outside with warm tallow. They were as soft as a tongue. When the shoe was relaced, he took out a new cut of Old Apple, and reflected on several points he had learned about chewing: it was better to bite tobacco than to cut it; was best never to chew at all, but to press lightly, for vigorous chewing brought out the taste of chocolate; was better in the open air than in a room; was always good after coffee, not quite so good after milk or iced tea. . . . He stopped considering and bit into the new cut. In spite of his acute knowledge of how to handle a quid, he often found himself chewing too vigorously. Feeling more secure after his reflections, he got up and started toward the house. His body ached.

But when he crossed the first strand of fence, he forgot the house and wandered aimlessly. At the back of the pasture he came upon a gap which had been cut for the corn wagons. Whoever had temporarily mended the break had done a half-hearted job. One slight push and every cow able to walk would be in the fields. He set about mending the broken strands. A few drops of rain warned him of the coming shower. But he remained, grunting and spitting, knowing he would be drenched. Aye god, a man had to fix his fence. The rain fell on him in a blinding sheet. It soaked through his jumper and shirt and underwear and ran down his body into his shoes. His chest was already clogged with sharp pains, but he stayed until the last barbed end was twisted into place.

Slushing across the grass in the pouring rain, he found two calves which he thought should be stabled in the barn. An hour had passed before he had them under the roof with two blocks of hay scattered at their feet. When he started to the house, he was already gasping and sneezing and his eyes were fringed with red webs. The juice on his tongue tasted better, sweeter, because he felt a certain triumph. At the back porch he painstakingly cleaned his feet and shook the rain from his clothes. Then he went up to his room, where Anna sat at her machine, making a dress for Ursa. She looked around, as if a ghost had entered and stood on the hearth. "My goodness! You're soaked and you're already sick with 'flu."

The fire began to draw steam from his clothes. He took off his hat and hung it on the poker. "I did git pretty wet." As if he had not noticed.

"Well, Rufus, don't stand there. Get those wet things off and put on some dry clothes."

He stripped to the skin and waited for Anna to bring him a towel and dry clothes. He rubbed himself briskly, and sat half-dressed with his feet stretched on the hearth. In spite of the heat in the room, he felt his lips grow cold and numb. He stared blankly into the fire. He mumbled his words. "I don't think I'll be able to go to the game to-morrow. I think I'll call Barney and git him to drive the boys down." He was suddenly exhausted, a limp heap, a fallen soldier whose ears still heard the battle. He looked on the dark side.

"Why don't you lie down?" Anna asked quietly. "You've been sick for two days. This is enough to kill you."

This? he said very clearly to himself, for his lips were asleep and his tongue was cold. You don't mean the rain, do you woman? The rain just washed the cover off; that's all. You can see the threads now; they're all twisted. Couldn't untangle them to save your life. "In a minute," he mumbled. "Wanta clean my shoes first."

"I'll clean your shoes," she said.

He opened his mouth to protest. There was no protest left. He got up and went to the bed. Before he could slip under the covers, she was standing beside him with pyjamas. As he dressed she held her hand over his forehead. "Why did you do this?" she whispered.

"Do what?"

She did not repeat her question. She covered his shoulders and a few minutes later brought a hot iron, wrapped in a towel, and put it to his feet.

"I'll git up after while," he said.

"You've got a high fever," she answered.

He heard her go downstairs and telephone someone. The doctor likely. Just like a woman to do that. But hell, what did it matter, if it pleased her? There was money to pay. The last time he could remember being bad sick with 'flu he was nine: there was hardly enough money for Red Rooster salve. He grinned, feeling the sluggishness of his lips. It all came to the same damned thing. It wouldn't have made any difference if he had died. All he needed now was a clean handkerchief and a good nose-blowing. The rest had nothing to do with young Dr. Sam Fitzwanger and his russet-coloured bag. That was modern. The old doctor had used a black one, of course. Now a woman had a lot of faith; a woman believed in doctors. But a man had to have his leg broke before he believed. He wiped a streak of sweat on to his pyjama sleeve. Parallel streaks of pain ran along his back, then branched into his arms. He would rest a while and get up in time to help Jim sack the cotton-seed he had put aside for spring planting. He closed his eyes until Anna returned.

"I called Dr. Fitzwanger," she said.

"Now what'd you do that for?"

"I know when somebody's sick."

"No; you don't. I've been sick for years."

"Not like this, you haven't. You're burning up with fever."

"Put your finger in my mouth and see how many degrees I got."

"See? You can hardly talk. Have you got any whisky?"

"No. They sold it all when I was sheriff."

She sat on the edge of the bed and looked down at him. Her round, sad eyes pleaded with him. He remembered a time when he could see his image in her eyes, when she laughed frequently, when they walked together at night and held hands and Rex lay buried in the dark tomb of her body. "Rufus, you're very sick. You don't know how sick you are."

Her words seemed to work a powerful spell. The room about him became unsteady; the covers became oppressively heavy. But his mind was clear enough to wonder what would happen if he should tell her what he had been thinking that morning, where he had been, and why. "I guess I've got the 'flu," he said to please her. A robust man with the 'flu: that had always seemed a bit strange to him, as strange as sudden trickery in an honest man.

"You've got to take care of yourself."

"Why, I don't need to do that. You can do that." He was talking with more ease now, but his head had gathered some of the ache in his back and was holding it. He became gentle; teasing, not mocking. The world slipped away from him for a few minutes and he slept.

He opened his eyes to a bowl of steaming soup, which he obediently tried to swallow. He managed three or four spoonfuls before it began to rise in his throat; he pushed the bowl away. "Boys come in yet?" His lips worked all right now, but a web of aching warned him that Anna was right.

"It's only twelve. You didn't sleep a half-hour."

The doctor came at one o'clock. He was a tall, slightly stooped figure with a perch mouth and slow grin. His clientele were chiefly country people, because he preferred attending them rather than city folk, who, he thought, remembered too many pranks of his childhood. He did not practise for money; he was driven by the need to play the role of a magician, a god. His nature was a quiet one and led him to tell much less than he knew. With Rufus, it did not take him long to find out what he wanted to know. He left an amber bottle of medicine, four capsules, a tube of pills, and instructions: the room must be kept warm, the covers up to the patient's neck.

"Reckon I'm gonna have the 'flu?" Rufus asked.

"Not until you get over this pneumonia," he answered.

Anna followed him outside. "I'll be back as soon as I can get back. This afternoon," he said. "Check his temperature every hour and record it."

"He's in danger, isn't he?"

"He ought to be in the hospital, but it won't do to move him. Yes, ma'am. He certainly is in danger. I'm not going to give him a shot right now because he'll need it worse about dark. A man like him, Mrs. Frost, can die before he knows he's sick. That's the big trouble."

She did not go down the stairs with him. She stood watching his shoulders and feeling the world grow dark, feeling it as if it were a wind. She returned to the room and stood on the hearth.

"Don't let him scare you," Rufus said. "They all do that so they can claim a big stunt when you're up again." But he was beginning to doubt what he was saying. A weak grin moved his face. "What would you do if I was to die?"

"Do you have to talk like that?"

"No; I don't have to. I just wondered if you'd marry again."

She went to the chair where the doctor had sat; she laid her hand on the ridge of cover that hid his hand. "If it would help you . . . tell me what's bothering you . . . tell me what's the matter . . . what made you go out this morning. I saw you standing in the rain. . . . I watched you."

"Did you? And you didn't run out to get me. You're like that."

"No. Don't talk . . . you mustn't talk. You need to rest. You can talk when you're well."

"That's right. I don't want to talk. I'm tired."

"Maybe if you closed your eyes . . . you could sleep."

"Seeing don't keep a body awake. It's remembering, Anna. If I close my eyes, I can remember better. Do you want me to remember?'

It seemed as if invisible fingers worked in the corners of her eyes, rolling the mist into crystal beads. She got up and went to the hearth to do her crying. She listened for the sound of the boys coming home from school, though she knew that sound was an hour away. In a few minutes she would go call Ursa; that would make three in the room.

Ursa came on heavy, noiseless feet. She sat at the corner of the hearth where, downstairs, churns were sometimes kept. Rufus saw her and closed his eyes. The rain began again, beating steadily, hanging a curtain of moving silver over the window-panes. If it kept up long enough, Rufus thought, he could go to sleep. Anna stood on the hearth, watching the clock at the foot of his bed. He was glad they did not watch his face. He would be all right by morning. He went to sleep.

When he awoke he thought he heard the boys in the house. Ursa had left the room (it was her job to keep the boys quiet) but

Anna was waiting patiently, watching the fire now instead of the clock. The change in breathing told her that he was awake.

"How do you feel now?"

"Like I'd been through a hay-baler." It was no joke; he felt as if his body had been pressed into a tight bundle and bound with endless strands of wire.

She gave him a capsule and a spoonful of the amber liquid. His temperature had climbed a full degree.

"Call the boys up here."

"All right. I didn't want them to wake you."

They came up in a rush. In spite of precautions, they could not believe anything could be wrong with a man who had never, to their knowledge, grunted, limped, or complained. There was a flurry of greetings, as if Rufus had been off on a long trip. "If you're sick," Jarvis said, "you can't take us to the game to-morrow."

"I'll git you to the game," he answered.

Wayne sat down and kept silent. His damp black hair was an uncombed, tangled mass, for he had barely had time to shower after basketball practice.

"Son," Rufus asked, "can't you find a comb nowhere?"

Wayne made no answer. He went to the dresser and combed his hair. Morris and Jarvis had been engaged in an argument over the passing abilities of Tech's Ludlow and their famous brother.

"Papa?" Jarvis demanded heatedly. "Is Ludlow a better passer than Rex?"

"I didn't say he was better," Morris corrected sharply. "I said he could throw it farther."

"I told you, you'd have to be quiet," Anna interrupted.

"Yessum," Morris said. "But Ludlow throws a longer ball. Papa knows. He can't hit his receivers as good as Rex and his ball takes a nose-dive. It's hard to catch. Rex keeps the nose of his ball on a level. Don't he, Papa?"

"Your mother won't let me answer questions."

Wayne finished combing his hair and returned to the hearth. Rufus watched the three of them. Wayne was going to be taller than Rex; taller but that was all. Jarvis was prancing about in knickerbockers, showing his magnificent legs. A little giant, Rufus thought, like me: like me a thousand years ago. More like me than Morris, even, whose shoulders kept the back of his leather jacket stretched tight. As long as they remained in the room, he would be all right. But, of course, Anna would send them away in a minute.

"I'll shuck your corn for you for a dollar," Jarvis said.

"A dollar?" Rufus said, beginning to feel the sway of the room. "Would you charge a sick man a dollar?"

"I wouldn't charge a pore sick man. But I'd charge a rich sick man."

"Ahhhh," Rufus grunted. "Looks like one of you'd do it for nothing. Flat on my back and 'bout to die."

Jarvis came and sat on the edge of his bed. "Are you bad off sick?"

He closed his eyes briefly. Sick, Lord yes, of a house I never built and chairs I never bought. "Why, son, I ain't never been sick. I just got the snoozle drips."

Jarvis thought it was funny. He set the room ringing with laughter.

I ain't going nowhere, Rufus thought: I never did mean to. He closed his eyes for a while. When he opened them, the boys were gone. Only Anna remained, like a sentry. She got more done with silence than anybody he'd ever seen. No doubt the boys were in the crib, fussing, shucking, tromping over his new corn. His breathing was becoming more difficult; he could hear the shucks rattle.

The real fear did not strike until darkness set in. The fact that the doctor was there made it all the worse. He stood as helplessly as the rest of them and listened to the feverish, random words. Rufus was delirious. They watched the tall, frowning man who held all the secrets; they waited for him to perform his miracle. He tried. He pushed the long needle into the solid flesh of his patient's arm. In a few minutes, Rufus was quiet, almost asleep.

The doctor sat at the table with the boys. They did not understand. They thought his miracle had been performed, and his presence was no longer needed. If he merely wanted a good meal —like the preachers—that was all right too. He talked about football with them; they saw right away he did not know much about it. Silly man with his little bag and monstrous needle: he ought to know Rex was not a quarterback. Rex was a left halfback who played in the tailback slot who quarterbacked. Nothing complicated about that at all if you understood the Tennessee single wing.

The boys thought it was not a very good supper, for it was the same old things they had been having: boiled ham, winter greens and turnips, butter beans, baked sweet potatoes, pickled peaches, hot buttered corn muffins, and apple sun-cake. The doctor kept both hands busy; it was exactly what he wanted: that was another reason he liked country patients.

"Mother's been busy all day or we'd have a good supper," Jarvis said.

"I believe I'm going to make out on this pretty well," the doctor answered. From habit he rushed through his meal, finished his coffee, and went upstairs.

Left to themselves, and feeling the crisis had passed, the boys began to mock each other. Even Wayne joined in the effort to banish the first death shadow that had ever loomed near their lives.

Jarvis occupied the doctor's chair and mocked his table manners; then he got up and pranced about the room, mocking the doctor's almost feminine gait. He seized Wayne's wrist and asked for a look at his tongue. "I say, did you have a good 'limination this morning?"

"Not that way," Morris said, and he went through the doctor's act.

Jarvis peered into Wayne's face. "Lemme see your teeth."

Wayne obliged.

"First teeth I ever saw in a hen's butt!"

Ha! Ha! Ha!

"Do you think it'll work, Jarvis?" Morris asked.

"What?"

"A windshield-wiper on a goat's hind end."

Ha! Ha! Ha! Their jokes grew rougher. They borrowed a few of their father's barnyard words. They laughed in brooding, hysterical whispers. Ursa came in to clear the table.

"I hear you. The good Lawd gonna hear you too. Liable to take somebody's daddy away frum heah. Ain't me saying it. Sumthin' come telling me. . . ."

A hush fell on them. The horrible shadow of death crept back once again. It could not be so, but the shadow was there anyway. They huddled together, tiptoed upstairs, and pressed against the closed door. They could hear the mumbling, the random words again. Their faces grew white and their eyes stared at one another. "You didn't need to talk the way you did," Wayne said. Their lips twitched, remembering, unable to refute him.

Ursa came up the stairs with a kettle of boiling water and an armload of towels. They made way for her, silently. Her huge, despairing eyes accused them. They knew. She entered and closed the door in their faces. She came out again, slowly, moving her men's shoes as quietly as she could. In her face was a flood of fear. Halfway down the stairs, she stopped and stared at them. "You better quit lookin' at me and start lookin' up at the good Lawd."

They pushed close together. They found it necessary to touch one another. "He said he was all right," Jarvis whimpered. "He said we could go to the game."

Wayne turned on him furiously. "Is that all you can think of? We're not going to no ball-game."

They leaned against the door again, forgiving each other. When a groan unrolled inside the room, they stepped back, as if to let it pass through the door. The room grew silent. Together they turned and looked behind them: they had visions of the ugly face of death crawling up the stairs.

"If he was to die, I'd run away," Jarvis announced defiantly.

Morris caught Wayne's eye. They could not help grinning.

Morris playfully stroked Jarvis's hair. "Where would you run away to?" A few minutes passed. They heard a train whistle dart through the grey, wet night. It was gone: the whistle, the train, everything except a closed door into which they stared.

Remembering the whistle, Wayne said, "I wish Rex was here."

They fastened on to the wish. It was like a prayer. Rex, the hero, the mighty one, the oldest, the strong of heart; Rex with his bright eyes and quick tongue and soul of fire; Rex with his flying heels and accurate arm and triumphant stance. If he was here, nothing bad could happen. He would tackle the bad angels who swooped down to take something away.

"I do too," Jarvis said.

And one by one they remembered Bayard, belatedly. They did not believe he could help; or perhaps they believed Rex would not need any help. But there was Bayard to be remembered, all the same. Strange, wild-eyed, with his girl-face brooding and sad. He could do no harm.

"And Bay-bay too," Morris said.

The others nodded.

The door opened. They almost fell against their mother. They expected her face to be filled with streaming tears, her hands to be ineffectual as moth wings. She was calm, tired; her eyes were dry and almost oblivious of them. She whispered clearly, "Tell Ursa to bring another kettle."

The three turned at once, but before they could go she stepped outside the room and whispered again, "Why don't you wait downstairs for a while. If your daddy gets any worse, we're going to call Rex and Bayard."

Anna returned to the room where firelight and fever struggled with each other. The doctor had off his coat and his shirt-cuffs turned up. "He's going to have to fight it. He's not fighting it," he said to Anna.

"He's never been sick," she said.

"Well, he's sick now."

Rufus opened his eyes, bright with fear and fever. He felt his body circle the room slowly and come to rest in the bed again. "Anna, I want to tell you about Jesse. I went to the well this morning. . . ." He decided there was no need to continue. It was all much clearer to Anna than to him, anyway. She sat down beside his bed and replaced his hand beneath the covers. Why would she do that? he wondered. He felt much cooler with one hand outside. The words spilled out of him with no effort. "You know I meant to leave. Walked and walked. Had to git sick before I got there. I made up my mind. Wanted to tell you about Jesse and the well, Anna. . . ." Then he slipped, past the white oak poles, down past the spider webs and into the circle of darkness. He thrashed wildly to keep the stagnant water from overcoming him. But part of it covered his face and seeped into his lungs. It paralysed his limbs.

"Try to lie still," Anna said. She pushed the covers around him again and tried to cover his hands.

He climbed inch by slippery inch from the bottom of the well, until his hands grasped the poles and assured him of freedom. He opened his eyes and saw her clearly. "Did you call Barney?"

"Not yet. But I will."

"You ought to call him, Anna. He'll take the boys. I don't want them to miss the game."

He rested for a while. Anna went downstairs and sent Wayne and Jarvis after Sidney. Morris returned with her to the sick-room; he could not remain by himself.

Rufus came to life again and fastened his eyes on the doctor's white sleeves. "Don't mess with that needle. Give me a good glass of whisky. That's what I need. I'll be damned if you don't let me die. You gonna assel around and let me die in a house I never built. . . ." He trailed off into choking, gasping laughter. Within a few minutes he returned to set his eyes on Morris. "They won't let your pore old daddy have a drink. Take you a baseball and conk somebody, Punkin. Doctor, this boy is going to the big leagues. I remember one day in Kerryville I had that ball breaking six damn feet. . . . Doctor, this boy's got a hop on his fast ball . . . curve . . . slider . . . git to any son-of-a. . . ." He continued, vulgar and profane. They stood, helpless before the madness that held the room. The powerful, pale body lifted itself from the pillows and fell back exhausted.

The doctor moved his finger across a chart. Anna looked at the figure: 104.

A rattle struggled through the silence. It was as if an invisible hand worked beneath the big man's shoulders, in a mattress made of shucks. The doctor shook his head slowly from left to right. For a long while he did not take his eyes from the bed.

The sound of voices in the living-room brought Anna to her feet. She went downstairs to meet Sidney and Amy.

They gathered before the hearth for a few whispered questions and answers. Their faces were frozen into a solemn, mute conspiracy against this sudden enemy. Their minds repeated Anna's words: "Only this morning. . . ." It was not the suddenness that shocked them, though that was stunning enough; it was the fact that Rufus was the victim. Who could ever believe that he would lie with his grey eyes flickering and helpless?

"Don't you think I ought to call Rex and Bayard?" Anna asked of Sidney.

"I believe I would," he answered. Though he had not entered the room where Rufus lay, he sensed the presence of death.

6

ON the night before big games, the new athletic dormitory was guarded by two watchmen. The two did less watching than one. They sat at a table in the small foyer playing checkers, giving neither thought nor talk to the Colonial-Tech game. It was eleven o'clock, and the only sound was the clump of a checker as one made a move, and the dripping of a shower down the hall. The regular watchman, a fat man with a long red face who had broken a leg while helping to construct the stadium, got up and limped toward the toilet to spit. He was no more than a yard from the pay telephone when it rang. Instinctively he lifted the receiver, and finding his mouth too full of juice to utter a word he spat between his feet, thrust one shoe over the dark blot, rubbing it into the concrete.

"Yes, ma'am. . . . Yes, ma'am. I'm sorry, you can't talk to nobody here to-night." He hung up the receiver, and before he could take his hand away, the ringing started again. He lifted the receiver and listened. Then he turned to the other watchman. "They say it's an emergency call for Rex Frost. Reckon what we orta do?"

"It's some ticky-tail girl calling that boy."

The regular watchman got an idea. "Operator, who's calling?"

"This is his mother," a third voice said.

"Just a minute." The watchman dropped the receiver. It swung like the pendulum of a clock while the watchman took his flashlight and went up the lighted stairs. Turning, leaning across the stair-rail, he explained to his companion that the boy's mother was calling.

Eyes fresh from sleep, Rex bounded down the stairs. He knew the call had something to do with Bayard. He was totally unprepared for the brittle news, calmly announced, that his father might be on his death-bed. "I don't know . . . what to tell you. I don't know what may happen. You get in touch with Bayard. . . ." He could do nothing but mutter one "Yes" after another. The line hung silent, except for a faint scratching, as if somewhere, in the miles between, birds walked nervously on the wire.

"I'm coming home, Mother!"

"I don't know . . . what to tell you," she repeated.

"I'm coming home. I'll get Fred's car."

For a second he looked down at the dark blot under his feet, then he broke furiously up the stairs. The watchmen looked at one another. It was their business to stop him. They put away their checkers, came to the foot of the stairs, and like good soldiers prepared to do battle. They had their orders: no one was to enter or leave the building.

Rex appeared on the stairs, dressed, holding a ring of keys. Instantly he read their eyes. His mind was set on a battle with Coach Kellogg, not with these two. He could tear them to pieces.

"You can't stop me."

"You know we got orders, Frost. What's the matter at home?"

"They're expecting my daddy to die."

"There's the 'phone. Call Coach Kellogg."

"I'm going to see him. You can call him and tell him I'm on my way over there now." The fight dissolved into nothing. He walked past them and out the door. He began to gear himself for a stubborn speech.

Sugar Bowl or no Sugar Bowl, if they couldn't win without him. . . . Well, they couldn't and Kellogg would shoot the fireworks. Looky here, Cornflakes (that was what the boys called him, and he did have a brown, crusty face), you might tie a trace chain around my ankle, you might keep me here, you can lead a mule to water, but you can't make him drink. I'm going home. Don't you ever think of nothing but first downs and touchdowns and points after? No, you crusty old bastard, you never had a daddy; you came crawling out of a football one September day. You've got a heart, a real ticking heart on the right side instead of the left. Bah! That's a churn of brown cream. You don't have a heart, right side or left. Run it again! Beat his guts out! You take that tackle out or you'll run this goddamned play till the sun comes up in the morning! Lemme hear some leather crack. What's the matter with you, Marshall? That block wouldn't knock over a cow lick. You know what's gonna happen to you, Saturday? That Tech tackle is gonna knock your teeth clean through your bunghole. I hurt my shoulder, Coach. Well, use your other goddamned shoulder. You got two, ain't you?

Marshall had a convertible (from a lumberman in Jackson, who played guard thirty years ago). He got it for making ten unassisted tackles in last year's game against Tech.

What do I care if it's your first chance for an undefeated season? What do I care if we miss the Sugar in the Sugar Bowl? What do I care about All-America (I'll be an All-American, anyway— already am)? I'm going home, Cornflakes. I'm fed up with it all, anyway. Change your heart over to the left side where it ought to be and maybe you'll feel better. Somebody might knock my teeth where you think they're gonna knock Marshall's. I've got nice teeth, all but one, and I'm going home, and you can't stop me. If they fire you for losing to Tech, and losing all that Sugar, you can join a circus and tame lions. You'd be a dandy taming lions . . . but you'd have to take that match-stick out of your mouth. They'd growl and you'd swallow it.

There was a light in the Kellogg house. He brought the car to an abrupt halt, left the lights burning. Few words, stubborn silence: that would be the best treatment. He hurried up the walk. The watchman had called, no doubt, and set the Coach astraddle of his fine high horse. He can't get too rough with me, Rex thought; I'll just pull the bridle off and leave. He knocked once on the door; the doorbell had been out of order for years.

The Coach opened the door. "Come in, boy."

Rex entered and waited near a coal fire already banked for the night. The Coach wore an old bathrobe that came a few inches below his knees. As always, he picked his dark teeth with a headless match. The pock-marks on his overly wrinkled face were barely visible in the muffled light. Rex wondered how such thin pale legs had ever carried this man to fame.

"What's the matter with your daddy?"

"Pneumonia. Double pneumonia."

"That's something will take you away from here. You want to go home, don't you?"

"Yessir."

He chewed the match stick into little splinters and spat them into the smothered fire. "If you go, you wouldn't get back."

"Nossir. I couldn't get back."

"I'm not going to try to keep you here, son. If he's that bad, there's only one thing for you to do."

Rex hesitated. His heart was suddenly running over, not for his father, but for the man who had made him into an All-American. "Coach, I. . . ."

"Go on," he said gruffly. "It's just a bad piece of luck. Lots of things bounce funny besides a football. I hope your daddy pulls through. . . ." He did not go to the door with Rex. He sat now before the hearth, snapped off a match head and pitched it into the coals. The head, finally rolling into a live coal, spewed a bright brief flame and died.

With the little brown stick he probed at his teeth. He had been in France when his daddy had died, and it had seemed that it would not, could not, have happened if he had been at the bedside. How could a man hold a boy back? So there went the game, the undefeated season, the Bowl, the chance of a lifetime. That was a lot to give up. But suppose he stayed and broke his neck to-morrow? Then what? Give him twenty years and the boy would be Governor: maybe he would remember something besides the cursing and the goading. Well, let the goddamned old grads lose when they had already broke out their bourbon for a victory and had been whining for ten days for tickets to the Sugar Bowl. That would give some of them double pneumonia of the bunghole and do them good. Let the fat-faced son-of-a-bitches lose a wagon-load of money: they were always sticking their tails in a crack. They were the ones who had ruined the game, the boys, and the coaches. If he had a boy, he wouldn't let him get close enough to a football uniform to read the numeral. Not even if he was a Rex Frost. He got up and threw the splintered match stick into the fire.

"Clark?"

He returned to the bedroom. Betty had awakened and was propped against the headboard smoking a cigarette. "What was it?"

"Nothing."

"Somebody else trying to find a place to sleep? I can't see why in the blue Jesus they come staggering in before a game like this and expect you to push a button and have their bed ready. Who was it?"

"Rex Frost."

"Rex? At this time of night?"

"I said, by God, it was Rex, didn't I?"

"What's going on? What's he doing here?"

"He's not here. He just went home. His daddy's got double pneumonia."

She flicked ashes over the covers. She was suddenly out of bed and struggling into her house slippers. Her eyes were wide and blurred with the fading visions of Antoine's, Arnaud's, the Court of Two Sisters, and the dozen little bars she had waited for for years. "You can't let him go! He won't get back in time! Where is he? Can't you do something? What'll you do?"

"I think, by God, I'll let you play tailback!"

"Now, that's cute! Isn't that cute? You let him go . . . just like that!"

He jerked viciously at the light cord, pulling darkness into the room, save for the feeble, sickening glow of her cigarette. "Will you get back in this bed," he whispered fiercely, "before you wake everybody in the house?"

"I'll get back when and if I want to. This is my room."

"Do you want them to hear you?" He had given up his own room that night to two old schoolmates: a newspaperman and a high school coach.

"You've got the least sense of any man I ever heard of. What earthly good could he do his daddy, even if the man's dying? He's not a doctor. You just mealy-mouthed and let him walk off. I know what happened. Get you away from a football field and you've not got enough guts to wring a chicken's neck. You remember very well Herbie Town played for you when his daddy lay a corpse. It wouldn't be. . . ."

"Will you shut up! Herbie Town didn't have as much sense as Rex Frost. And you haven't got any."

"Haven't I?"

"If I had a son. . . ."

"If you had a son. . . . You can't forget I never bore you a little Rex Frost to go breaking Conference records. You can't forget it. If for no other reason, you let him go home just to spite me."

"You ought to get you a cigar and a soap-box." A non-smoker, he disliked the sight of a woman smoking.

She stubbed out her cigarette. "He's got a yellow streak in him or he wouldn't have gone home. I've always said Rex Frost had a yellow streak in him."

"You've said a good many things about which you knew absolutely nothing."

"It's a fine come-off. I never heard of such a thing. If they fire you, I wouldn't lift a finger to protest."

"Oh, goddamn!" He got up, slammed the door after him and went into the living-room. Slumped in a chair, his head thrown back, he breathed the air of relief. Across his eyelids raced an image as luminous, as rare, as Halley's comet. They would not destroy it to-morrow, ever. The thing he had perfected was safe now; he was past the dread of seeing it broken.

Then he heard her at his bedroom door pounding, as if her little fists beat triumphantly against the face of fate. "Bob! Get up, Bob! Clark's got a story for you now!"

It was a few minutes past midnight. Bayard sat in the Moon Harvest Café reading "tomorrow's news tonight," or pretending to read. He was listening to two men, the only other customers, discussing the Colonial-Tech game, and the way tailback Frost, behind Colonial's downfield blocking, was going to leave a scattering of Tech arms and legs and teeth for the stadium janitor to rake up at nightfall. He wondered whether they would believe him if he should turn around and announce that Rex was his brother. Yes, they would believe him, because they were large, heavy-set men; it was the thin ones who would not believe. While he tried to summon courage to tell them, they got up and left. He turned to the classified ads (clumsily, with one hand in a cast) and looked for a small apartment.

Now he was living. Not for a minute had he regretted leaving the University. To be alone in a city of strange faces, among half a million tramping feet, was what he wanted. Within a few hours, you had become a man, you were on your own; and all the blaring lights and narrow streets and polished windows and lost, staring, friendly faces belonged to your kingdom. The noise cried down your throat and woke the things that had been asleep for a million years: the smell of newsprint recalled the low sea stench of the Nile, and a scorching hamburger crept up your nose like Nero's Roman smoke.

He had folded his paper, preparing to leave, when a young man entered the Moon Harvest and sat down three tables away. I know that face, Bayard thought; he is from the University. He was tall and thin, with a narrow face, extremely black hair, brooding eyes, and pale skin. One of the two waitresses, a tall girl with beautiful hair, turned from the cashier's counter and snapped off a small black radio that was pouring out its melancholy, hill-billy music. She went to the young man and sat down. They did not immediately say anything.

Bayard would not leave, because the narrow, pale face puzzled him. He checked his list of classes: history, algebra, chemistry, music theory . . . where had he seen the face? He ordered milk, a slice of pie, and waited.

"Long time, no see," the tall waitress said. She brushed at something on his hair.

"Only two days," he answered.

"Only?"

"Only two long, long days." He smiled.

"You want something?"

"No. Can you leave now?"

"I'm not supposed to till one. But sure. Stella won't mind. I'll go in a minute. How was the trip?"

"Okay?"

"I'll get you a cup of coffee and then we'll go. You're tired."

"I drove back. Driving gives me a headache."

She brought the coffee and stood for a minute with her hand on his neck. She went back to the counter and said something to the other waitress. The young man finished his coffee and waited for her. They went out together.

"You want something else?" the waitress asked Bayard. She was a large, neat girl with tortoiseshell glasses.

"No, thanks."

She switched on the radio. "You like music? He's funny. He don't like music."

"Who?"

"Jenny's friend. Oh, he's all right. Jenny's crazy about him. But he don't like music. Imagine that! Imagine a person that don't like music!"

It came to him very clearly that the young man favoured Wayne. That was it. He was glad to have it settled. Things like that would nag him to death.

"You know"—she leaned on the counter, absorbing the Tennessee Waltz while she spoke—"you'd think they were married. Only, folks are not so lovey-dovey when they're married. Least, the ones I know are not. You know any lovey-dovey married folks?"

"Well, I don't know many married folks."

"Hah, hah," she cackled. "That's a good one. I'm gonna tell that one to Jenny. You're new here, aren't you? I don't see you around before. I bet you go to school somewheres."

"I *went* to school."

"You done quich-u-ated, huh? Got a lot of degrees? I had a brother went to college for a while. Hey, I bet you don't know what B.S. stands for?"

"I bet I do."

"Hah, I bet you do too. M.S. is more of the same, and Ph.D. is piled higher and deeper. Ain't that a good one? Aw, flitter. . . ." She turned to the radio. "They gonna have the sports cast. Well, it's just five minutes. I got a girl friend used to date that sports announcer. But that was before he was sports announcer. He was just a little ole high school boy. How you reckon he ever got a job like that? You know, some folks. . . ."

Bayard was listening to the radio: ". . . matching the high-geared Colonial attack against the bone-bruising defence of the Techmen who stopped mighty Alabama two weeks ago with a skimpy one hundred and sixty total yards gained. The Indians will be fighting tooth and toe-nail, arrow and tomahawk, for a dish of Sugar and Colonial's first undefeated season. But all you Colonial fans hold on for this one: a late bulleting from the University reports that Rex Frost, their great All-American tailback, will not play in the game to-morrow. He has been called home to the bedside of his father, who is critically ill. Coach Kellogg, who confirmed the report, said, 'It's a bad piece of luck. Lots of things bounce funny besides a football.' Tech's Coach Walters, when asked for a statement a little while ago, replied, 'I guess we're a bunch of hopeful giant-killers without a giant.' That wraps it up sports fans, and won't you stop by . . ."

"What's the matter?" she asked. "Is it something in the water?"

He shook his head. The radio was pouring out its hill-billy music again:

> "Moonshine, you caused me trouble,
>   Moonshine, you got my man,
>   Right tonight behind them bars,
>   He's looking out upon the stars,
>   Moonshine, you put him in the can. . . ."

"Well, say," she said, "if you don't like this kinda music I'll cut it off. I bet you like classical. But you can't get that kind this time of night."

"I don't mind, but I'd like to use your phone."

"Go ahead."

The radio was still going strong:

"Ole man Judge,
  Couldn't you fudge,
    A little bit for me. . . .
Just a little bit, Judge,
Just a little ole fudge,
  And set my baby free. . . ."

She snapped off the radio.

He called the train station, then two bus stations. He could get to Cross City by six o'clock.

"Now," he said to the waitress, "could I make a long-distance call collect?"

She eyed him with mistrust. "We're not supposed. . . ."

"I guess I am acting funny. The news on the radio . . . about Rex Frost . . . did you hear it?"

"Oh, say, I bet you got money up on Colonial."

"No. Rex is my brother. I want to call home."

"Rex Frost! Really? I wish Greeky was here. If he was here he'd let you call for nothing. He cuts out pictures of Rex and puts them up in his room—I mean, I never have seen the pictures, but he says he does. Why, he'd be glad for you to use this phone."

He placed the call. The lines were busy. He had to wait almost half an hour, and while waiting he thought of all kinds of horrible accidents: Johnny and Nile Phelps driving off Polk Levee, Clarence Oldham falling under the wheel of a log wagon, Hillie Freeman blowing his foot off with a shotgun while rabbit-hunting, Roe Sewell catching his arm in a gin head, Charles Decatur Wilson falling on the spike that pierced his skull, three-year-old Tommy Knight tumbling into a boiling wash-pot. Yet, the announcer had not said an accident. The call came through.

"Rex?"

"I just walked in. Where are you?"

"Memphis. What's the matter with Papa?"

"Pneumonia. Wait a minute. Here's Uncle Sid."

"Does Mother know where I am?"

"No."

"Don't tell her I left school. Just tell them . . . tell them I came up here with Charles. Is he bad . . . ?"

"Wait a minute." Bayard could hear a brief conversation. "Bayard, Uncle Sid's going after an oxygen tank now. When can you get here?"

"I'm coming on the bus. It gets to Cross City at six."

"I'll meet you. You hurry on."

"Well, I can't hurry the bus."

"No. How's your hand?"

"It's okay. Listen. You tell Mother I hurt my hand playing

touch football, and I came up here to get it checked. That'll be better than saying I came with Charles. You hear?"

"Yes."

"Well, 'bye."

" 'Bye." Rex replaced the dead receiver. He had forgotten to ask Bayard how he knew to call.

The President of Colonial University, Dr. George McKeldon, was a short, thick man with weak eyes and a powerful vocabulary. He was reputed to be the master of fifty thousand words. The son of an undertaker, he had left home at the age of sixteen and spent six years in the Navy, where he was an expert wrestler. At twenty-three he entered Colonial as a special student, graduated three years later, and at the age of thirty departed from an eastern university with a doctor's degree in education. He climbed quickly: city school superintendent, junior college dean, state superintendent of education (the first ever to hold a Ph.D. degree), President of Colonial University. He was well into the fifth year of his régime, which was brightened no end by a dazzling football team (No, not dazzling; explosive was a better word for the Tennessee single wing system) that had conquered arch-rival Tech three times in four seasons and was all but a cinch for the fifth meeting. To put it modestly, his régime had flourished. The only real mishap he had suffered was the thirty-thousand-dollar loss two years ago to armed hoodlums. Fortunately, three members of the board of trustees had taken the loss with a sense of humour. As long as you could keep three of the trustees happy and laughing, you could eat high on the hog. It was a mistake to try to please five: sooner or later you would get your wires crossed. Three was the magic number, and quite sufficient.

And in the spring, when you went before the Legislature for an appropriation, it was important to carry with you the recollection of a November gridiron victory over Tech. It was an indelible mark of superiority. Did the trustees or the legislators care that young Dr. Thorton had made an important discovery in nuclear physics? That pint-sized Dr. Prince's study of minority groups was being recognized in sociology circles as a *chef d'œuvre*? That quiet, unassuming Dr. Traynor's American Literature text was now adopted by one hundred and seventy-seven colleges and universities? They cared all right. They gave it about as much attention as a fish gave a rainstorm. What mattered: Old Kellogg had a fine season; Old Kellogg beat Tech. The Legislature was full of University men, young and old, who had failed to make a living at the bar of justice.

Dr. McKeldon, I see you've got ten thousand dollars down here for the lyceum budget. Break that down for us.

Of course, gentlemen, the programme is not completely arranged at this date. Half that amount will be available for a symphony orchestra and concert artists; the other half will be chiefly for outstanding lecturers.

Dr. McKeldon, what does it cost to bring a symphony orchestra to the University?

About two thousand dollars.

Suppose we mark off the symphony and allow eight thousand? Does that suit the committee?

It suits the committee. Next item:

Repairs on Hemingsted Stadium. Thirty-two thousand dollars. Any discussion?

No discussion.

Recommended.

Gentlemen, Dr. McKeldon has requested, as you see, seven hundred thousand for the special building fund. It is my understanding that the Federal Government would furnish an equal amount. In other words, the Federal Government would put up dollar for dollar.

Old arthritic Jim Hodges rises like a jack-in-the-box. It won't go, Will. I'll fight it in the Legislature like a tomcat spitting tobacco juice in a bullfrog's eyes. All Washington's after is to git its foot in the door of our University. Next thing they'll be telling us who can enrol and who can't.

Shelved, for the time being.

Dr. George McKeldon arose every morning at exactly six o'clock. With eyes blinking, he went on flat, bare feet to the front door and found his paper. He suspected that some day somebody was going to get a glimpse of his bare feet, though six o'clock was about as quiet an hour as one could find on the campus. He hated shoes, particularly house shoes. From six to seven in the morning was the only time he could roam about freely with the lush carpets sprouting through his toes. He returned with the paper and had started into his study before he remembered that his two daughters—ages, twelve and nine—were sleeping there, for they had given up their own rooms to President Oscar Barron of Tech, his wife and daughter. The guest-room was occupied by the Chairman of the Board of Trustees.

He turned from his study and went into the spacious, overly furnished living-room. He always read the morning paper while standing, barefooted, digging his toes into the carpet. After a few minutes of searching for glasses, he found a pair and stood before the imported Italian mantelpiece reading first the stock market quotations, then the editorial page, and finally page one. The headlines in the sports box raked across his brain like an airfield beacon:

FROST WILL MISS TECH GAME
Father Critically Ill

He read the entire story, rushed toward his study a second time, and remembering the girls again, he went to the kitchen telephone. Coach Kellogg's line was busy. He was already being hounded, of course, at six-fifteen in the morning. What a damned shame the newspapers had got the story: it would cut the gate by a good five thousand. Newspapers got everything nowadays, down to the last bellyache. Then a new idea was conceived in the fertile brain of Dr. McKeldon. He squinted stubbornly at the paper and let the idea grow with cancerous effect: the blame could be placed squarely on the shoulders of Colonel W. B. Haverton, who, like all the military (officers, anyway), had a perennial fascination for the past and denied the future. The case of Rex Frost's brother was certainly at the root of it all. The boy had been virtually kicked out, and now Rex was retaliating. That was a splendid joke.

He dialled savagely. He could not fire the screaming eagle, but he could certain as hell wake him up at six-eighteen by the kitchen clock.

"Colonel?"

"Yessir."

"McKeldon speaking. Have you read the morning paper?"

"Nossir. I haven't. As a matter of fact, I was asleep when you called."

"When you get around to reading it, you'll find some repercussions from your 'walking walnut' case. Rex Frost is not playing to-day. He's at home. The Frosts have succeeded, quite appropriately, in tying your fanny, and mine, into a rolling half-hitch, because somebody didn't have enough insight to overlook the impetuousness of a sophomore."

"Why Frost can't . . . he's a good boy . . . I don't understand."

"But you understand that forty starving barristers, alumni of this institution, are members of the Legislature. When appropriations are set next spring, they'll still be remembering the Bowl we didn't get and the mauling we're going to get from Tech. They'll whack off half a million. What do you suggest?"

"Doesn't he know his athletic scholarship will be cancelled? Who let him go?"

"Who? You're looking at Napoleon's tomb now, Colonel. The problem is: he went. He doesn't hold a scholarship. He pays."

"What reason did he give for leaving?"

"A perfectly valid one. His father's sick." He softened suddenly. There was no need to make another enemy. "I wouldn't have called you so early, but I thought if we could do anything, we'd have to get on it right away. If you can think of anything, call me. . . ."

With the receiver safely cradled, he began to prepare a pot of coffee. Maybe he ought to call the Colonel again and transfer that "lack of insight" to Bowman: now, there was an old maid. Reminded him of a certain chief petty officer on the *Fargol* back in '17. No; he wouldn't call the Colonel again. He'd ask him to lunch Monday or Tuesday. A lunch would satisfy the old eagle. The damned Frosts. . . .

As the coffee began to perk, he heard steps. President Oscar Barron came into the kitchen. He was fully dressed, towering in the doorway, grinning sheepishly, and sniffing the aroma of coffee. Just an old clodhopper with a fresh shave and a hundred-dollar suit, McKeldon thought. It was true that Barron had been brought up on the farm, held his master's degree from a southern teacher-factory, could not have written a letter correctly punctuated if his neck depended on it, was a rank conservative, and among other things looked upon the electrical milker—which one of his professors had helped to perfect—as a crime against Nature and a monument to the slothfulness of men. When he was coming up, he often reminded his audiences, he got up at four o'clock and milked seven cows before breakfast. McKeldon often wished he could boast such a record when he went before the appropriations committee with his budget. Unfortunately, he had never squeezed a cow's teats, never thinned an acre of corn, nor harnessed a mule. It was a definite handicap.

"George, I didn't know you could cook."

"Morning, Oscar. Sit down, and I'll feed you a cup of coffee. We don't have breakfast around here till seven-thirty."

Barron sat down and gazed at his fellow president's bare feet. "You look like a bohemian."

McKeldon refused to be embarrassed. He poured the coffee and hid his feet under the table. "Secretly, Oscar, I am a bohemian at heart. I've always wanted to tell a few peckerwoods where to stick their institutions of higher learning, but I'm lacking in courage. That's where I fail as a bohemian."

Barron sipped his coffee, asked earnestly, "Have they been riding you too?"

Before there was an answer, Barron continued, "You know, George, I've had some bumps lately. I'll swear I believe they're going to put the pressure on me to take a leave and get my Ph.D. Can you understand that? After eleven years?"

"You're forgetting that old Kilgrow is no longer in the Governor's chair."

"You know I can't kick too much, George. He's kept me hanging on. But can you imagine a man my age starting out for another degree?"

"Don't worry, Oscar. You'll be all right after to-day. Read this." He handed the paper across the table.

Barron read with astonishment. Coffee dripped from his lips.

"Aw, George, that's a shame. You know we want to win. But after all. They tell me he's a mighty fine boy. You know, I've never seen him play."

"He'll be Governor by the time he's old enough to serve."

"You reckon?"

"So far as I can see, he has only one obstacle."

"What's that?"

"He seems to have an acute sense of justice."

"You know," Barron began, paying no attention to the paper nor to McKeldon's speech. His long nose was thrust into the coffee cup; he pulled at the last drop. "I'm learning to play golf. Can you imagine a man my age. . . ? It's absolutely fascinating. Why, I tell you I'm like a drunkard, with every green sprouting bourbon. The game. . . . You don't suppose it would hurt me. . . . I mean, politically. After all. . . ."

"How old are you, Oscar?"

"Fifty-four. Why?"

"I just wondered . . . wondered how you felt leading a crusade of three thousand young minds."

"What crusade, George? You know, this is excellent coffee. I'll help myself to another cup."

McKeldon made no move to serve him.

Wayne and Morris and Jarvis huddled in the kitchen around Ursa. It was almost two o'clock and she had not finished with all the dinner dishes. She dried her hands on her apron, broke three straws from a broom, and turning her back to the boys she planted the straws between two fingers.

"Whoever gets the shortest has to go," Morris said.

"No; the longest," Jarvis said.

"All right, the longest. One's fair as the other."

Ursa held out her hand. "Draw 'ccording to age," she announced with authority.

Morris drew the longest straw. He tiptoed up the stairs, opened the door inch by inch, and entered the sick-room. Anna sat between Rex and Bayard. They were leaning close to her while she whispered something. Morris moved around them and leaning over the back of her chair whispered, "Mother, is Papa better?"

She touched his face with her hand. "Yes, darling. He's better now."

"If we stayed in the kitchen, real quiet, could we listen to the game?"

"Yes; if you'll be real quiet."

Bayard whispered to Rex. "Why don't you go listen if you want to? I'll stay with mother."

"Both of you go," Anna said. "Amy will be back in a minute.

He's slept for over an hour now. You can tell his breathing is a lot easier."

"Come on," Rex said to Bayard. "We'll listen for a little while."

"I'll be down in a minute," Bayard said.

He was alone with his mother for the first time that day. He wondered whether she would pin him down about his hand: the cast was so gunglesome and obvious. To put her off, he whispered, "Mother, why does Papa keep talking about Uncle Jesse?"

"It's nothing," she said wearily. She had had only two hours' sleep since the night before. "It's just his fever."

He was sorry to bother her when she was so tired, yet he could not let this something slip past him. "I know it's the fever. But why Uncle Jesse?"

"You know we never did find out what happened to him. I suppose he's worried about it a lot, the way I did."

"Why did he keep saying he was going away? What did that mean?"

She laid her palm, damp and warm with relief, on his uninjured hand. As she spoke her eyes were half closed, set, not toward him, but toward the fire. "He did nearly go. So close. You don't know how close it was. I thought he couldn't live."

He had the feeling that she knew something she was not telling. But it was not like her to tell things. "It would have been terrible, wouldn't it, Mother? Terrible for you. For all of us."

"For him . . ." she said, and her voice trailed off as if the fire drew it and sent it up the chimney with the red oak smoke.

"Mother, why do they say I'm like Uncle Jesse?"

"Who said it?"

"I heard you say it once. I'm not what you think I am, Mother."

"How do you know what I think?"

"Oh, I know! I just know. I know all right. You think I'm sweet and kind. You think I have your disposition. I wish I did. No, Mother, that's not the truth. I wish I had Papa's. I would rather be like him. He's fair about what he sees, but he doesn't see what we see, does he? Everything bothers me. I wake up at three o'clock in the morning sometimes, wide awake, and I remember things. I remember things Uncle Jesse said to you and things Papa said to you before I was born. I know they're true. They're so clear. And I remember whole days that happened to me when I was four or six or twelve. And, Mother, I get mad . . . because I want the whole world to know me and treat me the way they know and treat Rex at the University. I think I couldn't stand to die and not be famous, like Rex. I do crazy things. I think nearly everybody is stupid. But they couldn't be. And then. . . ."

"What really happened to your hand, Bayard?"

"Rex did it. I made him do it. Mother, I made him so mad . . .

deliberately. . . . I enjoyed it. I wanted to. I spat in his face. I'm not what you think I am. I'm not good at all."

"I never thought you were good."

"Didn't you? No; you didn't. Because you're good, you love people who are not good. You can't help it. If Papa was a Sunday school teacher, you couldn't stand it. I know. You don't have to tell me. It's the half-good, half-evil; that's what you love. And that's why you can love so many things. That's exactly why."

They came to an abrupt, breathless halt. The fire crackled; Rufus was breathing regularly, with a faint, grating struggle. Bayard studied his mother's face; it held no struggle at all. He wondered whether she had really been listening to him. Maybe she did not yet understand that his fingers were actually broken, that he was finished with music.

But then she said, "Don't tell your daddy Rex hurt your hand . . . ever. I told Rex the same. There's no need. . . ."

"But, Mother . . ."

"It's enough that you left school."

So she knew that too. "What do you think Papa will say about it?"

There was the faintest intention of a smile. "You don't care what I say, do you? You only want to know what he'll say. Rex told me everything, but I haven't had time to think. We'll think about it to-morrow. Why don't you go down and listen to the game? I'm going to sleep a while when Amy comes."

He got up and kissed her. "I'm sorry, Mother. I've caused you a lot of trouble. But if I hadn't, I wouldn't have found out that I love you as much as I love Papa."

"Do you? Do you love me as much?"

"Yes, Mother, I do."

"Maybe the others will some day."

"That's a strange thing to say. But most things worth saying are strange."

To show him their talk was finished, she said, "Put some more wood on the fire before you go."

He chunked at the fire and piled on three or four of the quartered oak sticks. He was already into the job before she realized that he had only one hand to work with. The way he put wood on the fire, she thought, one would never know he belonged to Rufus Frost.

He opened his eyes and saw Amy and tried to wonder why she did not have a cigarette. He worked his lips to ask her, but not being quite certain of who was there and who was not, he grinned himself back to sleep. Not sleep exactly, for he could feel a worry hanging over him, and he knew he never worried in his sleep.

He remembered the pigeons on Court Square and on the

window-sills outside the sheriff's office and their jerking, iridescent necks. There was nothing to a pigeon, anyway, except his neck and his droppings inconsiderately scattered, like ugly drops of rain. Eight years and they never hit me once, not once, and Barney was always waiting to laugh when they did. He had never told Anna about the pigeons. That was another thing he should have told her long ago, and now it would be over with. A courthouse should never be spoiled, not by pigeons or anything. If he was sheriff again, he would catch all the pigeons and put them in the well with Howard's rifle. Let them fall like grey rocks into the dark water, and he would say, Look, Anna. Look what I've done. Spoil the water which was already spoiled and there would be nothing to drink. Scorching July and children crying at church for water and your own throat so dry you could not tell them to be quiet.

"Water. . . ."

Amy was Anna and suddenly there, holding the tube to his mouth. "Now," she said. "How do you feel? You've slept nearly three hours."

"Where's Amy? I saw Amy."

"She's gone. She left a little while ago. But she'll be back to-night. They just went home to do up the things. They'll be back. . . ."

"Did you ever smoke a cigarette?"

"Why, Rufus. . . . You're better. If you're able to joke you're a lot better."

"No; I'm not joking. Someday I want to see you smoke a cigarette."

"You get well and I will."

"I bet you wouldn't. You wouldn't do a little thing like that. Would you?"

"Oh, yes, I would. I promise you."

"No. You're not to pay attention to what I said when I was sick. What did I say? I didn't mean none of it. I'm not going nowhere. Did I talk about Jesse?"

"Yes."

"What did I say? Did I talk about Todda?" It was all very clear in his mind now: he had known for a week that Todda was going to marry Luther Whitmore.

"Todda? No, why? But it doesn't make any difference. I'm not jealous of Todda or anybody. Last night . . . early this morning, we thought you were gone." She seized his hand.

"Gone? You didn't call Barney, did you? They didn't go to the game. I saw Rex here."

"He's here. They's all here. He came in last night. They're in the kitchen listening to the game."

"They can't win without Rex."

"No; they're losing. They're two touchdowns behind."

"That's bad. Maybe it's good. I don't want them to win without Rex. Bring them all up here. I want to see all of them."

She rose to go. He reached weakly for her hand. "No, sit down. They're listening to the game. I know what they look like. I can wait."

He held to her hand and decided it was all right that she would never keep her promise to smoke a cigarette. It seemed that he could hear all the pigeons, imprisoned in the well with Howard's rifle, cooing and crying, "I'll keep still. I'll never jerk my neck again if you'll only let me out of here." After a while, when their hands loosened, or when his hand loosened, the pigeons were inside him. But he could wait. He remembered the boys' faces very clearly.

And still later, the pigeons flew over the stadium dropping their ugly rain. But that did not matter, for the crowds were gone (with no Rex Frost to hold them) and there was no sound except that of the two teams battling to a bloody standstill.

PART THREE: 1941. END OF A CIRCLE

I

UNDER the marquee of the Durmond Building the shingle rocked to and fro in the November wind. Thanksgiving shoppers passing along the wet pavement glanced up at the shingle as if it were a stop light. Some of them made a mental note of where they would go should they ever land in the middle of trouble; and they thought of the Yerby case, which was now history by the space of twenty-four hours. Upstairs and to the left, two doors bore the same sign as the shingle: Rex Frost, Attorney-at-Law. Behind the first door, a nineteen-year-old girl in a yellow dress typed slowly on long legal paper, remembering that twenty-four hours ago her boss, elegant in his grey slacks and navy blue coat, had performed for Noon Yerby a piece of magic which must have resembled Jesus at the tomb of Lazarus. He had calmly, slowly, cleverly snatched a man from the electric chair, the hangman's noose, ninety-nine years in Parchman. To-day Noon Yerby was back on his farm, feeding his chickens probably, while his name (and the name of Rex Frost too) flowed in black strips across a newspaper world. It was no wonder her boss had a new client already: a certain Mr. Joseph Tabor, who wished to bring suit against a certain Mr. Brinkley (initials unknown at the moment) for kicking his bird-dog.

"Mr. Tabor, I really can't take this suit. In fact, I would advise you not to sue at all, because . . ."

"But the law, son, the law states. . . ." Joseph Tabor, lean, brown, hollow-cheeked because all his jaw teeth were missing, was raging inside. If Brinkley had slapped his child, it would be a different matter: he would simply figure that his child had been impertinent and deserved it. His bird-dog, a gleaming Irish setter, had never been impertinent.

"The law, Mr. Tabor, is what twelve men in a jury box says it is. You just might happen to have a few men on your jury that don't care that much about dogs."

"I'll give you two hundred dollars. . . . I'll give you whatever you say. If you lose, that's my bad luck."

"It would be my bad luck, too, Mr. Tabor. I've never lost a suit in circuit court. Of course, I'm going to lose some time. That's not the reason I can't take it. I won't be taking any cases before the first of the year. I'm going to run for the State Senate."

Mr. Tabor did not read the newspapers, but he knew that

Senator York was killed in an automobile accident the week before, and the Governor had called a special election three weeks from next Tuesday.

"I'm going to give it a try. I may not win, but I'm going to give it a try. You could be a lot of help to me. In fact, my daddy told me to see you and ask you to help me at the Harmony precinct. He said you always rounded up a lot of votes for him."

"Well, I did. I did do that. I supported your daddy in both his races. You don't remember it, of course, but the last time he run, he got 219 votes at Harmony out of 337. That's pretty good."

"Mighty good, I'd say."

"I'll tell you what I'll do, son. I'll scout around."

"I sure would appreciate it. Papa would too. And you understand I just can't take any cases now. I'll have to cover four counties in less than a month. That's a lot of voters."

"Who's gonna run?"

"Jim Hodges announced yesterday. He's the one I'm afraid of. He's been representative from Tecumseh County for twenty-two years."

The buzzer sounded. Rex picked up the telephone, heard: "Mr. Harpole is here to see you."

"Tell him to wait. I'm busy with Mr. Tabor." Of course, he did not mean for her to say any such thing; he meant for her to say exactly what she said, "Mr. Frost will be with you in *just* a minute, Mr. Harpole."

Mr. Tabor moved to go. He was feeling much better, now that he had been asked to do something.

"Don't rush," Rex said. "He can wait."

"I better git on. You're right about that suit. You never can tell what's going to happen in a court of law."

"That's it exactly."

"Son, you're the first lawyer I ever saw that tried to keep a man out of a lawsuit."

"My daddy wouldn't like it if I let one of his friends get into a suit and lose it."

"That's right too. He always stuck by his friends. Much obliged for your time. And don't you worry about Harmony."

"I won't worry a minute, Mr. Tabor." He straightened a few papers on his desk and waited for Julian Harpole to enter. Mark up one neat stroke in his race. Rufus had told him to see somebody at Harmony, but he had not mentioned Joseph Tabor.

Uncle Sweetheart came in grinning. He had finally bought a two-hundred-dollar piece of bridgework for his front teeth, and the addition had the miraculous effect of making his neck seem longer—

also, he stuttered less. It did not, however, take away all the resemblance to a ground-hog. "How's the great c-counsellor to-day?"

"The counsellor is in an excellent frame of mind. I've just finished writing the announcement of my candidacy for the vacant seat in the Seventh Senatorial District."

"Unnhnn? Did you mention the late Frank York, distinguished and h-h-honourable lawmaker for many years?"

"The late Frank York was neither distinguished nor honourable."

"A truthful but not a p-particularly astute observation. Whatever your own p-p-personal feelings are, you can't afford to ignore the fact that Frank York meant a lot of things to a l-lot of people in this district."

Rex saw the direction quickly. "Papa asked you to talk to me, didn't he?"

"If you want to know the r-real truth, your daddy asked me to do everything I could to k-k-keep you from running."

"He thinks I can't win?"

"On the c-c-contrary, he thinks you can't help but win, unless...."

"Unless what?"

"I'm not supposed to go into details. I'll j-j-just say, unless Jim Hodges starts a lot of underhand s-s-stuff, which I'll assure you he'll start at the e-e-earliest possible moment."

"Like what?"

"No details, p-p-please. But may I ask you a decidedly embarrassing question?"

"Yes."

"How much money do you think it will take to be Senator?"

"I'm sure you'd be a better judge of that than I."

"Yes. I w-w-would be. I've had c-c-considerable experience in such manœuvres."

"But, Mr. Harpole, I think I ought to tell you in the beginning that I'm not going to spend one penny more than the law allows: that's one thousand dollars, which includes cards, posters, advertisements, radio time, everything. I don't mean to offend you. I know how you work, and that's all right with me, except I don't want to trade."

Uncle Sweetheart's face surged with red. He could count on his fingers the number of times he would get mad in a year. He was mad now, and he knew he would not stutter; he never stuttered when he was mad. He was mad because young Frost had not given him a chance: he had not come to make a deal at all; he had come to persuade the boy he ought not to run for a state office at all. He ought to keep up his law practice (always the defendant, never the plaintiff) and run for Congress when he was old enough (or when the war was over: for certainly there was going to be one). His eyes became two blots of mud between two narrow slits. He would teach this young turk a lesson in the very beginning. "Would you mind if I ask you a second embarrassing question?"

"No. I wouldn't mind."

"Good. Because I was going to ask it, anyway. I wish you would list for me two or three reasons why you won the Yerby case?" He held up one hand; his eyes did not waver. "Aside from the fact that you spoke like Demosthenes, that you had old men and old women drooling, that you cut the state's witnesses to ribbons, that you got under the jury's ribs . . . aside from that, why did you win the Yerby case?"

"I thought he was innocent. I still think he was."

"Come on, Frost. You can guess better than that."

"All right. I know that you and Papa did something. Or had it done."

"We had it done. We started working five weeks ago on the supervisors and then on the circuit clerk and then on the sheriff. Without them you had about as much chance as a soap bubble in a hurricane. Your daddy didn't tell you anything?"

"No."

"It's high time you learned something. We put paper-clips on the names of the men we wanted, or the sheriff did. When the sheriff put his hand in the jury box he felt for a clip, slipped it off, drew out the name. That's how you got your jury. Oh, I'm not taking a thing away from the way you handled the case, but be damn certain you give proper credit to your daddy. You had twelve men who stuck by you—or your daddy—and they didn't give a frown if Noon Yerby went to the pen or the chair or straight to Hell, innocent or guilty. You're twenty-three years old, son. . . ."

"Twenty-four."

". . . twenty-four, and bright as a star, but you don't exactly know how things are run."

"I didn't ask for things to be run that way."

"Be anything you want to be, but don't be ungrateful. If we hadn't got there first, the other side would have."

Rex's eyes bristled with cold scrutiny. In the first place, he did not like ugly people. "I was not the one on trial, Mr. Harpole. He paid me a flat fee, win or lose. If the court's decision . . ."

"How much did he pay you?"

"One thousand dollars. Exactly enough to run for Senator. I don't have to make any deals with you or my daddy or anybody."

"Son, you ought to leave your daddy out of that statement. You wouldn't have got the case without him."

"What I'm trying to get across is that I'm going to run my own race. Certainly I want you to help me. I want Papa to help. But I'm not going to make any deals. I'm going to the people with a clean record. I just happen to have a lot of faith in the people."

"The people! They don't know what they want, and most of all they don't know what they need. You mean you've got faith in folks who kept Frank York in the Senate for twenty-six years, who've kept Jim Hodges in the House for twenty-two years?"

"It wasn't the people. York and Hodges kept themselves in by scheming and buying."

"So now old Jim is going to turn good boy and quit scheming and buying?"

"No. I don't mean that."

"What do you mean? Did you ever hear of a politician buying a man who wouldn't sell? When Jim Hodges gets through with you and with your daddy and with you daddy's friends and with your brother and that book of his—when Jim Hodges gets through with all that, he'll make more ribbons out of you than you made out of the State's witnesses yesterday. He'll scrape you raw like a killing-hog, and burn your hair to fry you." His anger was gone now, driven away by the fear and doubt he had planted in the young lawyer's eyes; and he knew he was going to stutter. "You'll have to answer for a lot of s-s-sins, some you don't even know about. Things that happened when you were a little ole t-t-twinkle in Rufus's eyes."

"Suppose I dealt with you, what difference would that make?"

"I didn't come here to d-d-deal with you. I came to show you what you were up against. Wait four or five years. Go off to the w-w-war and come back a veteran. You could run for Congress. The t-t-time's not right now. There'll be a w-w-war; don't worry. We're p-practically in it now. When you get back, the people will be t-t-thinking about . . . well, they won't be thinking so m-much about sheriffs and books. You'll look like a h-hero whether you're one or not."

"The book won't matter. There won't be fifty people in all of the Seventh District who've read Bayard's book. Besides, he's not going to quit writing books just for me to be elected to office, even to Congress."

"Son, there are two issues which would defeat Jesus if he ran for Senator here: the liquor issue and the nigger issue. Your daddy's record will be hanging from one ear and your brother's book from the other. Two m-m-millstones instead of one. You'll have a h-hell of a rough swim."

"I'm not saying you've not got a point."

"Two points."

"Two points, then."

"But you're g-g-going ahead?"

"Yes."

"By me. I guess that's why you were an All-American. You'll a-a-anyway have some folks remember that—I hope."

When Uncle Sweetheart was gone, Rex sat down at his desk again and looked for the fourth or fifth time at the Memphis paper. It was a wonderful feeling to see his name in print again. For two years his star had waned, or at least it had been covered by a cloud of inaction. And Bayard's book had burst through (on the Hollow at least) like a blazing sun: *A Garden with Stones.* He took his personal copy from a desk drawer and leafed through it, noting the various marginal comments he had made of scenes he did not like or scenes he would have written a different way. The jacket design was all right: he supposed it represented a garden, with a grey overshadowing stone. But the title: he did not much care for the title. He must remember to get a copy for Mrs. Hamilton Hardy; he had faithfully promised her an auto-graphed copy, and already she had called twice asking about it, as if she couldn't go down to Benton's news-stand and wallpaper company and get all the copies she wanted. He couldn't blame Bayard if he refused to autograph a copy for the old witch. Let her keep calling. . . . On second thoughts, he ought to get it to her soon. She was President of the Catskill Club with its potential block of forty voters. A fine idea struck him; he loved to talk long-distance, anyway. He opened his door and called to Kay. "Are you busy?"

"Certainly I'm busy. I take your pay cheque every week, don't I? But I could spare a minute."

"Or two minutes?" He remembered Uncle Sweetheart's retort and grinned.

"Yes; two minutes." Or two hours or two years or two lifetimes, and that still would not be enough. So bright he is, with so little notion of what goes on in a woman's heart. She reached over and picked a fleck of lint from his coat.

"I'm going to quit wearing this coat. It picks up everything."

"Oh, no," she protested. "You look. . . ." What did it matter? Wouldn't he look like a god in a pair of overalls? "But they do catch everything," she added.

"Get Bayard on the phone for me."

"Do you know his number?"

"No; but he's got a phone in his apartment. It's listed."

He returned to his desk and waited for the buzzer. While he waited, he remembered a football game early in the fall: two weeks after Bayard's book was published. He had been sitting near a professor who had said to his wife, "Rex is Bayard's brother, honey. You remember seeing Bayard's picture last week. He wrote a novel." "Oh, yes, yes," she had said. "I understand they're going to make it into a play." "That's what I hear— or, rather, that's what I read," Rex had answered. "Bayard doesn't tell us very much. He's living in Memphis and we don't see him too often." *Rex is Bayard's brother.* It had been quite a blow, even if Bayard had studied chemistry under the man.

The buzzer sounded.

"Am I speaking to the Hollow's greatest writer?"

"I don't belong to the Hollow. I belong to the ages. Didn't you know that?"

"The Dark Ages. What're you doing?"

"What're *you* doing? Figuring up some scheme to obstruct justice?"

"Justice? Justice is like the moonlight: it shines on the just and the unjust alike. You don't believe in such things, do you?"

"No; but I believe in such a thing as the Southern Bell Telephone Company, and they charge so much a minute."

"Don't worry. I'm paying."

"Have you really made enough to pay your overhead? Or does Papa still have to carry you along the way he carries me?"

"I get along. Didn't you see that I won the Yerby case, or do you read the papers?"

"I don't read the papers. News is brief, but fiction is timeless. That's my motto."

"My motto is *Ad astra per aspera.* I break it down for you: To the stars by hard ways."

"You don't have to break it down for me. What'd you call me for, anyway?"

"To tell you I'm going to run for the Senate. York's seat."

"Hah!"

"You don't believe it. All right. I called to see if you had all the Stones out of that Garden."

"Not yet."

"What scene are you on?"

"Scene Two, Act Three."

"One scene to go?"

"Oh, many scenes to go, all combined into one."

"Could you take time out and autograph a book to Mrs. Hamilton Hardy and send it to her?"

"You called me for that?"

"Yes; and to ask if you're coming home for Thanksgiving."

"I'll be in on the train this afternoon."

"Autograph that book for me and I'll meet your train."

"I'm broke as you are. Suppose you borrow three dollars from

Mr. Frost—you know how it's done—and purchase said book and I'll. . . ."

"What do you do with your money?"

"I paid Papa my advance. . . ."

"You're not going to donate one book to my campaign?"

"No. Just a priceless signature. . . ."

"Aw, you kiss my south end while I locate the North Star."

"Bright, bright you are, bright. . . ."

Two loud cracks as each receiver went down a hundred miles apart. Rex always felt a curious sense of loss immediately after replacing the receiver on a long-distance talk. The whole business of a long-distance call was a little like getting drunk and getting over it. He hurried out to say something to Kay. The moment he said something to somebody his hangover would be cured. "Kay, I'm going to meet Mother and Papa. You can take off when you get ready."

"I think I'd better stay till four. A lot of calls are coming in."

"That's up to you. I'll be back Friday morning. Have a good Thanksgiving."

Have a good Thanksgiving. Was that all he could say? She watched him cover his beautiful navy blue coat with a more beautiful topcoat, which, she understood, his father had given him.

"You wear the nicest clothes." Then there was a moment of envy, much more intense than if she looked at a fine dress on another woman: if she had a father like Rufus Frost. . . ? It was no good remembering that her father was a drunkard and that her weekly cheque went to support two sisters and a brother. Anyway, the main worry was that he might never again come to take her to a movie or a football game and then drive out into country she had once—before she knew Rex —thought was wild and dangerous. She was aware that he was looking at the topcoat.

"It is nice, isn't it? Papa gave it to me."

She did not see where the present came from. There he was holding it out to her and she was filling the office with childish, delightful cries of thanks. It was the first present she had had in a long time. What it was did not matter. She would not open it until late to-morrow night: that would be a day and a half of wondering.

Rex went by the Post Office and dropped in a letter to Private Wayne Frost, Fort Hunterdale, Florida. The minute the letter slipped from his fingers, down the chute, he felt the same curious sense of loss as when he had hung up the telephone receiver a few minutes before. To-morrow would be the first Thanksgiving that the five brothers had not been together—either on Thursday or the week-end following. He did not know why the letter should remind him of his talk with Uncle Sweetheart. But it did, and he began to get angry.

He crossed the railroad toward the café. He paused for a few seconds beside his father's new Buick, then entered the café to find his father in a corner booth. He was irritable and nervous. He could not understand why any man who could afford a new Buick would choose a dingy hole in which to eat his lunch. "You been waiting long?" he asked.

"Just got here."

"Where's Mother?"

"I took her home."

"Did she go see the doctor?"

"Yes."

"What did he say?"

"I don't think he said much. She said it was her kidneys. Same kind of spell she had three years ago."

"Mother works too hard. She's going all the time. Ursa tries, but she's not much help to Mother. We ought to get somebody else to help."

Rufus nodded. "Your mother hasn't been well since Wayne left."

"Do you think that's it?"

"I don't know."

They ordered lunch plates of roast beef and vegetables. Rex had intended the lunch as a sort of celebration of victory in the Yerby case. Now he was glad his mother was not there. The smell of grease, mixed with the anger that welled slowly in him, was turning his stomach. He wondered whether he would be able to get down a bite. He hadn't won anything. If anybody had won anything, it had been his father, while he, Rex, had stood in the courtroom yesterday, imagining himself as the last thin straw of hope in a man's life, had mouthed like a puppet, calling on everything his mind could squeeze out; and the end of the matter was already inevitably fixed. He felt cheated, tricked by his own father. He would be anything but a puppet; he would be a failure first. Maybe his father was trying to trick him again, trying to keep him out of the Senatorial race, all because he wanted no skeletons exhumed from his two régimes as sheriff. He pecked at his food, refusing to eat. If someone had spat into his plate the food would have been no more nauseating.

"You're not eating."

"I'm not hungry." Then as if he must rush into the matter and get it over with, he said, "I was lucky to win yesterday."

"Maybe. You can't always tell which way a jury will go."

"Some people can tell."

Rufus knew immediately that Julian Harpole had had his conference with Rex. "What did he tell you?"

Rex stared at the hard, square, friendly face which he had always been able to defend, always. Now it seemed that he could have taken his hands and shaped it into anything he liked. Something from the web of anger inside him broke away and crept up his throat like a flame. "Why did you do it, Papa? Noon Yerby is not even a friend of yours. I thought that was all past. I thought. . . ."

Rufus did not stop eating. He did chew more slowly, however, and lowered his eyes to his plate. He wished he could remember more distinctly the first time he had sat in that booth, and the face that had been across from him; but he could not force his mind back in that direction. He said nothing.

"I wish you'd let me alone, Papa. I wish you'd just let them go ahead and tromp me in the mud, if that's what they want. I know they're crooked. I know half the people on the jury list would sell beeswax for honey. But you, Papa!" He would have gone on, for the flame was still in his throat; but he had reached the peak. To move at all was to come down.

Rufus pushed at his plate. He was beginning to feel a tinge of anger too, as if someone to whom he had given a bushel of corn for bread had trampled over his crib with manure-covered shoes. "You don't think they'd tromp you in the mud, do you?" Wanting no answer, he got up and paid the check.

As they walked to the car, Rex remembered, with another flame creeping upward, that he had asked his father to lunch and he should have paid the check.

"You want to drive?" Rufus said.

Rex drove. They did not say anything. The car moved smoothly with enormous power past the last fringe of buildings and along the paved road toward the Hollow. The rain had stopped completely, leaving a thick greyness over the countryside. On either side of the road there were snatches of cotton clinging like soiled wax to rotting hulls. Occasionally deep ruts appeared across the spongy fields where corn wagons had rolled. In a few places cattle stood hock deep near ditch-banks grazing on the winter-struck fodder.

Rufus watched the fields. Rex watched the speedometer needle move clockwise as he topped a hill two miles from where he would turn on to the gravelled road that led into the Hollow. As the car moved over the crest of the hill, Rufus turned his eyes to the road ahead. It was a nice block of bottom land, cut first by the canal and then by the railroad that lay like a freakish, endless ladder. The train pulling toward them from the left was hanging a rope of dark smoke that stretched back beyond the last box-car. Trains always stirred something in him; on grey, wet days their whistle sounds entered him like bird claws and scratched for what he had hidden.

Rex heard the whistle. He saw the hideous dark head ploughing madly forward, as if to recapture the sounds it had released. But the pressure from his foot moved the speedometer needle farther and farther. The flame had climbed up his throat until the white tip of it seared his brain. Everything he had ever heard about his father, from the first day in grammar school until this morning, fed the mad flame in him. A twisted mass of dealing and re-dealing and now he was in the middle of it. *My daddy told me to be sure and see you. . . .*

He could feel the enormous power at his control. It could not fix a jury nor mark a vote, but it could send them, together, father and son, tearing through that cold line of moving steel. And then they could come out on the other side, ragged but cleansed. His foot pressed down, farther, farther. The needle moved: eighty-five, ninety, ninety-five. . . . Why didn't his father say something? Why didn't he cry out? He could not look now, but what was on his face? The red lights were flashing and the bells were clanging and the whistles were ripping through the closed windows, but it was too late. His foot pressed with all his strength against the floor board. The needle quivered near one hundred. There was a springing jolt as they sped over the tracks. How close, how close? Rex thought. But he knew he was safely past and in another twenty seconds he would be turning on to the gravel road. His foot came up slowly. He could feel strength flowing out of his body, flowing out as the needle moved back and back. When it reached zero there would be nothing left in him. He turned on to the gravel road and stopped the car where sycamore limbs over-hung the road shoulder. His arms lay across the steering wheel; his head dropped down.

"You're that mad?" Rufus said.

"No," he answered as if nothing was left in him, no strength, no worry, no thought. "I'm that crazy."

"What got into you?"

Rex looked at him and the face seemed almost as calm as if there had been no train at all. "Don't you know? I was trying to scare hell out of you. I wanted you to yell at me. . . . I wanted you . . ." He dropped his head to his arms again. "You're my father and I don't know you at all. I don't know what you think or what you feel . . . or nothing. You've never really whipped me in my life. Why don't you break off a limb out there and give me a beating? That's my trouble. I've never been beaten . . . defeated. I've always won." He heard the car door open and for a split second he envisioned his father snatching a limb from the sycamore tree.

When he turned his head to look, he saw his father urinating into the edge of the gravel.

Looking back over his shoulder, Rufus said, "You scared me. Now are you satisfied?" He climbed back into the car.

Rex sensed the need to burst into childish, hysterical laughter, but he could not. He felt a blind new anger rising against this man who could forgive so quickly. Only those who had to be forgiven could forgive like that. "No," he said. "I'm not satisfied."

"Well, by god, just what would it take to satisfy you?"

"I want you to leave me alone. I don't care if I never win another case or never get elected to anything. I don't aim to be pushed around by Uncle Sweetheart wherever and whenever he likes. He's no good. I know he's a friend of yours, but he's no good. The first thing he wanted to know was how much it would cost me to be Senator. He's evil; his mind can't see a problem clearly. He's so evil he has no conception of the line that divides one thing from another. It didn't occur to him that I might be elected without buying and cheating and stealing and lying. An honest race wouldn't hold the slightest interest for him. They must have loved dragging you into things. . . ."

"Nobody dragged me into anything. But go ahead. I'll listen to anything you want to say."

"I'm not talking about you, Papa. I'm talking about the way things are."

"You asked me to leave you alone."

"I did; but I only meant. . . ."

"I know what you meant. I know from a long time ago, before I ever met Uncle Sweetheart and a few others."

"Papa, I didn't mean to say you were dishonest."

"You don't have to say anything. I know more about it than you do. Let's go."

"Do you want to drive?" Rex said.

"No. I don't want to drive."

Rex started the car slowly. Some of its power seemed to be gone. "Papa, I can't stand the idea. . . . I . . ." But he knew it was too late. He had driven the dagger home, through the hard flesh of all the years; and there it was buried, too deep to quiver. It would have been cleaner, simpler, kinder, if he had hurled both of them, a few minutes ago, into the churning mass of steel. He wished he could have caught his hand, like a child, but it was too late for that too. He had won, as he always won, only this time he wished he had lost. I was born to win, he thought. I break a body's fingers and he thanks me for it—almost. I drive a man within thirty yards of Hell or Heaven and then I accuse him and he pleads guilty. He wished very much that his father would bite a quid from his plug, roll down the glass, and begin to chew. After all, he was driving very slow and there should be no trouble in spitting the bright streams of juice through the window.

Rufus was glad of the silence. At least his son understood that he did not want to talk. Talk was no catharsis for the tangled web into which he had walked (not fallen) so long ago, and into which he had so lately dragged his son. The new smell of the car, hardly a month old, went down his throat like tobacco juice and set his stomach growling. When they turned into the driveway and stopped before the house, beside Rex's car, he sat for a minute looking straight ahead at the brown, lifeless yard. From the corner of his eye he saw Morris and Jarvis in the north yard pitching a baseball. Rex got out and went toward them. Another day, he might have followed, and he might have told Morris to be careful of his arm in such damp, cool weather. But he got out and went quickly toward the front steps. As he passed Rex's car he thought briefly that in it they would never have got by the train.

He was glad that Anna was not in their room. He punched at the fire, and then, dropping his hat and overcoat on the bed, he went to the door that led into a small, unlighted attic. Two or three times he bumped his head lightly against the naked rafters. Scrambling about in almost total darkness, he found the crib where five of his sons had lived so many hours of their lives. It was covered with dust and discarded clothes. Twice he had been prepared to give the crib to Sidney and Amy, though he had dreaded the thought of watching it leave the house. He brushed everything aside and knelt as he had knelt a thousand times to peep through the narrow ribs and rub his nose against one of their faces. All of them, except Wayne, had learned some prank before they were nine months old: a twist of the face, a peculiar grunt, something. Now all of them, except Wayne, excelled in something. Jarvis was going to be the football equal of Rex—if not better. He was more powerful, for one thing. Morris had already been signed into the St. Louis Cardinal farm system, and in three or four years what could keep him from going up? What, except bad luck? Only Wayne was left without a talent, and maybe that was why he had had to get away. Wayne and Dean: they had the same body, the same black hair and eyes. Wayne would be the last to accuse him and the first to die if there was a war. The thought of war—the certainty of it— burst on him there in the darkness like the train of an hour ago. If it had been the answer for Wayne, it might also be the answer for him. It might get him away. His going now was only a matter of time, and how slowly time leaked through the bright, curious, accusing eyes of his sons. He stood up quickly and bumped his head again. It did not anger him; it merely reminded him again that he lived in a house he never built.

Anna was in their room calling to him. He returned through the small attic door and startled her. "Oh, you've ruined that suit. What were you doing in there?"

"Looking for something."

"For what?"

He did not know. She did not press the point; she rarely pressed the point about anything. "Come here, and let me brush you."

"How're you feeling?" he asked.

"I'm feeling pretty good."

He stood on the hearth like a child while she brushed at the layer of filth and dust that covered his clothes. Why, he thought, should he resent her hands moving so tenderly and carefully over his body?

"When I get to feeling better, I'm going to take a whole day and clean that place up. But I just haven't felt like it lately."

"Let Ursa do it."

"Poor old Ursa couldn't get in and out of there."

"We'll get somebody else, then."

She finished with her brushing. "Bayard called to say he wouldn't be home until in the morning. Somebody planned a party for him or something. You needn't meet the train."

"I didn't know he was coming."

"He said he talked to Rex."

"I can't help what he told Rex. I said I didn't know he was coming." He had not meant to be cross, but it had spilled out naturally and there was no retreating, no retreating at all these days, even if she wasn't well.

He changed into khakis and work shoes and a heavy leather jacket. Though it was still early, he went to the crib and began his shucking. He wanted to take out his plug and bite off a chew, but he had a feeling it would not give him any pleasure.

2

THERE was no bell to ring, and when no one answered his knocking, Bayard found the key beneath the door-mat and entered. He left the door slightly ajar so that Jenny and Dean (when they returned from wherever they were) would know that he had arrived. The gas was on and the room was pleasantly warm: they had probably gone out to the store. He should have gone home, but Jenny had insisted: it was not easy to refuse Jenny.

He spent a few minutes looking about the apartment, which was already familiar to him. Jenny had a way of rearranging often, and almost every time he came there he had the feeling that a great deal had been added or replaced. It was one of the few rooms he had ever seen that completely pleased him. Oddly enough, it was really a man's room: the couch with its plaid cover, the plaid curtains to match, the natural oak lamps, the plain bookcase, the grass rug. He had always thought of it as Dean's place, planned and arranged by Jenny. But he knew that Dean lived with his mother and step-father, though he had no idea of the street or the house or the room that Dean called home. The truth was that he did not know very much about Dean or Jenny either, except that they both fascinated him. Offhand, he would have said that he knew everything— they seemed to have told him everything—but when he pinned himself down with a few questions about them, as he often did for no reason, he found himself without answers. There were times when he believed that they lived together as man and wife; yet that did not seem quite right, with a mother and stepfather so near.

In the beginning, two years ago, he had been overly suspicious of Dean. They had nothing in common, so far as he could see, and even so Dean had all but hounded his trail. When Jenny was working, they went to shows together; sometimes they walked for miles along the river together; sometimes Dean came to his apartment at the oddest hours, for no explainable reason, and without a word of warning. Once he had got up from his typewriter and looked around to find Dean stretched out on the couch behind him. He did not know how long he had been there or why he had come. It was eight o'clock at night, and he was sure the door had been bolted.

At first he had not thought about the bolted door. It had not occurred to him to be afraid. He was irked by the simple fact that his work was being interrupted. Dean lay with his head propped against the wall and with the latest copy of *The Atlantic Monthly* magazine closed over one finger. "Go on with your work," Dean said. "You're not bothering me. I'm just reading."

"It so happens that I don't work very well with somebody staring at me."

"I'm not staring at you. I'm reading."

"Anyway, I can't work."

"I'm sorry."

"What did you come here for?"

"I didn't come for anything. Jenny won't be off till midnight. I just came. I didn't think you'd mind."

"Well, I do mind."

"I'm sorry." He replaced the magazine on the small table, exactly where it had been, and went to the door.

As his hand touched the door, Bayard said, "No; don't go. I didn't mean to sound the way I did. I'm not going to write any more to-night, anyway. Would you like a Coke?"

"Sure, if it won't bother you. I mean, if you're really not going to work. I'll get them." He went into the small kitchen, returned with two Cokes and two napkins. Exactly as if he owned the place, Bayard thought; still, there was something about the gesture that he liked, just as there was something he liked about the fiery black eyes, the narrow face, the unruly heap of hair.

Bayard sipped his drink slowly and wondered why he had not let Dean go. He had a perfect right to say what he had said; if he had not retracted, Dean would have gone and perhaps that would have been the end of their relationship. For several weeks he had intended to put a stop to it. After all, he did not really enjoy going to the shows with Dean, or walking with him, or even talking with him. The chance he had wanted had come and he had not taken it. He did not like to offend anyone, but he had not retracted primarily to avoid offence. He was simply not able to break the bond, whatever it was.

"What do you do?" Bayard burst out. "What kind of work? I've known you for almost a year and you don't seem to do anything."

"I don't like to work."

"But you have to live."

"I'm living. I get along. Maybe Jenny keeps me up."

"Not on the salary of a waitress."

"How would you know what she makes?"

"I don't. But I know she doesn't keep you up. I could tell it if she did."

"Maybe my old man treats me like your old man treats you. Gives you money and lets you do what you want to. Only he doesn't. In the first place, he's my stepfather; in the second place, he works on the railroad and hasn't got it; and in the third place, I wouldn't take it, unless I was doing something like you. You know, you're going to be a good writer."

Bayard finished his Coke and set the bottle down beside his chair. Where had he got to? Where had he ever got to in finding out what went on behind that pair of fiery eyes, beneath that shaggy mount of hair. "Why do you like me?"

"I never told you I liked you, did I? I don't remember it if I did."

"No, I don't suppose you ever did. I just assumed. . . ." He felt the sinking, horrible feeling that he was being rejected. He was more than irked now; he was angry. "Well, you're always looking me up or calling or coming here. After all . . ."

"I'll tell you, then. I do like you. You're lonesome, and I'm seeing after you. Who would see after you if I didn't?" He began to laugh over the top of his Coke bottle, wild, friendly, explosive laughter. A warning that nobody was going to hem him into a corner. Continuing his laughter, he said, "Now you'll have to know *why* I like you. You'll try to slip up on my blind side and catch me off guard. . . . No, you don't slip up on people. You'll just ask me, and I'll tell you, but you won't find out. I'll tell you something, but it won't be the truth. You ask me."

"That would be silly if you don't aim to tell the truth."

"I'll answer, anyway. I like you because you don't like cheap, hill-billy music."

"You always manage to thoroughly confuse me."

"So what? We're enjoying it. You are enjoying it, aren't you?"

"I suppose I am."

"You enjoy my coming here too. You enjoy me. Period. You are the only person I know who enjoys me. Jenny loves me, and you enjoy me. You don't know whether to like me or not. But you're remarkably curious. As long as you allow me to like you, I don't really care whether you like me or not."

"I hope you don't mind if I say you're the strangest person I've ever seen in my life."

"I don't mind what you say. The only reason I'm ever careful not to offend you is that if I offended you, you wouldn't enjoy me—maybe. Then pretty soon I wouldn't have the chance to like you."

"I'm sure that's pure logic."

"Oh, no, just pure selfishness. Pure and undefiled. Which is the worst kind of anything. Well, I'd better go."

"Don't go. It's a long time before Jenny will be off." Now why did he have to say that?

And Dean had not gone. He had stayed on another hour, both of them chatting with no more form and sense in their talk than in an infant's array of blocks, heaped one minute and levelled the next.

That night Bayard had awakened in a cold sweat, knowing beyond a doubt that Dean had entered his apartment after he had bolted the door. The next day he had gone to a ten-cent store, bought a night latch, installed it himself, and had never used it.

As the months passed he began to see Dean alone or with Jenny regularly. And he found himself calling them as often as they called him. Their calls, or appearances, were no longer interruptions, any more than a meal would be. The two had become a part of his life, and he was thankful for having them. Sometimes, when Dean was away for several days (down in Mississippi at his stepfather's farm, he said), he went to the Moon Harvest or to Jenny's place, awaiting the return so anxiously that Jenny always noticed.

He had long since forgot to care what Dean did, if anything, other than take trips to the farm. And if Dean wished to keep his street and house and room and mother and stepfather hidden, that was all right too. Secretly (he would not whisper this even to Jenny), he believed that Dean might be ashamed of where he lived, and the fine clothes he wore might be a mask to hide his grey, porchless hovel. That, he told himself, was why his gifts for Dean were always much more expensive than the ones for Jenny.

Now, moving about in the apartment, still thinking of it as Dean's and not Jenny's, he was glad he had not gone home. He would be at home for Thanksgiving dinner to-morrow, and that was the main thing. He must remember not to stay too late: Jenny would have to work hard to-morrow.

Lying flat on top of the bookcase was a copy of *A Garden with Stones*. He could not help but touch it, and, reaching out, he lifted the cover and read the inscription: "For Jenny and Dean, with love and affection." He always squirmed a little when he read his own inscriptions. What was there to say, anyway? What was there to say for old Mrs. Battle-axe Hamilton Hardy? He was still holding the book's cover, as if he could not turn it loose, when the door swung back.

Both Jenny and Dean carried a bag stuffed with groceries. Bayard helped them stack away odd items in the kitchenette, and they set about immediately preparing supper. "We'll get it all set up," Jenny said. "Then we'll have a drink or two drinks or three drinks . . . only Dean never has but one. I can finish everything in jig-time." Turning to Bayard, she added, "We didn't treat you fair."

"How's that?"

"You meant to go home, and we made you stay."

"You didn't make me stay. I wanted to stay."

"You wanted to go home too. I can tell, Bayard. I meant to have a real party next Friday and celebrate the end of the play. But Dean has to go out of town, and he may be gone for a week . . . so we're celebrating to-night."

"That's bad luck," Dean said.

"What's bad luck?" she asked.

"Celebrating the end of something that hasn't ended."

"Child, you're too superstitious."

"I'm not a child."

Their glances crossed like swords. They said nothing else right away, but Bayard felt there was something wrong between them, and they had brought him there to help patch matters. They had their drinks and made small talk, but they could never settle into their usual comfortable state. Was the play nearly finished? Yes, it was nearly finished. So he would be leaving Memphis. Was he going to New York when the play was finished? Maybe. What would they do when Bayard left. Do like they do over the river, Dean said: do without.

Just as the steaks were placed on the table and they were sitting down, the telephone rang.

"If that's Cleve, tell him I'm not here. Tell him Mother's sick and I'm at home."

"He won't believe that," she said.

"Well, you think of something to tell him. I don't want to talk to him now."

Bayard did not understand, but it seemed no great mystery that a Cleve somebody should call and Dean shouldn't want to talk. Then he found out it was not Cleve, but Stella, who said that Greeky was worrying his lungs over the cranberry sauce that somebody had failed to order for to-morrow. And Jenny told Stella to tell Greeky to quit worrying his lungs and go to any one of a hundred grocery stores that were still open and buy a gallon or two gallons or a barrelful if he wanted that much. Yes, that cute writer was here and they were eating steak, which was getting cold.

They finally did begin on the steaks, and Dean thought they were not tender enough.

Jenny reminded him that he had selected them.

The dishes were finally washed and stacked neatly away, the broiler was scrubbed and dried, and ten o'clock came at last. Bayard began to make excuses that he had to get up early to catch the train home, that Jenny had a long hard day ahead of her. To his surprise, they made only the faintest protests, which was the same as agreeing with him. He felt the whole miserable weight of the evening descend upon him. It was punishment for not having gone home in the first place, as he had promised. Not that one evening mattered so much, but all the other evenings, all the other hours he had spent here or with Dean had become infected with a strange glare. It was like looking at a picture of the Last Supper hung beneath hideous, neon lights. After he had stood and put on his coat, he was still not able to make the final move. Perhaps a few more minutes and a look, a glance, would help to lift the weight. It was as if all his affection for them was based on the understanding that Dean and Jenny loved one another, and now he knew he had misunderstood, had misjudged their feelings, but his affection remained out there, beyond withdrawal, severed by the keen edge of a hidden knife. His departure

was awkward and cool. He went out as if he left a store from
which he had purchased a cheap and shoddy article at a very
dear price.

Dean lay on the couch, which Jenny had quickly made into a
bed, looking out at the river. He knew he had come to the end of
something, and somehow he would have to start all over again.
It was not easy; it was not easy to stop or to start again. It might
be impossible.

Jenny stretched out beside him. Her hand pressed against his
ribs. Why couldn't she leave him alone? Why couldn't she go to
the other side of the room and turn her face to the wall and stand
there until the feeling had passed? It would pass. It had always
passed. He was sick. His stomach cramped. He remembered that
long, dingy hovel of his childhood; he remembered the smell that
came up from the rotting, grey Negro houses; he remembered
squatting in the corner of the garden, behind the grey palings, and
turning to look, without astonishment or even surprise, at the milk-
white worm that had passed through his own bowels; he remembered
scratching a trench with a dead okra stalk and burying the squirming
white object alive; he remembered the sickening, though not sharp,
pain around his navel and the choking feeling in his throat and the
turpentine Lizzie had put on his tongue, and his mother coming
home in the rain.

"What is it, darling?"

"What is what?"

"What's the matter with you, with us?"

"Nothing."

"Of course it's something. You're tired of me."

"I'm tired of everything."

She moved her hand. That was nice of her. He took her hand
and put it back over his ribs, over his heart.

"Why didn't you want to talk to Cleve?" she whispered.

"I told you I was tired of everything. I want to get out."

"Aren't you going to Golden with him?"

"Yes; I'm going to Golden with him! I'm going everywhere with
him! I'm going to Hell with him!"

"Don't, please. If you want to get out, you can get out."

"Can I?"

"Yes, we both can."

"We said that a long time ago."

"Something has happened to you. It's something about Bayard—
because he's leaving—isn't it?"

"I don't know."

"Please tell me."

"Tell you what?"

"Tell me what has happened to you. I love you."

"You love me! You love me! Nobody has ever really cared anything about me but him. He believes in me! You . . . if you loved me would you stand for the things I do? How could you?"

"Do you love Bayard?"

"What does it matter?"

"I understand these things. Bill didn't go to California for the reason you think. Cleve . . ."

"I'm not like Cleve! Bayard's not like Cleve! What are you trying to do to us?"

"You think it's different?"

Her hand became a great claw over his heart; her eyes were steel. He raised up slowly and slapped her. "Bayard is my brother. Haven't I got a right to love him . . . to feel closer to him than anybody if I want to? You . . . you talk about all your understanding. You don't understand anything!" He got up and moved across the room; he kept his face turned from her.

When she spoke, her words were muffled. He thought she must be lying on her face. "Why did you wait until now to tell me? Why did you deliberately make me suffer . . . make me think . . . ? You don't understand anything either."

"That's right. I never understood anything. I never even understood how a worm crawls."

"What do you mean by that?"

"Nothing. I'm telling myself something about something that happened before I ever saw you." He went to the bed, bent over and kissed her hair. "I hurt you and you hurt me. We're even."

Her face was buried in the spread. "How could Bayard be your brother?"

"The same way anybody might be. We have the same father."

She lifted her face and looked at him. "You are telling the truth, aren't you?"

"Yes; I'm telling the truth."

She put her arms around him. She held him tight against her breasts. "I couldn't bear to lose you. I couldn't bear it. Lie down. Lie down beside me."

"I want to go, Jenny."

"Where?"

"Home. I want to go home."

"All right. Kiss me."

He kissed her with warmth, with some of the wild, tender childishness that was in him. She was almost glad he was going: the pain of his absence would make everything so real again.

She heard the door close; she listened to the sound of his steps on the stairs. She got up, locked the door, and prepared for bed. Alone, in the darkness, the bed seemed wider than ever before. The pain she had wanted and expected to feel was not there; in its place was a gnawing doubt whose hideous fangs sank deeper and deeper. She had lost him. How and why were not important. She had lost him: the last thread leading to him had snapped. His confession, his story of Bayard, floated in the darkness over her like a wild dream, a desperate concoction on which he would walk (or run) to freedom. He was at Nebold corner now . . . he was running now . . . the chill night was tearing through his hair. She must not . . . she simply must not. . . . But the next minute she was making her way across the room to the telephone. She managed, without the aid of light, to dial the number. The receiver shook about her ear.

"Bayard, this is Jenny."

"Yes. . . ." There was only the live sound of the telephone. "Is anything wrong?"

"You tell me."

"What's the matter, Jenny?"

"I want to know if Dean's there?"

"No. Why?"

"If he was to come by there, don't tell him I called."

"Why should he come by here? What's happened?"

"Nothing. We had a fuss, that's all. It's really nothing. He'll be in a good humour to-morrow."

"I'm sorry."

She was a fool, of course. She brushed past a chair into the kitchenette. A glass of milk and she could go to sleep all right. The refrigerator light startled her. The last swallow of milk tasted bitter and slimy. Moving to the faint outline of the sink, she ran water into the glass: glasses were so hard to wash when milk dried in them.

The bed assumed its natural size. There was absolutely nothing to worry about. She would be asleep in a few minutes. But he had gone . . . he had walked off. And hadn't Bayard sounded a bit strange? "I'm sorry." Nothing more. She must not . . . simply must not call his home. She got up and stood alone in the darkness.

Dean got off the trolley and walked down the slope that led to his mother's place, which was the west side of a small white duplex that faced an open two-acre lot used for a lumber-yard. Though the west side of the duplex was almost unbearable in the summer, that was the time of year he liked most to come there. Then he could smell the rich pine lumber that had baked all day in the sun, leaking its amber and crystal. The children played late that time of year, leaping and hiding and seeking until only their cries came up to him from the vast triangular wooden wells. One night

—the first summer he had known Bayard—he had sat on the front steps listening to them, because it was too hot to sit inside. All at once he knew they were singing, huddled together in the dark, their voices pouring from the deep lumber well like clear water. It was the first music he had ever liked. He imagined that he was one of them, that Bayard was another; and somewhere near in the faceless dark was Rex and Wayne and Morris and Jarvis—and perhaps Hershel. (Hershel had never really been his friend, but he was poor enough and the only other white boy within half a mile.) That was the same day that Bayard had asked him to go home with him for the Labour Day week-end. As he sat wondering what it would be like to go home with Bayard, the voices grew louder. A chill began to cover him, a chill with a hundred fingers that strummed on his muscles and set his body shaking. (He had felt the same violent seizure once before, lying beside Jenny with only his hand touching her.) He cried out against the voices: Stop! Stop! But the words rose through his dilated throat and spilled from his lips as silently as foam. The next instant he had fallen back into a sobbing heap with his nose and mouth pressing against the dusty grey floor. His mother had heard or had seen, and when she and Luther rushed out to him he was able to say it was his stomach. Stretched across the bed, he allowed her to put turpentine on his tongue, dab it in the hollow of his throat, smear it around his navel. She had learned the remedy from Lizzie, who said she had known a child who was choked to death in his sleep by worms. Luther did not understand what the trouble might be, but he stood by so sympathetically that Dean decided he might some day like him after all. He never brought himself to tell her that his stomach-ache was a sham, but he did tell her about Bayard and the invitation. He expected her to turn pale at the thought of such a visit; she did nothing except ask quietly, "Are you going?" He had laughed and laughed, though there was a moment when he wanted to say, "No, Mother, I'm not going, but it would be a lot of fun."

He had never again heard the children singing, but every time he came home now it was as if he had come to hear the children. Nothing else, he thought, bound him to that house.

Before he reached the corner he saw a light in his mother's room. A few yards farther on he turned off the walk, went like an insect toward the shaft of light, through it, and stepped on to the porch. Fumbling for the right key, he could still feel the light on his face, like one of Bayard's stares. He decided he was going to be nice to his mother this time.

"Luther? Is that you, Luther?"

"No. It's me." He made his way down the narrow hall to her open door. She was laying a magazine aside, pushing the covers back to get up. "Don't get up." He sat down on the foot of her bed.

"I thought it was Luther. He should be here by now."

"Did he have the Chattanooga run?" He had no interest whatever in Luther's runs, but he hoped to please her by asking.

"He didn't know what run he'd have. But I'm afraid something has happened."

He noticed then something that had dawned on him a year or two after his mother had gone to work as cashier in a large, respectable cafeteria: she spoke with assurance and correctness. He could not help reaching out for her hand, and for the briefest second he imagined it was a gesture Bayard would have made to his mother. "Oh, nothing has happened," he said. "None of the trains are on time now."

Though he withdrew his hand immediately, the gesture moved her almost to tears. She had failed him, just as she had failed his father, and now it was no wonder that he sat on the foot of her bed a stranger. She wanted most of all for him to talk to her, and yet she was afraid of what he might say. There was no need to pretend that she had anybody now except Luther. "He's never been this late before."

"Aw, Mother, I've seen him come in at all hours. Do you really care that much about him?"

"Luther is good to me—and to you."

"But you don't love him the way you loved Papa?"

They were both startled at the word; if he had ever used it so directly before, neither of them remembered. Just as they turned their eyes to each other, the telephone rang. The sound of it seemed to paralyse her. "Hurry. Answer it. Something's happened to him."

When he answered, she was beside him. "Dean? This is Jenny."

"It is?"

"I was calling . . ."

He turned to say, "It's for me." She remained at his side. Her presence annoyed him. Why didn't she go back to her room?

"What did you say?"

"I was calling . . . to see if you got home all right."

"Why wouldn't I get home all right?"

"I don't know. . . ."

"I know. You didn't believe me, did you?"

"No; but I do now."

A fury curled in him and leaped upward. He could hear the children singing; he wanted to tilt the lumber-stack and bury them alive. Bury everything alive with a few neat strokes of his okra stalk. "Well, you shouldn't. What you thought was the truth. Wasn't that a silly story I hatched up? Women are so clever. They see through us, don't they?"

"Dean . . . Dean. . . ." But the wire was already dead.

He turned and brushed past his mother, into her room. He was an angry, snarling beast. Why he went into her room he did not know.

"Was that Bayard?" she asked.

"Didn't you hear? You stood close enough. No; it wasn't Bayard."

"Who was it?"

" 'Who was it?' Why don't you let me ask you some questions?"

"I didn't know I'd ever stopped you from anything. Go ahead and ask." She was afraid of him. She wished Luther was home.

"Why didn't you ever let him do anything for me? Why did you hardly ever let me see him? Because you're selfish and jealous. You wanted me all to yourself. You're just like Jenny. You didn't care what I was so long as you had me . . . owned me."

"That's not true."

"It is true. He kept seeing you, didn't he? Do you think I don't know? Why couldn't he have seen me? I belonged as much to him as to you. But you did it for spite. He left money for me and you sent it back. Do you think I don't remember that?"

"Was it honest money?"

"I don't care what it was! It was something he wanted to give to me. You talk about honesty. The only reason you want Luther beside you is so you can put your arm around him and think of Rufus Frost. I know that too. But I don't blame you for that. I guess that's better than nothing."

"You've said about enough!"

"I've said too much. But I haven't said anything that wasn't so. Have I?"

She was trembling, trying to remember that only a few minutes ago he had touched her hand gently. "This is my house, and you're welcome to stay here. But you've said enough." She could not break down and cry as she wanted to. All that was past. It was too late to cry.

He went out into the hall and hesitated for a moment. He might call Bayard and ask if he could come there and spend the night. One night. He would never ask it again. One night would be enough to lie awake beside him, hearing his sleep, and thinking: This is my brother. But he would never call; he would never lie there.

"Mother? Would it help any if I said I was sorry."

"I don't know whether anything would help now or not."

He was tired, exhausted. He wanted only to lie down and sleep.

3

IT was time for winter to strike in earnest, and Rufus Frost was not ready. He had never been willing to let the autumn days end; certainly he was not willing now. He walked about the place, the barn, the fields as if some surgeon had said, "We can operate, yes. But where? It's been growing inside you for twenty years." He believed that the only thing he wanted was to escape. Yet, he knew that he had only to pick up his hat and start. What he really wanted was to hear a chorus of voices protesting such an idea; but how could they protest unless he made a move to go? He was willing to admit that every part of his obsession was ridiculous, but that had nothing to do with it. False angina was as painful as the real disease. A stray word from one of the boys would sometimes strike him cold, cast a shadow that hung over him until another stray remark would carry it away.

He had not yet been able to give the proper meaning to the incident last week with Rex. At the time he had been certain that he understood it. Several nights, in a recurring nightmare, they had not got by the train: in one of the dreams—the plainest one— the car had cut the train in half, and he had ridden off with the engineless part while Rex, safe at the controls, had gone in the other direction.

But day by day the entire incident had faded in his mind and the only thing that seemed important was that Rex had come to him for advice about his campaign. There had now been eight days of it, and not a day had gone by but that Rex had asked him something about a speech, an advertisement, a certain influential voter. He had fed eagerly on every question, every problem, betraying sudden interest when he had intended to remain coolly in the background. Then, just at the time he was beginning to come into the sunlight again, it became evident that old Jim Hodges was not going to run against young Rex Frost at all: he was really running against Rufus Frost. Where else could he find the proper fodder for his political cannon?

There were moments when he wanted to open his safety deposit boxes and pour so much money into the campaign that old Jim would shrivel up like a prune; at other times he believed a defeat would be a blessing for Rex; and, again, he thought Rex might win in spite of all the millstones—he might well be the very best speaker in the whole state. Jim Hodges had his points as a speaker too. His creaking, vulgar, incessantly angry voice pierced the skin of his listeners, telling them how they had been wronged, how he (usually alone) had fought their battles for twenty-odd years. Now, his young opponent was smart (to be sure), he was a great football player (never enjoyed anything more in his life than watching the boy whip off tackle for a touchdown); but was this boy ready to assume the responsibilities of a State Senator? Shouldn't a man be seasoned as a Representative first? (He had had twenty-two years of seasoning.) You good people are not going to turn a good mule on the grass now; you're going to give this old plugger one term in the Senate at least. You're going to let him fulfil his life's ambition, before the dark angel comes hovering to say, "Jim, ole boy, it's time fer you to go."

That was the line old Jim had taken at the first rally, and Rufus was puzzled. What he had expected from the man was not long in coming, however. At the second rally, old Jim asked the people to look at the background of his young opponent: His father was twice a county sheriff and was unquestionably "for liquor." Which was bad enough, but in his two terms of office, Rufus Frost—the records showed—had never allowed a nigger, no matter what he had done, to face a jury without an attorney—paid for by the state, paid for by your money. If that was not enough, look at the nigger tenant houses on Rufus Frost's place. (Better than most of yours!) And if they wanted to go deeper into the matter, read the book by one Bayard Frost, brother to his opponent. And bear in mind this boy was kicked out of their great University for advocating the enrolment of niggers. He could go on, but why? It was not his policy to sling mud.

He had timed his indictments expertly. They spread like a sedge-fire in a high wind. As Rex made his rounds, speaking at every small precinct, the wave of mistrust swept him back and back. He had ignored the charges; he had no alternative. He knew that even if he cried from every platform that he hated niggers, that he was bone dry, the effect would be to add more fuel for the fire. At the same time he would not give up.

On Saturday afternoon, three days before the third and final big rally, Rufus Frost had given up the last straw of hope. He finished feeding, latched the crib, and went to the house. He was alone with Anna (Morris and Jarvis were with Rex: his bodyguards, they said). He felt a need to explain to her that he had done everything he could to keep Rex from running in the first place. But explaining would cover none of his own shortcomings. He put it off as long as he could, until supper was over and they were in their room.

Then it was Anna who mentioned the race. "He hasn't a chance in the world, has he?"

"No; not if I'm any judge."

"It wouldn't be so bad if he lost by a few votes. But he'll lose by so much . . . he'll never get over it."

"I had no business letting him run."

"He had to run. The worst thing you could have done was to keep him out of the race. Then it would have festered in him."

"What would have festered in him?" He knew perfectly well.

"The fact that you kept him out."

"You mean the fact that I was afraid to look at my own record. They're all looking at it now. He's had everything I've ever done thrown into his teeth. They'll tromp him in the mud all right, deeper than I ever thought. He's gonna look at me when it's all over and point his finger, and I can't blame him. What am I going to answer?"

"You might ask Bayard what he's going to answer. He's in the middle of it with you."

He clung to the idea for a moment. He had been immensely relieved when Bayard's name was brought into the campaign beside his own. It seemed to border his shortcomings—whatever they were—with a bright strip of innocence. But later he felt a double guilt; it was simply that two of his sons were facing the fire instead of one. He had read Bayard's book, read it the way he might read an account of a dream. To accuse Bayard seemed as senseless as accusing a man for having a bad dream. He alone must answer: he must answer to his wife and to all his sons. Before he could say anything to Anna, he seemed to hear that imaginary surgeon's voice again, "We can operate, yes. But where? It's been growing inside you for twenty years." He took off his shoes, rubbed them clean, and began to smear them with tallow. "Let's don't talk about it," he said. But talk was exactly what he wanted to do. His mind was overflowing with it, and unless he got some of it out, somehow, it would drown him. He would drown in his sleep.

At that moment the telephone rang. Both of them got up quickly and both of them imagined the same thing: that Rex had had trouble somewhere. Anna, seeing that he stood in his sock feet, went ahead of him down the stairs. He sat down and put on his shoes. Returning halfway up the stairs, she called nervously, "It's long distance. Memphis. For you." Both knew there was really no cause for excitement; they had been expecting a call from Bayard, who was moving home in a day or two. Still, it was strange that he would call person-to-person.

At the head of the stairs Rufus said, "Why didn't you go ahead and talk?"

"The operator asked for you." She sat down, leaning against the stair-rail. All the reasons she could number did not quench one spark of the excitement in her. She watched him take the receiver.

"Mr. Frost, this is Luther Whitmore."

For a few seconds the name meant nothing to him. "Yes. . . ."

"Todda asked me to call you."

"Yes. . . ." His heart was unspinning, pumping his blood in too many directions.

"Her son was killed in an automobile accident this afternoon and she. . . ."

"Killed . . ." he repeated faintly. It was almost a question.

". . . she wanted me to call."

There was silence, nothing but all the distance between them, and Rufus felt as if he held half the weight of the line, which would soon sag to the earth.

"You understand . . ." the voice went on quietly, calmly, "you understand . . . we'd be glad if you could . . . if you would come. I mean, for her sake . . . I want you to feel . . ."

"Yes," Rufus said, weakly. "Yes, I understand. I thank you for calling. . . ."

She could see he was pale as a sheet. She was recoiling, she was backing up the stairs, she could not bear the horrible news his lips would shape in a moment. Death was the easiest thing to read on a man's face, and there it was: his son was dead. She was rising slowly, gripping the rail. They stared speechlessly. Her throat struggled. "Is it . . . Bayard?"

The name shocked him into understanding, but he could not move, nor speak for a few seconds. "No, darling. It's not Bayard."

Her hands loosened. She collapsed. He picked her up and carried her to their bed. "It's not Bayard," he whispered.

She held to him. "It is. You must tell me the truth."

"I've told you the truth. Nothing's happened to Bayard. It was somebody else."

The room was so oppressively still that both of them expected something to break—a vase, a window-pane, a mirror. If a spark could manage to fly past the hearth screen and land somewhere with a flicker of smoke, allowing them to move, that would help. Slowly he got to his feet, moved back toward the hearth, and sank into a chair. He stared down at the raw lump of tallow floating in a bowl. It might have been a gigantic iceberg in a more gigantic sea.

"Who was it?"

"It was Luther Whitmore calling. You don't know him. His stepson was killed in a car wreck."

Her voice came to him from far away; it came past a sawmill, across a vast field, over a hundred hills, and through a thousand doors, closed doors. "How old was he?"

"How old?" Yes, how old? Had he forgotten? Through this door and through that door and all the way back to a point in time, to a point as elusive and unreal as space in a dream. "How old?" he repeated. "Give me a few minutes, Anna. . . ."

"You thought it was Bayard, too," she said.

He nodded. It was the easiest, simplest thing to do. Now was the time to tell her, but he could not, not quite. But he would soon, in a few days, certainly.

And there was a heavy matter she wished to tell him, an uncertain thing, but terrible even in its uncertainty. She could not say it now. Heavy, Heavy.

In the funereal silence, they struggled like swimmers against the endless darkness, the endless waves, hoping to find each other by chance and go down—if they must—together. But neither could know that the other felt the overbearing waves, the salt wind; neither knew that the other was there; neither would cry out.

She lay back across the bed and stared at the ceiling. He leaned farther and farther until his fingers touched the sickening tallow; he rubbed one last touch of it over the toes of his shoes. And the silence continued its funereal pace. He could imagine himself saying: Anna, do you want to hear? It was in this house, your house, you in the hospital. . . . The imagining stopped. He must tell her that he had to go to-night: he knew the people well . . . well. . . .

He went to her and awkwardly, childishly, put his arms about her.

"Do you know how much I love you?" she said. "And them. Because they're part of you. I don't care what you've done or ever do. It's not the sins that matter, is it? It's the things they set in motion, isn't it?"

"I don't know what it is that matters so much," he said. "But there's always something that matters a lot." He had lifted his head. The tears ran down his cheeks and dropped on her neck. He did not know whether he cried for her or for himself or for his dead son.

4

DURING the night, Bayard was awakened several times, and his mind focused each time on the night Dean had entered his apartment with the door bolted. After several fitful awakenings, he went to the door and fastened the night latch. Then he lay awake remembering how small Dean had looked in his casket. He wished he had not gone to the funeral home with Jenny, but somebody had to go with her, and look with her. Now it was done, was stored in his memory for ever, a pale mask crowding out the image he would have chosen to remember: the narrow face filled with its pleasant mockery, the fiery eyes, the unruly hair.

Maybe Jenny had seen the fire, but he had not seen it; he would never see it again.

When morning came, he began to pack the few remaining articles that he had not yet prepared for moving. One was a small painting of the river above Memphis, which Dean had given to him. He had not planned to go home for another day or two, but staying there another night seemed impossible. The funeral would be at ten o'clock; after it was over he would call his father to come after him. If that plan did not work, he would pack everything somehow and catch the train. What he could not pack, he would leave with Jenny.

He was surprised when someone knocked at his door. It was barely past eight o'clock, and Jenny had planned to arrive at nine. He had some difficulty unfastening the night latch. There was Jenny, tall and dull-eyed, wearing a black coat that was a fraction too large and a fraction too short.

"You don't mind my coming so early, do you?"

"No. Come in."

"Stella stayed with me last night, and when she went to work . . . well, I thought you wouldn't mind if I came on over here."

"Sit down. Do you want anything? Something to eat or drink?"

"No; I don't want anything. I just didn't want to stay by myself. You're leaving too?"

"I was going to-morrow or the next day, anyway. I might as well go to-day. I'm going to call home after the funeral. Some of them will come after me. I can't take all this on the train."

"I know. I'm leaving to-night."

"Where are you going?"

"I called Bill. I'm going out there for a while with him."

"Bill didn't know Dean, did he?"

"No; but he was broken up about Cleve. I told him they had shipped his body to Cleveland. He wanted to fly up there, but I don't think he will." She waited for some reaction from Bayard. That Bill might fly to Cleve's funeral seemed to mean nothing to him. She did not know whether to go on with the questions she had planned or not. She took off the black coat and Bayard took it to the closet.

"That coat doesn't fit me. It's Stella's. I didn't have a black one."

"I don't have a black suit, or coat either."

They sat down. They were both uneasy, each half believing that the dead's spirit hovered with the other.

"Can you really believe it yet?" she asked.

"I don't think I can. I've never been close to a death before."

"None of your folks have ever died?"

"Not since I've been big enough to remember."

"Do you know who Dean's father was?"

"He never talked about his folks to me."

"It's strange. Last Tuesday he tried to join the Air Corps, and he couldn't get in because he didn't have a birth certificate. I'm going to tell you something . . . something I know. The accident wasn't an accident."

"How do you know that?"

"He told me he wasn't coming back."

He took her hand. "Why would he say that?"

"He had enough reasons all right."

"Didn't you try to stop him? What about Cleve?"

Her eyes grew chill and fierce. "What did Cleve matter? He was no good."

"But if he told you . . . I don't believe you."

"I didn't believe him either. He had told me so many things lately. I thought he was telling me a story just to hurt me . . . to make me suffer. But it wasn't that. He was the one who suffered. . . ."

There was silence for a few minutes. She cried quietly.

"Bayard, please don't ask anything about me or Cleve or anybody. Just remember that he told me you were the finest person he ever knew."

"Did he really tell you that, Jenny?"

"Yes. It was one of the last things he ever said to me. And he told me something else about you, something he was very proud of. I don't know whether it's true or not, but I hope it is."

"Don't be so mysterious."

"He said he was your half-brother."

Bayard began to laugh. "Poor Jenny. You'd believe anything, wouldn't you?"

"It doesn't matter," she said angrily. "The only thing that matters is that you were good to him. He had that . . . anyway." She stood up. "Let's go get some coffee."

"I could make some here."

"I'd rather go out. I'd like to walk a while."

When the time came, they took a taxi to the small chapel within the grounds of Cranwood Cemetery. Bayard whispered to Jenny, "Is it good manners to take a taxi to a funeral?"

"I don't know."

"Let's get out two or three blocks away and walk. We've got time."

She nodded.

"Dean would laugh at our worrying over a taxi, wouldn't he?"

She nodded again.

The day was deceivingly cold. A bright flood of sunshine poured over the leafless shrubs and trees and a wind pierced the stillness from time to time. As they reached the gate, the last of the funeral procession was entering. They were ushered into the small chapel, which was almost full, to a seat near the back. Bayard did not know the faces about them and he supposed that Jenny did not know them either. There were no children, not one face of a child that he could see. That was appropriate, for death came to the old, the toothless, the wrinkled of skin; to the dull, the watery-eyed, to him with stiff fingers. Once in a while, it came to people like Dean. (Oh yes, only once in a while.) But with Dean, death had not possessed him; he had possessed death. What bravery! Somewhere a hidden organist played softly; the minister read scripture after scripture.

We do not believe it, Bayard thought. We can not imagine it. We believe the Resurrection Day will come before our time—like the wild defences of children—or a giant whirlwind will carry us into Heaven, which we do not believe in either. It is only peacefulness, that is all; and peacefulness is nothing . . . nothing. If you cut off my finger, I may forget; if you cut off my arm, I may forget; if you cut off my head, I may forget that too. It is nothing . . . nothing. Dean, you are nothing, and that is the only peacefulness. We do not want peacefulness, we do not believe in it; but we will have it some day, with you, in spite of ourselves.

They were standing. The people moved slowly, respectfully past the casket. There was only the sound of their feet.

"I'm not going by," Bayard whispered to Jenny.

"You must."

"I'm not going by."

"Go with me, Bayard."

"No. I can't."

"I'll go by myself."

He did not answer. Those who did not wish to look were filing out the door. He stepped into the aisle and followed the stream. Outside, he moved with the others along a winding asphalt path toward the open grave. After a few yards he stepped aside and waited. As he turned, Jenny was there beside him. Her eyes smarted with tears and anger. "You should have. . . ."

"Don't tell me what I should have done. If you want to remember a grey painted mask it's all right. Is our memory so weak that we can't remember the fire in his eyes, his laugh, the hair splattered on his forehead? Have you forgotten that already and have to go looking to remember it? Well, I remember it, and it's not in his casket. They won't cover it up."

She took his hand. "It's all right. I didn't go look. You loved him, didn't you?"

"Why would you ask me that? It doesn't matter now who loved him; the only thing that matters is who he loved."

"He was not kin to you. I can see that." She wanted him to know her hurt. But that was such a hard thing to do.

He did not answer.

They moved into the line that led to the grave. She no longer held his hand. When he looked at her, to see if there would be something else about this curious kinship joke, he could tell that she was searching for someone. The procession stopped. They stood on the fringe of one group, twenty or thirty yards from another group that had formed to the left. "Greeky is over there," she whispered. "I'll go stand with him. I'll ride back with him. Goodbye, Bayard."

He was puzzled, but he was not sorry that she was leaving him. He had somehow lost all feeling for her. "Goodbye, Jenny." He watched her move to the other group and bury herself in the midst of it. If she looked back at him, he did not see her.

He heard the pall-bearers' feet and turned to watch. Some of the men used both hands and some only one, he noticed, but all their faces were fixed and solemn, as if touched only by the weight in their hands. After them came the minister, mother and stepfather. Then he saw the group of five or six, led by his father. The mental explosion in him did not come for fully a minute. Instinctively, he edged farther into the crowd, to hide himself. Needles of frozen light slipped down the hairs of his head, pierced his scalp, charged his brain. He lowered his head and waited. He understood, he said to himself; that was the beginning and end of it.

The crowd began to leave. He followed; he had the urge to run away. But before he reached the chapel, he stopped and waited. He saw his father shake hands with Todda and Luther and start up the path. Greeky and Jenny went by him. He turned so they would not look at him: let her go and take her mystery with her.

He lost track of them. It would be ages before his father got there. He stepped into the path. He was face to face with his father. "Papa, I want to go home with you."

The face engulfed Bayard. The red, swollen eyes showed no surprise. The lips remained not quite sealed, but motionless. His father made a step forward, then his hand went up and dropped lightly on Bayard's shoulder. "The car is over here," he said.

At the car, Rufus handed the keys to Bayard. They got in silently and waited for some of the traffic to clear. A policeman waved to them. They drove out. Within two or three minutes they were on a street with no traffic. "Did you mean to go home right away?" Bayard asked.

"Yes," Rufus answered. "Whenever you're ready."

They said nothing else until they were climbing the stairs to Bayard's apartment. "Don't let me forget to leave the key downstairs," Bayard said.

"All right," Rufus answered.

They entered. Bayard switched on the glaring overhead light. Suddenly every inch of the apartment seemed distasteful to him. He wondered how he could ever have been happy there. And yet he had been. He had been happier there than anywhere else. He remembered the strange, tangled, looping way Dean would lounge in a chair or on the couch, or the way he would stretch out in the middle of the floor on his belly. What had they talked about? What single thing under the sun? But the flow had been incessant. If I had known, he thought, if I had only known. . . . The corners of the room were hideous and gloomy now because it was all over. The mind might bring it back but it would be covered, always, with the grey painted mask.

"You sit down, Papa, and I'll carry these things to the car."

Rufus obeyed him without a word. He sat down, stretched out his legs, locked his hands behind his head and closed his eyes.

After three trips, Bayard had everything in the car except his suitcases, a few books, and a few pictures on the bookcase. He returned to find his father looking at a small snapshot of Dean and Jenny, taken on a cliff above the river.

"You know," Rufus said.

"Yessir."

Rufus kept his back to Bayard. "When did you meet him?"

"When I first came here."

"How did he feel about me?"

"I don't know."

"He didn't tell you?"

"No." He would never tell how the secret had come to him.

"His mother was an old sweetheart of mine."

"I know." He did not know at all. Why had he said that? But it was said, and he was afraid to undo it.

"You mustn't think . . . it was a long time ago. You are the only one who knows."

"Are you sorry that I know?"

"Not unless you are."

"I'm not. I'm glad."

"A secret . . . one like this . . . gets heavier than you might think. I need to know now what you want to do."

"I won't ever mention it, unless it's to you."

"Are you certain that's what you want?"

"Yes."

"Why are you so certain?"

"Because he meant something to me that nobody else ever will."

Rufus put the snapshot down. He had one question left and then he would be satisfied. "What did he do . . . work at?"

"I don't know, Papa. He never seemed to do anything. I don't know where he got his money. Did you give it to him?"

"No."

Rufus turned slowly to look into the face of his son. He felt a great relief: the living had been spared; God would have to take care of the dead. "You sent a nice wreath of flowers," he said.

Bayard drove home, with his mind focused ahead, actually on a short story he wanted to write: the story of an eighty-year-old couple in Natchez who had come into money via oil-wells on their impoverished land and had set about to recreate the world of their childhood. It was to be a funny story, in which the two old people pretended that Grant, not Lee, handed over his sword at Appamattox. While Bayard's mind worked forward on his newest creation, Rufus relived the night before.

He had arrived at the house a little before midnight. Not many people were there: a group of railroad men and their wives. After a few minutes he found himself in the bedroom with Luther and Todda. Though Todda protested that he should stay, Luther quietly left them alone. Rufus, too, had hoped Luther would stay, for then there would be no need, no possibility of digging into the past. They sat there alone, before a small gas grate, trying not to remind each other of the past, knowing that every breath, every movement could feed on nothing else.

"Did you ever give him any money, Rufus?"

"I never gave him anything."

"We went through his papers. He has a lot of money in the bank. It couldn't have been honest. Where he got it I don't know. I can't help but feel . . . this is for the best."

Her announcement was repulsive to him. They were born to uphold flesh of their flesh, blood of their blood, and to believe that death wiped away all sin. She should be weeping—she was a woman—and here she sat with calm, quiet eyes and pronounced judgment. He was angry, not with sudden, flaring anger, but with an ancient, grudging bitterness that sprang from the rock and clay that gave them life. He felt the vast, bottomless gap yawning between them. He wished that Luther would come back, but Luther would not.

"Whatever he was mixed up in, Todda, he was still ours."

"But don't you see . . . if I look at it my way, Rufus, it won't hurt so much."

How he hated her, he said to himself, how he hated the hours that would keep him there within the sound of her voice. Yet he knew—and then the hate turned suddenly upon himself—that if his son was not lying with his bloodless hands crossed, if there was no Luther, he could never sit there like an old woman; he would crush his lips against her, and feed on her, feed on the past, and the flame of desire would explode and flicker and finally die for a few hours. No one else could bring that flame to life so quickly, no one else could make it roar and consume with such completeness, no one else could smother it into a tiny spark. Even death in the house was not quite enough to extinguish it. He was angry a third time because he believed she knew what he was thinking.

He had slept that night, for a few hours, in his dead son's bed. He was glad when the safe light of morning broke. Not even the flowers with Bayard's card alarmed him. It seemed that nothing would ever alarm him again. He had lain awake that night not because he lay where his dead son had last slept, but because he could hear the muted voices of man and wife in the next room, voices that seemed to mock him.

He had forced the issue of burial expenses: he would like to pay everything, he said. He was glad she refused; he did not really want to give in death what had not been given in life. But it was another burden, another bond from which he would never be free.

He was prepared to meet Bayard in the path; he would have been disappointed if he had not been there.

Now on the long ride home, he had one face with him at least. He had not lost everything. They were guilty together; they harboured a secret. And nothing brought him so close to people as mutual guilt.

They stopped at a small tourist court café for lunch. A pleasant, handsome woman in her middle thirties attended them.

"Did you get your play finished?" Rufus asked.

"I finished two days ago. It's already mailed." And suddenly he launched into the new story he had in mind.

As they got into the car again, Rufus said, "That waitress was flirting with me."

"How do you know it wasn't with me?" Bayard demanded.

"I've had more experience with women than you."

"How do you know that?"

"How many women have you ever had?" Rufus asked, as easily as Rex might have asked it.

"Nine," Bayard said.

Rufus laughed, neither with belief or unbelief. They rode for a mile silently. It was a warm, tender interval with them, one that might never come again. Then they found it necessary to talk of Rex's campaign.

When they reached home, Rex came to the car to meet them and to announce that the Japanese had bombed Pearl Harbour.

5

THEY did not talk of the war at breakfast the next morning. Morris and Jarvis were rushing to catch the school bus, with Anna's help: she had to find shirts, fountain-pens, note-books—succeeding with the utmost ease, in silence. Rufus ate heartily, for he had been up two hours, one hour of which was spent at the barn. Rex was reprimanding Bayard for not having had a haircut.

"Don't say anything back to him, Bay-bay," Jarvis warned. "If you sass him before he's had his coffee, he'll cut your golden locks off with a butcher knife. It wouldn't hurt if he was to cut mine, because mine don't wave no-way."

Rex turned his fractious eyes on Jarvis and then back to Bayard. "I want to use your typewriter to-day, and your room too, so I can lock it. I don't want anybody to call me for anything."

"Oh, no," Jarvis said. "Not even if a squadron of Japanese bombers buzz the corn-crib."

Rufus announced that he was going to the woods to cut firewood, and as all the Negroes except Wren were busy pulling corn he needed another hand.

Jarvis, who would have loved staying away from school to take the job, had an answer for that too. "Make Bay-bay help you, Papa. He ain't paying board."

Rufus did not commit himself either way—merely grunted—and Bayard accepted the grunt as a challenge: a few hours' work with the crosscut saw was needed to put the final seal upon their new relationship. (And more, his typewriter and room had been commandeered for the day.) An hour later, he was jolting along in the wagon with his father and Wren on the road that led into the Shannon woods. He was well aware of the change in his father, now that he was in overalls and jumper instead of a suit, in a wagon instead of a car. Yesterday belonged to another life.

Once he was into the woods, once the huge red oak tree had been chipped and sawn and brought safely to earth (the felling of the smallest tree almost put him into a panic), he accepted the challenge seriously. It was no longer a lark. He and Wren handed the saw, Rufus the axe. After an hour his back ached and his arms became lead. Occasionally, as a cut was finished, he would straighten up to see his father's axe eat through a four-inch limb with one expert stroke; and sometimes he would see a mouthful of tobacco juice splatter on the bright blade, as if to sharpen it. His father worked with a steadiness and intenseness that seemed to tell them they had only a few hours to lay in the winter's supply of wood. Just as he was about to sit down on one of the cuts and rest awhile, Rufus spat on his axe and without missing a stroke asked, "Is he laying with you, Wren?"

"Yessuh, he doing purty good," Wren said. He was a short, stocky Negro of forty-five, with limitless energy. He knew he had already exhausted Bayard, who was riding the saw and shortening his strokes.

"Let him blow awhile," Rufus said to Wren. "He's not used to this, like me and you."

"Yessuh. Whenever he want to." Maliciously, Wren set the saw for another cut and waited for Bayard to take his handle. He was enjoying the sweat that dripped from the pale, girl-like face, while he had not so much as wet his own armpits. "Whenever he want to give it up, jist tell me," Wren said, half to Bayard, half to Rufus. He pulled the saw swiftly, expertly. He went from one cut to another, with no sign of letting up.

Bayard called on the last dregs of his energy. He whispered to himself, like a prayer: One more cut, one more cut, and maybe he'll stop. In the midst of it he could hear or see his father spitting and chopping, as if he had forgotten them. He felt superior to the black face opposing him, he hated it; he felt the battle. He would not call a halt. How he would continue, he did not know, but he would fall flat on his face in the leaves before he would give up.

The first tree was finished. They started on a second one.

"You better blow a while," Rufus said.

But already Wren had set the saw for the first cut. Depleted, almost blind with fatigue, Bayard dropped to one knee and seized his handle. "I'm all right," he said, dimly seeing his father spit a huge stream of juice, grunt, and go on with his axe.

When the second tree was finished, it was past noon. Bayard could see the face at the other end of the saw only as a tiny black dot. They began to load the wagon; he did not offer to help. He sat on a cut pretending he could not see them loading, and wondered if he would ever be able to get to his feet again.

"Tired?" Wren asked, grinning, with the keenest feeling of pleasure he had known in years.

Bayard got to his feet; it was a struggle, but he managed. He did not have the energy left even to hate his tormenter. "Not much. Are you?"

"Wore out," Wren said and began to laugh. He scooped up a heavy cut that would be used for a back log and threw it over the sideboard as if he were tossing his hat. "Mista Rufe, he jist need a chew of yo' Apple."

Bayard watched his father, who, he thought, did not even know there had been a battle. They climbed on to the wagon; the load had hardly diminished the pile they had cut. Rufus took the lines up front; Wren sat with his feet hanging over the back end-gate; Bayard sat in the middle of the load. When they reached the main road, Bayard lay back, looking up at the jolting sky. He could barely feel the sharp edges gouging into him.

"Bessie," Wren said, without looking around, "she read yo' book."

Bessie (she was Wren's wife), Bayard thought, can go to Hell. He did not answer.

Wren looked around. A cigarette dangled from his lips. A smile, thin as smoke, covered his face. As they drew even with the tenant houses, Wren hopped off the wagon without a word. The fire from his cigarette dropped into the gravel; he stooped to recapture it. Bayard turned to look at his father: the straight back, the wide shoulders, the thick neck. If this does not seal it, he thought, it will never be sealed. He was suddenly angry with Rex for having taken over his typewriter for the day. Speech or no speech.

"This damn' war," Rufus said, turning his head enough to spit over one wheel, "is going to be bad."

Bayard sat up, just in case the big grey eyes looked his way. A certain amount of energy had returned to his body. "I bet you'd like to go! If you could."

"If I could," Rufus said. The remark was like a knife in his back. Course to hell he could if he wanted to. Who was the one worn to a nub: father or son? He turned to look at Bayard, and on his huge face was the same thin superior twist of lips that Wren had used all morning.

The mules plodded automatically into the driveway, then turned again to the right and circled around the garden into the back-yard. Rufus did not have to pull once on the lines until he was almost even with the wood shed. He stepped off the double-tree on to the ground, laying the check lines across one of the mules. He looked up at Bayard, held his body straight; energy seemed to exude from him like a male odour. Tobacco juice stained the edges of his mouth and lips—something Bayard could not remember having seen before. It seemed like a deliberate ugliness, as if he had cheated someone and told it, laughing. He held no secret with this man; it was merely a hideous dream he had had the lack of sense to record. He felt the same anger he had felt that morning, plus a bitterness; and hate, maybe. Yes, hate too, he thought.

"You can go on to the house," Rufus said. "You're tired. I'll unload after a while."

"What are you grinning about?" Bayard said.

"At you."

"What about me?"

"You and the women you told me about."

Bayard was furious. So his father knew! He knew it had been a lie! He opened his mouth to curse away the humiliation, he who was not given to profanity. He fastened on to the vulgarity he had heard so often in the corn-crib; he would fling it back to its source. "I don't give a s— whether you believe it or not. I'll never tell you anything else."

Rufus had bent over to undo the traces. A raw, vulgar chortle leaked from his throat. "Oh, yes, you will!"

Bayard climbed from the wagon. He started for the house. He was stiff and cold and nettled with aches. But that could be forgotten.

He felt spiritually depleted, corrupted, and full of hate. He would not look back at the face. Yes, he told himself, he was full of hate now. The first time he had felt that against Rufus (He thought: *Rufus*, not *Papa*). When he entered the house and the warm air struck him, his thighs began to quiver.

Rex had sat all morning at the typewriter. The bed was still unmade and crumpled sheets of paper littered the floor. At noon he went downstairs long enough to eat a sandwich and drink a glass of milk. Then he hurried back to Bayard's room and worked until he heard the wagon pulling up at the wood shed. Quickly he got up and crossed the hall into his mother's and father's room. From the top dresser drawer he took one of his father's pistols, a small one of low calibre which had been designed for the pockets of revenue officers. He returned quickly to Bayard's room, locked the door, shoved the pistol into the desk drawer, and continued work on his speech; or, rather, he began to re-read it. When the knocks came, he got up and opened the door without a word.

"How's the crusade?" Bayard said.

"What crusade?"

"Your crusade for youth and honesty and progressiveness."

"Are you rubbing it in?"

"Possibly. I like to rub it in." He collapsed across the bed.

"I hope you realize it's partly your fault that a man with the brains of a flea and the integrity of a water moccasin has succeeded in beating me into a bloody pulp. I won't get a smell."

"I don't see any blood."

Rex got up. "Be serious for once, will you? I want to get

something settled. I want an answer to something. I want to know if you've been repaying me: an eye for an eye, and a tooth for a tooth?"

"Repaying you? I don't owe you anything."

"Oh, yes. You owe me something. You owe me for breaking your fingers, and I think you've repaid me by deliberately writing the one thing that would ruin me in politics."

Bayard did not raise his head; he was too tired. He was too tired to get angry or even to laugh. "You have no conception of art, have you?"

"I'm not concerned with art now. I'm concerned with a simple answer to a simple question."

"Well, I don't choose to be simple. Everything a man does is tempered with what's happened to him. Nothing exists in a vacuum—except politicians. Everything, including art, is created from good and bad motives. Art has its imperfections. It's not divorced from Nature and it's not an improvement over Nature. When it begins to improve over Nature it ceases to be art."

"I don't give a damn about your definitions and evasions. I don't give a damn if the answer is Yes or No. If it's Yes, my account is settled with you. And I think it's Yes."

"Think whatever you like. I don't know the answer."

"Don't be naïve. You know you know."

"I don't know! If you're asking me if I've always envied you, the answer is Yes!"

"Why?"

"Now who's being naïve? I could point out several things. I'm not six feet tall and brown-eyed. I don't have deep waves of blond hair—at least they're not as deep as yours. I don't have a perfect set of teeth. I never had forty thousand people looking down on me yelling their lungs out. I'm not an All-American. I never won eighteen lawsuits in a row." He held up his left hand. "I have two enlarged finger joints, slightly stiff. And when I pull a crosscut saw a few hours I feel like a dish-rag. Do you want any more reasons?"

"No. But if you deliberately wrote what you did, knowing what it would do to me in politics, aiming it at me, then our account is settled and you'll never . . . you'll never be a *great* writer."

"You're going to get your answer, aren't you?"

"Yes; I'm going to get it."

"Well, I'll give it to you. I never wrote a line to deliberately hurt you. I haven't got the guts." He suddenly leaped from the bed and stood beside the window looking toward the barn. "I haven't got the guts it takes to be a *great* anything. I hope that makes you feel better."

"I wanted an answer, that's all."

"You wanted *the* answer. You wanted the one you didn't get. According to your own calculations, you owe me something. It's too bad you can't pay me in guts, because I haven't got enough to pull a crosscut saw. And you think that doesn't matter, but it matters to me!" He was looking at his father coming from the barn, the face, the shoulders, the rugged hands. "If I was like him . . . if I had one-half, one-tenth of his. . . ." And he wheeled on Rex. A tigerishness flowed through his pale cheeks. "Why did I have to be the one? You answer me that? You tell me why I had to get the pink cheeks and broom-handle arms. You who are perfect from cow-lick to toe-nail. But you've got the guts to tell me I've ruined your political chances by happening to write about Negroes as human beings. The sooner you're soiled the better. Haven't you got sense enough to know that the most despicable thing on this earth is a perfect man? What do the flawless know about love and compassion? How could Jesus know what I feel unless He had tasted evil? There is no beauty in perfection. No, I take it back; I don't envy *you*. I envy the guts you've got." He heard the back door slam. He knew that his father was entering the kitchen. He fell back across the bed and buried his face in the covers, a trembling heap of nervous, exhausted flesh. "Don't talk to me. You don't understand what I'm saying. You could never understand. You're too much like Papa."

"I'm not blaming you for what you wrote, Bayard. I was simply going to point out what had happened and then tell you that you were right."

Bayard lifted his face. "You don't believe I'm right."

"You'll know whether I do when you hear me to-night."

"How will I know?"

"You'll know."

They could hear their father's voice below.

"Papa is calling you to come eat," Rex said.

"Let him call. I'm not hungry." But he got up immediately, rubbing at his face. The voice was pulling him like a gigantic magnet. As he moved down the stairs, toward the voice, his thighs began to tremble again with cold, erotic, delicious shivers.

Rex clipped the pages of his speech together, put the pistol in his coat pocket, and went down to his room. As he transferred the pistol to the navy blue coat which he would wear that night at the rally, Anna entered his room without knocking. He turned from the closet as if he had been caught pilfering.

"The President is going to speak in a minute." Without waiting for a comment, she added, "I had a letter from Wayne. I've been thinking, if you boys want to, and if your daddy wants to, maybe we could all go to see him the day after the election. School will be out Wednesday at noon. We could leave that night. I think we ought to. No telling when we'll all be together again. Would you like to go?"

"I'll need to go somewhere after they get through picking my bones."

"They may not pick your bones."

"May not? They already have. But I've learned something. I've learned what the people really believe. I've seen more Nazis here, I'll bet, than I'll ever see on the battle-front. We just happen to have enough democracy to keep them in check. I know what they think. After to-night they're going to know what I think."

"You'd better be careful," she cautioned.

"Yes; I'd better be careful. But I'm not afraid of them. They're cowards."

"Cowards kill people, you know."

"I'll be careful. I've got to save myself for the war."

She studied a minute. "What are you going to do? Are you going to wait your call?"

"No. I'm going to join something in a few days. The Air Corps, I think."

"Oh. . . ." She felt the same sensation that a pilot experiences when he has reached the nadir of his dive and the nose of his plane turns upward again. "Wayne already. You and Bayard now. Morris and Jarvis before it's over."

"I'm afraid it may be that way, Mother."

"How could the world have gone so wrong?"

"Does anybody understand anybody? Do you understand your sons?"

"Perhaps not. But I don't turn on them because I fail to understand."

"But, Mother, you have your great weapon of silence. Chickens cackle, dogs bark, people quarrel, and gods remain silent. You see, I've been thinking to-day. Aren't you impressed? You have to answer. I won't accept silence."

"Aw, come on in the kitchen. I want to hear the President speak."

He caught up with her and kissed her. "Mother, you won't do."

She stopped. His sudden warmth reminded her of the chief reason she had gone to his room. "Did you have a quarrel with Bayard?"

"Yes and No. Why?"

"I heard you two. And then . . . I saw him when he came down. He looked . . ."

"If you mean he looked like a rope of cellophane, that wasn't my doing. I didn't send him to the woods to pull a crosscut saw. It's his business to know what he can do and what he can't do."

"All right." She was annoyed. Sometimes she got through the wall that surrounded all her sons and sometimes she did not. Rufus had built it, brick by brick, without knowing, maybe; but she knew. And yet it had not really mattered through all the years, would not matter in the years to come—if there were years. She would love them whether they were for her or for Rufus, and there were times when they could not be for both. "I know it isn't easy to take a defeat, but if you start blaming people . . . then you've really lost."

"You're asking for a little more silence on my part?"

"No; I'm asking for a little more kindness. You two have always fought. But you're grown now. You're not children. If one of you shouldn't come back from this war, the other would certainly remember."

"What if both of us didn't come back?"

"You're being deliberately stubborn."

"I'm sorry. It's not Bayard and Papa I'm blaming."

Though they were not finished, both of them unconsciously moved on into the kitchen, where Rufus and Bayard sat eating.

"What are you two arguing about?" Rufus asked.

"About the Nazis," Rex said. "The ones that get their mail through U.S. post offices. Why don't they use Hitler's tactics and throw all the niggers in a gas chamber? That's what they believe in."

"Don't be rash," Bayard said. "Who would we get to chop cotton and sweep banks and wash dishes for seventy-five cents a day?"

Anna went to the radio and increased the volume. "I want to hear this," she said. Looking around again, she saw that some colour had come back to Bayard's cheeks.

It was dark and a wind was rising. It whipped around the corner of the house and whistled through the hedge of wild hawthorn. Jarvis and Rex were in the front bedroom, which they still shared. Bayard, dressed for the rally, came in and sprawled across the bed; every muscle in his body felt sore and stiff. Jarvis was standing in his shorts before the dresser, brushing his hair. Rex was moving about, fully dressed, cigarette in hand, as if waiting to make his speech. From time to time he picked up the tray on the dresser and shook off the ashes of his cigarette. "Get a move on," he said to Jarvis.

Jarvis's eyes remained fixed on the mirror. "I've got a presentiment," he said (he had got the word from Anna), "that if I could get my hair to wave like the rest of you rogues, I'd make All-State next year."

"I'll tell you your trouble," Rex said, pacing nervously, keeping his right hand in his coat pocket. "You can't do anything but run fast and straight. You can't fake."

"Can't fake? Why, when we played Golden, I faked their left end out of his jockey strap."

"Yeah; I know."

Jarvis continued to brush his hair. "Let me tell you I heard a certain person bet that I'd score more touchdowns in college than you did."

"Who?"

"Ah, a certain feller with beard on his face."

"Did he have any beard on his tongue? Do you know what they'll do with you—if you ever get to college? They'll make a running guard out of you. The only time you'll get your hands on the ball is when you block a punt or recover a fumble. That's the only place for you under the Tennessee system."

Jarvis turned to Bayard. "Ain't I glad he ain't coaching me? He'd make me into a substitute water-boy. No. . . ." He shook the comb at Rex. "If you'd been very smart you'd have signed that pro. contract and forgot the law."

"I'll tell you what," Rex said. "I hold five conference records. I'll give you a thousand dollars for every record of mine you break."

"Listen to that! You'd give me. . . . Why, you can't pay your office rent. Now, you might get Bay-bay or Papa to pay me. Bay-bay's going to be rich. I'm his buddy now. Say, Miss Hendricks asked me in class to-day if your play was a tragedy or comedy."

"What did you say?" Rex asked.

"Why, I didn't know what to say. I said I reckon it's a tragedy, he acts sad all the time."

"Get some pants on," Rex said, "and cover up those damn legs. They're big as your belly. Look, Bay-bay, just look! Now, I ask you if it's human. Morris is bad enough, but you're revolting. I can't stand to look at 'em."

"Bay-bay, would you take me to New York?"

"He's not going to New York. We're all going to see Wayne. You better get some clothes on. I'm leaving in five minutes."

"Uncle Sid's going. He's not here yet."

"Yes; he is," Bayard said. "He's upstairs."

Morris pushed the door back and entered. The minute Morris was inside, Jarvis ducked—as if dodging a baseball—and sat down flat on the floor. "You big lug," he cried. "You better quit throwing bean-balls at me."

"Ain't he a complete fool?" Rex said. "Let's leave him." But he was obviously amused. Glancing in the mirror, he began to compare himself with the other three. He could not help doing that when they were all together and ready to go somewhere. He was exactly six feet tall, brown-eyed, with deep waves of blond hair—the deepest waves. He was dressed in grey flannel slacks, dark blue coat, white shirt, sandy tie, black shoes. He had rarely looked so well, so keen and brilliant; yet, he never looked many degrees worse. He had a habit of drawing his lower lip and sucking a bit of air between his perfect set of teeth.

Jarvis got up, drew in his lower lip, sucked air, and said of himself, "Fellers, let's send him off. He ain't right."

"Papa and Uncle Sid are ready," Morris said.

The three started for the car. Two minutes later, Jarvis leapt off the porch, running after them, trying to pull on his sweater and top-coat at the same time. When he was seated in the back with Bayard and Morris, he ran his fingers through his hair and said, "It still don't jittle." Then mocking Rex, sucking air through his teeth, he said to Morris, "You know what the Cardinals will do with you if you ever get to St. Louis? They'll make a bull-pen catcher out of you."

Morris smiled, but he did not laugh so that Rex could hear. He was usually on good terms with all his brothers.

Rex drove. Jarvis leaned forward and asked, "What did you all do to Bay-bay, Papa? He won't talk."

"You leave Bay-bay alone," Rufus said. "He cut enough wood to-day to keep your hind end warm all winter."

Jarvis threw his arms around Bayard in a bear-hug. "He's a good thing, he is. Best brother I got."

"Quit acting a fool," Bayard protested. He was certain that in the secret world of no dimensions Jarvis's heart belonged to Rex. Rex's heart belonged to Rex. Morris's heart belonged to all of them. And Wayne's belonged to no one. His own, for the time being, did not matter.

"Reckon we gonna run late?" Rufus asked.

Rex glanced at his watch. "I don't want to get there early. I'm gonna say my say, listen to ole Jim, and then come home. I don't want to wait around."

There was a sudden hush in the car. Those who questioned Rex's mood and intentions did so silently. The car moved on at moderate speed. Insects flying against the windshield bounced off without splattering.

The Woodall County courtroom was enormous. It was rarely filled, except for sensational trials, county singing conventions, and certain political rallies. On the judge's stand were two microphones, a pitcher of water, and a tumbler which had not been thoroughly washed for ten years. People milled about, sat in windows, leaned on the rail that rimmed the public seats. They wore overalls and leather jackets, Army coats from World War I, ordinary business suits, coveralls labelled with the name of a garage or store or lumber-yard, khakis, and a few dark blue dress suits with shining shirts and ties. Among the four or five hundred men, there were thirty or forty women, none of whom appeared to be well dressed.

Old Jim Hodges sat at a table, to the right of the judge's stand, and whispered with a few of his cronies. Rex and his delegation sat at a table to the left. There was a great deal of caucusing among the men, but they talked of the war, not of the senatorial race. They hoped the candidates would speak chiefly of the war, explain the war, which had shocked and mystified them—just as the death of a neighbour always seemed to shock and mystify them though they knew he had been suffering from incurable cancer for a year.

The manager of the Cross City radio station introduced the two candidates with obvious impartiality, explained that Mr. Frost had bought the first thirty minutes of the hour, Mr. Hodges had bought the second thirty minutes.

As Rex mounted to the platform, with his hand in his right coat pocket, there was a warm and extended ovation. He had a complete copy of his speech in his left hand, but for fully a minute, as he looked into the graduated rows of faces, he did not believe he could deliver a sentence of it. He wanted to be loved! Above all, he wanted to be loved, to be their god, to be their magician; to score when all others failed. He had eighteen blistering pages. After the first one they would hate him; he could not stand seventeen pages of hate. If they did not have their eyes on him, it would be different. But their eyes were on him; he alone held their eyes. Those who sat before their radios—how many thousand?—did not matter. These before him: they had come to see as well as to hear. The ovation continued; his heart melted. What were they remembering? The last touchdown he ever scored: a half-spinner, and over guard for forty-six yards (broken field running at its best). What were they remembering? His charge to the jury in the Yerby case?

"My friends . . ."

He had not meant to say "My friends" at all; he could not give up now; he must win in spite of defeat. He would not let them cheer now and trample him into the mud next week. He would. . . . But they were remembering.

". . . what I have to say to-night will take only a few minutes. I don't know why I must say these things, but there comes a time when you must speak with your heart and not with your mind. That time has come to me. This afternoon, the Congress of the United States declared that a state of war now exists between our people and the people of Germany and Japan. Most of us do not know what that will mean. We know only that our lives will be changed, that we must now look in a new direction. I am a young man; my opponent is not young. He is neither legally nor morally obliged to wear a uniform in our country's battle. Not only that: he has already served our country honourably in one war. I am morally bound to withdraw from this race and enter some branch of the armed forces. I am going to do that. And because I am going to do that, I want to tell you for the first time exactly what I think and feel about the only issue in this campaign. All of you know that issue has been and is: white against black. My opponent has succeeded from the beginning in keeping me in the black column. I didn't want to be there, because I knew it meant certain defeat. Let it be said to the credit of my opponent that he told you in plain language what he believed; let it be said to my discredit that I did not tell you.

"I don't know how many people there are in this district who believe that all men are born and created equal, that God is no respecter of persons. But whoever you are, whatever your number, you are opposed by a vast horde in our own district who would fit like a square peg in a square hole in Hitler's Nazi Germany. . . ."

A tall, thin-faced man, with silver-rimmed glasses, wearing plough shoes, overalls, and a leather jacket, moved from the rail where he leaned, toward the microphones, saying, "I won't take that! I won't take that, by God!" The next second Rufus was on his feet, but the man had already retreated, muttering a streak of profanity, shaking his head; his eyes were glued on the pistol which came easily from the speaker's pocket and rested on the lectern. Rufus remained standing; Rex could not stop now—he did not care what they were remembering. The courtroom became a tomb.

"I know a lot of you are excited about this war; and that's the way it should be. But you are in a lather because you are afraid for yourselves, not because you are shattered and appalled that Hitler has killed three hundred, or three thousand, or three million innocent people. This is no time for ifs and buts and maybes. Every human being is a sacred temple; every human being is endowed with certain inalienable rights, and one of those is the right not to be pushed on to the back seat when the front seat is empty. I can't put it any plainer than that. Perhaps I didn't fully believe it when I started this race, but I believe it now, and I'll believe it if I ever reach the front lines and start fighting for those of you who stay at home and don't believe.

"Sometimes a revolution comes like an earthquake and levels everything into complete destruction. Sometimes it comes like a flood destroying one day and leaving the earth enriched the next. I hope when this war is over and when Fascism has been destroyed that there will be a revolution here in this county, this district, this state: not a bloody, street-to-street, farm-to-farm, hand-to-hand fight—not that at all—but a rebirth or first birth of good will in the hearts of men.

"Some of your sons are going to die in this war. And their deaths are going to be ironic testaments that you don't believe who I know you do believe. I hope that the next young man who comes to you asking for an elective office will not be penalized for believing what the Gospels teach: That all men are equal in the eyes of God."

He paused. Heads seemed to tilt slightly backward for a breath. "I'm almost finished. I have only one other point to make. I don't know what my opponent is going to tell you, but I'm telling him he'd better not mention my brother's or my father's name as he has done in the other fifteen or twenty places where we've spoken. That's all." He pocketed the pistol, crumpled his eighteen-page speech into his left hand and stepped down beside Rufus.

With hobbled, arthritic steps, Jim Hodges reached the microphones. He looked at the crowd, then he turned his cold, watery eyes on Rex. "Friends, don't get excited. Me and this boy are not going to have trouble. But, mister," he pointed to the man who had challenged Rex, "if I'd been in your shoes a few minutes ago, I'd a' fainted away cold as hell. . . ."

The spell was broken. A twisted, inhibited laugh issued from most of the faces. To Rex, it was like pus dripping from a sore; he did not care if all their sons died.

". . . Pardon me for that bad word, friends. I'm not given to profanity or strong drink, but I get excited when excitement's going on." Then, pausing for a few seconds, he said, "We're gonna have lots of excitement for a long time. The war clouds are over us now. The rain has begun to fall. I can think only of all the young men out there—soon to be out there—and you who grieve for them. The people have been good to me. If I were young in body I would go, gladly, and gladly would I spill the last drop of red blood in my heart of hearts, for your sons and mine. But I must stay. It is not for me this time. My time came twenty-four years ago. To-night, the spirit is willing, but the flesh is weak. That's all I want to say. God bless you, and keep your courage high." He started off the platform with the intention of shaking hands with Rex and his father, but Rex turned quickly, went past the jury box and through the first door, where three or four men stepped aside to clear a path for him. Rufus followed close behind him, and after Rufus came Morris, Bayard, Sidney, and Jarvis, several yards back. As they went down the courthouse steps, Rex cleared his throat and spat a spray of saliva that the wind caught and splattered before him. Rufus saw it and remembered and said nothing.

Jarvis was the last to get into the car. He kept looking back at the courthouse. No one else had come out yet. "Get in here," Morris said. "What are you hanging around for?"

The car started. Rufus was driving.

"I wanted to take a whack at that snaggle-toothed fishing pole that tried to jump on Rex," Jarvis said.

"Aw, shut up," Morris said. "They'd make sausage out of you and all the rest of us. Wouldn't they, Papa?"

The car was moving swiftly by then, for there was no traffic. Rufus let his right hand slip off the steering wheel and cup against the inside of Rex's thigh. "Let me tell you something, boy. . . ." He stopped. He had meant to curse and condemn such a stupid, dangerous act. But he could feel the thigh quivering and could say nothing. He stroked the thigh gently, as if Rex were a child. The car moved swiftly, out of town, on to the highway, and they heard only the high-powered purr lose itself in the wind.

"Well, what do you think? What do you think, Bayard?" Rex burst out, nervously.

"I think you've cooked your goose with the good people of this state for the next hundred years."

"Make it fifty," Jarvis said. "Bet a dollar it's fifty."

"Shut up!" Rex cried. "Will you kindly shut up!"

"Oh, you damned Communist," Jarvis said. "I'm not gonna sleep with you to-night."

"Don't worry," Morris said to Rex. (He had recently been exposed to the idea of the transmigrations of souls.) "Maybe you'll be Governor in the next life."

"Give me that," Rufus said.

Rex understood. He handed over the gun. Sidney drew a deep breath of relief.

Jarvis sucked air between his teeth, mocking Rex, "Papa, why don't you give this car away to somebody who ain't got no shoes?"

"Will you kindly hush?" Rex cried out again.

"Aye god, that's enough out of you, Jarvis!" Rufus was turning on his youngest son the fury he had meant for his oldest.

Jarvis understood he had gone far enough—perhaps too far.

"Slow down a little," Rex said quietly to Rufus. "I'm getting . . . sick at my stomach."

Rufus slowed the car. Automatically he dropped his hand to the thigh again, grasping the handful of wool and flesh as he would grasp a layer of shucks.

Anna moved about in the room preparing for bed. When she glanced at Rufus, she saw that he had one arm over his forehead, his eyes wide, staring at the ceiling. She heard Rex stirring below; he might be vomiting again. She must go see about him.

On the stairs she held to the rail and descended slowly, remembering the time ten years before when she had stumbled and badly bruised her knee. She had always had weak knees and to-night they were like water. But the boys and Rufus were home; they were safe; it was over. Her hand gripped the rail with each step. At the foot of the stairs she was breathing heavily; strange, it was always harder for her to come down than to go up. When Rex and Bayard left— and it was only a matter of days now—she and Rufus ought to move into one of the rooms downstairs. (But they never would, of course. It would be like moving to another house.) She heard Rex stir again and hurried on. Migraine headaches scared the living daylight out of her. She was much more afraid of a migraine than of anything that had happened at the rally to-night—which was bad enough. Well, now they could rest from politics for a while, but of course there was the war ahead of them. And she remembered the convulsions, the agonies Jesse had suffered every month or two: they called it a sick headache in those days. Whatever it was called, it reminded her of epilepsy. But thank heavens, Rex had not turned blue around the lips, had not shivered and groaned, and had not had his right hand grow numb—things that always happened to Jesse. And too, this was Rex's first attack since high school. It was the speech, of course. She tapped gently on his door, and entered.

There was still an acrid trace of bile in the room (he had vomited a great deal). "Are you feeling better?"

"Yes. I'm all right now."

"You're not cold?"

"No. I'm all right."

They could hear Morris and Jarvis talking in the next room.

"Is Bayard asleep yet?"

"I don't know. What do you want? I'll get it for you."

"I'm all right. If he's not asleep yet, tell him to come down a minute."

She looked to see that everything was in order. His eyes did not have that peculiar feverish stare that Jesse's always had at such times. She said good night again and went out. As she passed Morris's room she knocked once and said, "You two quiet down in there."

"Mother?" Jarvis called.

She turned back and entered the room.

Jarvis got out of bed, stood in his shorts—for he never wore pyjamas—and said, "I'm showing him how you wake me up every morning. Watch." He bent over the pillow where his head had lain a minute before and shook it. "Jarvis? Jarvis?" He called gently, and then he burst out, "Durn your blasted time, boy, I mean get out of that bed right this minute! You're gonna miss that school bus! You hear me? I'll take a stick of stove-wood to you, boy! Now you get out of there!" Then gently again, "And cover little Rex up."

"Oh, flitter," she said, and went out. She could hear them laughing.

Rex could hear her climbing the stairs slowly, and the sound transformed itself into a prolonged ovation. They did love him, or, rather, they *had* loved him. But now he had ruined everything. To begin with, he had botched his speech. He could hear it now as the frightened, memorized words of a high school valedictorian. What good, what earthly good could come of it? It was all right to say those things in books, for people in the Seventh Senatorial District did not read books—could not, some of them—and those who could read and did read would not believe. The season had ended, the last game was finished, the stadium was empty; the dust and peanut hulls and candy wrappers swirled up from empty whisky bottles and struck his face. It seemed that the blood gurgled in his temples.

He heard Bayard's steps; he breathed deeply. The door opened. Before Bayard had reached the foot of the bed, Rex said, "I told you this afternoon what I was going to do. Why didn't you stop me?"

"I don't remember your telling me."

"I hinted mighty strong."

Bayard sat down on the edge of the bed. "A word to the wise is not always sufficient. Sometimes it takes a sentence or a paragraph."

"Why did I do it? What good will it do?"

"Probably none."

"I made an ass of myself. . . ."

"But if you believe it. . . ."

"What if I don't believe it? What if I don't *really* believe it?"

"You'll have to believe it now."

"But do I?"

"I don't know. Maybe you don't. Did you ever hear of Herostratus? He was a Greek who burned down a temple because that was the only way he knew how to become famous. Whether you believe what you said or not, you've probably earned yourself a place in history as the first white candidate in this state ever to stand on a public platform and say a Negro is as good as a white man. That ought to hold you for a while."

"I'm going to join the Air Corps," Rex said abruptly. "Why don't you join with me?"

"Air Corps? I'll do good to make the infantry."

Rex was beginning to feel better. There were sparks in his eyes. "I want to fly the fastest damn' thing this country can build. I'll be an ace and come back with a bucketful of medals or come back in a box, one or the other. I'll show the son-of-a-bitches!"

The door opened and Jarvis burst into the room, chased by Morris.

"I wish you'd take this hoodlum back," Morris said. "I'd just as soon sleep with a bull."

All four were on the bed. Jarvis slipped under the covers beside Rex, and put his arm around him. With baby-talk he said, "You won't let 'em kick me around, will you?"

"Fool. Complete fool."

Jarvis patted Rex's stomach. "He's gonna marry Kay before he goes off to the ole war and I'm gonna be best man."

"Are you sure it's Kay?" Morris asked.

"Kay or Frieda or Estelle or Janice or Sudie. I forget which one he said. He changes girls like he changes socks, you know. But I'm fer you, Rex-baby. I'm gonna vote fer you. I don't care who you marry or how many votes you get."

"You go to hell."

A silence fell on the room. Jarvis sat up and looked into Rex's eyes. He was the last to know something; he could feel it. But what? And then he knew; it was so clear. The one who was his idol—who had been his idol since the days when he had first opened his mind to a vague notion of what it meant to be handsome, eloquent, chosen—had stubbed his foot like a common schoolboy and fallen with no more impunity than a snowman. He could not bear to think of it. The silence was so heavy he felt that none of them would be able to move, to utter a word. Then the hushed, intimate sounds from upstairs came through the ceiling like silver birds. His heart beat as if one of the birds were caught beneath his cage of ribs. His eyes turned to the ceiling, "Listen!" he whispered. "Listen!"

The faces of the other three were flooded with deep red. Lowering his voice, fighting the red that covered his face, Rex said, "You've got absolutely no sense of propriety."

Jarvis, feeling that he had been contradicted, feeling that he must free the heart-bird beating in him, whispered feverishly, "They are so too! They are making love!"

"Oh, hush," Morris said. "Mother's sick."

Rufus did not know the hour, whether it was to-morrow or to-day. There was no light in all the house; he heard no sound of steps. But he knew the woman beside him was crying.

He was not puzzled, for it seemed that nothing ever again would puzzle him. His heart was full of a heaviness. Did she cry because her heart was full too? A woman's way was strange. She was in his hands and his sons were in his hands; everything was in his hands, except himself. She would save him. She would be the one, though he could not weep with her, for such was not his nature. But his nature was so turned that he felt a heaviness for his son who would never again have thirty thousand voices in the palm of his hand, for his son who had boasted of women and knew no women, for his son whose only talent was honesty, for his sons who were not yet men and did not understand, for his son who was dead and unloved. He felt a heaviness for Anna too, whether she wept for him or for her sons who were going to war, or for herself; but he also felt a joy, knowing her innocence. He felt a heaviness for all men who spat on courthouse steps and frightened pigeons. And most of all he felt a heaviness for the weakness in himself, which if time were snatched back a generation, would make him travel the same road once again. Of that he was certain and ashamed. But he had loved, and in loving he had held back nothing. The woman beside him could bear witness.

His heart had enough to carry now without the added burden of a secret. He would tell her—he must tell her—and now he knew when: he would tell her as they lay in the pullman berth together riding toward warmth and sunlight—it would be easier then. He moved his hands over her gently, to stop her crying.

She wished to tell him something too, but she could not—not yet.

6

WHEN the telephone rang at eleven o'clock the next morning, it was necessary for Anna to go down to answer it. Ursa had not come at all that morning. Rex and Bayard were off bird-hunting with Rufus. Bessie was cleaning the attic. She went slowly, though she was afraid the ringing would stop before she reached the foot of the stairs.

It was Dr. Miller himself, not his secretary. "Mrs. Frost, I wondered if you could come by my office at one o'clock?"

"Yes. I could be there at one, I think."

She replaced the receiver and waited a minute to organize herself. Rufus might have gone off with the car keys. But she found them on the mantel and then sent Bessie for Wren, who would drive for her. Finally, there was the business of what she would wear. All her life, she had always been able to go to her closet and select what she wanted at a glance. But in the last few months, she would sometimes find herself undecided over such a simple matter as a brooch. Not long ago, she had gone so far as to change her mind about a dress after it was on her. Such indecision irked her immeasurably. To-day she would choose quickly. And yet, standing in the closet, it was some minutes before she finally selected a dark grey suit.

At one o'clock (after she had bought three or four items she would need on the trip to see Wayne), she waited in the rectangular room of the clinic, with its huge plate-glass window covered by immaculate Venetian blinds. On the wall, framed in olive green, was the motto: "No man has ever done anything worthwhile until he mastered the illusion he would live for ever." She remembered that the room in summer was cool and brittle.

Dr. Miller came in briskly. He was not worried about anything. He was like a young farmer who looks at a rain-cloud, not caring whether the rain passes or falls, because his cotton is at the stage where it will profit either way. He was about the size of Rex, with short, blond hair and very handsome hands. She had been told he was the finest golfer in Cross City.

"Nice day for December," he said.

"Yes; it is."

For two or three minutes he busied himself reading a letter.

"Did Mr. Frost come with you?"

"No; he didn't."

"I called because I'm going out of town to-morrow or next day. We're having a meeting in Dallas. I'm going to read a paper. I wish I had Rex to do it for me." He put the letter aside. "I sent your X-rays to Dr. Riehl in Baltimore. I had a letter from him this morning. Don't be alarmed about this, but I want you to go to Baltimore."

She showed no sign of alarm. "When, Dr. Miller?"

"I'd say next week, if you could."

"We had planned to go to Florida next Wednesday . . . to see my son who's in the Army."

His eyes betrayed his desire to frown. "Which son is that?"

"Wayne."

"There's no reason you shouldn't go . . . but it's a lot of travel, and . . . How long would you be gone?"

"At least four or five days."

"Let me think about it."

"But I have to go. You see, I've already promised him. And I somehow feel . . . I haven't seen him since he left."

"Is he going to be shipped out?"

"He thinks so."

He turned to the letter again, giving himself the chance for a well-knit frown. "I guess it would be all right. I'll be back Monday. You come in then. At . . . say, two o'clock."

She was ready to leave. She hoped he would not say any more, for there was not one single thing of beauty in that whole room to support her: not one vase or picture or chair or table or instrument but what was infected with the horrible and useless aura of clinical-ness.

"I heard your son . . . Rex's speech last night. I. . . ." He was caught on something as difficult to speak of as tumours. "I got quite a surprise."

"We all did."

"I think he's about the best speaker I've ever heard." Now they were moving toward the door and everything was going to be all right. He touched the door-knob and pulled and the winter sunlight came into the corridor as if he held it in his hand.

Wren drove slowly. She watched the fields, the grey, barren fields go by. There would be quail for supper (Rufus would not come back empty-handed) and very likely Bessie would not know how to prepared quail.

"Wren?"

"Yessum."

"Drive slower."

"Yessum. Was I driving too fast?"

"No. I just want to go slower."

There were little grey feathers on Bessie's hands.

"Where are they? Where is everybody, Bessie?"

"I think they went to the school to a ball-game, but Mista Rufe is down to the barn."

She went to her room and changed clothes. The sunlight was coming through the windows, a patch of it reaching almost to the hearth. She found Jesse's diary in the closet and leafed through it. She found the entry made not long before he died: "I cannot worry about dying in the war, for then it is for something. To go like Mama went, cell by cell and inch by inch, worries me a lot more. I sometimes feel that will be my luck. I wonder what she really thought about. . . .

She went to the hearth and dropped the diary into the fire. After she had straightened the chairs in the room she went down through the kitchen to the barn.

Rufus was in the crib. She stood looking at him, at his big grey eyes and the sudden flush on his cheeks because his mouth was full and he wished to spit. In one corner of his lips was the faintest bit of golden froth.

She moved aside and he spat.

"I didn't know you wanted to go to town. I would've carried you."

"There were a few things I needed to get for the trip."

The crib was so full of corn he sat almost in the doorway. He moved forward, put his feet on the ground, and prepared for her to sit in his lap. "Sit down. You look like you feel bad."

She sat down on his thighs, put her arm around his shoulders and felt his big hands about her. They talked with low, quiet voices.

"How many birds did you kill?"

"I got four. Rex got two. Bayard got one."

"Did Bayard really get one?"

"No; but I told him he did. I really got five."

"Didn't Sid go?"

"No. He's going with us to-morrow, if it's pretty." He leaned far to the left to let a stream of juice roll off his tongue on to the ground.

When he straightened, she closed her eyes as if she were sleepy and let her face rest against his cheek. It might be easier to tell him on the train.